ON THE ROCKS

MARJA GRAHAM

On The Rocks

This is a work of fiction. The events described here are imaginary: The names, settings, places, and characters are fictitious and not intended to represent specific places or persons, living or dead. Any resemblance to actual events or persons is entirely coincidental.

Editing: Sheisa Tapia (@authorsheisatapia)

Cover Design: Grace Steffen (@gracesteffenart)

Proofreading: Sheisa Tapia, Miah Onsha

ISBN: 979-8-9904635-0-9 (paperback)

First Edition: April 2024

10 9 8 7 6 5 4 3 2 1

To the little girl who learned that not all dreams come true and the woman who found a new
dream between the pages of a book.

This one's for me,
and all the other burnt-out dreamers who need a second chance.

PLAYLIST

Gimme Shelter - Rolling Stones

Cold Cold Cold - Cage the Elephant

Perfect Strangers - Cece Coakley

Sweet Nothing - Taylor Swift

Volare (Nel Blu Di Pinto Di Blu) - Dean Martin

Like Real People Do - Hozier

I Wanna Be Yours - Arctic Monkeys

Ode to a Conversation Stuck in Your Head - Del Water Gap

Scott Street - Pheobe Bridgers

Bandaid - Jackie Hayes, Billy Lemos

hate to be lame - Lizzy McAlpine, FINNEAS

Heavenly Kind Of State of Mind - Lewis Capaldi

Author's note

Dear Reader,

Thank you so much for taking a chance on me, my characters, and the story we share. Writing this story was a deeply healing and complicated process for me. Much like Drew, I was a musician (definitely not a famous one, though), and one day, I woke up and felt abandoned by the life and passion I had given everything to

But years later, I found a new dream, and by reading this, you are now a part of that dream. Thank you.

That being said, your mental health matters, and I encourage you to consider the following content and themes that are presented in the story:

Discussions of grief and grieving

Death of a parent (off page and before the start of the book)

Absent parent

Anxiety

On page panic attacks

Drug and alcohol use

Explicit sexual content

1

Lacey

I'm fairly certain my fight or flight instinct is broken. That's probably why I'm a little too excited about the pair of two-hundred-plus-pound hockey players hurtling toward me across the ice. Mentally, I beckon them closer as I stand my ground.

Just a little further.

I don't move a muscle, knowing it's worth risking another second.

Three feet away.

Two.

One.

Just a little more.

I press down with my forefinger, causing the camera's shutter to flicker rapidly as I capture the scene.

Done.

Satisfied, I yank my lens out of the photographer's hole in the glass, letting muscle memory take over as I slide the protective cover into place.

A breath later, the players collide with the boards directly in front of me. The sheer kinetic force of the collision causes the crowd to jerk back as if pushed by a shock wave.

But I don't flinch. Years of practice capturing perfect shots have trained my body to ignore instinct and trust the process. Flinching could mean missing the next crucial moment—that once-in-a-lifetime, career-defining opportunity. And if my awards are any indication, I never miss.

The second the players are safely away from my assigned station, I remove the cover and slot my camera back into position to track the action.

There are people who have asked me why I chose to pursue hockey and not weddings. I mean, sure, a kiss at the altar, sealing eternal companionship, is wonderful, but it has nothing on witnessing the raw power of a hundred-mile-an-hour slap shot flying down the ice faster than the human eye can process.

Weddings are magic. Hockey is *addicting*.

A tense battle for dominance. A drama unfolding in three periods.

Really what I do is a game within a game, where I have to be steps ahead. People always assume it's as simple as following the puck. But if you're doing that, then you're already behind. It's about reading the players, knowing the team and their movements so completely that you can anticipate the rising tide of action before it reaches its climax.

The crowd's collective cheer consumes the stadium as Jonathan Hernandez, the Cobra's right winger, digs the puck out of the corner and effortlessly passes it to our rookie center Aaron Nelson, all before Houston's defense can orient themselves.

With each camera click, my mouth curves further and further into a smile. Their hard work is paying off. With my guys faster than they were last season, the Houston team was stupid to think this would be an easy fight.

This season opener is a hockey fan's wet dream, last season's underdogs versus the early projected conference champions.

Atlanta Cobras 2 - Houston Knights 2

Anticipating another goal, I press the net cam's remote button as Aaron propels a shot through the goalie's defense. If there is one thing I hate the most, it's netcams. They break all the damn time because, really, what type of equipment is meant to withstand the full force of a puck?

But God, do they take some of the most breathtaking photos, making you feel like you're right inside the action. The puck appears larger than life in the foreground, while the players are still processing the moment in the back of the frame, all under a halo of dust-like ice fragments.

At last, the clock is spent, and the buzzer blares, marking the perfect first game of a new season.

After the tedious post-game press conference, I wait in the hall outside the locker rooms for Price. We've had the routine since high school. Long before he landed a multi-million dollar contract and I signed on to earn just above the median for a sports photographer, he was my best friend.

I'm sifting through endless emails on my phone when his massive form pops out, nearly blinding me with the flash of a disposable camera. It's an unfortunate new habit he's formed since he realized I managed to avoid being in all but one of his wedding pictures last spring.

But that's on him for expecting me to pose and look natural with the rest of the wedding party. He knows I've always been far more comfortable behind the camera than in the spotlight—one of the many unfortunate side-effects of being the only child of a rockstar.

When I'm not the one in control, I seize up, like my body is physically averse to permanence. I guess letting Price get away with the pictures is akin to exposure therapy.

"We really rocked their shit tonight," he says with his permanently lopsided grin, revealing his dentist's miracle work. If I had to bet, only half of his teeth are real after so many years of playing.

He tucks his camera away as we start making our way down the hall to the exit, Price waving at the other staff, who are all trying to rush home for the night. Though he's an intimidating guy on the ice with brown eyes that pierce through his opponents and lethal agility, everyone loves working with him.

"They rocked Houston's shit while *you* were doing splits in the crease. From the looks of it, you have a solid shot at that Cirque du Soleil audition." For being built like a brick house, he has the hip mobility of a ballerina.

"Mari has not once complained about my flexibility. Actually, I'd say she is the number one fan of my gymnastic abilities." Price lifts his eyebrows with the suggestion.

"On the list of images I don't need in my head, that's probably at the top. Happy that you're enjoying married life and all, but I don't need the details." I shudder. I love Price like a brother; we've known each other for nine years and there's a certain level of comfort, but there are lines we don't need to cross.

"You could go out with us tonight to wash that scarring image away with a beer or two. I know you believe in the separation of church and state, but it wouldn't hurt to do something social for a change. It'll be fun. You remember how to have fun, right?" he urges as we enter the elevator and I press the button for the first floor.

"I have plenty of fun." It's a lie and we both know it. My average night is spent watching back game footage, making minor adjustments on my Photoshop presets, or binging B-horror films and used paperbacks with a five-dollar bottle of Sauvignon Blanc. "And anyways, I have plans tonight."

"Shit, it's that thing with your father, right? Are you still sure you don't want me to go with you?" Price winces as he runs his hand through the mop of loose dark curls on the top of his head so they stick up at an odd angle. This isn't the first time he's offered, and though he's like a brother, I don't need to drag him into what is destined to be an emotional sucker punch.

"No, you go celebrate. And I mean it," I tell him, and his smirk only grows wider. "I better not turn around and see you in some half-assed disguise. After tonight, this will all be over, so it's really not worth worrying your pretty, perpetually concussed head over."

He's done it before, the disguise, I mean. You haven't reached peak teenage embarrassment until a six-five hockey player with absolutely no discretion and a tragically fake mustache tries to act like he's not eavesdropping on your date.

We share a quick laugh before his expression shifts to seriousness. "That's what I don't get. You're going through this extra stress and planning to let your father back in your life for one night when you've happily avoided his existence for years."

"You know I have to do this." My words are just as much a reminder for me as they are for him. As usual, during the game I was able to forget—forget the meeting, forget him.

"Bullshit. You've never had a problem laying down ego-bruising boundaries. You had poor Nelson looking like a sad puppy when you explained that you don't play well with others," he says as we walk out of the elevator, one step closer to that unfortunate reality.

It's not that I don't play well with others. It's that I only have room for a set number of people in my life and those spots have belonged to the same set of people for the last six years. I don't like bringing new people into my life unless I know I can give them the attention they deserve. Nelson, as sweet as he seems, was never going to make the cut.

"Nelson got over it." However, he did flash sad eyes at me when I took his promo photos two weeks ago. "And fine. I know I don't owe my father anything, but if it were me, I would want someone to do this in person." I take a second before continuing because I know that the next thing out of my mouth will be harsh, but no one has ever accused me of sugarcoating my words, "And maybe I'm being a little petty, too. I want to look him in the eyes and know that I'm right. That he's an asshole that didn't even show up to his ex-wife's funeral." I chew my bottom lip.

"And then what?" His question catches me off guard.

"I'm not sure," I admit, looking down, my mind racing over what to tell him. Funny how I'm always a step ahead during the games, but in my life? That's a different story. "Guess it's because he's a part of me."

"You're not your dad, Lace," Price says, reading between the lines.

"You say that, but you don't know him." Granted, I don't really either, but I've navigated through the rubble of him leaving for my entire life. The hazy memories of a four-year-old aren't what you'd call clear or reliable. But that's not where my fear stems from.

Even based on the limited information I have, every trait I have can be traced back to him or my mother with precision. If I mapped my personality out, it would look like one of those criminal investigation boards tying together culprits and evidence with thumbtacks and red yarn. I'm somewhere between my selfless, workaholic mother and flight-risk, undeniably talented father. The worries have burrowed deeper into my consciousness now that my mother is no longer here to help me piece together my identity.

"I think I'd know if my best friend was a womanizing narcissist who leaves when things get hard. But I also think that one night won't resolve a lifetime of questions." I glare at him, and he holds up his hands in defense. "Just don't be surprised if something more comes from this," he says as we push through the door to the employee parking lot.

The warm, thick Atlanta air is a shock compared to the crisp chill from the stadium.

"Decent people don't just flit in and out of your life every few decades on a whim. There's enough evidence stacked against him that I know he's no saint. That's all I need to know." I remind him. Price is no stranger to the situation, but he's also generally a better person than I am, and I'm not really in the mood to emulate his sainthood. "Anyways, you know, I'm not doing it for me."

He just looks at me. "You'll call when it's over? I'll even let you brag about how the night sucked and that I'm a hopeless optimist." At least he's self-aware. Still, his optimism doesn't change the fact that nothing more is coming out of this.

Our dynamic is balanced. Price has always had his head in the clouds, dreaming big for the both of us, while I have both feet in reality. He's the helium-filled balloon, and I'm the paperweight that keeps him from floating away. But I do think sometime in the last few years, I became less of a paperweight and more like a five-ton boulder.

"We both know you'll last a grand total of one beer before going home and curling up with Mari. You'll be asleep before I have anything to report; I'll talk to you tomorrow." I wave him off as I head in the direction of my Subaru.

I wasn't being honest but it's better this way. To have him think I'm doing alright, rather than have him check in and dealing with another reminder that something is wrong.

The wave of anxiety rises from my stomach and crawls up my throat. The familiarity of the experience is utterly exhausting. But it's the price I have to pay for not wanting to take the medication a psychiatrist prescribed after my mom's accident.

The medication did its job too well, making the world feel slightly out of focus. To the point where I couldn't take photos the way I needed to. And I need this job not just because I love it but because it's one of the few things I have left. I can deal with temporary discomfort if it means everything stays the same.

I wait for it to pass, breathing and attempting to ground myself. The last thing Atlanta needs is one more anxious driver on its labyrinth of roads. I take one last glimpse at the letters resting in the passenger seat.

The little pieces of paper that have managed to disrupt my reality. I found them this summer stashed in my mother's vintage writing desk. The one where she used to sit and write out lengthy thank you cards to anyone who had ever brightened her day. I was sorting through stacks of mismatched stationery, trying to find anything worth donating and found them.

One for me.

One for my father.

It had been just after the two-year anniversary when I was sure I was ok enough to pack up the house and sell it, but the letters took me back to the morning I woke up to a dozen missed phone calls and the news that she was gone.

The letters could contain anything. A family recipe passed down for generations. A document that we're secretly royalty from a small European country. But I was scared. And I still am. Scared that the truth would be much more painful. So I didn't open it, gladly delaying any more heartache, even if that meant keeping a final part of her sealed away.

Because if hope is the thing with wings, grief is the thing with claws. Claws that sink in and refuse to let go.

And after tonight, one of the letters will no longer be my problem.

Maybe those damn claws will let up a bit too.

2

Drew

"You signed the contract," Hartly yells from her side of the phone, her voice cracking in frustration.

We've been going back and forth for twenty minutes, and I'm honestly impressed it took my mild-mannered agent so long to finally snap. After all, she has every right to be mad at me. I'm technically in breach of the agreed terms of said contract after missing today's meeting.

I can only imagine the reaction that rolled through the room when they realized I wasn't coming. Just another piece of evidence of what the guys expected me to do in the first place—being the letdown of the band. Something that has come far too easily these past few years, even though Fool's Gambit is only a memory these days. Well, until the stipulations of ancient contracts officially came into effect today.

"I was twenty-three when I signed it. How good do you think I was at making decisions back then?" My defense sounds flimsy to my ears as I say it, but I don't care.

I was a different person when I signed it ten years ago, back when I was still in love with music. Hell, when I was still able to *play* music. And being able to play is a primary factor of this deal that I haven't found the strength to reveal might not work out.

It's not that I have a broken arm or something physically wrong. No, that would be too simple, something people could readily see and understand. Instead, ever since the day everything ended, there is something loose in my brain that hasn't fallen back into place.

"I can't wait to tell a room full of lawyers that my client forgot that his frontal lobe wasn't fully developed when he signed a legally binding document."

"Thank you for taking one for the team," I joke, hoping the splash of sarcasm will lighten the mood.

It doesn't, and I can tell she's holding the bridge of her nose like she does whenever she's exasperated with me when she says, "Please listen for once. Everyone else has agreed. They all showed up, except for you. And the execs are giving me hell. I have other clients too now, thanks to you."

"Even Jared?" Not that it's really a question. Our rhythm guitarist has always been a rule follower.

"Yes, even our favorite stay-at-home dad is sacrificing family time to make this work. Now, can you just agree to the reunion? It's one night." Yeah, one night plus the rehearsals and the meetings that lead up to it. "You can sit in the corner with your drums and shake a few hands before forgetting you were ever a superstar."

The reunion. One of the terms for Fool's Gambit breaking up. And one last way for the label to eke out a little more cash, though we'd already returned their investment in spades.

Fool's Gambit: Four boys from Tennessee that would break your heart then rebuild it in just one song.

That headline marked the start of everything.

Our music still makes solid rotations on pop-hits playlists. My sister, Evelyn, makes it her mission to send me the latest fan fiction she's found in the bowels of the internet. Though I'd rather claw my eyes out than read one, I'm genuinely impressed by how many continue to spring up with new and outlandish plots.

"Popstar," I correct just to set her a little further over the edge, but there is a difference. Popstar is a job description. Superstar is an accolade you earn by oozing charisma and kissing babies. I've never been one for handling infants. Fan interactions never came easily to me, and for some reason, the semantic distinction matters.

Semantics aside, I've officially been backed into a corner. I know I signed that contract, at least conceptually. I just thought I would have more time—granted, I have been procrastinating hiring a legal team to get me out of this obligation, but as the years passed, it felt less and less urgent. That is, until now. And with the label apparently pouring money into this project, I'm fucked.

Absolutely fucked.

"I don't care if you want to be recognized as the King of Lithuania. Just show up." Hartly sighs, her patience nearing its end.

"Ok, then we're having the after party at Half a Memory." It's a stupid stipulation, to demand my bar be the venue, but I have to come out of this, winning at least one battle.

"Works for me. I'm happy as long as I don't have to hire someone to haul your ass to the venue." And I don't doubt for a second she will if she really thinks it's necessary.

"Fine," I concede out of resignation.

"I swear if you don't show up, I'll kill you myself. Your multi-million dollar ass might be able to recover from it, but I won't."

"I said I'll be there, so I'll be there."

"Good," she says, finally sounding relieved.

She's a great agent and an even better person for putting up with me after all these years. The world might see me as the most irrelevant member of Fool's Gambit, the band member who never brought much to the table and is devoid of personality as far as they're concerned, but Hartly has held my hand each step of the way, and I won't let her down now when it's her head on the line and not mine.

"Hartly, please tell me they don't have any more surprises up their sleeves or hidden in the contracts after this."

"This wasn't a surprise, no matter how much you think it is. But no. Once this is done, so are you." She acts like I'm being paranoid, and maybe I am, but I would have signed so much stupid shit when I was twenty-three. The evidence of that is the fact that we're even having this conversation.

"I'll be done," I say, almost to myself. In January, I'll be free. It's not like I've had much to do with the band these last few years, except my bar.

Two years after the break-up, my twenty-five-year-old self was desperate when he threw together a bar dedicated to the past. A way to relive those old days, the joy it once evoked. Still, he wasn't thinking long term, as now I'm stuck with it, witnessing it age into more of a ghost than happy nostalgia. The novelty makes it a destination spot for tourists and super fans who still listen to our music.

Soon, I won't have to think about picking up a pair of drumsticks or singing about issues that haven't been relatable since my early twenties ever again.

"Yes. And I understand if you don't think you'll need me anymore," Hartly adds in a serious tone, breaking me from my thoughts of freedom, "but you still have so many things to handle. Do you know they're still trying to make toys with your face on them?"

"The answer is still and will forever be no about the dolls. Hartly, I swear I'm never going to let you go. You handle all of the shit that makes my head spin. Even if you raise your fee by one thousand percent, I will still pay it."

"Don't tempt me."

"I know you won't, just like I know you'll take care of me." I pause. "Can you just triple-check that there are no more sneaky clauses?" That's the last thing I need, to think I'm out for good only to get pulled back in.

I can practically hear the eye roll in Hartly's voice when she replies, "I'll get right on that."

"You're the best."

"I know," she says before hanging up.

Exhausted, I press my head against the cool glass of my window. The slow drizzle outside starts to bring down the temperature of the simmering, Atlanta night. I know the air will be impossibly heavy with humidity tomorrow, but it's more than likely I won't even go outside to experience it.

I'll stay cooped up and do the bar's inventory or some other task that doesn't really need to be done for a few more months. Just *something*. Anything. So that I can pretend that I'm making a difference after so long.

Although I wasn't the favorite, together, we made a real impact. Yes, a part of me is eager to move on. Still, taking that final step is terrifying because it all started out so well. And now, all that remains are four burnt-out dreamers who figured out too late that the world is cruel when it doesn't love you anymore. But frankly, it felt like the world was ready to love us forever while my bandmates were prepared to move on.

The story fed to the media about the breakup was that it was amicable. Everyone wanted to go on with a new phase of their life, chase new passions, and keep the band as fond memories of the good old days. It was almost true.

Jared wanted to start a family. Garrett wanted to show the world that there was a brain somewhere beneath his head of quaffed hair. Wes was getting too big to share the stage with anyone but his ego.

I was the outlier. I had no second passion. I didn't want to move on, but I also had no chance of going solo. So, when they told me what they decided, it was a betrayal that spiraled into something I couldn't recover from. But I've never been one to voice complaints.

The irony of it all is that when I signed the damn contract, I craved this reunion more than anyone. It was a chance to keep the dream alive. The one I never wanted to say goodbye to in the first place. Yet, here I am, all but incapable of participating.

Do any of them know that? No.

Will I have to admit it eventually? I don't need to know the answer now.

What I do need is a drink, and conveniently, I live above a bar.

A bar that feels too dangerous to enter unarmed, especially with the announcement of the band's 'One Night Only' event spreading like wildfire across every social media platform imaginable—my phone blowing up all day as a consequence.

At the top of the list were my parents' explanations of how offended they were that I didn't tell them the news in person but proud because, in their eyes, I was getting my life back together. My sister is probably dancing around right now, knowing that I'm taking my parent's attention off her. And, of course, there are the ex-hookups and friends who only lasted a season reaching out, trying to nudge their way back into my life.

I've since silenced everything except for my work email and the separate work phone number I made years ago. My bar isn't going to take a backseat to this mayhem.

I snatch a hoodie and a baseball cap from one of the various piles on the floor and slip them on before I descend the creaky stairs to the bar. I don't miss the music changing from the Willie Nelson song to the pop playlist that Craig has been endlessly reminded to play.

Patrons expect a specific experience, and if that experience includes top forty hits from the last two decades, so be it.

"Wow, Captain America. You're a master of disguise," Craig says when I settle into my usual spot on the barstool furthest from the door.

He has a point. I created a location, unfortunately, optimized for being spotted by fans on nights like this when they are extra excited about the announcement and probably thinking it means the band will get back together, which, no, will never happen.

"It's called hiding in plain sight."

"It's called bringing down our collective IQ. I'm already the pretty one; I can't be the smart one, too."

"Very funny, but last time I checked, I don't pay you to make fun of me when there are thirsty customers," I joke.

Craig is the best damn manager and friend I could have asked for. He's dependable and doesn't give a shit about my past and even less of a shit about his paycheck because, underneath the tattoos and one-liners, he's the heir to a fortune that makes my bank account look like pennies. At the end of the day, we're just two idiots hiding from the expectations of others.

"If you're too much of an ass tonight, I'll throw some tipsy fangirls your way. I'm not sure how much good the hat and brooding will do you then," he threatens as he wipes down the bartop in front of me and sets down a cocktail napkin.

"You wouldn't." He would, and I really shouldn't tempt him to try, but I'm in a worse mood than usual, which means that my self-destructive tendencies are a little too close to the surface.

In response, he winks and meanders away to actually do his job.

It might surprise people that I can casually hang out in the bar without having to sign an endless stream of autographs, but it's by design.

I know exactly what the Fool's Gambit fans want: something flashy and nostalgic with Wesley Hart and Garrett Larsen's faces blown up to dramatic proportions. Being on stage and seeing the majority of posters with glitter hearts around their names hit me harder than it should have back in the day. But now I think of it as knowing the exact audience to ensure the bar stays afloat.

All the posters are either of them, and occasionally, Jared is at the forefront. Only one poster exists that has me posing solo and it's banned from this place. Even if people focus on me in the background of group photos in the dark lighting, I've changed. I was a shy kid who was a PR nightmare with how I avoided the spotlight, the girls I dated, or the lack of charisma that didn't come naturally compared to the others—leading many to wonder if my exterior was hiding some dark past.

It wasn't. I have a good relationship with my family and come from a stable suburban upper-middle-class home. With my parents being Italian immigrants, there was always some pressure to succeed as they reminded us of the hurdles they've faced. It was their way of showing their love, and although we've had our differences about the merits of music as an actual career, it was never in a catastrophic way.

So, no, I don't have any secret that has scarred me for life or trauma that makes a girl look at me like I'm a puzzle to fix. People wanted to like me so badly that they came up with backstories that would make it into some tabloid before being debunked. They had this idea of me they wanted to cling to, but honestly, it just highlighted that there wasn't much about me worth knowing.

Once he's done prepping a round of orders, Craig slides a beer over to me without asking. The silent act means one thing: it's going to be a long night.

To add insult to injury, Craig turns on my favorite channel on the TV nearest to me as if he anticipates I'll be here alone long enough to watch a few episodes.

He's probably right. There's nowhere else I go.

Nights are always the same. Inevitably, someone will come up to me. We'll go through the motions of small talk as they pretend not to recognize me. In the morning, I'll get tagged in some gossip post from an account that, in the grand scheme of things, doesn't matter.

Then I'll do it again tomorrow.

Repeating a meaningless cycle of pointless interactions.

I catch one episode of *Seinfeld* before a woman carrying a cloud of disdain storms into my bar and sits her sexy ass two seats away from me.

I'm transfixed as she slides off the seat, claiming a death grip on my bar. Her evident disgust immediately makes her the most interesting thing in the place. For most people, the building is an escape or a neon fever dream, and they usually ignore the sticky floors and uncomfortable chairs.

But her mood isn't the only thing that pulls me in.

I recognize her eyes, but her face is unfamiliar to me. Quickly skimming through my memories, attempting to find her. Her soft, pink lips, her prominent cheekbones—home to a galaxy of freckles—all framed by wisps of dark hair, broken free from her tight ponytail.

I am sure I would remember a face like hers.

3

Lacey

He's late.

Twenty years late, if I'm being picky, but I'm more concerned about the thirty minutes he's left me waiting in the rain. It might be generous to call it rain. It's more like a lingering mist that fills the air with suffocating moisture.

Whoever made the uninformed proposal to romanticize Southern summer nights should be sued for false advertising. There's nothing beautiful or alluring about the dense air and thin layer of sweat that clings to your skin the moment you step outside.

I recheck my phone as a car speeds through a puddle of rainwater, the resulting spray coating my worn combat boots with street filth. Even though the water doesn't seep through the leather, a sensation jerks up my leg at the cool, uninvited rush.

I shouldn't be standing so close to the street, but I wouldn't be standing outside at all if he was on time. Mentally, I make a mark against him, an imaginary tally I anticipate will continue throughout the night.

Him.

My knowledge of my father scrolls through my mind as a spitefully written Wikipedia page: Martin Hall, the chart-topping rockstar turned music producer known for his Midas touch—turning nobodies into artists with sold-out stadiums and more awards than they can carry.

His fame has always been inconvenient for me, if not parasitic. Even when Martin wasn't physically there, his presence defined so much of my life that I felt like a footnote in my own reality. It's like when you see a famous couple on TV and they always address the equally famous, arguably more fabulous, woman as "the wife of."

They are never recognized for who they are individually but, in my case, by who they are related to.

Condemned to be known as the daughter of Martin Hall.

As the rain starts to pour in earnest, I remind myself why I'm here—my love for my mother. It has crossed my mind a million times to keep this last fragment of her, to hide it so he cannot shatter it as he did with all the other pieces of her.

He had enough notoriety when he married my mother to justify a prenup that left her high and dry after a drawn-out public divorce. He was the villain who contributed to why Mom was either working, sleeping, or making sure she never missed one of my soccer games. His absence dimmed her.

It only drove me to give her a distraction, attempting to do anything to draw her attention and convince her she had something to be proud of. I think I was always going to be an overly critical overachiever, but there's no discounting how the power of daddy issues factors into the equation. In the end, my respect for her wishes outweighed the resentment, and so I'm here.

Bringing me back to reality, my phone pings. I hold it up, shielding the screen from the rain to reveal the worst-case scenario.

Martin

Plane is stuck in Baltimore because of the weather. Won't make it tonight.

I can't exactly blame him for the weather. He probably has plenty of connections from working with music industry royalty, but I doubt he has a direct line to God. I tamp down the rage that comes with knowing this situation will last longer than tonight.

Lacey

Are you still coming to the city?

Martin

Won't be there long enough to meet up. Soon?

Lacey

When?

I need a date. A finish line. Something to guarantee the end.

Martin

I was going to invite you to this tonight.

Attached is an e-ticket to an event marked for January 14th.

My gut twists, doing uncomfortable and queasy acrobatics as I read who the event is for.

Fool's Gambit's Ten-Year Anniversary Reunion.

For so many people, this is essentially the equivalent of Willy Wonka's golden ticket. But for me, it's a slap in the face.

If he was the producer for anyone but Fool's Gambit, I might have forgotten him altogether. The band notably consisted of floppy-haired guys in their early twenties who made teenage girls swoon with cheesy lyrics, or at least I assume they did. I never broke down and listened to their music to evaluate its poetic complexity.

In fact, I avoided anything with their faces, but escaping the names and questions was impossible. If I had a dollar for every time someone asked me for a small favor in the form of a VIP ticket or Wesley Hart's phone number, I'd be able to afford one of their overpriced meet-and-greets.

Still, my mom and I liked to pretend we lived in an alternate universe where the band never existed. One where she never married my father and I was simply a product of immaculate conception.

But secretly, her heart was still in the past. She tried to hide the tabloids and how she switched from *E!* to *Wheel of Fortune* when I entered the room, while I pretended not to notice the discarded magazines and the split-second channel changes. Our love ran so deep that we, without realizing it, created a chasm to hide our emotions. Yet that same distance blurred the lines of our relationship, leaving us unsure who was caring for whom.

My finger lingers on the phone keyboard, going over the information. His new invitation means I'll have to endure more than a simple handoff where I can walk away when things inevitably become too emotionally draining.

But those are problems for future Lacey. I've spent weeks hyping myself up for tonight, and now I'm back where I started.

I could go home or meet up with Price and the team, but I don't trust myself around them with my current excess of negative and volatile emotions. Then again, I'm already here. I thought a bar was an odd place for this moment between us to go down, but Martin insisted, so I might as well make the best of it.

Pushing through the entrance, I almost leave when I see the interior. But the idea of walking in and immediately back out feels rude, especially now that I've made lingering eye contact with the heavily tattooed bartender. Maybe one day I'll be able to have an *I don't give a fuck about social conventions* attitude, but today isn't that day.

As it turns out, the bar's name, Half a Memory, isn't a reference to alcohol-induced amnesia. It's a damn Fool's Gambit hit song, because why the hell wouldn't it be?

This type of nonsense is very on-theme for the night. Why wouldn't Martin take the opportunity to stroke his ego and remind me of my parasocial nemeses in one fell swoop? How humble and utterly insensitive of him.

I make another mental tick on the *so my father really is an asshole list.* Impressive how he can do so without actually being in the room.

The bar room is a 2010s fever dream come to life. Signed band posters and cartoon flames plastered on as wallpaper. Buzzing neon casts a pink halo on the patrons sitting at the bar.

The memorabilia alone must have cost a small fortune because everything is stained with oversized, Sharpied autographs. The immersive aesthetic half convinces me that if I grabbed my phone from my back pocket, I would have to flip it open to use it.

Still, there's a bright side to this. I don't give a shit who sees me fuming because there's no way in hell I'm ever coming back.

When I reach the bartop, I slide on and nearly right off the slick, sparkly vinyl barstool. Does someone polish these things like a bowling ball?

But I won't be defeated by a piece of furniture. With my pride on the line, I grasp the counter for support to prevent further slippage. Looking down, I notice more images of the band members staring up at me through Teen Vogue clippings and scattered band stickers.

"Can I get you something to drink?" The bartender from earlier sidles up to me, a lean Korean man with high cheekbones and an easy grin. The mirth dancing in his deep set eyes gives me the impression that he's perpetually amused.

"Just a house whiskey on the rocks," I tell him, my words pulling a snort from the man a few seats down, and I catch him looking my way. "Have anything you'd like to say about my drink order?"

"Nothing. You're just brave for ordering it," the grump says. His baseball hat is drawn low over his face, casting a shadow obscuring his features. His gaze flickers between me and some Seinfeld rerun.

"Whiskey is whiskey," I defend.

"You'd probably like the taste of straight ethanol then."

"And I bet you'd like the benefits of therapy, but I don't think it's worth listing things neither of us will try." I never try to put up a filter if I'm around strangers. At work, there are times that I just have to smile and shut up. I'm a woman in sports, and being talked to like I have no clue what I'm doing was practically in the job description.

But I don't have to play nice in these random interactions, knowing I'll walk away at the end of the day.

The bartender sets my drink in front of me and I take a healthy sip to prove my surly companion wrong. It turns out to be a bad move because it is the worst drink I've ever had. Liquid fire runs down my throat as I swallow and nearly choke.

"Told you." The man smirks, turning slightly towards me.

"It'll do the job," I insist, still determined to make a point.

"What job is that exactly?"

"It helps to wash away bad days, usually." Whiskey for bad days, tequila for celebrations, wine for everything else.

"That makes sense. It could probably be used as a household cleaner. Anything in particular worth wiping away on this particular occasion?"

"I got stood up." Not exactly, but the sentiment is the same. A buzzing high of anticipation crashing into a pit of disappointment.

"Their loss is my gain."

"By my *father.*"

"You could call me d—"

He's cut off by the bartender. "I swear to God, if you finish that sentence, I'll throw a drink in your face even if she's too nice to."

"I definitely would have thrown the drink, but I appreciate it." I make sure to give my new best friend behind the bar a genuine, if not a little evil, smile.

"I'll behave, Craig," my companion says, sounding chastised, but the look on Craig's face makes it seem like he doesn't believe a damn word.

"Don't tell me you're a regular at a boy band bar," I wheeze with the effort it takes to contain my laugh. Honestly, who would camp out in a place like this for fun?

Now that he's fully facing me, the man feels sharper, like our exchange has pulled him from the fringes of reality.

The adjustment lets me appreciate that he doesn't fit in here. He probably would look more at home as one of the celebrities on the wall instead of sitting here next to me.

His chiseled features and square jaw are graced with a hint of stubble. The angles of his face are cast in an intoxicating, haunting glow from the neon light. The waves of brown hair peeking out from under his cap soften his sharp edges.

But what gets me are his eyes. They are a rich, deep green that feels like getting lost in a forest.

When I lower my gaze, it's an effort not to stare at the tattoos that take up his toned forearms. Who knew forearms could be so hot?

"What if I am?" He doesn't seem the least bit offended.

"He just likes to bum off our WiFi and shitty cable," Craig calls out.

"Whose side are you on?" my companion complains.

"Whatever side you aren't on," Craig quips, sending a smug sense of victory through me.

"Ouch. And I thought we were friends." The guy pretends to act wounded, throwing his hand over his heart and leaning back as if he's just been shot. "Craig knows he loves me; he just won't admit it." He gives me a wink, his long lashes nearly brushing his cheeks.

In a seamless burst of motion, my stranger hops to the seat next to me. I'm not sure what part of our conversation gave off *let's be friends* vibes. I don't give it much thought because as he settles into place, my attention snaps to where his leg brushes against mine.

"I'm Drew," he says, holding out his hand. I briefly take it before turning back to my drink. "You know it's customary to respond with your name after someone introduces themselves?"

"I don't give personally identifying information to strangers. And hasn't someone told you that shaking hands has been out of fashion for a while now?" I tell him, deflecting.

I make it a habit of not telling people too much about myself; all of the key parts of my life often lead to conversations I'd rather avoid. Let's think: Famous dad, Dead mom, or tell them about working for the NHL, only to end up talking more about the players than my actual job.

In lieu of being a buzzkill, I'm not above lying to supplement a conversation. But I like the raw rapport that we've built and I don't want to ruin it with unwarranted dishonesty.

"But we're not really strangers. You know my name, and I know that you're too stubborn to admit when you're wrong."

"If that's all the information it takes, I'd be besties with my barista."

"Good to know I'm not getting special treatment, but I bet the barista gets to know your name, at least."

"How else would I know when my order's ready?" I roll my eyes at having to explain the obvious.

"I guess I'll just have to take you out to coffee then."

"Not going to happen. And even if it did, I would expect you to order, so it would be your name on the order, not mine, and that would negate the entire purpose of your scheme."

"You're forgetting the secondary and more important purpose." He pauses. "buying a beautiful woman a drink. But I can do that now, too, if you let me."

"I can buy my own drinks. Thank you."

"Based on the current evidence," he says, pointing to the amber liquid still in my glass. "I don't trust you to buy your own drinks, and you owe me."

"Why's that?"

"I gave you my name and I'm working with nothing here except knowing that you're the key demographic for this place, but that's not a ton to work with."

"What ways do I fit into the 'key demographic?'" I'm trying my best not to bristle at the comment. I'd be offended if I didn't know he was right in ways I'll never admit.

"Hmmm, you were probably a teenager when bands like Fool's Gambit were popular. You probably got tickets for one of their shows for Christmas, spent the week before making some predictable sign like, 'I heart Wesley Hart,' and probably have some overpriced memorabilia that you keep for nostalgia's sake in a cardboard box that you can't bring yourself to get rid of." He counts out each reason with one of his fingers and gives me a cocky look; so sure he's got me pinned.

I laugh, ready to dismantle his expectations. "I hope they don't pay you for market research. I'm not a music person, I've never been to a concert, and I have far better things to spend my money on than memorabilia that will end up in a cardboard box under my bed," I tell him. I swear his grin grows, like proving him wrong was precisely what he wanted. "You, on the other hand, are pretty damn easy to read. Probably peaked during or right after high school. You live for happy hour because it's the first acceptable time to come here and drink alone. You probably go home with whoever thinks you're hotter than you are annoying, and then you do it again the next night."

"How do you not like music? It's like a basic human need." The question doesn't come out accusatory. When I tell people, they usually take personal offense, as if my aversion is some commentary on their personal taste. But this man just sounds miffed.

I try to pick an explanation that's not: *You see this bar? Yeah, my dad worked with the band and gave me a general bad taste for music.*

I usually don't dwell on these facts this much, but I guess current circumstances have made them glaringly relevant.

"I just never really connected with it. There's always been this thing that hasn't ever let me get lost in it. It's not like I don't listen to music. I've never had that experience of being carried away by it." That *thing* being, I was always scared of falling in love with a song on the radio and learning that my father had some hand in creating it. I didn't ever want to think of him as capable of creating beautiful things.

"So, no to boy bands then?" He gestures with his drink to our surroundings.

"This moment." I mimic his movement "Me being here is some cruel joke pulled by the universe that I don't have the mental energy to explain. Honestly, I don't get why someone would make an entire bar glorifying them. Like whoever owns this place must be obsessed. Don't you think it's a little creepy? What rational person thinks about opening a bar and settles on an ode to a band that hasn't been together for the last ten years?"

"I heard the owner is one of the old band members." He shrugs like it's common knowledge.

"So, *self-obsessed* and probably has a tiny dick. I'll make sure to never meet him then."

He chuckles before adding, "Yeah, probably can't even hold a decent conversation."

I suffer through the rest of my first drink before ordering a margarita. We continue to fight about nothing and everything from the merits of raw fish in sushi—that he hates it and I think that he needs to grow up—to why sitcoms aren't as good as they used to be.

When Drew sets down his drink, some sloshes on the bar. He leans forward to grab a napkin, and in the process, his hand moves to rest on my thigh. I don't stop him or shift out from under it. I would have no problem returning his hand to him, but when his fingers tease the seam of my jeans, I can't help but think what his long, thick fingers would feel like teasing other parts of me.

He lowers his head, lips brushing my ear as he says, "If you're going to keep staring at me like that, I'd prefer if we did it somewhere more private so you could do it properly."

That's it.

I've forgotten how to breathe.

In shock, I stand up, but my foot catches on my stool. As I start to fall, I brace for the impact that never comes as large hands grip my waist. I look up into Drew's eyes and almost stumble all over again from the way they burn into me.

"Falling for me now? You didn't have to go that far to touch me." The rumble of his voice pulls me from the spell.

"Oh, fuck you."

"I'll let you if you ask nicely." His grin is so cocky, but that does nothing to stop the image that flicks through my mind, sending a flush of heat through me. The damn grin only widens when he clocks the blush taking over my face.

When my feet are firmly beneath me, he removes his hands. I retreat toward the bathroom, hoping the distance will help me regain my senses.

God.

This night is not going in the direction I planned. And the funny thing is that it's been nice. I had been prepared for a tense, forced get-to-know-you session, not a verbal match that had me forgetting my worries.

What's the harm of leaning into it? I could definitely do worse than a hot stranger for the night.

When I get back, it's the fourth drink that's my undoing. It's the one that has us pressed together in the dimly lit back corner under a neon sign shaped like a microphone.

Hungry and desperate, each touch ignites my body and stirs up emotions I've suppressed for far too long.

As his warm hand plays with the hem of my shirt and he nips down the length of my neck, I make noises that would make two or even three drink Lacey utterly fucking embarrassed. But I can't think of anything else but the hard length of him pushing me into the wall.

He pulls away to look at me, leaving my bruised lips wanting more.

"If you're going to keep making those sounds, we better go somewhere else before we're not so politely asked to leave," he says, before leaning in to speak against my lips. "If the next words that come out of that pretty little mouth are, 'I don't do one night stands,' or 'I'm not that kind of girl,' let me know right now so I can order you an Uber home, and I'll go take care of myself."

I can't help the smile that slides onto my lips just before I lift up onto my toes and whisper into his ear, "It's just your luck. I only do one-night stands."

4

Lacey

I only have time to set down my keys in the dish in the entryway before my back is pressed against the solid surface of my door. His lips find mine with an enthusiasm that makes me feel like I'm the only thing that can satiate him.

I savor the light prickle of pain as he grips my ponytail and teases at the delicate skin at the juncture of my jaw with his teeth. In response to the sting, my back arches, grinding against his thigh.

He takes the opportunity to graze the sliver of exposed skin on my stomach, and I feel electric. I'm a lightning rod being hit repeatedly, feeding my growing desire.

"Are you just going to spend the next hour kissing me or actually put your money where your mouth is?" I ask, wanting more. Needing to fade into him. To know what he can do with his clever fingers and vicious tongue.

His emerald eyes narrow. "Don't you worry. I'll put my mouth wherever it will make you moan the loudest."

I know the devil must have green eyes, because I've never seen anything more sinful in my life than how his gaze devours me. As if to emphasize his words, his hand snakes up my shirt, finding my pebbled nipple, rolling it between his fingers, and pulling a startled gasp from my lips.

Before I can fully process the sensation, he hitches my legs around his waist and carries me to my kitchen then sets me on the counter.

My shirt and bra are easily discarded, but my jeans are plastered against my skin, damp cotton clinging to my thighs like their sole purpose in this universe is to bar me from having sex tonight. Running through the rain feels like a damn movie until your clothes get in the way of the real magic happening.

I struggle at first, attempting to slide them off my hips, but Drew takes over.

No tinge of awkwardness disrupts the tension between us as he peels back the fabric, making me feel like I'm being unwrapped. A gift for his enjoyment as he takes his time exposing each inch of skin, letting his touch trail down my inner thigh.

Fully bare before him, the chill of the marble sends a shiver through my skin. When I glance up, his eyes are locked onto me with a blazing intensity that threatens to set my skin on fire.

He reaches out, running a finger over my center. "Look at you, soaked already."

"That's just from the rain." The retort comes as easy as breathing at this point.

"Oh really? The rain got you all ready to be fucked?" Cocky, so cocky. Before I can form a response, the pad of his thumb circles my clit. My hips surge off the counter in a way that requires one of his massive hands to anchor me in place. "Did our little sparring match turn you on? I bet you've been like this the entire time we were at the bar. What would I have found if I checked?"

"Nothing," I say, despite the fact that there has been a heat building low in my belly for the better part of an hour.

"Liar. You may think I'm infuriating, but your pussy is practically begging for my attention." My mind goes blank as a finger sinks into me, curling, hitting me exactly right to shut off my entire brain.

A second finger has me grinding against his hand.

"That's it. Ride my fingers." The praise is absolutely dangerous, sending a bolt of heat through me that I feel all the way to my toes.

I do as he commands until my thighs shake, and I tip precariously closer and closer to the edge of release.

Then he stops. He fucking stops, pulling his hand away, leaving me empty and absolutely needy.

A sound of rage halfway between a scream and a whimper erupts from my throat. "Fuck you."

"Soon, I promise. But it will be fun to see how mad I can get you first. You might have thought I was driving you crazy earlier, but trust me, I'm not done making you squirm."

More. I need more. Everything. Any sensation at all.

I reach out my hand to unfasten the button of his jeans, but he catches my wrists with a single hand just as my fingers graze the fabric of his pants. Fabric that strains with the evidence of his own desire.

The daggers I throw at him with my eyes only seem to make him amused. "Oh, I'm not giving my cock to you yet, you greedy thing. You have to earn it first."

Still holding my wrists to the side, he sinks to his knees and it's a damn beautiful sight. His lips brush against the tender flesh at the crease of my hip, encouraging my legs to open for him.

An invitation I'm happy to give.

He buries his head between my thighs. His tongue dances around my clit, teasing me, not quite hitting where I want him to. Not out of ignorance but part of the battle of wills we've thrown ourselves into. I shift my hips, desperate for the pleasure he's given me a glimpse of.

"Fuck. You taste so sweet despite all your venom," The gravel in his words vibrates through me. This time when he lowers his head, he devours me, tongue plunging into me, thumb meeting my clit, making those same precise circles.

"That's perfect," I gasp, a tide of ecstasy threatening to pull me apart. Feeling nothing but how he's setting off every sensitive nerve like I'm a damn fireworks show as I come. He pulls away, releasing my wrists before rising and seizing my chin in one hand.

"You almost had me convinced you're a good girl. You looked damn near angelic after coming on my face. Too bad I know the truth." He leans closer, so his words brush against my cheek. "You're a little demon."

When he presses his mouth against mine, I taste my own arousal as our tongues clash. He's infuriating, but I have to give him credit. There are competent men, and then there is this man who seems to have an atlas of my body burned into his mind.

"I never would have expected you to be such a giver. Even if you weren't, I'd make sure to get what I deserve," I say with the confidence of someone who didn't just fall apart against his mouth.

"I'm nothing if not a gentleman."

"You're no gentleman."

"You're right. It's a good thing you know that because I don't think either of us wants me to be gentle with what's next."

True. I don't want to feel like a rose to be crushed and discarded. I want him to bite into me so I have an excuse to bite back.

My eyes trace his movements as he lifts his shirt, revealing a mosaic of dark tattoos and sculpted muscle contours. There's not a doubt in my mind that God is a woman because there is no other explanation for how well he's crafted.

My mouth goes dry when he undoes his belt and lowers his pants.

"You're—"

"If you say too big, I'll be disappointed. I thought you'd like a challenge, or do you only talk a big game?"

"I was going to say adequate." I wasn't, and from his lazy, self-satisfied expression, he knows that too.

"*Adequate?* I can't wait to prove you wrong."

Once again, he lifts me into the air. This man and his obsession with carrying me is a little addicting, feeling feather light and utterly taken care of.

"Are you ready?" he asks, resting me on my mattress.

"Yes. I have condoms in the top drawer of my nightstand." I direct him, but he already has one in his hand, tearing the wrapper and rolling it onto his impressive length.

Hands wrap around my calves, and he slides me toward the edge of the bed, eliciting an embarrassing squeak from my lips. Once I'm where he wants me, he grips my thighs, spreading them apart so he can stand between them. I watch as he pumps a hand down his shaft before he lines himself up and eases into me slowly so I feel every inch.

"God," I moan as my body adjusts to the size of his cock.

"Not God. I gave you my name, and I expect you to use it," he commands as he starts to rock his hips, moving in and out of me at an excruciatingly slow pace compared to what I'm craving.

"Ok then, *Drew*. Stop taking your time and fuck me like you hate my guts." My words seem to snap the last strand of hesitation between us, and he thrusts forward, snapping his hips with brutal force. He works my body into a frenzy, having me writhing beneath him.

"Do you feel how much you irritate me? Are you convinced?" he demands.

"I barely feel anything," I lie, using my words to push against him on instinct. This only prompts him to guide my legs over his shoulders in a way that simultaneously makes me feel whole and that I'm about to be split in two. I want him to break me apart. I want him to take control and eliminate my need to think.

"What about now? Does this feel *adequate* to you?" he asks, twisting my words against me as he buries himself in me in a deliberate stroke.

My ability to form words vanishes. I can only succumb to the sensations pouring through me, letting loose another needy moan while sinking my fingers into his biceps, relishing his skin under my nails. Making him feel me as much as I feel him. Demanding that I won't be forgotten.

"I hope you know I'm using you for your body," I say in a breathy voice I hardly recognize. I want to reinforce that no matter how good this is, how many stars I feel rushing under my skin. This is just sex. Top-shelf sex that I will have recurring dreams about, but that's it.

"I'd let you use my body anytime you want." He punctuates by lowering my legs before leaning over me and taking my nipple in his mouth, skating his teeth across the sensitive skin.

His touch effortlessly draws me in, and I get lost in those eyes—in him, in someone. But just as quickly, the desperate need for control tightens its grip around my throat as I push him away, only for a moment.

He shifts back, letting me take the lead for the first time tonight as I guide him onto the mattress so I can straddle him before sinking onto his cock. The new angle is utterly euphoric.

Strong fingers press into my hips as he tries to guide my hips, but he's already had his turn. "Stop moving and let me use you how I want."

I pin his wrists on either side of his hips and hold them there, using them to stabilize myself as I take exactly what I need.

I sense his admiring gaze tracing my movements, focused in a way that implies he could see right through me, questioning everything I've been adamantly selling him tonight.

Moving one of my hands to the firm surface of his chest, I throw my head back and close my eyes, quickening my rhythm to match my racing heart. A part of me hopes it's a sufficient distraction to divert his attention from looking too closely at those fragile pieces.

"Fuck, *sconosciuta.* You feel so good. Take what you need, take everything." The praise is the final push needed for a second orgasm to wrack through me and he quickly follows.

When we finally pull apart, there's an emptiness, and I'm struck with the realization that I can't remember the last time I've been so completely satisfied. I have no problem telling a guy exactly what to do so I can come. There's no use wasting a night on someone who doesn't get me off. I'd rather slightly bruise their ego and help out the next girl they're with in the process.

Exhaling, I turn to him to let him know he can leave. But before I can even utter a word, he starts gathering his damp clothes, and I shamelessly watch him as he dresses. It's a relief that neither of us are under any illusion that this is anything more than it is.

"Did I finally earn your name?" he asks, catching me in the act of surveying him.

"We've made do for this long without it. Why ruin a good thing with unnecessary trivia?" I don't give anyone my name during these types of encounters. It's easy enough to put it off; names and other throw-away facts are just the pleasantries people hand out to get into each other's pants.

"Maybe next time?" he asks, and I'm surprised that my first thought isn't immediately "no," given the times it never worked out well for me.

"What makes you so sure there will be a next time?"

He quirks one of his full eyebrows. "Do you want me to give you a play-by-play? I'd stay to prove the point, but I have somewhere to be."

"Don't hold your breath. I'm a one-and-done kind of girl. One night with you didn't change that." An uncomplicated, clean break is how it has to be.

"You know where to find me when you come to your senses."

"Sure. Unless someone else makes a habit of haunting Atlanta's tackiest bar."

"I think I've monopolized that niche market." He wraps his hand around the back of my throat, pulling me in for one last kiss that leaves a searing impression on my lips. I'm almost disappointed as I watch him leave, his touch still lingering on my skin.

By the end of the day, my shoulders are usually so stiff with tension they arch up to my ears. Considering how the night started, I should be feeling drained and tight, but doing a mental full-body scan, I don't feel anything but light.

Free.

Drew gave me a release, a target to let out all the emotions battling for attention inside my head. Sex has always been an excellent way to work off stress, but it's never done it so entirely before. He didn't stick around for pillow talk or niceties like most people try to do, which is nice.

That blurry limbo between pleasure and goodbye is tricky. It's tempting to spill your soul to someone who has no stock in your life. I had a guy once practically beg to be my therapist for the night. The end result was a full head instead of an empty one.

It's why no one gets to stay the night. No one gets to ask the personal questions that seem like a good idea until they go too far. And no one, not even my ex Henry, got to say I love you.

I love you—words that have enough weight to sink a ship.

Yet, some people toss those words around like coupons, as if they're easy to use up and throw away. Maybe some people genuinely have that much love to give out, but I don't believe them. How could anyone be so full of any emotion?

During one horrific encounter, Thomas, some artsy guy who insisted that smoking cigarettes was 'European,' said the words during hook-up number two. It was definitely one of those heat-of-the-moment things that probably meant, I love your body or I love fucking you, but I didn't, and still don't care. I politely moved off him, handed him his clothes, and reintroduced him to the door.

The one-night stand rule is law and has yet to fail.

I pull on an oversized t-shirt and shoot off a text requesting a girl-talk debrief with Cara. Despite the post-midnight hour, I know my only girl friend is awake grading assignments.

She's one of those people who is productive at the most unconventional hours. During the semesters when we lived together in college, she was hardly home, either at whatever girlfriend or boyfriend's apartment or at the library. But our shared drive for academic validation was part of why we clicked so well. The fact that we were in entirely different fields helped ensure that instead of being competitors, we were each other's biggest supporters.

Now, she's at the forefront of research finishing her PhD in molecular physics in Ithaca. Even at twenty-five, she's making internationally recognized contributions to the field. One day, I'll probably be in the crowd at some award show for a discovery she makes that will be immortalized in textbooks.

As I wait for her call, I grab disinfectant and a rag from under my sink. Call me high maintenance all you want, but I can't comfortably look at my counter again until it's been cleaned.

"Hey," I hear a subtle clattering of keys from her end. She has one of those keyboards designed to feel like a typewriter; it's unnecessarily loud, but she loves it. "Just kick another stranger out of your apartment?"

"Yeah, but I hate that you call them that. It's creepy." Thinking about bringing strangers to my apartment is far more enjoyable when I don't consider the implications associated with said strangers.

"Well, you need to be more wary about it."

"Are you watching *Criminal Minds* again?" Her concerns about my life are based on her current TV obsession. When she rewatched *Gossip Girl,* she was hell-bent on breaking me out of my black tops and jeans fixation. My constant decision fatigue makes my minimalist closet more of a necessity than a rebellion against consumerism.

She counters with her own annoying but accurate accusation, "I bet you're cleaning right now. It's what, two in the morning? You just had sex good enough to distract you from your change in schedule, so your first response is to clean.

You know, disinfecting every surface doesn't wipe away the remnants of intimacy. When will you stop going for strangers at bars and find something sustainable?"

The conversation was always going to divert into this. The *when are you going to open up and let the world see how amazing you are* conversation that I have to take with a grain of salt because my social circle has been two people for the last six years.

"The moment that I can talk about my job without getting the fourth degree about player stats and the possibility of meeting the team," I tell her, the same way I always do.

"Is it really that bad? You like those things too. Think of it as a bonding experience. You'd be able to run laps around any of those guys at trivia."

"And we both know men take a blow to their ego like that really well. Remind me what that chemistry professor did after you pointed out a problem in his research methodology?"

We were friends before we settled into our respective careers. But there's a special type of kinship that comes from both of us working in male-dominated fields—sharing in the times when people constantly question our abilities as if verifying that our years of credentials aren't just elaborate fabrications.

"At least tell me how it was. Your love life is my favorite reality TV show. It always cheers me up."

"Are you saying that my romantic life is so bad that it makes you feel better in comparison? Because I'm content with my situation," I insist.

"I'm not. You're torturing both of us with your bad decisions."

"It's completely logical."

"Lying to people at bars and not giving them your name is not the behavior of a well-adjusted person."

True, but it doesn't mean I don't get exactly what I want from the interactions.

"It's your mistake for assuming I'm well adjusted," I tease.

"I'm still waiting for the details."

A smile creeps onto my face as I recall the last few hours. "Fine. Have you ever been so annoyed by someone they turned you on? Like you couldn't decide if you wanted to smack the shit out of them or fuck them so they'd just shut up."

"No, but you're really making me want to. It could be fun going into a bar with the goal of annoying someone."

"You're too lovable to get anyone that riled up." Cara's considerate yet driven nature is why we make a great match. She's understanding and doesn't get defensive when I'm too blunt.

"Like the rude shit he was saying in the bar had nothing on the filth he was telling me in my bedroom. Well, the kitchen too, thus the cleaning. I feel like I should get a priest in there or something."

"You just killed my vicarious high by talking about disinfecting surfaces," she groans in disappointment.

"Whatever, the details aren't super clear now that the adrenaline is wearing off, and I'm still a little buzzed from drinking." I open the cabinet under my sink and return the cleaning supplies to their proper place.

"There is a simple solution to this. You just have to sleep with him again, take notes, and report back."

"Now that's hilarious."

"Just go back to the bar," she nearly begs.

"Not happening." With my apartment back in order, I move to my bed, curling beneath the sheets, where faint traces of his cologne remain.

"But you should. You better keep me updated. I don't care if the man is naked in your bed. You better let me know if it happens again."

"If I have a lapse in judgment, I'll give you a full voice memo and everything," I relent slightly.

"You better make it like one of those horny audiobooks so I can listen to it again later. You should also keep a journal, like for field notes," she says, getting carried away.

"Cara, please don't use my exploits for nefarious reasons," I say, not that I'm agreeing to this at all.

"Only educational ones. If it was that good, like the alleged life changing benefits of yoga good, I want to learn how to replicate it. I think you should go back and finally consider a relationship, especially if it was as fun as you're saying."

"I've already done the relationship thing,"

Cara huffs. "We both know Henry was more of a bandaid than a boyfriend. I'm just happy you tore him off and threw him away before I had to do it myself."

"He wasn't that bad," I defend him, despite everything he pulled in our relationship. I could never be with someone like him again, controlling and self-righteous. But he was exactly what I needed at the time.

Henry and I met at a fundraiser six months after my mother's funeral, back when I was barely keeping my head above water. He was charming enough, which is pretty much guaranteed since he's a beloved sports commentator. More importantly, he had no problem telling me what to do and who to be at a time when I didn't want to do those things for myself. The only reason I left was because he eventually pushed too far, leaving me with no other choice.

"I've gotta go. My students are organizing a mutiny over their grades. Don't they have beer pong to play or something?" She groans, likely dreaming about the day when she'll be done TAing lectures and can just focus on research.

"That's what you get for being ruthless."

"Forgive me for wanting them to have a fundamental grasp on the basic laws of the universe. Bye."

No matter what she says, it's best to let tonight remain a memory. The kind of thing that is best left untouched by further discoveries.

5

Drew

The remaining trickle of rain does nothing to dampen the pleasant hum buzzing through my veins. I'm buoyant, nearly levitating off the sidewalk as I return to the bar.

When was the last time someone glanced at me like that without that subtle glimmer of recognition? A flash in their eyes always lets me know the person is thinking: *Are you worth it? If so, what do I want from you*? Those looks always make me feel like a used-up tube of toothpaste, the type someone is determined to force just a little more from, pressing and contorting the package until they get what they need. Leaving me a little more empty in the process.

Her raw, honest conversation was the opposite, giving me back something I wasn't aware I was missing. I'm still giddy as a teenager over introducing myself to her, even though I wasn't entirely truthful. But I didn't see a point in potentially ruining a good thing before it started. And it was a damn good thing too.

I can still feel the phantom press of her soft skin against my fingertips, the delicious tug of her fingers in my hair, and the way she looked when she came apart. I'm certain it will be etched into my brain forever.

When I get back to the bar, Craig is already at the end of closing up, sweeping stray cocktail straws and garnish skewers. I almost feel guilty that I ditched him, *almost.* The guy looks too smug for his own good like he orchestrated tonight's sequence of events.

"If you open your mouth and ruin this, I will set the TVs to a home improvement channel and hide all the remotes," I tell him.

"I was just going to ask if you could help mop with all the water you brought in." His smile tells me he wasn't planning to talk about mops. "But if it had crossed my mind, I would say that girl has you looking fresh as a daisy."

"It's good that it didn't cross your mind then because that's cheesy as hell. I think I'm more of a rose."

"I kinda like the look on you. It's been a while since you've been that distracted by anyone. You need a break sometimes, boss. And no, sitting at your own bar with your bandmates' faces posted up all over it doesn't count as a break. It's probably considered some form of self-inflicted torture. I literally have nightmares about this place turning into one of those carnival funhouses. We could live without so much pink." His eyes go glassy for a moment, his shoulders shuddering as if he's imagining said nightmares in vivid detail.

"Beyond your unsolicited interior design advice, if those thoughts did cross your mind, I'd probably tell you you're a good friend." I move to get the mop from the cleaning closet, and when I return, I tell Craig, "Get your ass out of here before we're hit with another wave of this storm. I really don't want to add finding a new manager to the list of shit I have to deal with at the moment. I'll finish up closing."

"Don't forget you'd also have to find a new best friend. And that would be impossible because I'm irreplaceable," he says, gathering his stuff and throwing on a rain jacket.

"Oh fuck off," I laugh.

As I soak up the puddle I tracked in, my mind sticks to what Craig said. One-night stands usually end up with a missing t-shirt and getting tagged in a picture someone took of me passed out on my pillow. They're sleeping with a name, a piece of nostalgia that will become their favorite party story, not a person they give half a damn about.

The feeling of anonymity I had tonight meant no digging up secrets or leading questions.

Maybe she was right and I am obsessed with the past. I created this bar to give me a reason not to keep moving. It was nice to hear her brutal honesty instead of just being fed what I wanted to hear.

I need more of that in my life. I have Craig, but I can see that even he softens his blows sometimes, as if sensing I only have one foot in the present.

I want her words to keep cutting through all the bullshit cluttering up my life.

I sleep so well that it takes an earthquake to wake me up. Or at least I think it's an earthquake until I'm met with Craig's crooked grin looming over me. It's sinister, really, sadistic joy radiating off him.

"How the hell? And *why*, it's like seven in the morning?" I ask, knowing full well how he got in.

Though Craig has keys to the bar, he doesn't have anything that should let him into my loft. But like so many times before, he's proven that doors aren't a barrier he needs to worry about. In the same way other rich kids stole for fun, Craig became a master at breaking into wherever he pleased.

I guess today, wherever he pleases, includes my bedroom.

"You can't fault a guy for wanting to see his best friend, but you should probably stop wasting money on replacing the locks. Also, it's eleven," he says, still too cheery even if it isn't as early as I thought.

"You saw me less than twelve hours ago. You could have just texted."

"Yes, that makes sense because last time I checked, people can reply to texts in their sleep now. Here." He hands me one of the to-go coffee cups he's brought, branded with a little mug logo from The Cup down the street.

I take a sip of the quad shot of espresso and gag. "What is this?" The espresso is acidic, nothing like the rich blend with notes of chocolate and cherry that I was expecting.

"New barista," he explains. "Poor kid looked lost as hell, sweet though."

"And you trusted him to make our drinks?"

"I trusted him to make *your* drink. I tipped extra, so Sarah made mine," he says, referring to the pretty Master's student who is our usual barista.

"Thanks for letting the kid practice his skills on my taste buds," I groan, not excited to start my day with bad coffee.

"That reminds me of what I came to talk to you about."

"I thought you just wanted to see your best friend."

"It's a twofold mission." He leans against the wall, shifting from playful to serious in the blink of an eye. "When are you going to be done with the bar?"

"Done, like shutting it down? Why the hell would I do that?"

"No, I wouldn't ever suggest going that far. Just ditching the old shit. Making it less them and more you."

Instead of admitting he's probably right, I feign ignorance. "You just want an excuse to play different music."

"I play whatever music I want when you're not there. And sure, I think I might go blind from looking at the day-glo color scheme, but I'm here for mostly selfless reasons."

"I'm docking your pay."

"Go ahead. Knock yourself out and take my entire check if you want. Just once this reunion bullshit is done, give yourself a chance to move on. Or think about it. That's all I'm asking." He moves, making himself comfortable, stretching out his body on my couch. "Which brings me to my third mission."

"You said you only had two," I remind him.

"I just needed to lull you into complacency for this one," he says, which only means one thing. "What the hell are you going to do with the reunion since you can't fucking play or sing?"

That has been why I've avoided the calls and emails reminding me about the meeting I missed.

"I'll fake it."

"Yeah, because that won't be obvious at all. There's no equivalent of lip-syncing tracks for drummers, you know. You have to figure this out. Or, you know, tell them the truth." Craig is the only one that knows what's wrong. He's seen the ugly result of what happens when I try to play.

"That's funny. I sometimes forget how funny you are because that has to be a joke. I'm not telling them shit. Imagine the field day Wes would have with that."

"Ok, Wesley is categorically annoying and can kiss my ass, especially with all the other shit he's pulled. But you know everyone else, especially your own sister, will be there for you."

Though Evelyn isn't part of the band, she's been there since day one when we were still practicing in our parent's garage. But letting her see this part of me would only represent another way I've failed her as an older sibling.

"Can we just drop it for now? I hear you, and I heard Hartly yesterday. I'll figure it out." I sigh. The brief conversation is already draining my reserves of energy.

"Whatever." Craig rises from the couch and heads to the bathroom, carrying a small black box.

My mind slips back to last night, to that feeling of being unknown. I was a nobody, a version of myself that I crave to be again, but it wasn't long ago that I would have hated the idea.

Things change.

The paradox of being seventeen and holding the keys to the world as you know it is that you're still a kid, even though you deny it every chance you get. Then, one day, you wake up, and you're not a kid anymore, and you can't get the time back. The world keeps moving, even if you're stuck at the top. And I'm not sure if having all the money I'll ever need while the world flows around me is a curse or a blessing.

Maybe I wouldn't be weighed down if I had a reason to keep moving. Just something to keep me from feeling like a rock at the bottom of a turbulent river, too stubborn for my own good.

If given the chance, would I have given it all back? Would I still have signed the contracts and taken the money to live out my dream? There's never been a right answer.

I became everything I ever wanted but at a cost. I didn't sell my soul, but definitely a fragment of it. But is that any better? A life that destroys you slowly instead of all at once? Besides, in another universe, there is more than a slim chance that I'd be doing exactly what I am right now: spending my nights sipping a beer and letting my mind go blank. The only difference would be that I wouldn't be the bar owner.

Martin Hall was our idol when he started working with us as a producer, giving advice and support throughout our journey. Once, I overheard him tell Wesley that you know when you *arrive*; it's a gut feeling so undeniable that it couldn't be anything else. None of us had thought about the reality of arriving too early.

Because once you arrive, what else is there for you? By the age of twenty-three, I had fulfilled my life's purpose and the rolling expanse of years ahead of me became crushing.

It's Martin's fault, really. He heard us singing along together and saw a vision with dollar signs. I don't mean it in a bad way; he was a good guy who cared for us better than anyone could have hoped for, but it was a job, and our success determined his.

The plan was set in motion once it was confirmed that none of us had two left feet. And we succeeded. As a boy band, we were stars—everything we wished for. But like a falling star colliding with the atmosphere, I eventually burnt out and became dust, broken down into nothing but fragments of who I used to be. It's like I've been walking around holding my breath out of pure stubbornness, and this woman walks in, punches me in the gut, and says, "Breathe, you fucking idiot." It's not that she knew anything about me. It's the fact that even without knowing me, she could see it.

I continue to sip on the espresso mostly because it's in my hand, and I keep forgetting how terrible it is. I run through the list of things I should do today, starting with following up with the liquor distributor and the missing shipment of cocktail shakers. Two things, but still, those two things begin to weigh me down.

An abrupt buzzing sound starts from my bathroom, where buzzing should probably not be coming from at this very moment. Or ever.

"Craig!" I shout, finally hauling myself out of bed, not bothering to properly clothe myself before investigating. I find my friend missing the middle section of his hair, a limp reverse Mohawk.

"What?" He turns to me with an innocent look that seems to say *No, my hair isn't covering every inch of your bathroom, just most of it. This is perfectly normal behavior.*

"Care to explain where the hair clippers came from and what drove you to do whatever the hell you are doing in my apartment."

"Sarah said something about liking guys with buzz cuts, so I thought it was worth a try."

"The twenty-two-year-old barista told you she likes guys with no hair, so your first instinct is to go bald?"

"She's hot. I make it a rule in life to listen to hot women," he says, like it's the most logical reason in the world.

I just leave him to it, heading to what I think is the pile of clean clothes in the corner to pull on a shirt and a pair of sweats.

Not long after, he needs me to help with the hard-to-reach portions on the back of his head. I'm tempted to make him live with his impulsive decision and leave the awkward patch of hair, but the guy is trying his best.

However much this was for Sarah, the barista, it was also for me. He does shit like this to make me laugh, going to extremes to force emotion out of me. To his credit, he does it really well. Coming up with ideas that usually involve sacrificing some part of his dignity to do it. I don't try to make sense of it.

Trying to make sense of Craig is like trying to solve a Rubix cube blindfolded; someone out there can do it with pure dumb luck, but that sure as hell isn't me.

Granted, most of his antics don't leave me with piles of hair that I know I'll be cleaning up for the next few days.

6

Lacey

It's easy to fall into the trap of thinking you know people from how they're portrayed in the media. The photos and interviews, woven into vivid stories about athletes and celebrities, are all designed to convince you you know them like best friends. A cleverly constructed facade for people to forget that these public figures have teams of people training them on how to present themselves.

The average person doesn't see how poised posture slumps when someone knows the camera is no longer on them or how the sweet boy-next-door defenseman has a mouth that should be washed out with soap.

I'm reminded of this as I crouch in the hallway, capturing the guy's walk-in outfits. My knees groan as I shift my weight, adjusting my angle just as Jonathan walks towards me in a purple suit jacket over a charcoal turtleneck, his hand lightly grasping an empty water bottle. The moment he's next to me, his focused expression morphs into a grin. In one swift movement, he taps my head playfully with the bottle before jogging to the changing room.

They pay me to make the guys look good, but it would be far easier to show the world that they're just a bunch of idiots—my idiots, but still.

Aaron is next, wearing a slate pinstriped suit that does wonders to make his sky-colored eyes pop. Unlike the others, his movements are less refined. His casual nature hasn't been scared out of him with media training. I love it, though, seeing someone who hasn't carved away parts of themself to fit a specific image.

When he reaches me, he hesitantly whispers, "Did that look weird? Should I do it again?"

I meet his eyes. "I'll never let you look bad. I swear you're about to break hearts with these pictures." This is also part of the job, reassuring them that this is for me to worry about and reminding them they have a whole team supporting them.

I intimately understand the anxiety. Martin stopped living with us when I was four, but my parents' divorce was drawn out and unnecessarily public due to his fame and selfishness. I have cloudy memories of walking out of school only to find a slew of cameras hunting for my mother and me. And although things got better after we moved to Phoenix, I've never been comfortable when someone takes my picture.

A psychologist would probably say something about fear leading my career choice and how I want to switch roles with my tormentors. Maybe they're right, or maybe I just love the thrill of being privy to the behind-the-scenes reality of perfect moments.

The rest of the guys follow the same pattern, shifting back into themselves once they know their picture is taken. And then there's Price, shooting finger guns at me the moment he turns the corner. He's never let this life get to him, never even tried to pretend.

Price is just Price.

Once the guys are all inside, I rapidly upload the pictures to send to the social media team and touch base with Tessa, the intern I've mentored for the last few years. She's sweet and has a sparkle in her eye, even after working with us for two seasons.

I walk with her to capture footage of the guys' pregame soccer warmup routine, which helps them loosen up before games. As we arrive in the open space, the team passes the ball to each other, and she holds up her phone to film. When I catch Price's eye, he breaks away and grabs an extra ball from the corner.

I've updated him about the events that unfolded a week ago at the bar. Admittedly, I left out a few details. Talking to Price about relationships only makes me feel like a failure; he gives well-intentioned advice but doesn't quite get my commitment-phobic tendencies.

I follow him to a spot a few feet away so we can talk with at least a little privacy.

"So what have you decided?" Price asks, dribbling the ball back and forth and then passing it to me.

"I'm going to go. The results are going to be the same either way." I shrug, trying to downplay my emotions about surrounding Martin's invitation.

"The reunion will be different. He has the home turf advantage in that scenario."

"It's not like the bar was any different. Get this, it was some shrine to Fool's Gambit." I catch the ball as it overshoots, then return it with a light kick.

Price doesn't catch the ball because the idiot is doubled over laughing. He barely gets out the next few words. "You've got to be kidding me. There's no way a place like that exists."

"I promise I couldn't dream it up in my worst nightmares. You should take Mari there for a date night." I'm only half joking.

Mari proudly declares herself the band's number-one fan. So, it's fair to say that Price and I decided to wait until they were serious before revealing my relation to her idols. To her credit, she's never pried once.

He's still trying to force air into his lungs when I scoop up the ball and hand it back to him. "I need to set up the net cam," I say, ready to retreat into my work.

"You really are dedicated to taking pictures of my ass."

"The defense. The net cam takes pictures of the defense. I take no joy in editing pictures of your ass."

"Why must you kill all of my dreams?" he complains, a smile creeping onto his features.

"Because you'd be utterly delusional without me. It's my job to make sure you never let being a pro athlete turn you into an asshole, remember?" It's part of the deal we made when everything started clicking into place for us. He asked me to make sure he never got corrupted by this life. I told him I doubted that was even possible, but I promised because it was one of those rare times when there was no levity in my best friend's voice.

Sometimes, I wonder why I stick with my job when I hate some of its unfortunate side effects. Then I remember that conversation all those years ago and the similarity between Price and me: we do it because there's not a single other thing in this world that makes us feel whole. The same rush and freedom he experiences on the ice is what I feel capturing it. It makes it all worth it.

7

Drew

It's been nearly a week since I banned hair clippers from my loft, and I'm still finding pieces of Craig's hair in my bathroom. As I give up on a broom and move to find the vacuum to solve my problem, my phone buzzes. I let it go unanswered because the only thing worth focusing on right now is making sure no more of Craig's scratchy ass hair finds its way into my shirts.

I spent the better part of yesterday doing laundry, facing the clusters of clothes that take up permanent residence on my floor. That was probably part of his masterminded scheme to force me to do a basic task. But that was only after I threw on a shirt that had me itching like my skin was crawling with fire ants.

My phone goes off again, but still, I don't want anything to do with it. On the third set of insistent vibrations, I give in and pull the phone out from my pocket, ready to gauge whether to turn it off or accept my fate with whoever is calling.

My father's contact flashes across the screen.

One of the major downsides to people knowing that you have nothing going on in your life is that they also know you're available to pick up the occasional phone call. Taking my time, I consider delaying whatever discussion he's prepared to force down my throat.

Finally, I press the green accept button and my father's lilting, accented voice floats through the speaker. "Why haven't you called about the band getting back together? You know, we're proud of you for getting your life back on track." That pride is exactly why I haven't called; I haven't earned it. "You should have told us, but instead, we learned from one of my coworkers who saw it on the internet."

My parents were the ones who welcomed a group of teens to practice in their garage, even going the extra mile to soundproof the space. So, after all of their support, hearing the word proud now feels like I've been stabbed. There's nothing I'm doing with the reunion to be proud of. I'm dragging my feet and praying for a solution to fall into my lap.

"The band isn't getting back together. It's just for one night," I remind him, but I doubt he'll drop it.

"That's too bad. I was hoping you would start doing something with your life again."

"I run a business," I get out through gritted teeth. It's a conversation I can count on every few months, and it never fails to grate on my nerves.

"But you are so much more than that. I've seen you do great things; that bar isn't one of them. It's a hobby; you'll find something." His words have my hackles raising, wanting to defend everything I've built. But there's an ounce of truth to what he's saying. The bar is far from great. There are some seasons when I have to funnel my own money into the place, especially when profit margins aren't ideal and most earnings go to the employees and general upkeep.

But it's mine, and I'm the only one allowed to call it inconsequential.

To shield my ego, I lie, "It's been open almost ten years. I think I'm doing just fine with it."

"Then turn it into something bigger if it's as successful as you're saying. It's not like you to limit yourself. You're our dreamer."

"I'm not going to make the next Margaritaville." Although, that would be something. A slew of Half a Memory bars scattered across the country, neon pink bar rooms filled with last decade's top hits. "Is there something else you want to discuss besides my career trajectory?"

"I just wanted to confirm that your sister is coming to the event and not planning on fleeing the country again."

"Yes, she's my plus one, and we've gone over this. She didn't flee to Europe. She was on a study abroad that you signed the paperwork for, and that was seven years ago." I improvise, playing along with what Evelyn likely just told him.

I have no doubt that the moment he hangs up, she'll call me, asking me to cover for her. We've been playing this game since she first visited me on tour. She only visits about half the time she says she is and spends the other half solo traveling the globe, filling the pages of her passport.

For Evelyn's sake, I hope my parents will stop treating her like a kid. She's twenty-eight and head of design for the PR company she works for, yet they still treat all of her trips like she's sneaking out in the middle of the night.

It's mostly my fault. I left home at seventeen and got my GED simply to ease our parents' worries. But, in doing so, my sister had to compensate for everything I wasn't—becoming a present, straight-A student who's now a successful woman with a conventional and successful career. They always told me they were proud of me, but I could tell there was a tinge of disappointment and fear surrounding my choices.

"Good. Let us know when she gets in."

"God. It's not for months, Dad. You could just track her phone instead of checking in with me," I joke, but I'm sure they've attempted to at some point. "I'll keep you updated."

"I can always count on you," he says with misplaced confidence.

"Talk to you later." I hang up, and not even a second passes before a new call comes in.

I take a moment to breathe and sit on my couch before answering, ready to be pulled into the other side of this family mess. "So, you're my plus one? Thanks for letting me know."

"Shit, he moves fast. Thanks so much," Evelyn says, then adds coyly, "But if you're offering, I'd gladly take you up on it. I'll be in Atlanta for a few days and was going to ask if I could crash at your place anyway."

"Sure. That shouldn't be a problem. What did you do to piss them off?" Because knowing our parents, there has to be a secondary reason for their check-in.

"Remember Shawn?" she asks, and I can practically hear her wincing.

I groan, "How can I forget? Please tell me you broke his heart."

"Yes. I think he cried, but I didn't stay long enough to know how long it lasted. But that apparently also broke Mom's heart a little bit. Apparently, she thought you'd be married by now, so anyone I bring home is now in the line of fire," she says, reminding me of another thing our parents are putting on her.

"Well, I'm proud of you for getting rid of him." Shawn was a slimy leech of a boyfriend and, once upon a time, a part of another band that wanted so badly to be our rivals. They were one-hit wonders at best. Now, he's some low-level record label producer. If she ever showed up with a ring, I would have thrown it in the trash and bought her next ticket to Milan. "Where are you headed this time?"

"A ranch in Montana."

"If I'm gonna cover for you, I at least expect it to be for something interesting."

"They teach you how to make your own cheese on this cute little farm, and you get to pick your own eggs in the morning for breakfast. They say we might even get to see the northern lights."

I try to yawn loud enough for her to hear. "Please tell me you're not paying to do farm chores."

"It's a wellness retreat with thousands of five-star reviews. One of the women said it was the best thing to ever happen to her, including the birth of her child," she explains, her tone growing defensive.

"It's rich people bullshit."

"*You're* rich."

"And you don't see me spending money to milk a cow."

"You don't spend money on anything. You're hardly a model millionaire," she says confidently. "If I were you, I'd be the one owning the wellness farm. Besides, I need a break. You could come, you know. It could be good for you."

We used to travel together all the time, either on tour or on random trips she planned using top ten lists on travel blogs. Now, my life exists in a five-mile radius, and breaking past that to go to Montana and listen to lectures on holistic wellness sounds like hell.

"Whatever. Just let me know if you need a ride from the airport." I pause. "And I really do mean it about Shawn. You're better off without him."

"Thanks," she says softly before bouncing back to her normal bubbly energy. "So, I heard you didn't make it to the first meeting. Is everything ok?"

"I'm fine."

"Seriously, if there's anything that you need to talk about, I'm here. I bet it's weird to go back after all this time." I can practically feel the concern dripping from her words.

"Like I said, I'm fine." I grit out.

"Like even the small stuff. I want to hear about it. If there is—"

I cut her off. "How many people do I have to tell that I'm ok? I'm fine. It's going to be fine."

"Sure, cause you sound like someone who's fine," she says, her tone matching the fire in my own. "If you aren't going to tell me what's happening, then I'll find someone who will."

"Ev—" I start, but this time, it's her turn to cut me off as she quickly hangs up. *Shit.* We've always gotten along, but no one else can get under my skin as quickly as her, and she's never been one to take it well.

I hold up the phone to text an apology to Evelyn until I am met with a lovely distraction from Craig. *Thank fuck.* I need to get out of here before my mother decides it's her turn to give me a call.

Craig

I need you to go on a citrus run. If I see another lemon drop martini tonight, I'm quitting.

8

Lacey

Water ripples under my feet. Something that would be expected if I was taking the shower I've been in desperate need of since a fan accidentally poured their soda down my back in the middle of the first period. My shirt has been plastered to my back for hours, and I was really hoping to wash away the sugary residue before meeting up with Price and a few of the guys.

No.

The water is in my living room. Just a few inches, but who really *wants* water in their living room?

My front door opens and the man I contacted from the management company, Trent, splashes in. Neither of us even attempts to smile. He's made it apparent that I'm an inconvenience for calling right before the office closed, and I've made it clear that I'm not all too happy that my apartment has turned into a live-in aquarium.

"So?"

He adopts the tone of someone trying to calm a wild animal, saying, "So, we'll have someone to inspect it tomorrow."

"Ok, what are you thinking? One day? Two?" It's just some water. How long should this really take?

"We won't know for sure until he comes in, but I wouldn't get your hopes up. Because you let it sit for so long, it leaked into the unit below. We'll likely have to replace more than a pipe or two."

"I'm sorry. Do you think I've been playing in this water all day? That I chose this?" I welcome the ice that coats my voice. Screw this guy and his one-star customer service skills and non-answers.

"Ma'am, that's the reality of this situation." *Prick.*

"Do you at least have any open units that I could use for the time being?"

"No, we do not. If that's all, I'll be going. We'll email you updates as they become available," he informs me before promptly leaving.

When he forces the door closed behind him, my pulse starts to race. Without the asshole in the room with me, I no longer have a target to direct my emotions at. I clench and unclench my hands.

I need a plan. I need to do something.

When no immediate solution comes, I channel my agitation into packing. It doesn't take long since I don't need much as a chronic outfit repeater, so I tightly fold the necessities in only a few minutes.

Just before I zip my suitcase closed, I tuck in my mother's letters. I hate touching them and hate what they represent, but I also have no clue when I'll be back.

As I head out the door, I collect the ancient coffee maker from my counter, the only thing I took from the house in Arizona before I sold it.

Once I get to my car, shrouded in the darkness of the underground parking deck, I start to cry. Because I'm still sticky, and even if my apartment is cold and impersonal, it's the only home I have left.

I try to stop it, but I'm losing the battle. Tears flow freely as the wall I've built crumbles.

Every day, I try to show people that I have everything under control, and most of the time, I do. It's not because I want to. It's because I have to. Control and pushing forward are what always keep me together.

When I broke my right arm playing soccer during my freshman year of high school, I couldn't stand not being able to use my dominant hand. It wasn't just the frustration of being unable to play but also the feeling of falling behind—recovering for four weeks while everyone else was getting better. It didn't take long before I found myself pacing the house, so much so that my mom gave me her old digital camera and practically pushed me outside.

Whether she knew it then or not, it changed everything. That push helped me discover photography and ignited this insatiable hunger. Photography became a way to capture the world on my terms while hiding just out of frame.

It was exactly what I needed to keep going, like a shark swimming through anything in its path. And if I did just that—kept moving, pushing, swimming—nothing could go wrong.

But something did go wrong.

And now I'm more like a hummingbird. It's a myth that hummingbirds die if they stop moving; I looked it up once. And yet here I am, scared of what will happen if I slow down, even for an instant. Frantic and fragile in any moment of uncertainty or stagnation.

My attention is redirected when my phone screen lights up from the passenger seat with a text from Price telling me he's on the way to the team's favorite sports bar.

I told them I would meet them tonight to celebrate the first wins of the season, especially with two of the three opening games being in their home city. It's been a long fucking week, and they deserve some fun. I agreed to join, thinking if I go out tonight, then I can turn down invitations for the rest of the season with fewer complaints.

It gives me a direction, at the very least, and a chance to ask Price about his spare room. I hate asking him for another favor since I've leaned on him so much over the last few years, but it's that or a hotel.

I wipe my eyes and stare in the rearview mirror until my face is no longer red and splotchy. The sports bar is only a few blocks away, so I opt to walk off the last of my nerves. With each step, the gears in my head turn faster.

Forward.

I can call the insurance company in the morning.

Forward.

I don't own anything that can't be replaced.

Forward.

I will catch all the pieces because I have to.

I arrive before all my thoughts have been properly sifted through. The sound of laughter and cheers leak from the bar, promising escape and a damn good time to anyone who crosses the threshold.

I guess it's whiskey again tonight.

As I step to push open the door, Price lightly grabs my arm, stopping my momentum. "Hey, I have something to tell you real quick."

I force my whirring brain back into the moment. If Price needs me, I can compose myself for a few minutes, but I don't think it's anything bad based on the smile taking up his entire face.

"Sure. I actually have something to talk to you about, too." Before continuing, we step to the side so we're not blocking the door.

He grabs me by the shoulders and says with hushed awe, "Mari's pregnant."

"Oh." The lone syllable is all I can manage. My mind goes blank before I can form an appropriate response. Of course, I would mess up hearing my best friend's pregnancy announcement. Going silent instead of jumping up and down with the excitement the moment deserves. It's a mix of everything hitting me at once, coupled with the strange feeling of witnessing my high school best friend grow into an adult. Sure, we've been adults for years, but it doesn't always feel that way.

One day, you know that every girlfriend is temporary and that you're his best friend, not in the way that you'd be a better fit for him, but in the way that you're each other's number one, no questions asked. Then they have that one girlfriend, the one that works and becomes their wife, and you're so damn happy because he deserves only the best things in life.

And Mari is so good for him, but at the same time, I'm slipping down his list of important things, leaving me lost in a reality I once knew. The thought is oily, landing uncomfortably in my chest, selfishness competing with joy.

Too much time passes before I say, "That's amazing. Amazing. Congratulations. This is amazing news." Apparently, the shock has sealed away all access to my vocabulary.

He runs his hands over the hint of stubble on his cheeks, oblivious to my lackluster response. "I know. I can't believe it. Like I've always dreamed of this, and it's happening. But please don't tell anyone yet. The only people who know are our families."

"No, this is literally everything you've ever wanted." It is. We used to sneak out and smoke on his roof in high school, and he'd tell me about his big, happy plan. The one with a perfect family and perfect hockey career. I was cynical, but here he is proving me wrong. It seems like he's been making a habit of it lately.

"I know." Price pauses, finally looking at me. His expression of awe shifts to concern. "Are you ok?"

"Yeah. I'm totally fine. I'm a little shocked that I'm about to be a godmother," I offer, abandoning my plans to ask him for a room, not wanting to ruin his happiness with my problems.

"Lacey, I love you more than 99.999% of people, but there's no way in hell you're going to be this kid's godmother." I know he doesn't mean it as a jab. We both know that I can't keep a plant alive and that I almost burn down the kitchen anytime I even think about using a stovetop.

I give a forced laugh. "I know. I'm not fit for that."

"Hold down a relationship for a month, and then maybe I'll put your name in the running. Maybe even get a cat."

Hell, I know he's trying to be funny. Under any other circumstance, I'd probably be the one telling him he better not even consider me as a godmother. I'm not suited for anything but being the single aunt who tells slightly inappropriate stories while sipping on a perpetually full glass of wine.

But today, it hurts. It fucking hurts.

In moments like this, I wish I could call up my mom; her voice would feel like a hug, and I could cry until she said some cheesy fortune cookie advice like 'the hard things will pass if you stop to smell the roses,' and it would all work out. She just had that type of magic.

I was supposed to be her fairy tale ending. But instead, I'm falling behind. I keep looking at Price, oscillating between a strange mix of hurt and genuine happiness—he has someone who loves him, a perfect job, and soon a lovely family. These are things I like to imagine I wanted at some point, things my mom wanted for me, but even when I consider trying, I always worry: what if the want becomes a need? What if I need someone and fall apart so completely that I can't piece myself back together again?

I can't process the rest of Price's words as I watch his lips move, and his hand gestures exude excitement I wish I could share.

Before he can continue, I take the opportunity to escape. "I left something in my apartment." My sanity, probably. "And I should honestly get ahead with work. I'll see you tomorrow. Congratulations again. If anyone deserves to be a dad, it's you."

I watch his face fall in disappointment. "We'll miss you. I know they were really looking forward to spending time with you. The guys all think you're funny as shit when you're not trying to focus at work."

"Next time," I say, and I can tell that neither of us believes it for a moment.

I walk back toward my apartment but only make it around the corner before the internal dam breaks again. I'm not a crier, but when the tears start, they don't seem to have an off switch.

I grab the wall next to me, and the rough texture of the brick is my only hold on reality. My chest heaves, but I can't get enough air into my lungs.

I should be fine. I haven't had a panic attack for months. I'd made sure everything was under control.

Somewhere in the background, there's a soft thudding sound. A form moves in front of me, and I back away on instinct. Wouldn't tonight have the perfect ending if I got robbed?

"Hey, hey. What's wrong?" The voice is familiar but more tender than I remember. I look up to find concern in the man's sparkling green eyes.

The embarrassment of running into an ex while hungover and wearing worn-out sweatpants has nothing on having a mysterious one-night-stand find me having a borderline panic attack in the middle of the sidewalk.

"I'm fine," I say, like the liar I'm turning into.

Instead of making a huge fuss, he reaches out to rub my shaking shoulders and says, "I've had my fair share of shit days too. Come on, you look like you need a drink." His casual acknowledgment soothes an aching part of me.

"Fine. But only if you're buying," I try to quip, but my voice comes out weak.

"Must be the king of shitty days if you're letting me buy your drinks." He leans down to pick up a white plastic grocery bag of . . . lemons and limes? He tracks my gaze and explains, "For the bar. Craig has me out doing his dirty work."

We walk the short distance to the bar in silence.

Once inside fan girl heaven, he tells me, "I need to prep a few of these real quick. I'll be right back." Which my desperate brain immediately translates to *I'm not leaving.*

I sit at the end of the bar, leaving one seat for Drew on my other side.

"Rough day, Lacey?" Craig asks as he rinses his cocktail shaker.

My back goes ramrod straight. He said *my name*, something I haven't given either of them. How the hell—

"Damn. Chill. I got it from swiping your credit card to start your tab. It's amazing how much information credit cards hold," he says. "I didn't tell him, and he didn't ask. Don't worry. Your secrets are safe with me."

"What else do you know?" I ask, narrowing my eyes with suspicion.

"Enough. I won't take sides unless you make me. I just like having the advantage." His carefree smile drops, and he leans against the counter. "Just remember I do actually like the guy, so don't fuck him over."

"I didn't come back for him. I'm obviously here for your charm and now very shiny head."

"Sure. Keep telling yourself that," he says, absentmindedly rubbing a hand over the smooth surface of his scalp.

"I'm serious."

"I bet an unlimited bar tab that you two won't be able to keep it in your pants tonight." His attention abruptly jerks to the side, and he starts moving to the other side of the bar. He calls out in the practiced patient tone reserved for toddlers, "Jamie, for the love of God, stop trying to put that glass in your purse. We just did this last week, and there's no way it will fit!"

Though I promised never to come back here, I have to admit it's really hard to cry when surrounded by so much pink and glitter.

9

Drew

I've never been so grateful for lemon drop martinis and grocery runs.

Would I have preferred to see her again under better circumstances? Sure, but the moment I saw the tears streaming down her face and the rapid rhythm of her breath, there was nothing I needed more than to ease her burden.

I suspect I know the exact chest-crushing sensation she was experiencing. No one should have to go through that alone.

I set the prepped citrus peels and lemon juice behind the bar where Heather and Craig can reach them as needed. Free of my bar owner duties, I turn to the woman who hasn't left my head since the night we met.

Most people look worse when you haven't had a few beers. This isn't the case for her. It looks like someone has captured a thundercloud in her eyes, gray and shifting. Pillowy, pert lips. Toned, lean muscles shift with each subtle movement. And tense, definitely tense.

I'll have no problem working the knots from her shoulders.

She looks up with a half smile, the expression a flicker compared to the fire I know she's capable of.

"Are you really allowed to be back there?" She looks genuinely appalled at what she must think is a health department violation. It would be if I didn't own the damn place.

"Let's just say the owner and I have an agreement." Her eyes narrow as if trying to read between the lines. "Whiskey?"

I grab my favorite bottle and pour a little more than the standard one-and-three-quarters ounces we claim to put in our drinks.

"You remembered?" She quirks an eyebrow.

I remember everything in technicolor detail, but she doesn't need to know that. "Yeah, and from the looks of it, today is a good one to burn away." I point to the other end of the bar where Craig and his shaved, glistening head are chatting up a blonde. "And if you need a distraction, look at that."

"What the hell happened to his hair?" she asks conspiratorially.

Craig swaggers towards us as if summoned by the mere mention of his baldness. Just before he gets within earshot I whisper, "Intrusive thoughts and no self-control. Ask how he's doing."

She raises an eyebrow but goes with it. "Craig, how are you?"

"Life was far simpler back when I had hair," he replies. It's been like a fucking broken record, but it was entertaining enough the first time.

“When did this get old?” she asks, a real smile finally pulling against the corners of her lips, and that slight movement feels like victory.

“About ten minutes after I helped him shave it all off.” I was tempted to make a drinking game out of it. One shot for every time he used the terrible line on a new person. I know how to hold my liquor, but if I had followed through, I would have been in the hospital after the first night.

“You were much nicer to me back when I had hair,” Craig whines.

“You got on my nerves a lot less when you had hair,” I mutter, and my comment is what finally does it.

Her tight shoulders ease back just a hair, and she takes another drink, her small laugh like music to my ears. Our banter flows effortlessly, just like when we first met.

It isn't until she's on her third drink that I finally ask, “What are you drinking to drown tonight?”

“I’m homeless,” she says, causing my eyes to widen slightly at the news. “Well, apartmentless would be more accurate. I came home to discover that the pipes busted and ruined everything. I have no idea how long it will take, and I’m fairly certain I’ll have to buy all new furniture.”

“You don’t have somewhere to stay?”

“I have options, but they’re all shitty. Have you ever been around newlyweds in a confined space for any period of time?” she says, spinning her glass so the ice cubes clink lightly.

"No, but that sounds like some special type of psychological torture."

"And they just found out they're pregnant. I was told not to tell anyone, but I don't know you, so who the hell cares?" She keeps going, and it seems like she has more than one thing bottled up.

"So, there's no one else?" I ask, a stupid idea taking root in the back of my mind.

"I'm really trying to find an alternative. I've been told I'm exhausting to live with, so I'd rather save anyone I know from that fate." She tenses, lips pulled into a tight line like she's repeating someone else's words.

"You don't know me. Well, you know me better than a stranger from the internet. And if I can deal with Craig, I can handle anything."

"Taking pity on me now? This is great. The fucking regular of Atlanta's tackiest bar is taking pity on me."

"It's not the tackiest bar. There's that line dancing place a few blocks over that definitely has the top spot." It's spaghetti western-themed, and yes, it's as bad as it sounds. "And it's not pity. I don't think someone could pity you if they tried. I'm just attempting to build up some good karma."

Yeah, karma, not the fact that I feel like myself around her. That's not quite it. I feel like someone new, like reality has split, and this is the version of me that would have existed if I had lived a normal life, where I'd be a regular guy at a random bar lucky enough for her to give me a second glance.

"So you're going to rent me a room because you want to make good with the universe? You must have some major cosmic debt," she prods, amusement settling across her features.

I shrug. "I have the space, so why not?" Not in the loft. But I have another place that's more of a guest apartment than anything, staged in the style of my once-upon-a-time success but largely devoid of any personal touches.

"I'm not going to sleep with you," she says with the force of a slammed door.

"That's not why I'm offering. Karma remember? Well, and maybe I have the ulterior motive of learning your name."

She smiles at that, and I can feel her walls slowly coming down as we go back and forth. Her limbs visibly loosen as I reassure her that I really don't mind eccentricities and point out that she doesn't like me all that much, so what's the worst that can happen?

She ponders the question, and all the while, I pray my desperation doesn't leak through the conversation—although desperate is precisely what I am. I've only been around her in short doses, but those moments have been transformative.

And I want more; I want to pull her into my life to see what might happen.

Maybe this is my equivalent to Evelyn's wellness retreat.

"Craig," she calls out, catching my friend's attention.

"How can I be of service?" he says as he whips a towel over his shoulder.

"Would you consider him house-trained?" she asks, and I can't tell if she's joking.

Craig tilts his head back and forth as he weighs the question. "Hypothetically."

"I'm not a dog," I remind them.

But she just looks down at her drink, swirling it as she makes her decision. I do my best not to hold my breath.

"Fine," she finally agrees. "We can try this out for tonight. It's already too late for me to go anywhere else but a hotel." I won't let the resignation in her voice get to me. Would I love it if she agreed with more enthusiasm? Maybe, but her lack of rose-colored glasses is one of the reasons I'm so drawn to her.

"Ok, so what's the name of the woman I'm about to let into my apartment?" I ask, excited to have the answer to my new favorite mystery.

"Lacey," she says, holding out her hand, mimicking my actions from the night we met. I take it, and her hand slips into mine like it was specifically designed to fit there.

"Ok, Lacey," I say her name slowly, testing how it tastes on my tongue. "Let's grab your stuff and go."

As I make my way to the door, she asks, eyebrows furrowed, "Aren't you going to pay for your tab?"

"Oh yeah." I wrestle my wallet from my back pocket, leaving a few crumpled twenties on the bar, catching Craig's eye, seeing a telltale glimmer of mischief. He's loving this too much.

I follow her to her car and grab the three bags she plans on using for however long it takes for her apartment to get fixed.

It's promising that she grabs it all, even though she's only trying this out for one night.

10

Lacey

The reality of what I agreed to sinks in as the Uber driver yells their way through downtown traffic. The last time I saw Drew, I was naked and properly fucked while watching him walk out of my apartment.

If I do stay longer than one night, will there be a constant specter of awkwardness? Do I need to shave my legs every day to maintain some image he has of me? Should that be on my list of priorities? Probably not, but my brain can't help but scramble. I might be jumping from one problem to another. But honestly, I don't care about him. We're practically strangers, so this could work out fine.

He offered a place to stay and with my limited options, it's a convenient agreement. *That's it.*

I'm not worried about Drew getting annoyed with me or my habits because, at the end of this arrangement, he'll still be a stranger that I don't care about. Nothing more.

The drive has me so lost in thought that when we pull up to a luxury apartment building, I assume we're at the wrong address. But Drew slides out from his side and helps to unload my bags from the trunk.

We get into an elevator and when it opens directly into his apartment, my jaw hits the floor. I was expecting some sort of frat castle, laundry flung into corners, and a weird smell that gives you the impression that a cat lived there at some point.

Instead, I'm welcomed to an airy penthouse with floor-to-ceiling windows and a cherry red couch shaped like a teardrop, designed more with aesthetics than comfort in mind and probably worth more than my car.

My eyes wander, and I'm not sure what I pictured Drew's place to be like, but it isn't this. As I walk further in, I blink in confusion as my eyes focus on a single massive photo on the far wall.

It would be less surprising if it was some naked woman taken in a pose that is deemed as 'tasteful.' But instead, the subject is a familiar acquaintance—a ghost town.

But why is it here? A photo I took years ago.

It was part of the collection of photographs that catapulted me into the life I have now. It's what made everything possible, boosting my confidence enough to chase something that I was so certain was impractical.

I took a gap semester before going to college, wandering around the deep South and hunting for hidden and forgotten places. My only companion was the new film camera I received as a high school graduation gift, and I was ready to use it to embrace the freedom of being eighteen.

On a whim, with plenty of pep talks from Price, I submitted my work to a young artists' program. The application required a three-piece portfolio, and if you were selected, they would choose one to display and for people to bid on at auction.

It's not the most prestigious recognition I've received, but it changed everything.

Initially, I was determined to pursue medicine, not because I loved it, but because it symbolized the success and recognition I was desperate for. But everything changed with that picture, and the validation that came with it led me to pursue a career in sports media.

And now, staring at it years later is surreal, like I've been displaced in time.

Drew walks up to stand beside me, and it's like we're at a museum, not in the middle of his living room. "You like it? I stumbled upon it at an auction and had to have it. I've been told I overpaid, but every time I see it here, I know it was worth the price tag."

"Patron of the arts, huh?" I ask, still trying to shake off my shock.

"Not usually, but finding it felt like fate. I haven't checked to see if the photographer ever became something, but I really hope they did." His words pull a smile from me.

Fate.

In the small transition from the bar, I've been trying to figure out if this is the right choice, but his words and the photograph give me an odd impression that I'm supposed to be here.

"That's something special. I bet you made their entire existence by buying it."

"I hope so. I've been considering reaching out to see if they have any recent pieces." Instantly, the whimsy of my thoughts turns to a subtle dread. This is too good to be true; the situation might be ruined before it starts.

He wouldn't kick me out if I told him it was my work. But if I choose to admit it, then there will be questions.

Questions and answers that could change everything.

I tell him a version of the truth. "I imagine they would love hearing how much their work has stuck with you over the years."

He smiles at my words and says, "It's one of the few things I picked out for the place. Always nice to know it was a good choice."

"You mean you didn't color coordinate your living room all by yourself. I'm shocked."

"Damn, Lacey. Glad you feel at home enough to taunt me before you unpack." He nods to the few bags that contain my camera equipment, clothes, toiletries, and, very importantly, my coffee maker. "Is that really all you need?"

"I travel a lot for work. It pays to know how to pack light. I guess that's something else you need to know. I'll be in and out often, sometimes back really late."

"That's fine. I'm a heavy sleeper," he says, and a little more tension releases from my shoulders. This would normally be where the questions would start, but he's not trying to pull anything from me that I don't want to give.

As I shift, I'm reminded of the sticky shirt still plastered to my back, and now that my primary problem has been resolved, my need to be clean dominates my mind.

"Could you point me to a shower? I had an unfortunate encounter with a Diet Coke earlier, and I didn't really have a chance to wash it off."

"Sure, there's an en suite in your room."

He walks me to the room, placing down the bag he insisted on carrying, the one with clothes and books, because it doesn't matter that I'm starting to trust him; no one is allowed to touch my camera equipment.

"Thanks," I say, and he gives me a curt nod before leaving.

The bathroom is luxurious and minimal, following the white and gray of the rest of the apartment. I quickly turn on the shower, not waiting for it to heat up, and rinse away the soda residue from my skin, letting the mess of the day wash away with it.

Finally alone, I take a moment to think about what has to come next. After all, being adults doesn't wipe away the awkwardness of living with someone who you had sex with less than a week ago.

I get as comfortable as possible in a set of navy sweats before reentering the cavernous living room.

I walk through the open balcony door to find him sitting on the edge of a lounge chair, smoking a joint, and ask, "How are we going to do this?"

"What do you mean?"

"Well, last time we were alone together, there was a lot less clothing, and we're complete strangers. So . . . maybe we should figure this out?" How is he so casual about this whole thing, letting me waltz in and do whatever I please?

"I kind of liked that, if I'm being honest." He offers me the joint, and I take it, inhaling deeply and releasing the smoke from my mouth to curl into the sky.

"Which part?" I roll my eyes. Honestly, I walked myself into whatever he says next.

"Both. Definitely both, but since you've made it clear the first thing is off the table, I'm also a big fan of the second." He sounds eager, but that might be me grasping at something. It might be the whiskey or the weed twisting his tone into what I want to hear.

"So you don't want to get to know me?" That's completely fine by me; putting some distance between us might make this easier.

He takes a moment to collect his words. "If you put it that way, it sounds like I don't like you as a person, which would be a lie. I like that we don't have all that baggage. You don't know my shit, and I don't know yours."

"I like that. There's no pressure."

"How about we make a deal then? The moment either of us walks through the door, we leave the shit behind. Work, stress, the heavy stuff doesn't cross the threshold with us."

I hesitate at his proposition. Is it really possible to exist in a space without questions and tricky explanations? I let this idea rattle through my mind as I sit across from him. It would be nice not to hide behind the occasional white lie or tactically made omissions.

"So we stay strangers," I say, abandoning my seat to go inside to grab a yellow legal pad and pen from my bags.

When I return and lower back into my seat, he asks, "What are you doing?"

"Making a lease agreement."

"You're not leasing the room. It's yours for free." I can tell his words are genuine, but I hate owing people anything. Whether he likes it or not, he'll be getting a check.

"I'm not staying here for free. I'll have an insurance payout that I can give you. If we're really going to do this, we need to agree on terms and conditions for us being roommates. Number one, leave the bullshit and reality at the door. I think in the spirit of things, number two is no last names." Because last names lead to internet searches, and unfortunately, I'm fairly easy to find. "And number three is that you understand that I have my routines. Your turn."

"If this was a movie, this sounds like the part where I'd say 'don't fall in love,'" he jokes.

"You can fall in love all you want; just don't tell me if you do," I say.

I'm not too worried about his stupid movie joke. I'm like a magnet, one that's positioned to repel instead of attract. Pushing and pushing the people in my life until I'm sure they'll stay no matter what I do.

"What a fun challenge." His voice goes thick, sending an uninvited heat through me.

I stammer as I try to navigate to safer, less tension-filled waters, "I-I don't know when I'll have my place yet, so I'll just leave this part blank until I get an estimate."

I scrawl the word *"Until"* followed by two lines for us to sign our names. As if running out of time, I rush to sign my name and push the paper toward him. My eyes trace each movement of his hand as he scratches out sharp, angular letters. Once he finishes the *W,* I feel more secure.

The deal might be silly or impractical to him, but for me, it's soothing. Clear-cut lines and boundaries have always helped me stay safe.

11

Lacey

As of this moment, I have a newfound appreciation for home gyms. I never really got the point of having a room with a random assortment of equipment thrown together when you could go to a high-end facility.

But seeing my very sweaty, very shirtless roommate on the treadmill, is doing a damn good job of changing my mind. I take a moment to appreciate the beautiful artwork covering his torso. The metamorphosis of a butterfly that starts at his right hip bone and floats up his ribs. The small illegible quote on the other side hugs the well-defined curve of his left pec.

I remember running my hands over those tattoos. The way his muscles tensed and rippled under my fingertips. How powerful I felt pulling the reaction from him. It really is a shame I can't get one more taste.

The only thing keeping me in check is the signed set of rules that we made three days ago. Adorned with sloppy signatures and stuck to his fridge with a magnet so that when I wake up, I remember what the hell we're doing here.

"Are you going to keep lurking in the doorway, or do you need something?" I can practically hear his smirk.

Our eyes lock in the mirrors that span the expanse of the far wall. So, yeah, he's probably been watching me watch him for the last couple of minutes.

"I was just going to ask how to get out on the balcony. I can't seem to find the door," I manage to say as I swallow my embarrassment.

"Oh yeah, it's not exactly user-friendly," Drew says, a light smirk continuing to pull at the corners of his lips. He turns off the treadmill and grabs a towel to wipe the sweat from his brow as he walks towards me.

And he doesn't make any move to put on a shirt.

It's so infuriating not to be able to turn off that part of my brain that thinks of that night. No matter how much I yell at myself, *He's your roommate*! it doesn't help.

When he reaches me, I move out of his way, allowing him to lead the way to the elusive balcony door. And not a second later, I realize it's a miscalculation as his back muscles direct my attention down his torso and to his toned ass.

He's your roommate.

He's your roommate.

I repeat a million more times, trying to drown out the memory of how nice that ass felt underneath my hands as I—

My traitorous train of thought is cut off by his voice. "It's a little weird."

"What?" I ask, hoping that there's no sign of my daydream on my face.

He raises an eyebrow, hinting that he knows exactly what's roaming my mind. "The door handle." He points to a bit of black window trim. No handle in sight.

"Umm, am I missing something, or are you imagining door handles?"

"You have to press this in," He pushes on the bit of trim that he was pointing to, and a handle does, in fact, pop out. The invisible device makes me feel slightly less stupid about being outsmarted by a door. "It's some bullshit minimalist design that practically guarantees that you can't get on the balcony while intoxicated, which is probably for the best." He grimaces as if recalling a memory.

"Thanks."

I shuffle outside and lean against the balcony's edge with my phone cradled in my hands. Maybe if I accidentally drop the phone, then I won't have to send the text.

I take a moment to embrace the rare bite of the false Autumn air while the sound of the city wraps around me. It will be like this for a few more days, cold and wondrous, before reverting to the stubborn heat of late summer. Early October in Georgia really is a temperamental bitch.

After having to deal with my apartment, the subsequent long calls with insurance agents, and back-to-back games on the West Coast, I haven't been able to take a moment to respond to Martin. Sure, I could just type out a few words and call it a day, but it's hard to wrap my head around how something like *I'll be there* can mean so much.

The train of thought is claustrophobic, thus the need to be outside.

Once I resolve that I really shouldn't destroy my perfectly good phone, I open the text thread and type out different versions of the same thing until I settle on:

Lacey

I can make it. Let me know if there's anything else I should know.

Concise. Professional. An attempt to make it read as warm and cuddly as a business email.

I don't know how long I stare at the screen, waiting for some response. An old but familiar feeling settles over me, one that I push aside before I analyze it any deeper.

Seconds pass.

Minutes pass.

Just before I shove my phone back in my pocket, a text bubble finally dances at the bottom of the screen.

Martin

Excited to share this with you.

Sure. Excited to show off.

It's not the first time I regret doing this on his terms and schedule, but I don't have enough fight left to do it any other way.

I catch myself staring out into nothing when the sound of the balcony door and outdoor lights flickering on pulls me back to the present. At some point, the sun fully vanished, leaving me alone in the vast dark night.

Turning so my back is pressed against the rail, I find Drew striding over to me, holding two steaming mugs.

"Here," he says. "Chamomile. Not as good as other things for stress relief, but it tends to do the job."

He holds out one of the mugs to me, and I mutter, "Thanks."

I grasp the mug, and my cold fingers welcome the sudden rush of heat.

"Another rough night?" he asks, settling beside me. I have to resist the urge to lean into the warmth radiating off him as a breeze nips at my skin.

"Yeah, you could say that. I wish there were some way to switch off my brain. Like a 'Lacey will not be accepting any more intrusive thoughts until nine A.M. when we resume our normal business hours.'"

"I'm right there with you. Remember, I'm a guy who *lives to drink alone.*"

I wince at his words, thinking about how ruthless I was when I thought I'd never speak to him again. I should probably work on that. "Sorry, that was a dickish thing to say."

"Nah. It was what someone should have told me a while ago. Your honesty is pretty fucking refreshing." He looks down at his drink as if he'll find an answer in the amber herbal liquid. "And to your credit, you were spot on."

We're silent for a moment, the air going stale between us as we both try to figure out what to say next.

Taking a sip from my mug, he shifts slightly, his voice gentle as he asks, "Want to talk about it? Whatever has got you freezing out here?"

At his words, I register the goosebumps in my arms and my body's slight shaking. Without hesitation, he removes his thick fleece hoodie and hands it to me. I take it and wriggle it over my head as it swallows me in a comforting, protective layer.

"I thought we agreed to not let the outside world in," I counter. That's the whole point of this situation: enabling each other's need for escapism.

"It can go both ways. Whatever we say here stays between us. Also, I think I know you pretty well."

"We've known each other for about a week. How much can you really learn about a person in that amount of time?"

"Sure, but I learned a lot that first night. When you don't intend to see someone ever again, it's easy to stop hiding behind the walls you put up for other people. Would you have said all that stuff to me if I was someone else, someone you actually wanted to know?"

"No. Probably not. I guess that means I know a lot about you, too." I try to think of all the pieces that I've picked up. But with everything I've learned, he makes less and less sense. It's like each new glimpse contradicts the one that precedes it.

"Maybe, but unlike you, I was definitely hoping for another meeting."

"I'm starting to think you care about me," I taunt.

"Or maybe hearing about your shitty day will help me feel better. I could have completely selfish intentions," he jokes back, a wry smile pulling at his mouth. It has the intended effect, though, helping the knots in my stomach loosen slightly.

"You really give a shit about my problems, huh?" My free hand rests on the railing as I fix a skeptical gaze on him.

"This is how I see it. We're in this together, so why not embrace it? We can keep being strangers like we agreed, but we can also—" His eyes lock with mine as he comes closer. Is he going to try and kiss me? He leans a little further, and I hold my breath as my heart races. My eyes land on his lips just as he begins to speak, "Look, listen, I watched this documentary on weather patterns."

I can't help the snort that escapes, picturing him casually enjoying some commentary about clouds and tropical storms. "What are you, eighty?"

"Thirty-three, but some days, I can't really tell the difference." He places his hand over mine. The contact sends a simmering heat racing through my arm. "But that's not the point; it's soothing. The narration is calming as fuck."

"Where are you going with this?"

"My point is that despite how disastrous hurricanes can be, the eye of the storm is the calmest part. I guess what I'm saying is that we both have our own storms and here we can be in the eye of those storms together."

"So, you and me in the eye of the storm?" I like the sound of that, our own little pocket of calm.

"Exactly. You don't have to tell me what's wrong, but I'm here." His eyes soften, reflecting the comfort radiating from his voice.

What's the harm? When this is all over, I get to walk away from this and any secrets we share. I lean into this moment. Lean into the companionship he's freely offering and the comforting presence of the hand he still hasn't removed.

"I'm getting back in touch with a person and a part of my life that I've lived without for a long time. It's not that I want to do this, but I need to do this for someone I care about," I say, and it's nice not to cover the sentiment in bravado and pretend it's under control.

"Yeah, I get that. I'm personally over the nostalgia thing. Sometimes thinking about the past just sucks."

It's nice to be on the same page with someone about that for once.

12

Drew

Lacey looks so damn good in my kitchen.

I lean against the doorframe of my bedroom as I track her routine. She uses the custom pot filler faucet attached over the gas range to fill her coffee maker, then moves to sit on my butcher block counters, nearly banging her head on the overhead brass cookware. She exists so casually in a space I've been interviewed about for various celebrity home tours.

All that's to say I have a gorgeous kitchen, but Lacey puts it to shame wearing her cropped hoodie and shorts, hair in its state of being perpetually tied on top of her head.

Out of the seven days she's lived with me so far, she's only been here four nights. I've gotten this view a handful of times, and I still can't get enough.

Welcoming her here might be the best and worst drunk decision that I've ever made. A temptation and blessing wrapped up into her tightly wound body.

She's starting to make me understand why someone becomes a morning person. I'm drawn in by how the soft glow of the sun seems to catch on her freckles and the sound of her off key hums as she drinks her abomination of a cup of coffee.

Yeah, people get up early to see a view like this.

It all started that first morning when she played jazz music at full blast. She warned me about it, but I wasn't really expecting to be woken up by a blaring saxophone riff.

The volume wasn't her fault. I helped her connect her phone to the wireless speaker system and neglected to tell her that it tends to play louder than you would expect. So, that morning, I found myself abruptly awake at an hour I hadn't seen in ages.

It's been the same consistent routine each time she's here. After the first two times, my body woke up at the ungodly hour on its own, whether she was around or gone for work.

My current guess is a flight attendant. With the Atlanta airport being a central hub and how random her days seem, it's possible.

"Are you going to keep lurking in the doorway, or do you want me to make you some coffee?" she recycles my words from the other day as she moves off the counter to wage war with my toaster. She's going to burn her toast again.

"I'll take a cup," I accept, although the coffee she guzzles down each morning is criminally bad. I have a cafe-grade espresso maker in the corner. I offered to teach her how to use it, but she turned me down. She warned me how she likes her routine. And nothing will get in the way of her sacred burnt toast and coffee.

So, I drink the damn bitter cup with her and enjoy it because she's the one who makes it.

"I'm still surprised you get up so early," she tells me, handing me the steaming mug.

"Are you calling me lazy, *sconosciuta*?" I've kept the nickname I've given her in my mind. We've agreed to stay strangers in this weird way that has us balancing being intimately familiar yet distant. The name reminds me of that: *sconosciuta*, stranger.

My stranger.

"You don't give off the impression of someone who's awake before noon. And you don't really seem to have a reason to either."

She's right on both accounts. Some days, it might be noon or later before I'm up. Between late nights at the bar and not having much going on, there aren't many reasons to be awake longer than needed each day.

Being awake for more hours means having more hours to fill. But at this moment, being awake and seeing her like this, in her natural state, it's like uncovering a hidden part of her. It makes everything worth it.

"Where are the cutting boards?" she calls over her shoulder.

I have to think far harder than I should about where it might be. "On the upper left side of the fridge."

"Moments like this still make me half-convinced you don't live here," she says. Not far off. I only come to this place once a month, max.

She dances on her tiptoes, trying to get the cutting board she's selected. Her fingertips nearly brush the edge, but it remains just out of reach. I move to get it for her just as she climbs on the counter to grab it. I snag it easily and make a mental note to move all the dishes to make them more accessible.

"I could have gotten that," she protests while snatching it from my grasp.

"Well, I do prefer my counters without feet on them."

"I was only going to kneel on it."

"It's the principle of it." My loft back at Half a Memory might be on the rougher side, but even the kitchen there is always pristine.

Sliding off the surface, she lands in the gap between me and the counter—a completely reasonable distance until she fills it with her body. Feeling the curve of her ass slide against me has me jolting back, though all I want to do is linger.

It's torture.

So she might be trying to kill me; I wouldn't put it past her. This is why it's a bad decision. A painfully bad decision if my dick has any say in it.

Each night I hear her turn on the shower, I can picture exactly how she looks, remember the dimples in her back, and imagine how she might throw her head back in the stream of water just like how she looked when she came apart while I was buried inside her.

So this might be an acute blend of torture and pleasure, specifically designed to test my damn patience. But hey, it does one hell of a job of distracting me from what I should be worried about.

"So what's the death-defying stunt for a cutting board for?"

"Avocado toast if I'm lucky. Burnt avocado toast if I'm not. I don't have much of a winning streak." She glares at the toaster.

"I would have never guessed your nemesis would be a kitchen appliance."

"I like to think of us more as rivals trying to outsmart each other. My actual nemesis is the bird that hunts down my car every day at work to take a shit on my windshield."

"Sounds like a long list of enemies. Do you have any I should be worried about?"

"There's this grump I met at a bar who sometimes doesn't leave me alone. But I think I can handle him."

"Are you sure about that?"

"I've done a round with him before and handled him pretty well. He's nothing to write home about." She shrugs.

I fight the urge to comment on how well she handled me. Instead, I say something that's been on my mind since the first time she left for a work trip, "I know we agreed not to tell each other what we do or where you're headed, but can you at least tell me when you get there safely and maybe give me a general idea of how far? It might be useful to know if I need to file a missing person's report."

"I guess if it helps in a hypothetical investigation, I can do that much. What's your number?" she asks, quickly tapping the numbers as I recite them. A moment later, mine vibrates in my pocket.

Lacey

800 miles

"So you're going to Texas, Chicago, New York, or somewhere in between? Could you at least give me a cardinal direction?"

"No. I have plenty of people who know where I am, so you really don't need the information, but if it makes you feel better, I'll tell you when I land. Also, you can probably rule out east because that would put me in the Atlantic Ocean," she says before taking a bite of her toast.

I'm starting to realize that in the same way I want to be seen, she wants to be hidden.

We promised no outside bullshit, but my intuition tells me I'm getting close to something that's writhing under her skin, so I don't push.

My phone pings, and I pick it up, anticipating Lacey checking in.

Jared

I'm gonna be at your building in 10 minutes.
I have the kids.

Out of everyone in the band, he's the one I've kept in contact with, partly because I love his kids and partly because he doesn't have an ego the size of a skyscraper. Still, his mentioning the kids is easy to interpret as *you're not getting out of this.*

I quickly read his messages, sensing he's more concerned than angry about my absence from the first reunion meeting. He sounds like such a dad. It turns out he's in Atlanta on a layover with his kids, so I invite them over. Not that he's giving me much of a choice.

Thirty minutes later, I welcome them in. Jared's youngest, Liam, barrels into my legs while Fern hides behind her father. Each of them has Jared's wild auburn hair.

"Where's Alyssa?" I ask, noting that his wife is nowhere to be seen.

"At a conference in Chicago. We thought we'd surprise her for the weekend and got tickets to a hockey game tonight. Liam's been obsessed since last winter, so we thought we'd show him the real deal." He comes over to where his son is still clinging to my leg and ruffles his auburn hair. "It's against your team."

"My team?"

"The Cobras. The rising stars of the league," he says, explaining in a tone implying that I should already know this fact.

"Oh, sure." I nod. I might have seen something about that a while ago, but sports haven't ever been my thing. I lift Liam off my legs and crouch down so his tiny body can clamber onto my shoulders, then I ask his dad, "You just come here to talk about sports?"

"We missed you," Jared says, but it sounds a lot like *you should have been there*. Jared truly has a gift for communicating in subtext. "What about we set these guys up with a game and talk."

"I'd rather join them," I deflect.

He gives me one of those looks that must come naturally the moment you stay up late changing diapers and cleaning baby puke off every shirt you own. It's a magical look that has me shutting up, turning on the TV for the kids, and following him outside.

The moment the door shuts behind us, Jared starts. "Is it Wes? Is that why you're not coming? He's better . . . not good, but he knows how to keep his mouth shut now. I understand why you wouldn't want to be in the same room as him anymore, but you need to show up."

"I'm past that."

That.

There were many things that made our last show fucking awful. One of which was walking in on Wes with my girlfriend, Emily. I didn't want to make our relationship public because I hated the prying eyes and speculation. In past relationships, cameras and tabloid write-ups made everything play out more like a performance, leaving me wondering if the kisses and handholding were for me or the picture I'd find plastered on some gossip column. Emily was eager, in hindsight probably too eager, to agree.

Right before the show, I walked into the green room to find them with her naked on Wesley's lap, facing away from me. But I had made eye contact with Wes the moment before I retreated. It wasn't the first time he did it, but it was the first time I saw it happen. All I could think was, at *least this is the last time this will happen.*

I never said anything when people used me as a stepping stone to get to the guys. I never really thought much of myself back then. I rationalized it, reminding myself it was just the cost I needed to pay to pursue my passion. That causing drama would only lead to losing what mattered most.

Jared blinks and jerks back as if I've eliminated the only possible reason for avoiding this mess, "Then what is it?"

Shit. I should have just played into his assumption. But ten years is a long time to hold a grudge, and I was never as upset as I should have been. The relationships never felt genuine, like I was bracing for the end before they even began. I held them to the standard my parents' relationship set but never expected any woman to be that perfect other half.

"There was an emergency at the bar, and I forgot to check in. I forgot that the reunion would probably mean we'd be busier. I'm interviewing a few new bartenders next week to keep up."

It's mostly the truth. I intend to go to the next meeting under the threat of Hartly hiring a hitman, and we are hiring new employees to keep up with the bump in business, but Craig will be conducting the interviews, not me.

"You'll be there next time?" The suspicion in his voice is apparent and justified. The reunion isn't the only thing I've blown off. There have been plenty of vacations and invitations to spend Easter and Thanksgiving together.

"I'll be there. Did you three pull straws to see who would confront me? Was there a layover at all?"

"I volunteered, and there was a layover, but I planned it this way." His words remind me of what I've always liked best about him. He's never lied or dug himself so deep into the early grave that fame pushes you towards. He's the best of us. The one who got out relatively unscathed. "You know I have an extra ticket to the game."

I glare at him, "What makes you think I'll say yes?"

"If you do, I'll fuck off and tell everyone you're doing fine."

"No more ambushes?"

"Unless you do something else that requires one."

"Any chance you have a plane ticket too?" I scrub my face as I give in. If this is the price of peace, so be it.

"Yeah, Liam is really excited to have the opportunity to tell you all about his first hockey game," Jared grins, his eyes gleaming with pride and victory.

"Fine. Let's get it over with."

One turbulent plane ride later, and we're walking into the stadium. The last time Jared and I were here, our names were up in lights outside, the ticket holders ready to scream our names. Now, we're just faces in the crowd. Jared made sure to cover his fiery red hair and ensured I'd taken similar measures to blend in. For him, it's less about being recognized and more about letting his kids live outside the public eye.

Liam has been bouncing with excitement since we set foot in Chicago. During the entire plane ride, he rattled off facts about each player and told me enough about the game that I now had a basic grasp of what to expect. The kid is making me damn jealous of a time when I was filled with joy for my passions.

We settle into our seats on the stadium's lower level, close enough to get a good look at the action but far enough away to just be faces in the stands.

"Even though I had to twist your arm to get here, it's good to see you," Jared leans in and says as the stadium goes dark and is filled with colored spotlights as the players skate onto the ice. Something rattles in my bones as I remember how those lights felt against my skin, leaving stars in my eyes if I accidentally looked directly into one. I'm just thankful for the cold radiating from the ice, reminding me that this is a different time and place.

Liam tugs on the sleeve of my hoodie and points to the goal. “That’s Price Aetos. The Cobras are ok, but he’s the best. I’m gonna be the best, just like him.”

“Your mom lets you do that?” I ask, my mind trying to envision Liam blocking flying pucks, just like the goalies in front of us.

“Yup. She says it’s the most important position. Because I get to save the team.”

“I bet that you’re great.” I’m getting the impression that Alyssa supported it because it means that Liam gets extra padding.

As the game continues, I’m easily sucked into the constant action. All the while, Liam gives his commentary, explaining the different penalties and his personal critiques of the players. I’ll never tell Jared this, but I’m thankful I decided to come.

13

Lacey

I've been to Chicago enough times to know what to expect from the wind chill that rolls off the water to the fanbase's profane vocabulary.

So I'm convinced I must be seeing things when I sweep my camera across the crowd.

Why the hell is he here?

Drew must be so in my head that I'm starting to imagine him. There's no way it's actually him. I zoom in. No, I'd know those eyes anywhere. He turns to me and stares directly into the lens.

Fuck Fuck Fuckity fuck.

I duck down, holding the camera body in place to block my face.

"Lose something down there?" Aaron smirks from his place in the penalty box. He shouldn't look so cheery after getting into his first fight of the season.

"Shh. I'm thinking," I hiss.

My mind racing, I text Tessa, asking if she wants to switch spots for the next period. Even before she responds, I know she'll agree; Tessa is above on the catwalk, which is not the best assignment for someone who hates heights like she does. I nod to her as she approaches and bolt up the stands.

Once securely on the catwalk, hovering above the action, I finally catch my breath. The game looks so small from a bird's eye view. I usually avoid coming up here because I hate being so removed from the action, but for now, it's a haven.

Without players flying by in front of me, my mind and camera wander. I find myself searching for Drew again, but this time on purpose. Once I spot him, I allow myself a moment to watch him react to the game.

He's on the edge of his seat, his eyes watching the action like a cat tracking its prey. And I can't help as a smile pulls at my mouth, watching as he falls for the sport I love so much.

I press the button to capture a picture, and as soon as the shutter stops, I zoom out, trying to refocus on my work. But during the game, I can sense his presence, my heart leaping when he momentarily looks toward the catwalk, his gaze so close but never quite meeting mine.

The final buzzer rings out, prompting the mass of fans to rise from their seats. It also signals that it's time for my next task—avoiding Drew as I head down to the press room. Despite how enjoyable it was to watch him during the game, this crossover only validated my reason for not telling him more about my life. I just hope this was a one-time thing instead of something that will force me to sneak around my own place of work for the foreseeable future.

I'm most of the way to where the press conference is being held, but before I can turn the corner to safety, I hear an unmistakable rumbling laugh. "Sure, just make sure to hold on." I peer around the corner in time to see Drew walking away with a little girl perched on his shoulders.

I really don't need the image of him with kids in my head. Maybe I'm just ovulating; yeah, that has to be it. It has to be the hormones pumping through me; I'd probably have this same reaction to any above-average-looking man with a child.

I shift around the corner and meet a few stares from passersby about my admittedly suspicious behavior.

On the bus to the airport, Aaron leans over his seat and asks, "Successful with your mission?"

I don't have a chance to answer because Price whips around in his seat and takes a picture as Aaron poses. I just give him a *'do you really have to do that right now?'* look.

"Mission?" Price asks when the camera is tucked safely out of sight.

"Yeah, Lacey was hiding from someone at the game. For the record, I think you'd make a terrible spy," Aaron explains.

"I'll keep that in mind if I ever consider a career change," I grumble.

"Who were you hiding from?" Price asks.

"No one you know," I snap, maybe too forcefully, but I'm still not over the godmother conversation. I want to talk it out with him, just not while I'm still on edge about everything going sideways in my life.

"Obviously. Pretty much everyone you know is on this bus or went to college with us," Price presses. He has a point; pretty much everyone I know is also a contact on his phone.

"Maybe I decided I needed a break from you fools," I say, raising my eyebrows and challenging them to ask more questions.

"Good for you, getting out there meeting new people." Price nods slightly before shifting forward in his seat.

My keys jingle as I push through the front door. Drew is on the couch, leaning on his arm in the most comfortable position he can manage and watching something narrated by an old British man. At the rate he consumes docuseries, he must have an encyclopedia for a brain.

Walking to the kitchen to grab some water, I can't help but glare at the couch. God, I hate that sorry excuse for furniture. It's like he never left the space. It makes me wonder what he's off doing when I'm gone if he can just jet off to Chicago for a day trip. He doesn't look like a trust fund kid. Maybe he's some sort of tech genius who sold his company?

"How was work?" Drew asks as he presses pause on his documentary.

I take a sip from my glass and look up at him. "Is that a trick question?"

"Just trying my best to catch you off guard," he supplies with a wink.

I take a risk and say, "Obviously, you didn't go on any grand adventures today." If I wasn't looking for it, I wouldn't have caught his slight flinch.

"Nah. Why would I need to go anywhere when I can learn about deep cave expeditions from the comfort of home?" he asks, gesturing toward the screen.

"You keep doing that." I could go back and forth with him all night, but I'm ready to collapse into bed. I give him a quick wave as I grab my glass and head to my room.

I close the door, but instead of continuing into the room, I stand and wait, listening for what I know will come next. The soft sound of the TV goes silent, followed by the light shuffling of Drew as he gets off the couch and heads to his own room. It's the same pattern he follows every night when I come home. It doesn't matter if it's ten P.M. or three A.M.; he's on that couch watching something about how surgical robots are manufactured or Bigfoot lore.

I want to dislike it and feel like he's overstepping by making sure I get back safe. But I can't.

Because that would mean lying about how good it is to know someone is waiting for me.

14

Lacey

The image is just slightly out of frame.

The thought cycles through my head over and over until it tunes out everything else.

I'm sitting cross-legged on the foot of the bed, laptop balanced on one knee, clicking through images of Jonathan just as he scored the final winning point against North Carolina yesterday. The image in question is almost perfect.

You can see the force and pure athleticism of his body being translated from the hockey stick to the puck as it makes contact, shards of ice adding drama to the moment.

Almost perfect, which is more irritating than if I could easily delete the picture instead of fixating on it. The blurry pictures, the boring pictures—those are easy to discard.

I was probably only a millisecond behind in following his movement. I study these mistakes religiously, visualizing how to make improvements. Everyone on the team is slightly faster than last year, not just in their individual movements but also in their decisions made as a unit, allowing for more efficient plays.

I'm falling behind; even if it's by a millisecond, it still matters.

I go back to the footage from last night's game and compare Johnathan's movements to the moment I captured, taking notes of what I could have done better. I've been told that this is just an exercise in beating myself up and that no one can be perfect at what they do. But for me, it's therapeutic to break down the problem and find a solution, pushing towards the future.

Otherwise, I dwell on the past.

As I get lost in the routine of editing and rewatching old game footage, my mind starts to drift. I think about the unread words folded into an envelope with my name on it. And more so about the three words I regret not saying enough to the one person who deserved them the most.

A knock on my door draws me back to the present. My immediate reaction to the sudden sound is to slam my laptop shut and tuck it under the sheets. Heat rushes to my cheeks, feeling guilty for getting caught. Because there's a nice little list on the fridge that says I'm not supposed to be working right now.

I can't help it.

It feels like everything and everyone else in my life is in disarray. Work has always been the one area of my life I've always felt in control of, and I need it to stay that way.

I look up to find Drew leaning in the doorway, arms crossed, in one of his endless supply of hoodies. “You’re not supposed to be working.”

“What’s the harm? It’s not late or anything,” I say, trying to play it off. But the fact that he’s taking the arrangement seriously has a comforting warmth spreading through my chest.

“It’s nine P.M.,” he corrects. “Don’t you do anything for yourself? I’m kind of disappointed seeing how the first few times we met, you seemed like you got out more often.”

"Sorry, but those were my two scheduled fun days for the month. Every other day, I'm just plain boring. Apologies for the false advertising," I say with a smile, ignoring the fact that on one of those supposed fun days, he found me crying outside a bar.

"For someone so vicious, you sometimes act like a little old lady," he smirks. I retaliate by grabbing one of the decorative pillows beside me and launching it at him in full force. He effortlessly catches it with one hand, not even glancing away from me. "All I'm saying is that you might want to slow down a bit. If you're always at 100%, you'll be running on fumes before too long." Even without knowing the entirety of what's going on, his concerns sound like everyone else in my life. "I actually came to see if you wanted to watch a movie. Catching you breaking our rules is just a happy accident."

“I’m not *always* at 100%”

"You've probably never said that in your life. I'll have to start giving out punishments if you keep this up, and I have a feeling that you wouldn't like that."

"What makes you think you know what I like?" I regret the phrasing the moment the words pass my lips. He moves into the room, his legs eating up the space between us.

Right as he's close enough to cast a shadow over me, he speaks in a rumble that sends shivers down my spine. "Don't ask questions you don't actually want the answers to. Maybe one day I'll stop biting my tongue and tell you."

He lifts his arm, and I brace for him to touch me. Briefly remembering the euphoric sensation of his skin against mine, I find it difficult to pull away.

But he doesn't touch me. Instead, he grabs my laptop and walks into the other room, calling behind him, "Time for that movie! I'm feeling generous, so I'll even let you pick."

My rising frustration has me wanting to grab the nearest pillow and scream into it.

Instead, I follow him into the living room, holding out my hands. "Fine. I'll do the movie. Can I have my laptop back first?"

"No, I'm keeping it until you head to work tomorrow." He sounds so proud of himself that I don't even want to fight him on it.

Letting him win this battle, I make my way to the damned teardrop couch, pausing momentarily to strategize because there's no truly good way to sit on it. After grabbing the remote, I settle on the wider section of the couch, curling my legs underneath me. I queue up *Jaws* and wait for Drew to emerge from his room.

When he reappears, his lazy grin gives me the impression that my laptop is thoroughly hidden. It being in his room is enough of a deterrent. I can't imagine there will ever be a reason big enough to justify entering his space.

"You know this couch would probably be better in a modern art museum than a living room." I fidget, trying to maneuver into a position that will be comfortable for the duration of the movie. In addition to its shape, the backrest is half the height needed to give any semblance of lumbar support.

He sits next to me and then tries out his own set of different positions.

"It really isn't all that comfortable," he finally says as if genuinely noticing the peculiar piece of furniture for the first time.

This reminds me of how he's not entirely sure about where certain things in the kitchen are or how his wardrobe of sweatpants and plain shirts doesn't fit the luxury interior of the space, as if he only sort of lives here. I honestly wouldn't be surprised if someone walked in one day claiming to be the real owner.

"We'll survive for a movie," I relent with a sigh and press play.

Drew goes rigid beside me as his impressive speaker system immerses us in the first notes of the iconic theme song. The

TV itself is so big that it's curved to give you the impression of being inside the movie.

"Oh fuck no," he says, reaching across me to grab for the remote as I pull it out of reach.

"What, it's just *Jaws*. It's like the most family-friendly horror film."

"I can do horror, just not," he waves at the screen, which features a frozen snapshot of tangled kelp.

"Not what?"

"Not sharks, ok! I don't do sharks." He sounds resigned with his admission. I try my best not to laugh. I swear I try, but I fail miserably. "It's not funny. Those things are monsters. You just have to look at their eyes. Tell me you can look at a shark and claim it has a soul."

"But you're literally the size of one of those things. I bet you could wrestle one and win," I manage to wheeze out.

"Sure, but I don't have multiple rows of teeth designed to shred flesh."

I lean in, pretending to inspect his mouth, "Damn. I could have sworn I saw a few rows in there."

"I think you would have felt it when I bit you. I bet it would have been pretty memorable." His eyes darken, my breath hitching in response.

"Yeah. I probably would have had a hard time forgetting that." I pull back because I've gotten too close, both physically and to the memory of that night, that should just be left alone.

He makes another move for the remote, so I slide off the couch, my feet landing on the floor. It only takes a moment before he's chasing after me. We run around the island, circling one way and then the other in a childish game of keep away.

I move, ready to dart past him and into the living room, but my socks betray me on the polished floor, and I slide. I brace to catch myself, but I never hit the floor.

Instead, two firm hands grip my waist, keeping me upright. My mind flashes back to the bar and how he caught me in a similar way.

Is it such a terrible thing to know he'll catch me whenever I need it?

I swallow, trying to steer the conversation to safer waters, "So, new rule: no sharks." I slip out of his grip and walk a bit faster than necessary to the list on the fridge. With his eyes following me, I add the word "sharks" with a big X over it. "It's a shame, though, because I still haven't gone to the aquarium."

He looks moderately offended when he says, "You're kidding me, right? You've lived here for how long, and you haven't gone to the aquarium that people literally travel across the world to see?"

"Excuse me for not having the sudden urge to pay to watch fish swim in circles all day." It's somewhere on the list of other activities that seem largely wasteful, like stamp collecting and bird watching. Why would I spend an entire day looking at fish when I could be doing something productive?

"We're going. You're off Wednesday next week, right?"

"I thought you said 'Fuck no' to sharks?" I ask, pointing to the freshly-inked word.

"That's just one exhibit in the entire place. I'll survive."

"I'll hold your hand and keep you safe from the animals that are literally behind glass specially designed to keep them inside."

"You promise?"

"Big baby."

"Old lady."

I've never seen the point of aquariums, zoos, or most places where visitors just stand and stare at things all day, which is probably hypocritical for someone who used to want their work featured in museums.

I never had a reason to go, and my mom and I never did many day trips. She was always stuck working at the hospital, and it always felt unfair to ask her to take her days off to walk around a building for multiple hours when I knew she'd already spent fifty hours or more on her feet.

Maybe at some point, I wanted to, but I guess that desire got buried deep inside as the years went by. It's not like she didn't do what she could. She showed up when it mattered, never missing a soccer game or the few gallery shows I had been featured in.

As an adult, time felt too precious to waste in a place like this. If I wanted to look at fish, like some cat sensory video, I could livestream something on my TV.

Now that I'm here, I want to take it all back.

From the moment we join the crowded line, the collective excitement becomes infectious. The aquarium buzzes with activity, filled with vibrant colors and the gentle sway of the water. Standing inches away, Drew has his phone pulled up, occasionally glancing at me to ensure I'm enjoying myself. It almost feels like we're a couple—although the addition of a singing bald man in a fish-covered Hawaiian shirt does an excellent job of shattering that idea.

I'm not sure at what point Craig invited himself on this little trip or when he took the edible that has him staring at everything like he's a toddler in a toy store, but the effect has Drew and me feeling like parents trying to pull their child from one exhibit to the next.

I don't blame Craig's lingering, especially with the immersive exhibits that pull you away from reality. Rippling reflections of water and dim glowing lights in one room give way to the chattering of otters in the next. If someone told me you can crawl through the sea otter exhibit, I might have come years ago.

I chase Craig through the otter tunnels as Drew watches us with a faint, amused smile.

We end up with both of our heads in a plexiglass bubble face to face with one of the otters.

"You know, I'm kind of happy I lost our bet," Craig says, not breaking eye contact with the cute creature in front of us.

"Our bet?"

"Yeah. I was sure you would go back and sleep together again," he casually reminds me.

"How do you know we haven't?"

"Cause you guys look at each other in that awkward yearning way that reminds me of high school. But it's nice to have you around, so I'm happy you guys are keeping your pants on."

Suddenly, the small space feels claustrophobic now that Craig has invited the awkward truth into the cramped space with us. "We better move before a parent comes and yells at us."

"Fuck those kids," he declares, but follows behind me as I crawl out.

I fall back into place next to Drew, letting Craig guide our trajectory through the space.

We stay mostly quiet as we go through the exhibits until Craig tries to convince a kid that goldfish are venomous. The kid just stares at him, calling Craig a hairless idiot.

As we navigate back and forth, I start to notice how fidgety Drew is. If we pass a group of people, he'll pull at his cap or hang back if there's a crowd around a particular tank.

After the third time he lowers his cap over his face, I tug at his sleeve to get his attention. "Hey, we can go if you're not feeling ok."

"No, I want to be here. How else would I see you gawk like a little kid? I forgot what it's like for someone to see this for the first time." He gives me a reassuring smile that I nearly believe.

I won't push if he doesn't want me to. I give Drew one last look before weaving through the crowd to catch up with Craig before he gets bullied by more preteens.

Our next stop is the moon jelly room. Of all the creatures we encountered, these pull me in the most. I could stand here for hours, just watching them drift aimlessly, their translucent bodies pulsating rhythmically. I'm almost jealous of their brainless, hypnotic forms.

What would it be like to care so little? To simply exist? If reincarnation is real, becoming a moon jelly in another life doesn't sound half bad.

There is something otherworldly about how the glow of the tank reflects in the deep green of Drew's eyes. I can't help myself; the impulse to capture perfect moments is a deep-rooted habit.

I only have my phone, and I quickly adjust the exposure before holding it up. I click the capture button twice before he turns his attention.

"Beautiful, right?"

He's asking about the luminescent jellyfish, but that doesn't change my answer, "Yeah, absolutely."

"You know that they only live about a year." He points to the aimlessly moving creatures.

"Your documentaries talk about that?"

"Probably, but I'm just reading the plaque," he says with that same smirk. Before I can respond, Craig's voice grows louder as he reaches us, urging us to hurry up.

Tension radiates off Drew as we reach the final exhibit. I thought Drew was joking about the sharks and that it was just something that he liked to avoid when given the chance. But from his bone-crunching grip potentially causing permanent damage to my hand, I'm changing my evaluation to full-blown irrational fear. He snatches my hand up the moment we enter the exhibit and doesn't let go until we're all the way to the gift shop.

Craig, in a stroke of genius or insanity, decides we all need matching hats that look like a tiny shark is biting the top of our heads.

"I'm not wearing it," Drew says, crossing his arms.

"It is literally made of fabric. Just for the picture, and then you can take it right off!" Craig whines, dangling the hat in front of his friend's face.

I raise my hand, drawing their attention to say, "I'd like to veto the picture."

"C'mon guys, you're no fun. I had fun and just want something to remember it by," Craig continues, practically begging.

"I'll do the hat if you get in the picture," Drew says to me, his voice turning softer, picking up on my discomfort. "It would be nice to remember today."

"Fine. But only if you wear the hat all the way home," I concede.

"Deal."

We buy three of the stupid hats and take a picture. Craig and I smile for all we're worth, and Drew tries his best to look upset and fails. Sure, I usually hate photos of myself, but some moments are worth remembering.

15

Drew

Atlanta holds a special place in the band's history. It's where we headlined our first major venue, and thus, the main reason for choosing it for the reunion. Despite the city's vibrant music scene and the multitude of talented artists who call it home, it often doesn't receive the recognition it deserves, especially compared to cities like Nashville and LA.

Back then, even after the sting of Fool's Gambit parting ways, I was still optimistic. I had my apartment designed when I first moved to Atlanta, throwing myself completely into the process, determined to make it my new home.

Out of all the rooms, one has remained unused for years.

With my hand resting loosely on the knob, I can already picture the interior—walls layered in a mix of thick, jewel-toned Persian rugs and geometric sound-absorbing foam. An array of instruments resting on stands in the far corner, still waiting to be played for the first time. And against one wall sits studio monitors, a computer, an audio interface, and all the other essential production equipment that has only been turned on a few times to check if they still work, all long overdue for upgrades.

I push through the door before I lose my nerve, not bothering to waste time by flicking on the lights. Walking closer to the drum kit, I focus on controlling my rapidly quickening breath, just taking in the place and feeling the familiar weight of the drumsticks in my hands.

Jared's words wriggle under my skin and through my mind as I sit silently on the stool.

I have to do this.

Maybe it will be different this time. Right?

It's been three years since I tried. A lot can change in three years.

I start the way I always do, creating a solid backbeat with the bass drum and snare, letting the sound become as familiar as a second heartbeat. A beat that could belong to any of a hundred songs. The movements are no different than the thousand other times I've run through them, but somehow, the sound feels hollow.

I push past the thought, transitioning to the lead-in to "Funny Thing," the lyrics scrolling through my mind like a karaoke prompt screen.

It's a safe choice with its upbeat feeling, emphasized by a bright sound that comes from each strike of the cymbals. I play the happy pop anthem almost as if hoping the energy of it will seep into me.

Like every other song, it's drenched in memory.

People always talk about how scents bring you back in time, the smell of cinnamon in the fall, or your grandma's lavender perfume. Music has that same propensity, a time warp caught in a handful of notes.

One moment, you're out for a run listening to an old favorite as your feet pound against the pavement, then the next, you're back in the car zipping through the night with your arm slung around your first girlfriend, nervous that she'll think you're a terrible kisser.

As I play, I'm transported back to the coffee shop where Jared first met Alyssa. The warm aroma of freshly brewed coffee mingles with their laughter.

Then I'm at the studio with the whole band together, a smile spreading across my face as Martin plays a rough cut of our newest single. We exchange glances, feeling the excitement building within us for the new journey ahead. One of those *I can't believe we're the lucky fucks who get to do this moments.*

Finally, I'm on stage, basking in the heat of the lights on my skin and the sound of the roaring crowd. But I don't pay too much attention to them. I never have.

Music has always been a selfish act for me, a sanctuary—something that saved me from the depression that threatened to pull me under as a teenager. Music was a lifeline.

I blink, and I'm back in the dark room, alone with the harsh reality.

Because nothing is the same, and it will never return to how it was.

I miss a beat, and then another, and another, until they're all wrong, and I can't get back on track no matter what I do, no matter how much I need them to be right.

The feeling of wrongness washes over me in waves, and I can't outrun it even as I pick up the tempo, even as my hands start to shake and something deep in my stomach starts to seize up.

The drumsticks fall from my hand, barely making a sound as they fall into the thick carpet.

I nearly trip over the pieces of the drum kit in my haste to escape, but it's too late.

I pushed too far. The lifeline snaps all over again.

I stumble blindly out of the room. This is how it always ends, no matter how good it seems at the start. I never make it through a whole song before it slips out of my control, tormenting me with what's no longer mine.

Like clockwork, I rush to the nearest bathroom, barely managing to close the door behind me as my hurried steps carry me to the toilet. My stomach churns, and acidic bile creeps up my throat as I finally release the contents of my lunch into the bowl, the sight of it staring back at me before I flush it away. Collapsing onto the cool tile floor, I welcome the chill against my clammy skin.

There are a few things I remember about our last performance. I blame the concussion for the blur, and ten years later, I can't decide if it's a blessing or a curse. I remember waking up, deciding it would be best to savor the last nectar I could pull from the dream; I had just wanted it to be perfect.

That is, until Wes and Emily. Until I walked onto the stage, looking at my friends, at the guys who had become my brothers over the last five years, all smiling in relief.

I couldn't help the anger boiling in my blood, wishing I could hurl something at them. Because how could they be so happy about it ending? They were so excited to leave the best time of our life. For it to become a distant memory, one you talk about years from now.

Then the opening song, "Ronnie," started and . . . Nothing.

I know there's a video out there about it that could fill the gaps in my memory, but I've never thought it was worth hunting down. I might wallow in the ruins of who I've become, but I don't want to relive how I got this way.

The last thing, the most brutal thing, was waking up in the hospital afterward. My family clustered around the bed, knowing the show finished without me. That I never got to say goodbye, especially when I didn't want to let it go in the first place.

After that, I tried to practice like everything was normal, like my entire life hadn't been disrupted. But each time I tried to sit back behind the drums, I'd just relive that day over again like a movie in my mind. Instead of credits rolling at the end, my body would just give out.

For a while, the doctors thought it might be focal dystonia, a neurological disorder that is rare but impacts plenty of musicians. It affects fine motor movement, so I was doubtful because the problem never seemed to be my hands. Still, I sat through extensive tests as they looked at my brain's electrical signals.

Some specialists were so determined that there was something wrong with my inner ear, potential damage from constant exposure to high volumes, and from the concussion I sustained from my final performance. The outcome was that the doctors became a few thousand dollars richer, and I learned that my hearing was actually better than it should have been.

With time, it's just gotten worse, each failure snowballing, leading to the point I'm at now.

I've never really confessed to anyone but Craig what was going on. I wouldn't have told him either, but he let himself into my apartment just in time to see the aftermath. My head resting on the lip of the toilet in my loft, drumsticks abandoned on the floor.

After that, he treated me differently, as if I were something cracked on the verge of shattering. As if one more thing would tip me over the edge.

It's one of the many reasons I've never told my family the truth. It would feel the same as telling them that I'm defective, that all their years of support have gone to waste.

It's been easier to let them think that my retirement from music was a choice. That I had some control over my failures. That I wasn't fucking broken on some chemical level.

When I'm sure the room won't spin if I sit up, I slowly open my eyes as the unlit space gradually comes into focus.

It's plain and sterile, but the smell of burnt vanilla coming from the large bottles of shampoo and conditioner lets me know it's Lacey's bathroom.

I stare at those bottles until my phone pings in my pocket. My eyes take a moment to adjust to the bright light of the screen. When I read her name, I feel pulled back into the present instead of lingering in the past.

Lacey

I just landed. Home soon.

As I shift upright, I feel every place my shirt adheres to my chest, sticky sweat coating every inch of me. I can't let her come back and find me like this.

I'm tempted for a moment to use her shower and the products she's left behind, leaving me smelling like a damn sugar cookie.

I've barely gotten myself cleaned up and situated on the couch before she enters, going through the familiar motions. The predictability of her movements grounds me. The jingle of her keys, the thud of her heavy boots as they hit the mat.

"Can we get pizza?" Lacey asks over her shoulder as she crosses to her room and sets down her work bags.

"Yeah. Pizza sounds nice," I call back.

She pops her head out the door and asks, "Mushrooms?"

"No mushrooms."

"Dare I ask why?" Her eyes flick to the list on the fridge while a knowing smile teases the corners of her mouth. That smile and her casual air do more to calm my nerves than all my efforts combined.

"Probably not, but knowing you, curiosity might kill you."

"I think I'll survive until after I change to hear the explanation."

She disappears back into her room and comes out a few minutes later, her body drowning in a t-shirt and gray sweatpants. Instead of sitting on the couch, she settles on the floor, sinking into the plush rug with her head resting against the red upholstery, gazing up at me with furrowed brows.

"Are you ok? You look a bit pale. Did you just work out or something?" she asks, her inquisitive eyes still roaming over me, searching to pinpoint what's off.

I nearly stutter over my words with my haste to speak. "No, just scared of the prospect of you welcoming mushrooms into this place."

"Ok," she says, her voice still wary. "So, mushrooms."

"If something eats dying things, I don't want it in my body. I respect the food chain."

"Are any of your fears logical?" She sighs and gets up, making her way to the kitchen and her ever-growing list, writing no mushrooms somewhere beneath no sharks. It's becoming an odd mix of rules and things we're learning about each other.

In my defense, the list isn't just full of my illogical fears. She has her own additions, too, such as banning lemon-scented cleaner because it makes her sneeze and requesting more Oreos in the apartment.

“Plenty of them, but those are no fun to share.”

"You could share them with me." Her gaze briefly meets mine. "I mean, if you want to. Like you've already mentioned, who am I going to tell?" She shrugs, walking back towards her spot on the floor. As she settles back in, her stomach growls softly, a reminder of the task at hand.

“Right now, I’m more concerned about you eating,” I say jokingly, a small, gentle smile emerging on her face.

Maybe one day I'll tell her. But not now, not when she hasn’t seen any of the cracks threatening to split me in two.

The greasy pizza box lays open on the counter behind us as we flip through movie options. I’m trying and failing to convince Lacey to watch something other than one of her horror movies.

“That’s going to put me right to sleep,” she says about the documentary on the history of space travel that I’m trying to convince her is worth watching.

“Good, you look like you could use some rest.” She’s already crashing from work, slightly slumped against me. I don’t mind the weight. The pressure of her body reassures me that she’s here, that I can move past my failure from earlier.

“Fine, but at least put on something with animals. And wake me up when it’s over.”

She dozes off before the narrator even finishes introducing the hierarchical dynamics of African watering holes. My attention dips from the screen to where she's resting on my shoulder. I carefully shift her form so her head rests comfortably on my lap, taking a moment to brush away loose hairs behind her ear.

I just look at her as I lose myself in thought, memories of my childhood spent attending mass with my parents flooding back. I'm not sure how much their devotion to Catholicism was out of faith and how much it was to feel connected to the culture and family they left behind in Italy. I rarely listened to the sermons, except one that has stuck with me throughout the years. It was about miracles and how they come to those in desperate need.

Lacey is a miracle, and I'm not convinced I'm someone worthy of one.

She's a miracle, and I'm just a man who she so happened to fall asleep on—a man she's rebuilding from dust. Each time she walks through the door, I immediately feel sturdier, maybe even a little more whole.

I watch her chest rise and fall, taking in the full, slow breaths of a deep, unworried sleep as if I'm someone who can protect her, but I'm not sturdy enough for that. I wish I could shield her from the storms within her mind, but I know I can't. Even then, I'll stand with her in the eye of the storm, making sure she's never alone.

It takes everything in me not to pull her against my chest and wrap my body around hers. To not fall asleep on this couch and learn what it feels like to wake up next to her.

Instead, I gently lift her from the couch and carry her to her room before tucking her under the covers and hoping she knows she's safe with me.

16

Drew

"Who are you trying to impress with the sunglasses and hat indoors? Just because you're built like a superhero doesn't mean you have to dress like one, too." Lacey grabs the shades off my face, resting them on her head.

The disguise is lame, as I've been reminded twice now, but I'm not sure what to expect. It's not like we're in LA or New York, where it's a random Tuesday if you run into a celebrity at the grocery store.

I don't bother responding to her comment because her food choice demands my attention. I've noticed over the last few weeks that, honestly, she eats like shit when she's at the apartment. Normally, I wouldn't risk going out in public for such a prolonged period, especially after all the close calls at the aquarium, but I have to put an end to her dietary sins.

"You're not buying those." I snatch the box of frozen four-cheese mac and cheese from her hand and put it back in the freezer. "No fucking way that's taking up real estate in my kitchen."

"Then what am I supposed to eat?" she asks, defensiveness leaking into her tone.

"I don't know. Maybe something that doesn't resemble what you'd find in a high school lunchroom?"

"I can't really get fresh groceries. They go bad before I can use them. These," she reaches for the freezer door again, but I hold it shut as she attempts to jerk it open, "keep for God knows how long so I can eat them whenever. Food is just fuel anyway, and these do the job."

"You're not a car. You have taste buds for a reason, so maybe try to enjoy them every once in a while." Though, she does tend to treat her body like a machine, moving with a determined intensity from point A to point B, with little care about how fast she's being worn down. "What the hell is on the list that you made?"

"That's none of your business. They're *my* groceries," she retorts, clutching a piece of paper. Instead of using her phone like a normal person, she wrote it all down the old-fashioned way. Though it does work to my advantage when I quickly seize it from her. "Hey, give that back!"

"*Sconosciuta,* what the hell?" I ask as I scan the contents of the slip of paper. "Are you shopping for an eighteen-year-old frat boy or the apocalypse?"

The list consists of beans, bread, frozen meals, and canned soup, with the only fresh item being avocados. Things that, in all honesty, you don't really need a list to remember, but she has a thing for lists. If someone could have some sort of organization kink, I have no doubt it would be Lacey.

"I'm just being practical," she huffs.

"Do you actually enjoy eating any of this? Wait, I don't want you to answer that because if you say yes, I won't be able to look you in the eyes ever again." And that would be a shame because those eyes do wicked things to me. "But also, you're not buying this shit."

"Then what should I do? Let the fruit rot and the meat go bad? Even if I wasn't worried about adding to the world's food waste, I can't cook." I've guessed as much since the apartment now permanently smells of burnt toast.

"I'll cook for us," I say before giving it a second thought.

Cooking has been one of the few things I've been able to motivate myself to do over the years. Partly because it would be a snub against my mother's hours spent teaching me family recipes if I let those skills go to waste.

But she raises an eyebrow, looking more suspicious than impressed. "You cook? Like, it won't give me food poisoning or send me to the hospital?"

"I'll make you never want to touch that prepackaged shit again. If you ever meet my sister, though, run in the other direction if she offers you anything she's had a hand in making." A ghost of a shiver runs through me at the literal kitchen nightmare that is Evelyn Mariano, who has sent loved ones, yes plural, to the hospital because of her infamous culinary skills.

"So what's on the menu then, Master Chef?" she asks.

"I guess you'll just have to find out. Guesses will also be accepted."

"Why won't you just tell me?" she pouts. I hate it when she does that. It only emphasizes how full her lips are, like they were designed to be kissed and bit and wrapped around my—fuck, I'm standing next to goddamn chicken nuggets. I shouldn't be thinking about my roommate like that right now.

That's what we've felt like in moments like these, just roommates, despite having to tamp down the hope that we could be so much more.

Today, we're just two regular people doing ordinary things together, as if we've done this a hundred times before and will do it again without a second thought. It's comforting and scary, like a safety blanket with a looming sense of uncertainty. She still hasn't heard from her apartment's management, making every day feel like it could be the last. I'll be more than happy if they keep taking their sweet time.

Instead of answering, I take over the shopping cart, putting one foot on the bottom rung before pushing off with the other, skating away from her, and leaving me feeling carefree and light like a kid. The aisles pass by in a blur, the fluorescent lights above casting a soft glow, her rapid footsteps echoing close behind. She catches up to me two aisles over.

"You can't just do that," she protests.

"Why not?" I ask as I scan the shelves for bronze-cut pasta. I could probably make it from scratch, but I don't know where my pasta maker is collecting dust these days.

"It's against the rules."

"Since when were there grocery cart rules? I don't think the workers here get paid enough to care about that kind of thing. And you're missing out." I raise an eyebrow as I toss a few packages of Fettuccine and a can of San Marzano tomatoes into the cart. "Your turn. Hop on."

I step away and gesture for her to take my place.

"No."

"*Please.* Come on. Let me prove you wrong."

She hesitates momentarily before responding. "Well, as long as you're begging. But don't think you'll change my mind about this shopping cart nonsense."

"If I knew that all I had to do was beg—"

She claps a hand over my mouth. "I'm going to stop you right there before you say something potentially scarring inside this store," she scolds. My laugh comes out muffled against her hand.

When she pulls away, I ask, "Who am I scarring exactly? You've heard worse from me before." And if she gives me the option, I'll do it all over again with however much begging she wants. My words cause her cheeks to burst into perfect patches of pink. "You blush a lot for someone so serious and competitive."

"I can't exactly help it. If I had a choice in the matter, I'd never blush." She reaches up gently to cup her cheek with the same hand she used to cover my mouth. It's almost like I'm kissing her through some diluted transitive property.

I lean in so the tips of our noses are barely an inch away. "Do I make you nervous, *sconosciuta*?"

"I'm not going to answer that." She doesn't back down. Instead she meets my gaze with heat in her eyes.

"Why not?"

"I don't want to have to lie to you," she admits in a hushed breath that brushes against my skin.

I match her breathy tone. "It's okay. You make me nervous, too."

"I meant what I said that first night. I don't mix sex with emotions."

"I remember. You're the one jumping to less than-innocent conclusions," I tease, though my head is in the same place. It nearly kills me not to close the distance and taste her lips again, but I respect her too much to cross that line. "If you want to shut me up, take the cart for a whirl."

She tears away from me and climbs on, copying my earlier actions half-heartedly. She barely moves more than a foot before coming to a halt.

"Ok, that was pathetic. You've got more than that in you," I tell her. I have no doubt that she could send herself hurtling down the aisle if she wanted to with those toned legs of hers.

"I did it, ok? You can take the cart back now."

"It seems fundamentally against your character to do something half-assed. I'm disappointed." I cross my arms, knowing that it will push her perfectionist buttons.

"If we get kicked out, you're reducing my rent."

Yeah, the rent she's never going to pay. No matter how many times she mentions she doesn't want to owe me, she's doing plenty for me without paying me a dime.

She repositions the cart and finally commits, flying down the empty lane, turning around at the end, and rushing back towards me without any sign of stopping. I quickly catch the front edge of the cart just before it hits me full force.

"Are you trying to run me over?" I pretend to complain, taking in the wide smile that's cracked across her face. "The wild side looks good on you."

"I can try again if you want." A smug pride rings through her voice. "And this is nothing. I've done things that would make you piss your pants."

"Is that so, then what had you so worked up?"

"I just like rules," her tone comes out with a sharpness that doesn't feel entirely aimed at me. "They give me a structure to fall back on when I need it." The words sound practiced rolling off her tongue as if this is a topic of past arguments.

"Fair enough. Though it's hard to picture my granny of a roommate doing anything that would make me piss myself." Honestly, the person she is during the day is at odds with the image of who she is at night, softer yet still so focused.

"I've skydived three times, each in a different country."

"I could handle that." I shrug.

"I swam with sharks once too."

"I thought we had a no-shark rule in place?"

"That's just for the apartment. See, rules are important. It helps to know when they do and don't apply."

She looks at me as if she's just won some debate, but I can see her. The parts of her she hides from the world, and how she tries to contain her life in certain boxes. That's why I like pushing her to have some harmless fun. If it was up to me, there's one specific rule I'd want to convince her to break, but that's off the table while she's living with me.

Just roommates, I remind myself, because although I want her, I would never want her to feel uncomfortable where she lives if it were to go wrong.

"I bet you don't speed either."

She huffs a laugh before saying, "I like my rules, but I'm not insane. Not speeding on Peachtree is just asking for trouble."

We continue to zip through the aisles, grabbing what I'll need for the week to convince her to stop eating garbage. The cart skating comes to an abrupt stop when a little old Southern woman glares at us.

"Sorry, Ma'am, she's just a bad influence on me." I grab Lacey's hand as she glares at me. Her body tenses with the effort it must take her to not tell the woman that I'm the corrupting force in this scenario, not the other way around.

The woman gives us one more bone-chilling glance before making her way out of the aisle.

"See, she knows the rules," Lacey mutters loud enough for just the two of us to hear.

"Maybe you should go live with her then," I grumble.

"I would, but unfortunately, my current roommate is more fun to look at." The compliment fills me with warmth.

Lacey never seems to see how she's forming me back into a human being. The idea of being here in this store for so long would have completely drained me months ago. Who would have guessed being treated like a normal human being would be so damn healing?

Finally moving again, we turn into the coffee aisle to restock Lacey's supply of what is essentially pre-ground jet fuel.

"Why do you buy this stuff anyway? I'd expect you to pick something way nicer," I ask as she reaches for a bag and puts it in the cart. I grab a second one for her. It's better to be stocked than learn what happens when we actually run out.

She bites her lip briefly, and for a moment, her eyes turn glassy and distant. "It's not that I think it tastes good. I know it's terrible. But it's what my mom and I used to drink every morning. She worked nights, so breakfast was the one time we'd always spend together. So it doesn't taste good, but it tastes like home. I can't imagine waking up without knowing that's how I'll start my day. It's not about the taste at all. It's about consistency, knowing it will be the same every time." This is the most she's told me about her family, but I have a feeling that this isn't an invitation to ask more questions.

"I can understand that."

Consistency seems to be one of her core components. Ever since the day I met her, she's stayed in the same uniform: black top, jeans, and those scuffed-up boots. Well, except when we're at home, she wears sweats, which now includes the hoodie I gave her on the second night she was here, the one that she never gave back.

The stability of her routine is like a *Groundhog's Day* remake, but instead of wanting to break the loop, I'm starting to want to do everything in my power to ensure it will never end.

Once the cart is full of everything I'll need to convince her to let me cook for her forever, we head to the self-checkout, falling into a natural rhythm of scanning and bagging. I steal glances at her occasionally, and in those moments, I realize I could live every day like this, no matter how many rules I have to follow, as long as she's there.

But the moment shatters when I spot a phone camera pointed in our direction and make eye contact with the blonde woman in her twenties who's angling for a shot. She's obviously trying to be discreet, pretending to take a phone call, but the way she's honed in on me and the phone position are giveaways.

This isn't my first time dealing with this sort of situation, but it's the first time I care enough to divert it before it escalates.

I snag our receipt and start heading towards the entrance, turning so our backs are to the woman, preventing her from getting a photo with either of our faces in it.

"I'll race you to the car," I whisper into Lacey's ear, and she nods at the suggestion before sprinting off. It's nice to be able to rely on her competitive nature.

I hate how even going out into the real world for an hour encroaches on the bubble that we've curated. Though being spotted in public gets under my skin, I won't let it affect her.

I also know that if the reunion wasn't fast approaching, this wouldn't be an issue at all. People tend to recognize you more when your face is splattered across social media. What puzzles me is why Lacey, even as adverse to Fool's Gambit as she first appeared, hasn't figured it out yet.

The shadowy obscurity of a drunken one-night stand is entirely different from living together in broad daylight.

I'm not complaining, definitely not, but I sure am curious as hell.

"I'm putting them away," Lacey insists.

"Absolutely not. If I'm the one cooking, then I have to know where the ingredients are. The chef makes the rules." But she doesn't budge, so I try a different angle, "I cook. You do the dishes."

"I can make that work, Chef," she agrees and walks to the island, where she boosts herself up to sit on the counter. I tried to get her to stop climbing on the surfaces intended for food prep, but the combination of her stubbornness and the fact that she looks more delicious than any meal won out.

She idly swings her legs as she watches me unload the groceries onto their proper shelves. "What's on the menu for tonight? I'm emotionally attached to my frozen mac and cheese, so you better aim to impress."

"My family's secret red sauce recipe."

I can't help the grin that takes residence on my face. This recipe immediately came to mind when I thought about cooking for her—simple, but special. Food has always been something of a love language in my family, a way of taking care of the people that matter most.

In the band's early days, I would cook all our dinners on the road armed with a hot plate, an old set of pans, and a notebook full of my mother's recipes. I loved giving the guys a reason to smile after a bad show: the ones on weekdays in dingy bar rooms with only a handful of patrons that left the guys downtrodden.

This red sauce recipe was the first thing I learned how to cook when I was a kid. I used to help measure ingredients and butcher onions in an attempt to mince them.

Lacey doesn't talk as I work, which I'm thankful for because, despite all my practice, I might slice a finger open if she distracts me.

As I toss the garlic and onion in heated oil, the fragrance fills the room. Once the aromatics are properly sauteed, I add the rest of the ingredients and reduce the heat to a simmer.

"What's the secret ingredient?" she asks, leaning to peek around me and survey what's left on the counter.

"I'll only tell you if you promise to help."

"You drive a hard bargain, but ok."

"Before you say no. Remember, you promised." I hold out a hand in her direction, hoping she won't back out. "The secret is that you have to dance while the sauce simmers."

Though it may seem that way to her, it's not some contrived way to get her to act out a romantic scene. It's a tradition bordering on superstition. While playing sous chef with my mother, I would try to lead her through a stilted, awkward waltz as Pavarotti's enchanting tenor flowed through the kitchen.

On the occasions when dancing was neglected or put off, the sauce always seemed drained of flavor. I've never been sure if the secret was actually dancing or the joy that came with it.

17

Lacey

My gaze flicks between his outstretched hand and his eyes. The moment stretches like a rubber band, growing taut and thin with tension as seconds pass.

I look at his eyes one last time and see that look I'm becoming intimately familiar with. It's soft and pleading, a small *I need this* that I want to interpret as *I need you.* It's a version of the look he gave me at the store when he asked me to ride the cart like a kid.

Each time he looks at me like this with a soft crinkle around his deep, forest eyes, I'm powerless. But I don't mind being needed instead of the one in need.

"So, will you help?" he asks again, his voice causing time to snap back into place. I move off the counter to stand in front of him, pausing for a moment before I give my answer. I'm so close—too close—I swear I can count his eyelashes one by one if I tried.

I take his hand, his calloused fingers are gentle as they fold over mine. "But there's no music."

"*Sconosciuta*, I don't need music when I'm with you." There's something hopeful in the light tone of his voice. "But we can turn some on if you want."

I nod, and he calls to the voice-activated speaker system to play the version of "Volare" sung by Dean Martin. The tune has a joyful swing that whisks us away. Though I have an aversion to contemporary music, there is a small special place in my heart for songs made decades ago.

It only takes a moment of stilted awkwardness before I find my feet and follow his effortless lead. I've seen men larger than him move gracefully on the ice, making sharp turns and precise striking slashes.

This is different.

Drew moves without restraint or caution, casually knocking his hips into mine as he sings the mix of English and Italian lyrics. The silky sound of his voice grabs me by my heart, threatening to never let go.

We keep dancing as Dean Martin gives way to a staccato Spanish opera and then to a swooping aria. Half of our steps are more like glides, our socked feet sliding on the glossy wood floor.

He unfurls me into a spin, and a light string of laughter bubbles out of me making me feel like a shaken bottle of champagne. When I'm pulled back into the circle of his arms, I'm acutely aware of how his hand lands on my mid-back and not any lower. I should be happy he's not attempting to use this moment to cross any lines, but a seed of disappointment settles in my stomach.

My mind takes this opportunity to ruin everything as it drifts to think about how happy he'll make the person he ends up with. Whoever they are will have endless perfect moments like these. I hope they don't take them for granted.

We stop abruptly, and I look up at him as he brushes a strand of hair out of my face and then wraps it around his finger. "Where did you just go?"

"Just wondering how someone hasn't snatched you up as the perfect house husband yet."

"Are you proposing?" He smirks, and my stomach flips at his words.

"No. I'm not marriage material. Who'd want a wife who's gone every other day?" I force a self-effacing laugh. "Never mind. The answer is obviously someone who intends to use the opportunity to cheat on their wife. Besides, I'm not exactly built to open up to people in the way they want me to."

I've never been able to picture myself as a wife. I can conjure up everything else—a home with glowing, inviting windows even on the darkest winter nights, children in matching pajamas running through the halls, and a man with the most beautiful smile lighting up his whole face.

But when I picture myself as the final piece, the image shatters. The children don't resemble me, and the man's expression is like he's looking at me but seeing someone else.

No matter what I do, it's never mine.

Drew releases the strand from his finger and brushes it behind my ear. "Anyone that would do that to you doesn't have the right to call themselves a man. That shit shouldn't matter because the right person would make it work."

"I guess you're right, but that's assuming you meet the right person. That's the tricky part. Sometimes, you stay with the wrong person since you're convinced it's better to be wanted than to be yourself." I clench my teeth.

"So what, you figured out you deserved more? Good for you." He nods with his approval

"No, that's not why it ended," I say, my voice steady, but I'm not entirely able to disguise the hurt that comes with the memory. "He was convinced I was sleeping with someone from work, which I would never do. But I knew if he hadn't acted like a major jerk, I might have stayed. Even though he made me feel so small." I pause. "He just felt like my only option and after him . . ." I trail off.

After Henry, I came to terms with the idea that I'd already met everyone I'd ever love, and it wasn't worth risking trying again.

"The one-night stand rule," Drew finishes for me, his jaw flexing in irritation.

I force a smile in an attempt to break the somber mood, "What about you? What demons are in the way of your happily ever after."

"You know how something happening twice is a coincidence, but three times is a pattern?"

"Sure."

"Well, after my girlfriends cheated on me three times with people I knew, I decided that, just maybe, it would be worth taking a break from trying to find a genuine connection." My heart splinters at the words.

White hot fury and sorrow rip through me. I've seen how trusting he is, how easily he let me into his life. I want to shred anyone who's abused that kindness.

"So, we're pretty much made for each other? The universe just wanted to push together two people with the worst damn luck and trust issues, then said go live together and see how it works out." I force my words to sound like a joke because this is starting to feel like something more.

Drew opens his mouth, but before he can say anything, his phone timer sounds. His chest brushes against mine as he reaches around me to turn it off. I linger for a second as my heart skips a beat. It's an effort to duck away and put a safe distance between us, but I do it because I have to.

Wordlessly, he moves to boil the water, and I return to my place on the counter, swaying slightly to the music still filling the room around us.

Once done, he serves the finished pasta and sauce in one of those dishes that can't quite decide if it's a bowl or a plate. We remain in the glow of the kitchen, him leaning against the counter opposite me.

With rapt attention, he watches me take the first bite. Theoretically, I know what it should taste like, but there's something unmistakably more to it. Something that can't be attributed to the basil or the garlic.

"So?" he asks once I've swallowed.

"I think you're hired. You're spoiling me, you know. I don't know what I'll do if I get used to this and then have to leave." I take another bite, and it tastes like a hug. How the hell does food taste like a hug?

"You deserve to be spoiled, and I'm happy to be the one doing it." And there goes my hummingbird heart again, thrashing with emotions I don't dare put into words.

"You deserve that too. Someone who doesn't doubt for a second you're worth it." I want to inject how much I mean my words into his bones. We don't have control over who ruins us, but I hope that, in some way, I can show him that their actions don't define who he is.

After the plates are scraped clean, I wash the dishes, and he packs away the leftovers. We weave around each other as we complete the tasks, the soft clinks of cutlery and the gentle swish of water creating a soothing rhythm in the background.

Our movements have a similar but slower cadence to the dance we shared. It's like we're both trying to stretch each moment, catch the grains of sand in the hourglass before they can fall and slip away.

But the night has to end. No matter how long we take, tomorrow will come. So, reluctantly, we part ways, each heading to our respective rooms, lingering before we enter.

His warm and genuine voice carries across the distance as he says, "Thank you for today."

“For letting you buy groceries and cook dinner?” I ask, even though that description doesn’t do justice to describe the time we spent together.

“For giving me a reason to.”

The words hang in the air before he turns and shuts his door.

18

Lacey

I usually wage war with myself on the flights to and from games. Long expanses of time where sitting still is the default makes my skin crawl and my mind spin.

To combat this, I would normally take candids of the players passed out in their seats or playing cards. When I finished that, I would look over my notes about the other team. I don't actually need to do as much research as I do, but understanding the other team makes me feel prepared and steady. Price has told me on more than one occasion that I watch old game footage more than he does; it's probably true.

Despite his teasing, Price gets it. The drive is a combination of doing what you love out of passion and fear of failure. I see it on my friend's face each time he gets off the ice.

On bad days, he'll blame himself for a loss, the hard set of his brow telling me he's thinking about what would have happened if he had only blocked one more shot. On good days, he'll struggle to take credit for his own work because, on the good days, it doesn't feel like work at all.

Today is different.

Today, I'm replaying memories from the last month like a favorite movie. I welcome the fragments of old conversations, not for the sake of analyzing them to determine where I messed up and should have said something different, but for how comfortable they felt. Somehow, without trying, the edges of fantasy and reality have blurred, and I'm not sure which one I prefer.

Before the broken pipes, the tacky bar, and finding the letters, I always had my sights set on the horizon, always hunting down the next goalpost.

I've done more in the last three years than most people do in their entire careers: traveling to new places, capturing stunning memories, padding my resume with photography awards, and seeking thrills that set my heart racing with adrenaline. I was always scared of the day when I couldn't find the next logical step. The day when I hit a wall, and I'm not sure where to go next.

It's such a stark contrast to the person I'm turning into, lingering in soft moments. I used to dread grocery shopping, only doing it out of necessity and distrusting anyone else to do it for me. But now, the weekly trips fill me with excitement. Walking down aisles bathed in fluorescent lighting and skillfully dodging the occasional toddler shouldn't be so enjoyable, yet somehow it is.

Once the plane lands, I text Drew, letting him know I'm safe. At first, it was an adjustment to know someone was waiting to hear where and how I was.

My independence often cuts like a double-edged sword; for every inch of freedom I get, I also know I'm less and less of a priority. Something as simple as a check-in text has flipped something in me, and it's a feeling I'm tempted to let consume me. The amount of times I have to remind myself this isn't a forever thing is slowly becoming dangerously high.

I don't bother waiting for a response because, from this point on, I need to be ready to work. We go through the motions of reaching the bus and then the stadium. During the bus ride, I touch base with Tessa about the content she plans to capture specifically for the team's social media during the game. It's sometimes hard to imagine how I was in her exact position just a few years ago. And how, in those years, I've grown so much.

There are times when she talks about her college boyfriends or the elaborate theme party she attended with her friends, and I wonder if I've ever sounded like that. Wonder if I ever allowed myself to be young. In college, I never felt like hooking up in a shared room with a twin-sized bed was a reputable rite of passage. I've always thought there were some steps worth skipping, some experiences worth passing up to get ahead.

I'm reminded of this again a few hours later as I wait to check in with Tessa before the final period. Her fingers fly across her phone screen, typing out a caption for her newest post. In the flurry of movement, my eyes catch on a sparkling glint. I do a double take, staring at the ring that is, in fact, on the ring finger of her left hand.

"Is that what I think it is?" I ask, pointing and stumbling over the words.

"Oh, I thought you would have seen the Instagram announcement," she says in that casual tone people use when they want you to be the one to ask more.

"I deleted my Instagram three years ago," I remind her. Acquaintances had a tendency to message me about things I wanted to forget, so it was a simple solution to delete everything from my phone and not look back.

"I always forget that."

"But oh my God. Congrats!" It's what I should have said first, but it took a minute for the right thing to break free from my tangled thoughts.

"Thank you!" she beams. "I honestly thought you didn't say something on purpose, but now I hear how petty that sounds. Like, I know you're intense, but you're not a bitch."

I wave her off, "No worries. I'm just surprised. I didn't know you were seeing anyone that seriously."

"I got back with Devin." Her words prompt me to sift through the catalog of her past relationships.

Devin.

He's the boy from her hometown in Arkansas. While I've only had one serious relationship in recent years, Tessa has had a few more, judging by all the stories she eagerly shares with anyone who asks. Still, it's always been more enjoyable than I care to admit, living vicariously through her experiences instead of pursuing my own.

She giggles, drawing my attention back in, "My mom and aunt were totally in on it and had a whole party set up for after the proposal. My roommate is giving me that 'Ring by Spring' crap, but I just love it." She says the last bit with an outstretched hand to examine the impressive diamond. I'm still processing. I can practically feel the little buffering symbol pop up in my brain as she adds, "He's got a job lined up next year in Lexington, and I told him I won't move my life for a man I'm not married to. A week later, he asked."

She lets out a dreamy sigh while I inwardly cringe.

I'm shitty at relationships. Being perpetually in casual hook-up situations has become such a facet of my personality that I know that if someone asked my friends about my favorite things, they would say meaningless sex, my vintage camera, and making vacation itineraries. Even with my limited expertise, what Tessa is talking about doesn't feel like love. Yet, maybe for her, it truly is love and not just an ultimatum, especially if the sparkle in her eyes is genuine.

I look at the ring again and am terrified because if this is love, then I'm happy to keep running.

"Oh, but that means I'm not coming back next year. It's a bit of a shame that I'll have to turn down the full-time offer to be your assistant. I mean, assuming you accept your new contract for next year, but we all know you will. Still, I'm excited to stay home and start renovating this cute little place we've picked out. I'm turning on HGTV the moment I get home for inspiration."

"You're not working when you get there? I can absolutely reach out to my contacts in the area if you'd like," I offer with an odd sense of desperation.

"No. I think I'm ready to make 'wife' my job. It's cheesy, but isn't that what love is supposed to be?" Her words are so sincere that I feel bad about the horror in my heart. I get the allure of a white picket fence and her idea of a perfect marriage. I had those daydreams sometimes when my little apartment felt so empty it could swallow me up, but realistically, that type of life wouldn't work for someone like me.

She continues in her customary bubbly excitement, "Oh, I wanted to ask. I've always loved Fool's Gambit. I was a little too young to go to their concerts when I was growing up, but I still have all their posters in a box in my parent's attic. Anyway, I heard that your dad works with them. Well, I guess he *worked* with them. I was wondering if I could get tickets to their reunion event. I would buy them myself, but they cost more than I have budgeted for my entire wedding. It would be the best gift ever if you could."

The request is innocent, but it throws me back in time, forcing me to relive the highlight reel of every time I've gotten a similar request. Tessa means well, but that doesn't change the sinking feeling that washes over me, the one that came when I realized someone was more interested in what I could get them than who I was.

"I'll see what I can do," I say instinctually, with little intention of following through. "Could you go to the catwalk and take overhead shots during the next period?" I ask before turning away, because we need more overhead shots. Absolutely not because the catwalk is her least favorite assignment.

The pictures from the first two periods are amazing and highlight everything I love about the game: power, force, agility—and all the other adjectives that could also be used in an energy drink commercial.

As the team battles it out in the third period, I can already tell that my last collection of images misses the mark. Chatting with Tessa got me more in my head than I'd like to admit. And because of that, my work turns to shit. I don't take any particular joy from being hard on myself, but it's how I got where I am in my career so fast.

I worked and delivered.

Every. Damn. Time.

With my thoughts so scattered, I don't see the puck coming my way until it's too late. Hockey glass is strong, meant to protect the crowd against rogue pucks, but the holes designed to fit a camera lens are also big enough for pucks to fly through.

I see it hurtling towards me with enough time to move my face from getting pulverized. My camera is wrenched from my grip, and I hear the sickening crunch of my lens shattering upon impact. The forceful blow shoves the heavy body of my camera into my chest, knocking the wind out of me as I tumble onto the sticky, hard stadium floor.

It's always a risk that this will happen, but it's a one-in-five-thousand kind of risk. I'm honestly more pissed about my lens than the bruises I'll no doubt find later. Bodies heal, cameras don't.

"Shit. Lady, are you ok?" A middle-aged man in a Detroit Comets jersey asks, his hand extended, waiting for me to take it. A small crowd circles around me, half with their phones out and the other half looking genuinely concerned for my well-being. I brush them off, getting to my feet on my own. I know this will be one of those viral sports fail moments, especially with how my face is splattered across the big screens.

Seeing my face stretched in shock is haunting. I feel naked in front of the thousands of fans in the crowd. My vision starts to swim, and my knees feel like toothpicks, not strong enough to hold my body.

A loud tapping on the glass catches my attention. I look up to find Johnathan pointing down the ice towards Price. Despite the distance, my eyes lock with Price's, and I feel my body grow steady again like he's lending me some of his strength.

I make sure to give him a wave that says I'm fine. I would hate it if this shook him up enough to cost us the game in the last half of the period. We do our best to keep our friendship professional at work; if we didn't, I'd be far more stressed about potential injuries.

I force air into my lungs before replying to the man in the crowd around me. "I'm fine. All in one piece."

It doesn't feel like anything is broken, so I don't see why I can't jump back in. This could have ended completely differently if the puck had hit me directly.

The hit does me some good; it is a literal knock back into reality that allows me to regain my focus for the remainder of the game.

Like he usually does after games, Price sits beside me in the staff section of the charter plane. Thankfully, it was an afternoon game, which means I'll be back home before midnight. After being intimately acquainted with the disgusting stadium floor, I can't wait to sit in the bath and soak my aching body.

"So what are you thinking about?" he asks.

"Did you know Tessa is engaged?" I blurt out.

"Well, that's not exactly what I was expecting. If you're focused on that, that puck must have hit you harder than I thought."

"I guess it just doesn't make a ton of sense to me, going back to someone when it failed the first time."

"Some shit like that doesn't have a ton of logic to it. Don't give yourself a headache trying to understand it. But I would have paid good fucking money to see your face when you found out," he laughs to himself, then he stops and examines me again. "Is that really all that's on your mind?"

"Honestly, it's a bit of everything: you and Mari, Tessa, my dad. I haven't thought about him in years. Now it's like he's living in my head, demanding the attention he never cared to give."

Price grips my hand, squeezing it once. "Not that much longer, and it will be over." His words give rise to an unexpected thought: *what if I don't want it to be over?* I don't have a chance to dwell on it as he keeps talking, "And I'm sorry about the godmother thing a few weeks ago. I shouldn't have said that. I just never would have thought you would want it."

"It's fine."

"Really? Lace, you looked like you were about to kill me during that conversation, and I kept digging myself into a hole while I was trying to joke about it. I'm not good at those serious conversations, and not knowing what to say has been eating me alive. You're a part of my family, with or without it."

"It's ok, really. I know you didn't mean it like that, just with everything going on, I've been on edge."

He nudges my foot and says, "So, will you finally tell me what you were going to say before I dropped the baby bomb?"

I consider what version of events to give him and where to start, but then I remember this is Price and opt for the truth, "I was going to ask to stay with you and Mari. My apartment essentially flooded before I came to meet you guys."

"Shit." His voice is louder than I expected, his eyes widening as he continues in a softer tone, "Is your stuff ok? Do you still need a place? Wait, it's been weeks. Where the hell are you living?"

"Probably will have to replace everything, but that's what IKEA is for. I appreciate it, but I've got it figured out. I've got a roommate who cooks and everything. And with the baby coming, I didn't want to ruin that big moment. You deserve to celebrate without my life getting in the way."

I nearly jump when Price grabs my face, squishing my cheeks together and forcing me to make eye contact with him, his deep brown eyes piercing into mine. I know we look nothing short of absolutely ridiculous. "Lace. I need you to listen to me right now. Your life doesn't get in the way of ours; it's a part of ours. I don't give a shit if you can keep a plant alive or not. This kid will call you their aunt, just like they will call Collin their uncle. You're family. Nothing's going to change that, no matter what. You've done so much for me over the years. So many times, I've felt like quitting, and you swooped in to save me from myself."

I've never thought that Price wanted to quit. There have been bad days, but this is a shock to me.

He lets me go, and I rub my cheeks. "That's different though. That's the simple stuff."

"The simple stuff. The hard stuff. That doesn't matter. There's no threshold for this shit. It's not like I'm gonna wake up one day and ask myself, 'Have I reached my limit on how many times I want to help Lacey?'"

"Maybe one day you should. It's not like I'm easy to keep in your life."

"Easy is overrated. We're in this for the long haul."

Long haul, huh? I can't help but feel my heart soar as he says those words.

At last, the plane lands, and I reach for my phone to text Drew, but a new notification catches my attention.

Craig

Hello, internet star. Are you ok?

Lacey

That fast, huh?

He sends a video link titled "Pretty Photographer Pucked Down".

Craig

At least they call you pretty. It does sound like hockey porn.

Can you come get your roommate? It's late, and he hasn't left me alone all day.

Lacey

I can be there in thirty as long as you never mention hockey porn again.

Craig

You drive a hard bargain, but he's annoying enough for me to agree.

19

Drew

Craig flops down on a navy L-shaped couch in front of me before continuing with a new version of the lecture he's been giving me all day, "But what if you get the couch but also a banner that says 'please fuck me, I'm absolutely obsessed with you' then right under it 'cause Craig needs some damn peace and quiet,' I think that would work well."

I sit down next to him and sink into the cushion. This is the third store we've visited, and nothing has been quite right. "Can you sit so your legs are on my lap?"

"Again?" I give him a look that says it will be less painful for him if he just goes with it. "Fine. At least you're giving me the princess treatment."

He moves to mimic how Lacey and I end up most nights, a necessary part of my evaluation process.

"So . . . are we about done? We didn't shut down the bar to spend the entire day furniture shopping. We still need to do inventory."

As I take a minute to mull it over, a sales associate walks by and glares at Craig until he swings his legs off me and plants his feet on the ground.

"I think I'm going with the one from the first place," I decide.

"You're fucking with me right now. We just spent the last few hours sitting on every sofa in the city just for you to pick the first one we tried?"

"I had to make sure it was the right one." I shrug.

I call the first store to charge the card I put on file with them and get the couch delivered before Lacey gets home tonight. But as Craig has kindly reminded me, we spent a better part of the day on this excursion, so the store is about to close.

"Any chance you have an after-hours rush fee?" I ask.

The worker sighs, giving me the auditory equivalent of an eye roll. "Sure, $1,000."

"I'll make it $1,500 if you haul the other one out of there too."

"Yes, sir," they say, and I have no doubt they'll be pocketing every dollar of the made-up fee. But as long as it gets to my apartment, I don't give a shit. I'd pay twice that just so the space can be as comfortable as possible.

Craig clears his throat, calling my attention to where he's started to do inventory behind the counter.

"Huh?" I murmur as I force myself back to reality.

I've been daydreaming like I used to, tapping my fingers on the bar top to the rhythm of some unwritten song. But this time, I wasn't thinking about running away to practice. I was thinking about Lacey.

Whenever she leaves for work, it feels like there's a taut string between us, as if a part of me is stretching to be wherever she is. Today, she's 720 miles away, and I feel every single inch of distance.

"We have to do something about that new poster of Wesley," Craig explains as he continues marking down numbers on his clipboard.

I raise my eyebrows in a *what are you talking about* way. The poster in question is a signed version of the promo merch for Wesley's upcoming tour with Avery, which he sent without me even asking. I'm not sure why the poster itself is such an issue besides the fact that Craig thinks he's a prick.

"God," Craig groans, letting me know he's about to repeat himself. "I've had a notable amount of customers kiss, lick, or try to steal it over the last week. Fuck this reunion."

"You're not appreciating the extra tips."

He completely glosses over my comment and says, "How much longer do I have to deal with this bullshit?"

"At least until January." I don't say that this will probably get much worse as the reunion approaches.

"When can we just make this bar into something relevant?"

"Are you calling me irrelevant?" I taunt.

"I say this with no love in my heart. If you start caring about your pop culture relevance beyond trying to make it non-existent, I'll hand in my resignation." He would never, but the number of times he'd threaten to would likely increase exponentially.

"Good. I can't have you going all star-struck on me."

Craig lowers his voice in a rare moment of complete seriousness. "I mean it. When you're ready, we can make this place yours."

"Unless I'm mistaken, my name is on all the documents for this place," I remind him, knowing fully well what he's trying to convey.

"Tell that to the pictures of your bandmates that haunt my dreams." He moves in to inspect a very photoshopped image. "Are Garrett's teeth really this white? If so . . ."

"I'm in here too." I tap the bar top.

Craig traces the foiled pictures and then points when he finds the one he's hunting for. "Finding your face is like the most challenging game of *Where's Waldo.*" A laugh slips from between his lips. "But I'm so happy we have this to commemorate your frosted tips. You know you were in a 2000s band, not a 90s one?"

"I lost a bet," I huff.

"You don't bet, yeah right. You won't even touch a fantasy football league."

"Have you ever wondered why I don't bet? I'm not exactly lucky."

Craig looks like he's going to take the bait for a moment but then pushes on with his original argument. "Stop changing the subject. My point is that you need to move on. This place looks like my sister's middle school locker, and there's barely any of you here."

"You keep saying that like it's a bad thing." But this time, his words strike a chord. I glance around, taking in the scene: the younger version of myself, the feel of the bar, Craig's words hanging in the air, and everything that's been unfolding. Things are shifting in my life for the better, and perhaps it's time to think about what else needs to change.

When I realized I wouldn't be able to work directly with music anymore, the bar seemed like the perfect solution. It could have been any theme or concept, but the homage was what I settled on.

I think, in some ways, that I just wanted to see how much joy the band could still bring to people, how they could come here and relive a bright spot from their lives—serving as a reminder that I was part of something that mattered.

"Lurking in the shadows of your past is not cute anymore."

"You think I'm cute? I didn't know you were that obsessed."

"Whatever. I'm asking Lacey to pick your sorry ass up so I can actually get some work done," he mutters, shifting his attention to his phone for a few minutes. "She'll be here in thirty minutes 'cause she's off work already."

"Wait, she tells you about her job?" An unjustified flash of irritation hits me. It's irrational, I know, because there's nothing between them, but I can't shake the feeling of frustration, knowing he has access to a part of her life that is completely off-limits to me.

"Just because you two are being obtuse, it doesn't mean I am going to be willfully in the dark. But I must say I'm happy she's keeping you busy. Your liver is also probably over the moon that it's not working overtime since you stopped spending every night here draining our reserves."

Now that he mentions it, I've woken up with fewer hangovers and have been up to see the sunrise more often than not. My energy levels are definitely better than they have been in a long time. The last time I felt like this was when I started the bar, back when I thought I had a future and a purpose.

Almost exactly thirty minutes later, Lacey strides through the door with her shoulders pulled back in her standard perfect posture, head held high. It's the image she shows the world, far from the slightly undone woman I get to see. A hum of possessiveness flows through me, washing away my earlier jealousy, thinking about how few people have gotten to see her the way I have, the version of her with fewer walls up.

"I'm here to collect the package," she says to Craig in a business-like tone, leaning against the bar and not acknowledging me in the slightest.

"Why is everyone in a mood today?" I grumble half-heartedly.

Craig goes along with Lacey and talks like I'm not even here. "Sorry, he hasn't been fed yet, so he's a little grumpy."

When she throws her head back and laughs, I couldn't care less about the shit that Craig's giving me. I would stand up on a stage and be heckled if it meant I could hear that full, uninhibited sound.

"Don't worry, I'll cover it," she says with a wink. Like shit, she will. I'm still genuinely concerned about how she fed herself before moving in with me.

"Let's go before you two tear the rest of my dignity to shreds," I say, looking at Lacey and catching the twinkle in her eye. It's like catching a star breaking through a patch of clouds on an otherwise overcast night—unexpected and utterly captivating.

After Craig basically kicks us out, we start heading towards her car, and I notice her pace slowing, her body slightly shifting from side to side. "You're limping. Why are you limping?"

"No, I'm not," she insists, straightening her posture and attempting to match my pace, as if that will camouflage her uneven gait.

I move in front of her to stop the painful progression. "Waddling then. Why are you waddling around like you're in pain?"

"I'm not waddling either."

I stare her down. "Zombie shuffling then. I can keep going if you want."

Long seconds pass before she huffs, "I just bumped into something at work."

"Was that so hard?" I ask, and for her, the admission probably felt like a root canal. "Ok, get on my back." I turn and crouch down without a second thought.

"I'm a grown-ass woman. I'm not getting on your back in the middle of the sidewalk."

"Even grown-ass women need someone to take care of them sometimes. Get on my back, or I'm carrying you over my shoulder."

And we both know I will, so instead of fighting it, she climbs onto my back. My hands grip her thighs, securing her in place. *God.* The way her body molds against mine is dangerous. My jeans tighten at the contact, and I'm thankful that she's not able to see the evidence of what this moment is doing to me.

As I return to a standing position, she mutters, "I'm starting to see why Craig was over your shit for the day."

"I heard that," I say, turning slightly to her. I hope she doesn't catch how my eyes flick to her lips as I note the minuscule distance between our mouths.

"You were supposed to. I'm literally right next to your ear."

When we reach her car, I try to insist on driving, but there's no way in hell I was ever going to get behind the wheel of her precious Subaru. Whenever she shifts in her seat, a wince twists her expression. I try to open my mouth to comment, but she glares as if anticipating what I am about to say.

I've started to note how much acknowledging weakness bothers her. She would rather almost have a cutting board fall on her head than ask for my help, so I've lowered all the dishes in the cabinets so she can reach them easily. Did she glare at me when she noticed that, too? Absolutely, but that's a fair price to pay to ensure she doesn't get concussed while making her breakfast every morning.

Dishes are one thing, but if she's actually injured, that's a different story. I'm willing to lose the small, insignificant battles, but I will win the war when it comes to making sure she's ok.

We park, and before she can move to do it herself, I grab her suitcase and bag, earning me, you guessed it, another glare. But this one is touched with just the slightest hint of relief.

Once inside, I settle on the new tan leather couch while I wait for her to get ready for the documentary she agreed to watch. For every four of her horror movies, I get to put on one episode.

Now that I'm paying attention, her stiff movements are apparent as she settles next to me on the couch. She looks down, blinking a few times in confusion before running her hand over the soft brown leather. The motion causes the neck of her t-shirt to slouch off her shoulder.

I take in a sharp breath, noticing the deep blue bruise on her skin.

"Lacey. You said you were fine," I say in a clipped tone, trying not to scare her off with the rage building in me, not directed at her but at however she got this way.

She tracks my gaze and adjusts her shirt so the bruise is covered again. "It's *nothing*."

Her movement causes her to shift, revealing another bruise as her shorts ride up.

"That doesn't look like nothing." I have to resist the urge to reach out and touch her, to search for any more places where her perfect skin is marred by angry, discolored splotches.

"Like I just said, I fell at work."

"No, you said you bumped into something. What happened, Lacey? I'm not just going to let you brush this off."

Her gaze flicks down. "What's with the new couch?"

"You said the other one was uncomfortable. Now would you answer my damn question?"

"Fine. My coworkers were playing around with . . ." she trails off, "a stapler, and it hit me pretty hard, so I fell over, ok? Really, it's not a big deal. Like it does hurt like hell, but I'm ok." Besides the obvious lie about the stapler, her answer feels true.

Still, I check one last time. "You swear no one did this to you on purpose?"

Her eyes hold mine for a tense heartbeat and then another before she speaks, "I swear no one hurt me on purpose. But if they had, I could have taken care of it myself."

"Can you just tell me when you're hurt? And I never said you couldn't take care of yourself, but I'm here to take care of you, too. You know that, right?" I'm close to begging now. I just want her to let me in, to give herself permission to lean on me and bend the rules a bit. I don't know much about her life outside this place, which, yes, we both agreed upon when we signed our names, but it's easy to see that she's not off with friends or fielding calls from family. So, if there's no one else, I need her to know that at least she has me.

"You don't have to take care of me."

"Maybe I don't have to, but what if I want to? What if it makes me feel better knowing I can help you?" She seems to grapple with my words, being pulled between not wanting to be an inconvenience and wanting to give in to my request. "If you don't do it for yourself, do it for me. It will make me feel better knowing you'll come to me if you need something." That last request does it.

"I can do that," she says almost to herself. Her shoulders release, and she sinks into the couch.

"Thank you." I reach out and squeeze her hand once before getting up to grab ice.

When I return, her legs stretch over my lap to keep the ice from falling off her chest and hip.

I really meant it. I want to take care of her.

I want to tuck her away from the world and roll her in a protective layer of bubble wrap so it could never happen again. Of course, she would hate me for it. I've been learning that she treats adrenaline like an essential vitamin from the horror movies to whatever she's off doing. I guess it's no wonder she has shocked me back into motion.

The narrator hasn't even finished setting the scene before Lacey opens her mouth again. "So, what's with the couch?"

"What do you mean? I told you I got a new one because the last one wasn't comfortable."

"You can't just buy me a couch."

"Well, technically, I bought *myself* a couch. But also, you were uncomfortable," I repeat for what feels like the hundredth time. Shouldn't that be reason enough? We've spent as much time complaining about the damn thing as we have spent sitting on it.

"It's kind of annoying how good of a person you are sometimes." The way she says it makes me believe that it could be true.

"I am the best, aren't I?"

"You know what a good person would do? Put on a horror movie for their healing roommate," she says, fluttering her lashes with a smirk.

"Fine," I relent, handing over the remote, and immediately, I'm rewarded with a grin that only cements the feeling that I've been absolutely duped. The documentary that had promised cute Capuchin monkeys and primate politics turns into a scene slowly moving in on an eerie, desolate church.

The thing is, I'd do anything to see her genuinely happy, to let her enjoy the things she would otherwise feel insecure about. So I guess in the end, I'm the real winner, even if she doesn't realize it.

20

Drew

I showed up, and all I got was a shitty headache. It sounds like a cheesy t-shirt, but it's also how every band meeting has gone since our first chart-topping release. But as Hartly reminded me with an email signed, *Remember I'm not above kidnapping you.* I'm required to be here.

"The setlist is all out of order. We should do it chronologically," Garrett says, rising to his feet and staring down Wes. It's easy to picture him in his new life as an entertainment lawyer. Though there's no suit in sight, his navy pants are meticulously ironed and obviously tailored, and his browline glasses make him appear more professional than artistic.

This argument is nothing new. He and Wesley have always battled for the limelight.

Garrett because he's always believed he's better and deserves the credit, and Wes because out of all of us, he's the unmatched star. Wes, before his solo career, was insufferable, and now, with his fan base growing even larger, he's become even more unbearable. Yet, when there's no one watching, they somehow put their egos aside to be friends.

When I walked into the bland conference room two hours ago, no one tried to conceal how their glances bounced between Wes and me. I wasn't lying when I told Jared I wasn't holding anything against Wesley. I don't trust him, but I also have no desire to make a bad situation worse.

Wes reclines further in his seat, raking his hand through overgrown brown hair as he counters Garrett's idea, "The fans aren't coming for a history lesson. They're coming for the best. So, we avoid the deep cuts no one actually cares about and give them the top ten."

"We could pull out an unreleased track?" Jared cuts in, completing the next step in the tedious game we always play.

He's the peacemaker in Wes and Garrett's hot and cold routine. Many years of taming their tempers must come in handy now with his kids.

Then, they turn to me to play my role, finding the quick fix. Martin once told me that the drummer is the backbone of the band. I just have to convince them that Fool's Gambit doesn't have a broken back.

"Yeah, it would be great to do something new, but it's not worth performing something we haven't played live yet since we only have a few live rehearsals. We could release a new track for fans on streaming services." I have no doubt that's already part of some plan. It doesn't take a marketing genius to know we can capitalize on tracks we already have. "I say we bring in our landmark songs. 'Funny Thing,' 'Golden Hour,' 'Half a Memory,' and 'Ronnie.'" I finish and brace myself for their reaction. I never used to care, but for a reason I can't pinpoint, I need to get this right.

Martin finally chips in from where he's set up on the video call. Why the rest of us have to be in the same room while he's on some European tour is beyond me. 'Team bonding' bullshit, probably. "I like it. Your first Grammy, something from the debut album, and whatever else takes them down memory lane."

I tense as I make eye contact with Garrett, whose knowing smirk always puts me on edge. Garrett's gaze discretely flicks to my hands, which I hadn't noticed were balled into white-knuckled fists. *Nosy motherfucker.*

"Now that we have everyone in one room. I have some personal news I'd like to share with all of you." Martin continues, "My daughter will be joining us for the reunion. If you weren't already planning on being on your best behavior, please do so."

We've never met Martin's family. It's one of those subjects we've always left untouched. He started working with us after his divorce and a lost custody battle. You'd see the updates about it if you walked through any grocery store checkout line. Headlines like: "Rock Legend Upgrades" and "Return to the Spotlight."

There's one in particular I remember, years before I met him. I was out with my mother, and she picked up one of the glossy-covered magazines and tutted her usual sound of disapproval. On one side was a picture of Martin and a Victoria's Secret model, and on the other was a woman in a robe pulling a small girl with a blurred-out face behind her.

My mother's words adhered to my brain.

"Poor girl."

Back then, I used to think she meant the mother, comparing the disheveled woman in a robe to the supermodel on Martin's arm, but now I'm certain she was talking about the little girl. It's one thing to willingly share your life, but being forced into the spotlight is entirely different.

Yet, even with all that, when we met him, we grew to feel we were like his family, never once giving a second thought to the one he already had.

We keep talking, and with the reunion only three months away, this is the first time we've had a chance to go over logistics. Well, it's also my first time attending one of these meetings, so I'm not sure what's already been discussed.

But what I focus on the most is the fact that I still can't play.

If this had been a rehearsal, I would have been utterly fucked.

In addition to the setlist, we all agree that we'll go back to our roots for this performance, just playing instruments without dancing. Everyone argued about rehearsal times and days for future meetings, further emphasizing our differences because no matter their decision, I'll always be available while everyone juggles their busy, fulfilling lives.

Distance really does make the heart grow fonder because, damn, I forgot how much the technical side of this shit sucks.

I think momentarily about texting Lacey, but I don't want to disrupt her plans. It's the first time since she moved in that she's gone out with friends. I won't drag her back when she's finally doing something for herself.

Once the meeting is over, I head outside to get the hell away from this place. It went fine, but my body doesn't quite feel like mine, as if I spent the last part of the meeting on autopilot. I turn the corner of the building just as Garrett slinks out from the dark corner where he's smoking.

I try to move past him, but then he opens his damn mouth. "Eve said you turned down another trip."

He's the only one to call Evelyn by that nickname, and it never fails to make me roll my eyes. Garrett releases a snake of smoke as his lips curl with satisfaction.

"Why are you talking to my sister about that shit?" I bite out then try to move past him again.

He says one of the few things that could stop me in my tracks, "She's worried."

"Why the hell isn't she talking to me about that if she's so worried?" I grit my teeth and regret involving Garrett in any part of my life. He's deep enough into everyone's shit to run a gossip column. Always has been. Now, it's just under a layer of swaggering disinterest.

"Because you're pushing everyone away, and she knows I've never cared about tip-toeing around your delicate feelings. I thought that little bar thing would be helping you, but it seems you're still focused on licking your wounds." I guess he's who she ran to when I wouldn't tell her what she needed to know. My skin crawls as I consider how much he knows. It can't be much because Ev is pretty much in the dark, but if there was anyone who'd put two and two together, it's Garrett. "You need to hear it from someone, and I guess I'm the designated villain for the occasion."

"I have Craig and Ev." *And Lacey.*

He laughs to himself, cracking a Cheshire grin. "Craig is practically your fucking babysitter. You literally pay the guy. And your sister's fucking pissed at you. She'll never admit it because she thinks she owes you for getting your parents off her back. She doesn't see that you're the reason that they're always on her shit. I hope you pray she never figures it out."

Garrett has always acted like he was also her brother, which I usually preferred because it means that he doesn't view her as some woman to sleep with and then dump using a message scribbled on a hotel notepad.

"Like you know anything. Maybe you should stop messing with my business and crawl back to your fancy office in New York," I practically spit the words at him.

"I'll stop when *you* quit acting like a fucking martyr. You sit around in that glorified time capsule of a bar, wallowing and playing the victim. You know what?" His eyes narrow, his grin slightly faltering. "We all lost shit. We were all part of the band.

Wesley lost Avery. Jared lost his shot at a normal life. You're no different."

"What did you lose then? You got the fame, then the fancy job. People get to call you a genius and a star. What did you lose?"

He used to be able to pick up any instrument and play flawlessly within an hour. He took all that ability and freedom and tossed it away. Maybe he did lose something, but I doubt it feels like he's been cut open and bleeding out for the last decade.

"I lost my family. You fuckers were my family," he says more to himself than me. The words are loaded with more emotion than he likely means to convey. Immediately, his bravado slams back into place as he says, "I won't give you a sob story over it because I grew up. I became better. We were in a boy band, but we're not boys anymore. Get that through your thick head and don't make us look like idiots." He taps his temple for emphasis.

"I won't make us look stupid if you and Wesley promise not to fight for attention on stage."

"That's rich. We're not the ones who almost did a swan dive off the stage the last time we performed. If no one else is going to say it, then I will. Take care of your shit, and I'll take care of mine." He stamps out his cigarette and leaves me with that parting blow.

I gaze down at my hands, fists clenched once again. It's not like I'm not trying to take care of my shit.

For the longest time, I believed music was a vital organ, something I needed to live. But one morning, I woke up and realized that I could keep breathing without it. In some ways, learning I could keep going without being a musician hurt more than the hollow feeling in my chest.

Before, when I thought about the future, I thought I'd have kids one day. I'd sit on the floor with them as they learned they could use pots and pans to make their own drum set. That dream now feels permanently out of reach.

My interaction with Garrett has left me numb. I've almost forgotten the feeling after weeks brimming with happy moments. But the hollowness is more consuming than ever now that I've had a taste of simple contentment. It was probably inevitable, this crash after riding the high.

I head back to Half a Memory. Once I arrive, I have to maneuver through the bustling crowd of customers to pour myself a drink. I should probably help Craig and Heather, but I'm not cut out for dealing with anyone tonight. I'm not sure if I'm even cut out to deal with myself.

I drink until I can't taste the burn of the liquor anymore, left only with swirling thoughts and fleeting images of Craig's concerned looks.

I barely notice when a redhead appears and starts saying things that don't matter.

"You're in that band, right? The drummer?" she croons, sliding into place next to me.

Yeah, the drummer.

I'm not sure if I say it out loud, but she keeps talking. I see her hand fall over mine, but I don't feel it, or anything at all.

It doesn't matter.

I know who I wish was next to me, but she's not here.

That's what matters.

She's not her. She's not her. She's not her.

21

Lacey

I'm not sure when game night turned into going to a club, but here we are with the lights and music assaulting my senses. Price promised *Settlers of Catan* and friendly rivalries over fictionalized barter systems.

I hesitantly agreed at first, but once Drew told me he also had plans for the night, I didn't have a reason to sit at home like a sad puppy waiting for him to return.

No. Not home.

As the email in my inbox reminds me, it's the place where I'm currently staying temporarily. The apartment management finally got back to me about the timeline, and a part of me felt a twinge of sadness. It's been over a month, and with everything going on, I'd completely forgotten they hadn't given me a clear estimate. But as soon as I opened that email, a real countdown began, reminding me that it was always going to end.

Two weeks.

Two weeks, and then this is over. I'll have to pop the happy little bubble we've created. We started this arrangement because he was someone I didn't care about knowing. Now, he's the thing I'm most scared to lose. I can't picture how I'll tell him. If he was anyone else I'd just . . . leave.

My phone chimes three times in quick succession, giving me an excuse to focus on something other than the guys seeing how many ice cubes they can sneak into Aaron's hoodie—the current count is at seven. I have no doubt they'll get to double digits, especially with Aaron's current zombie-like fixation on the brunette in a silver dress, who keeps doing suggestive laps around the table.

Craig

SOS

Drew is getting very close to the not-fun side of drunk. I can't do anything for him while I'm on shift with so many people here.

Like seriously SOS

For an instant, the world is drowned out by the rapid beating of my heart. I don't panic. I don't have time to.

"I've got to go!" I yell to Price while gesturing toward the door. He nods and gives me a thumbs-up. I'm certain he won't last long after I leave.

Thank God I hadn't planned on drinking and drove myself, so I don't have to wait on an Uber.

I keep promising myself not to freak out. If Drew needed it, Craig would call someone else. I'm likely only the second line of defense—I'm only his roommate. Craig wouldn't call *me* for an actual emergency, right?

I park farther from the bar than I'd prefer, and I'm all but sprinting down the sidewalk.

When I push through the doors, I see the first problem. If there were only a regular amount of patrons in the place, a drunk Drew wouldn't be an issue for Craig. But the place is more packed than I've ever seen. All I can see is a sea of bodies jostling each other to get their next drink or swaying offbeat to the pop mix flowing through the speakers.

Craig gives me a nod of acknowledgement, but doesn't have the opportunity to do much else with all the impatient customers vying for his attention.

I weave through bodies, dodging elbows to make it to Drew's usual spot at the end of the bar. I breathe a sigh of relief when I see a mess of brown hair and tap on his shoulder.

"Yeah?" he says, turning to me with a flirtatious smile. But the man isn't Drew. Fuck.

"Sorry," I call over the music and scramble away. The panic threatens to rise like a wave to choke the air from my lungs.

No, not yet. Not until he's safe.

Somehow, Drew's voice cuts through the clattering din of the bar. "And her eyes. They're like these little storm clouds, but when I make her laugh, they clear, and that's all I want to do. Make her laugh and make her food. That's how she makes me feel, you know?"

I'm less concerned with processing his words than I am relieved to have located him. A pressure lifts from my chest as I follow his voice like a lighthouse in a storm.

He's tucked into one of the leather-upholstered booths, his head tilted back and eyes closed like he's trying to recall some dream. A red-headed woman sits across from him, twirling a cocktail straw in her sapphire drink.

"Yeah," the woman replies, sounding resigned as if she's been listening to him ramble for a while.

Jealousy threatens to mix with my already mounting anxiety before I take stock of the situation. The distance between them. The look of disinterest on her face. The fact that he looks closer to falling asleep in the booth than sleeping with anyone.

"Hey. It's time to go home." I tap his shoulder, and his head flops towards me.

"I'm not gonna go home with you," he slurs, his eyes not focusing on my face as he tries to wave me away. "No sex. Not for me."

"Drew. It's me." I say, and the moment he recognizes me, it's like I've lit up his entire world. I'm still trying to forget what he was telling the woman next to him, trying to keep my heart from melting over the drunk mess he's become.

"He belongs to you?" The woman looks drained. She probably sat down intending to go home with Drew before realizing he was past the point of no return.

"I belong to her," he answers before I can. I swear, his sloppy smile is so big that it might break his face. He turns to me. "Can we go home?"

I guess he does belong to me, and maybe I belong to him a little bit too. He's transitioned from being some random guy with a convenient room to someone I need to take care of.

Someone I *want* to take care of.

"Yeah, big guy. Let's go home. Should I be scared about you puking in my car?"

"Nope. No puke." Despite his confident tone, I find myself hesitant to believe him. Especially when I have to catch most of his weight as he stands and drapes an arm over my shoulders.

As we hobble to the door, Craig rushes out from behind the bar as the wave of customers subsides and says in a rush, "Thank you. He had a pretty bad day. I'm just happy he's not going to be alone tonight."

I glance between Craig and Drew, noting Craig's troubled expression before he walks away to resume his work. I shift my attention to Drew, wondering what could have made his day so bad.

What wounds can't I heal because I don't know the whole story?

We half stumble, half walk the distance to my parking spot, moving with all the grace of competitors in a three-legged race. I might be strong, but he's built like a mountain.

I take a moment to catch my breath before opening the door and lightly placing my hand on his head so he doesn't hit it as

I tuck him into my car. I run to the other side and climb in, watching him fumble with the seatbelt. I take over the effort, reaching over and fastening it for him.

Fuck.

I feel so lost, and I just wish I could fix this. If only I had let him in, maybe he wouldn't be hurting. Maybe I could've been there with him before it was too late. Because all I can do now is make sure he doesn't end up covered in his own puke.

Tears prickle at the back of my eyes, but I can't cry—not now. This is everything I've been trying to avoid, and it's caught up to me in a way I can't ignore. Instead of pushing it away like I would have done months ago, I want to dive headfirst into finding a solution.

Taking a deep breath, I prepare myself and start the car, reminding myself that he will be ok. He hums along to the radio throughout the whole ride, and when he steps out of the car, he is a little more steady, but he still clings tightly to my hand, refusing to let go until we're safely inside.

Once inside, I guide him to the couch and help him out of his shoes. Checking for his phone and wallet, I realize he's probably left them at the bar, so I text Craig, also letting him know we've arrived safe and sound.

Drew remains silent as I walk him to his room and place a glass of water and painkillers on his nightstand. I make sure to roll him onto his side and that there's a trash can next beside the bed for good measure. When I start to walk to the door,

I pause. Sure, my room is just across the hall, but I can't leave him like this. So, I stay.

Still in my clothes from my night out, I lay on the other side of the bed, staring up at the ceiling. I doubt I'll get any sleep.

"I have a secret," he slurs, his voice jolting me out of my thoughts. I was so certain he was sleeping.

"Please don't tell me. You'll regret it," I softly plead. Even if he forgets it, I won't.

"I'll wait for you." Wait for me to what? He doesn't say, but I have a creeping suspicion I know. "I wish this was forever."

Forever. Forever isn't something I'm capable of. It's a load too heavy to even conceptualize. He's given my heart a place to land, but I don't think I can offer him the same thing, especially after I failed him tonight.

"You're making breakfast," Drew whispers in awe from behind me. When I turn to look at him, he looks like shit, or at least as shitty as someone with his face and body can look. "Real breakfast."

"I've learned something about breakfast. It doesn't matter if it's toast or bacon. Even when I burn it, it still tastes good." Maybe not good, but a burnt breakfast is better than a burnt dinner or lunch. "How about you take a shower? I'll have everything ready by the time you're done."

"I'm just going to stay here for a while," he says, settling into a seat with none of his usual grace.

He leans his head down on the countertop and watches me as I cook up a greasy mess. An almost-chuckle rumbles through him, not entirely passing his lips when I jump back from crackling grease.

In the end, the sandwich is stacked so high with eggs, bacon, cheese, and hash browns that it's far from structurally sound, but it still doesn't feel like enough.

"God," he moans as he takes the first bite of the masterfully crafted breakfast sandwich.

"Should I be jealous of this sandwich?"

"I didn't think you were capable of jealousy."

"After last night, I don't think I have anything to be jealous about." The words slip from me without a second thought. *Shit.* I was planning on just letting us both forget about the drunken confessions.

"What do you mean?"

"Nothing. It's fine. You just said something funny last night," I say, turning away slightly to conceal my blush.

It's not only his words clinging to me, but I woke up with his arm draped around me, and it was almost too tempting to nuzzle into him. Instead, I made sure to leave before he woke up.

"I don't remember shit," he says more to himself than me, and I can tell that he's annoyed. I guess that's good in some ways. At least he won't remember me falling asleep next to him last night, and we won't have to navigate an awkward conversation.

After he devours the, admittedly singed, sandwich and looks the slightest bit better. When he's done, he finally decides to take a shower.

I take my time cleaning up the kitchen, clinking utensils providing a comforting rhythm as I try to steady my thoughts. One of them being Drew's missing wallet and phone. He's going to assume someone stole them and start freaking out, his amnesia from last night annoying him even more.

Quickly, I dry my hands on a nearby towel and head towards his room to reassure him that they're safe with Craig until—

I don't know what I expected to find through the ajar door, but the scene before me carves a hole in my heart. He's pulled off his shirt and pants, leaving him in his boxers as he sits on the shower floor, water lightly falling onto his face.

I want to shake him and ask what's wrong.

I want to tell him I was wrong, and I want to know everything. Every damn thing.

I want to glue him back together, but I don't know how. So, my arms will have to do instead.

All I know is that one moment, I'm standing here, and in the next, I'm rushing to him. The water falls over me as I step into the shower and kneel behind him, fully clothed.

The moment hangs open, vulnerable and raw like a wound. I can feel the weight of unspoken emotions hanging in the air as I pretend not to notice when he cries, letting any tears get lost in the rest of the water.

I hold him like he held me on the street all those weeks ago. My embrace tightens as I wonder if anyone has held him like this before or if his pain is as solitary as it is silent.

Slowly, his hands find mine, and I hope he knows I'm here—that he isn't alone, not anymore, because if this is his storm to weather, then it is mine, too.

"Could you wash my hair?" he asks, his voice thin and choked, catching my attention.

"Of course. Anything you need."

I reach for the bottles on the rack in the corner of his shower, but he stops me, "Can you use yours?"

"Why?"

He hesitates before he says, "I just don't want to be myself right now. I'd rather be a little like you."

"Ok." My chest clenches, and I don't ask any more questions.

I don't waste time drying off, letting the trail of water I make from his room to mine become a problem for later. The only thing that doesn't have me running to get back to him is the fear of slipping on the slick floor.

"I've got them," I say as I return to my spot, letting the floor's tiled surface bite into my knees as I sink to the ground beside him.

I run my fingers through his hair, and his head follows my touch. I try to direct the suds of the shampoo away from his eyes. His curls feel like silk as I massage in the conditioner, and he moans softly like my touch is the only meaningful thing in this world.

Once I'm finished, he leans into me, closing his eyes, and I weave my arms around his middle, silently promising him that I'll stay as long as he needs.

Here, for a single moment, I can admit we've never really been strangers. From that second night of knowing each other and admitting that we craved the freedom of anonymity, we bore our souls to each other, showing some naked, vulnerable thing. It was a shared weight that forced us closer than we intended.

"It's just too much sometimes," he says.

"I know," I reassure him, pulling him tighter against me.

I don't know *what* exactly is too much or what did this to him, but I'm well-acquainted with the feeling of being overwhelmed by my own existence. It's why I've trimmed back my life to a formulaic, plain thing. I've thought all this time that only having a few things to care about meant I would have less to lose, but I guess that also means that there's less to love.

We sit on the floor in the steam-filled shower for what feels like forever—a type of forever I can handle, made of moments that stretch and last. Or it could simply be my way of talking myself into staying because it's less painful than letting go.

I know I can't leave because I'm scared of what will happen if I do—not just to him but to me, too. I'm holding him now, but he's done the same for me. The difference is that he's there every single time, and I'm only there when he's hanging by a thread.

22

Drew

My pillow smells like sugar cookies. It has me turning to hold the ghost of someone who's no longer there as disappointment washes over me when my arms find the empty space.

Reality creeps in, punctuated by the splitting headache of a well-deserved hangover.

With some effort, I wrangle my body out of the sheets and through my door to the main room. The space is cast in a golden glow as the sun dips toward the horizon.

"Why didn't you call me?" Lacey's words greet me like a slap from where she's sitting on the couch. She's staring down at the coffee cup in her hands, her eyes glossed over with exhaustion. There's no steam coming from it, but it's still full. I have a feeling she's been stuck like a statue for a while.

Staring.

Thinking.

I did that. Disrupted the peace she asked to create here with me.

"You said you were busy last night and wouldn't be back until late. I didn't want to bother you," I say, taking a spot on the far end of the couch to give her distance.

There's so much pain, so much hurt held in the lines of her face. "Drew. When I said that, I meant that you shouldn't call me about what to do for dinner or if I was going to meet you at the bar last night. It doesn't mean that I don't want you to call if there's an emergency."

"Last night wasn't an emergency."

"Do you remember last night?" she snaps at me.

"No. I—"

She slams down the coffee mug, sending the contents sloshing over the edge and onto the table. "Then you don't get to decide. You might not remember, but *I* do. I remember carrying you to my car and putting you to bed, not knowing how it got that bad. And this morning. God. I've never seen someone still drunk the next morning. In the shower . . ." her voice trails off, and her lips form into a tight line with the words she's holding back.

"I could have handled it." I don't want her to worry about me. This space we've created is supposed to be uncomplicated. It's supposed to be a happy escape that we can slip into at the end of the day, no questions asked.

"Obviously, you're wrong. I should have been there the moment it got that bad. I could have helped."

"You don't owe me that. You didn't sign on to be my nanny."

Garrett's comment about Craig only sticking around to take care of me is still cutting deep. I don't want her here out of obligation now that I've slipped and let her see what's beneath the surface.

I already know I've said the wrong thing before she speaks. "I don't owe you that? You're acting like you didn't offer a complete stranger a room in your home for free. You're acting like we didn't agree to do this together. I thought we agreed that the things we carry with us are too heavy. What happened to us being in the eye of the storm together? Or was it just some bullshit to help me feel better about opening up to you? Am I just a charity case to you?" Her voice quivers at the end, her gorgeous eyes starting to go liquid with unshed tears.

"Never. I have never thought of you like that. It just would have been selfish to ask you to come get me."

"Then let me be selfish and take care of you. It hurt seeing you like that. If you actually care about me and want to protect me, then don't do that to yourself." Tears start to roll down her face. I'm doing this to her, and I can't figure out how to stop it. "I'm scared to leave for work tomorrow. I'm scared you won't pick up the phone and call if you need me. I feel so fucking powerless."

I crawl to her from my corner on the couch, burying my face in her hair. "I promise I'll call. I promise I'll take care of myself while you're gone, and I won't even have a reason to call." Her shoulders shake, and I hold her through the tremors, rubbing slow circles on her back.

This isn't how it's supposed to be. We're not supposed to hurt like this. Not here.

"There's something else," she says with a chilling somberness. She pulls back from me, her eyes red-rimmed and puffy, but her features set with determination.

"There always is," I say, bracing myself for the blow.

"I got an email from my apartment complex," she says, pausing as I wipe away the tears I never meant to cause. "They said it'll be ready in four weeks."

In the back of my mind, I always knew our time together had an expiration date. But four weeks? It's not enough. She could have said a hundred years, and it still wouldn't feel like enough.

She's leaving. Something that felt impossible, like something we joked about, but now it's actually happening. It's like she's already slipping away, and in four short weeks, she'll be gone.

Because who am I to ask her to stay? I've hurt her so much already without even intending to, and with the time ticking down, I just hope I can make it up to her before she vanishes from my life.

23

Lacey

I've had a sour taste in my mouth for days now. And I can't tell if it's from the fear of leaving Drew alone after what happened or the lie.

They said *two weeks.*

It should be a relief, shouldn't it? With them ahead of schedule, I could return sooner. But instead of telling the truth, I lied to him. Why?

I had every intention of coming clean that day, expressing my gratitude to Drew, and preparing both of us to go back to our normal lives. But when I looked into his eyes, my plan fell apart. I keep trying to convince myself it's harmless. But is it?

Lying to him like this feels like uncharted territory for us because although we generally skirt around the truth in the apartment, I haven't outright lied to him like this before.

The stress of the situation has thrown me back into old coping mechanisms and taking full advantage of my access to the practice rink.

Feeling my skates cut into the ice gives me a temporary sense of control. There's no music, just my breath and the whooshing of cold air around me as I sprint on the ice.

At the end of the day, Drew might see all I am and accept my odd schedule and perpetual need for control, but even then, he could still find a new reason to leave, mirroring the familiar cycle like those who came before him.

So, I push away any hope that we could make it work, or at least I try to, cataloging every reason why it might not. I've learned the hard way that when you let something truly exist, it will always prove to you how fragile and breakable it is.

And it always breaks. Always.

A thud from the opposite end of the ice pulls me out of my head. "Fuck. Are you trying to kill me?" Craig groans from a prone position. He's fallen. Again. For about the hundredth time. I sigh and turn to make my way over to him. Thankfully, we're the only ones here, or he'd be taking innocent skaters out like dominoes.

At this point, his jeans are covered in a perpetual thin layer of frost, and his head is adorned with a purple glittery pom pom hat that he 'found.' Beyond knowing that skating alone would just wear me down more than reduce stress, I also brought the bald wonder to get more information about what happened the other night.

But before I could even ask, he just said it wasn't his story to tell and left it at that. It's nice to know he has Drew's back, but worry has been incessantly gnawing at me.

What else haven't I seen in all the moments I've been away?

I asked him that, too, and he reassured me that there's nothing else he's aware of—subtly suggesting that I should talk to Drew if I want to know more.

So, maybe I'm getting some type of petty joy seeing Craig fall.

"Sue me for thinking you'd be good at this," I say as I stop in front of him.

"I'm from Florida," he pouts, playing into his pitiful state.

"I learned in Arizona. Come up with a better excuse."

"I stayed in the South for a reason, and it wasn't for the sweet tea." He lifts his arms like a baby instead of getting to his feet by himself.

"You two are made for each other," I say, crouching, helping him up, and almost crashing down with him in the process.

"Why? Because we're devastatingly handsome and make your life inconvenient?"

"I'd phrase it differently, but for the most part, yes."

I watch as he clutches the edge of the practice rink, his fingers tracing the cold metal. "I'm going to the bathroom, by which I mean I need a break from this sadistic pastime that you're forcing me to take part in. Not to say I don't appreciate a look into your job, but I also have a feeling there's someone else you wish was here," he says, his voice a pointed mix of sarcasm and sincerity, before finally clambering through the door.

I stay silent, not bothering with a response because he's right. I came here to . . . I don't know at this point. My thoughts always drift back to him, thinking about how graceful Drew is when he dances and the way his arms felt on my skin, just us wrapped in a blanket of music and joy. I bet he'd move just as seamlessly on the ice.

One of the external doors loudly slides open, and I quickly turn.

Price's voice echoes through the rink. "Thinking about Martin?"

"Not this time. What's going on?"

"I asked where you might be, and they said you were blowing off steam here. Invite me next time." I guess my secret skate sessions aren't so secret after all if I'm this predictable. I skate up to meet him, and Price's eyes narrow as he scrutinizes me. "Holy shit. It's a guy, isn't it."

"Nope. I'm not telling you anything. Not since the Roy Taylor incident of 2021."

"I know I laughed, but you literally fell off him and onto the floor. I promise if you tell me, I'll be better this time."

"I'm not talking about that one." I guess, in hindsight, there were multiple Roy Taylor incidents. "The one where you Instagram stalked the guy and liked his photos, forgetting that you are, in fact, a professional athlete." Roy wasn't the first or last guy to ask to meet players, but after he saw Price 'accidentally' like all of his pictures going back four years, he wouldn't shut up about anything else. Needless to say, Roy lasted about three weeks in total.

"Oh yeah. I still follow him on everything. He comments on all of my posts, really sweet too. He's definitely coming for your place as Friend of The Year."

"I'll skate him for it," I say, sending us both into a fit of laughter. The one time I gave into Roy's nagging, we went on the ice at his insistence, and he spent more time on his ass than on his feet, not quite as bad as Craig, but close.

"Oh, please say more about the Roy Taylor incident," Craig says from behind me. What marvelous timing.

Price's attention doesn't waver from me, "Roommate?"

"Not Roommate," Craig shakes his head.

"Hi, Not Roommate, I'm the best friend, Price."

"Prove it," Craig says, accompanied by a quizzical glare.

To my dismay, Price pulls down his bottom lip, showing the stupid yet permanent proof of our friendship. It's our worst inside joke. He still has the brilliantly thought-out words *"you'r mom"* etched into his mouth.

Don't get me started on how the artist and Price didn't catch the obvious grammatical error. He blames the concussion he had just gotten. Twenty-one-year-old Price thought the joke was worth it, but six years later, the comedy has faded far more than the ink.

I sigh. "I'm guessing you want to see mine?"

I turn to find Craig fluttering his lashes, "If you would be so kind."

I pull my bottom lip down with my middle finger to reveal a jagged, dull-looking smiley face.

"Happy?" I say with my lip still pulled down.

"Oh. I'm fucking giddy. But don't you worry, I won't tell 'The Roommate,'" he says, his voice stretching to emphasize the last words, "unless you ask." It was the wrong thing for Craig to say.

Price immediately perks up, beckoning Craig, the traitor, off the ice, "So, The Roommate. Tell me more."

"Have you ever seen two people so in denial that it makes you pull out all of your hair," Craig does a grand reveal of taking off his hat, ready to tell Price a fabricated sob story about how Drew and I are the culprits behind his hair loss.

Instead of indulging him, I propel myself as fast as I can to the other side of the rink, the cold air whipping against my face as I skate lap after lap until I'm sure I'll be sore for the next eternity.

Finally, as I slow down to catch my breath, I spot Price waving his arms to flag me down, signaling the end of their gossip session.

"We're going to be late for that press thing," he says as I maneuver off the ice.

"Tessa is taking care of it for me," I tell him as I sit and undo my laces, attempting to make it sound as insignificant as possible.

"Excuse me, Tessa? You can't be serious." I look up, and Price has the expression of someone who's just been dosed with ice water.

"Tessa's good at her job. That's why we brought her back for a second year." She is. That's also why I'll have no problem being a reference if she changes her mind and chooses to work again.

"She's good, but *she's not you,* which I thought you'd be very aware of," Price says, not buying my attempt to fly under the radar.

"It's not a game or anything. She's done plenty of these with me, so there's nothing to worry about. I have somewhere more important I need to be." I feel his eyes on me as I pack my bag and tug on my boots. "What?"

"I'm just wondering what act of God it took for you to finally take a step back from work."

"Oh, he's definitely not a god," Craig mutters.

I don't see Drew immediately when I come in or after I go to my room and change out of what I wore to skate in. But a door hangs open in the far corner. I've never tried and looked through the rest of the place. I just assumed the other rooms were for guests or storage.

But I know that's where he must be. His keys are on the hook, and his favorite sneakers are set by the door.

I set my bag down before moving to investigate. When I push through, it reveals a room full of instruments, soundproofing foam lining the walls, and Drew hunched over a drum kit, arms hovering like he's about to play. His form trembles from the exertion of being stuck in the position. How long has he been like this?

He looks up with a look full of strain. When I meet his eyes, it feels like all the oxygen has been sucked from the room.

I choke out, "I'm sorry, am I interrupting?"

"No, I was just getting started. It's fine." His voice is thin and soft. I'm not sure who he's trying to convince with his words.

"Can I listen?"

He takes a moment before responding. "You don't have to. I thought you weren't going to be back until later." That would be true if I hadn't asked Tessa to take over today. Something tells me that if I had told him about the change, I wouldn't be witnessing this moment.

"Yeah, my meeting got canceled, so I got back early," I dig myself into another lie as his gaze shifts to his hands, a moment of reflection passing over him. Despite my reservations, a persistent voice in my head prompts me to ask again. "So, can I listen while you practice?"

"Drums aren't anything like guitar or piano. They're not all that impressive by themselves."

"Since when were you insecure about anything? I thought the only thing you were a big baby about was sharks," I try for another tactic. "If you don't want to play, then at least give me a lesson."

"How do you know I'm any good?"

"I don't. This could be some eccentric rich person's hobby room. But I don't know shit about music, so even if you aren't any good, you could at least pretend for me." I doubt that he's new to this. It was in the way that he was poised above the drums, the look of someone gearing up to explode. It's all too similar to players coiled up for the puck to drop at the start of a game.

"Will you let me leave the room if I don't?"

"Probably not." I shrug. He has that look on his face, the one that tells me he needs this. And for whatever reason, making a big deal of it feels like a bad idea.

He stands and adjusts the stool, presenting it to me with a flourish once he's done.

I walk over and sit, feeling small and lost behind the instrument.

"Here." He hands me a fresh set of drumsticks, and I grasp the pale wood. "Loosen up. You don't have to hold on so tight; they aren't going to run away," he coaxes, and the mood in the room instantly shifts.

"But couldn't I accidentally throw one?" I picture a stick flying out of my hand and embedding itself into the abstract blue and silver painting on the far wall.

"Sure. That's a risk, but easing up will help." He moves to hold my hand, then pauses. "May I?"

I stare at the space between us for a breath. "Yes."

He drapes his hand over mine, guiding my fingers into a lighter grip. "It's easy to think that playing the drums is about power, about being heard. The truth is it's also about being restrained and structured. Sure, some moments feel like a thunderstorm, but those matter more if they're rare, breaking through at the right time." His words only work to confirm my initial impression.

There are people who have hobbies. Then there are people who talk about their passions like living, breathing things. This is *something* to Drew; I just don't know what.

"Now what?" His face hovers next to mine, anticipation washing over me.

"Now you let it out. Make some noise."

"What if it's bad?"

"Probably will be, but who am I going to tell?" He smirks, stepping back.

I'm hesitant at first. Striking each piece of the set as if sampling an appetizer. I let his words sink in. There's no expectation here.

Music has always been purposefully foreign to me, kept at arm's reach. So, for the first time in a long time, I'm trying something new. Something that I will fail at. The thought breaks the last threads of hesitation. If I'm going to fail anyway, I'm going to at least do it spectacularly.

I'm less conscious of the sound and more of the freedom.

Moving. Hitting. Creating.

There's a twitch in my chest. A deep and innate sensation of understanding.

Understanding who? Drew? Martin?

It's not long before my arms begin to tremble. Between ice skating and this, my limbs are nothing more than jelly.

"That's one way to do it," he says, face crinkled into an expression of pure joy.

"It was terrible, wasn't it?"

"Objectively, yes but I'm a fan." I can't stop staring at that smile. I haven't gotten one like it since picking him up from Half a Memory. "How did it feel?"

"Honestly?" I pause. "It's like there's less pressure in my head. You know when you were a kid, and you stopped the garden hose with your thumb? The water would build up, and then it's so satisfying to watch it burst out."

"I know exactly what you mean. That's why I did it."

My mind catches on the past tense. "What do you mean by did?"

I watch as his throat works, as he opens his mouth, and nothing comes out.

"This," he gestures around the room, "is something I'm coming back to. It's been missing for a long time."

I nod, my understanding deepening with his words. Photography used to bring me pure joy, even with the pressure of turning a creative passion into a viable career. But everything changed after my mom passed away—it became a refuge and a shield that allowed me to hide behind the lens instead of facing the world in front of it.

"Will you play for me now that I've made a fool of myself?"

"I'm not sure that's a good idea . . . I'm out of practice."

I resolve to give one more nudge before leaving it alone. I look into the depths of his eyes as I remind him, "There's no pressure here. It's just us. You don't have to be perfect for me. I want to see this part of you if you'll let me."

"It might be bad."

"It might be great, but either way, I'll listen because it's you." I wouldn't care if it was a collection of pots and pans as long as it was him.

His jaw ticks, and he releases a shaky breath. "Ok."

I relinquish my spot, and time turns to liquid as he adjusts the seat and returns to his place behind the instrument. I'm not sure where I should stand, but I settle for the couch near the opposite wall.

Nothing could have prepared me for how the initial crash of sound rings through me. The vibrations course through my skin and bones, straight to my soul's core.

Even from the first ten seconds, I recognize the song—it's from one of the few modern artists I've included in my playlists.

I was tapping away, merely creating noise, but this. This is music.

And I can't explain it, but in that moment, as he continues to play, it's like my heart reset itself, syncing up with the song's rhythm, as if it understood the music as language, *his language*, and responded accordingly.

24

Drew

I'm dreaming.

I must be dreaming because there is no other logical explanation for what is happening in this room.

I'm playing.

There's a beautiful, perfect girl curled up across the room, absorbing each sound.

Because I'm playing. Not just half a song or an endless cycling beat.

It's a lot like flying, or I'm guessing as someone without wings or any fundamental means to fly. To do something so inherently woven into my being.

I wonder if birds with clipped wings feel this way, that the sky and open spaces are calling to them but that they are just out of reach due to forces out of their control. But somehow, that limiting force is gone, and I'm worried I'll lose this all over again if I fixate too much on the why.

I sink into the feeling as if it's a well-worn leather couch. Vibrations flow up my arms, and I become nothing but a conduit for sound to be born.

For a moment, looking at Lacey, I wish I was like my sister, who has such unquestionable grace as a pianist.

Evelyn's fingers dance across the ivory surface when she plays, stirring a flurry of emotion as she effortlessly summons the notes of etudes and minuets. Lacey deserves something beautiful, full of delicate arpeggios and tragic dissonant chords.

Yet those feelings drift away as quickly as they came when I look up and see how her eyes sparkle, realizing that it probably wouldn't matter if I was banging away at a cowbell. Though she can see and freely point out the flaws, she doesn't care about the music. For her, it's just a small part of who I am, not my core defining quality. I'm just a regular guy who plays the drums, not some star who people are surprised to discover is a person.

I think that might be why I can access this part of myself again. Her look alone gives me permission to fail, letting me know that if I miss a beat, my worth in her eyes won't decrease with each mistake.

She might be the one person in the world with no expectations about my playing. What are the odds that she's here with me?

The silence at the end of the song feels louder than the cacophony I created.

"That was 'Just for Kicks,' right?" Her smile is similar to what she looked like on our trip to the aquarium—childlike and vulnerable. Joy, awe, and wonder mixed together on the universe's most perfect face.

"Yeah. I'm impressed. People don't usually pick out anything but the guitar or keys from a song." I am impressed. Drums may not always steal the spotlight, but they sure look cool, playing the background role on stage and in people's minds. At least, that's the general sentiment I used to get.

But her focus on it, noticing it, noticing me, feels different.

"I, uh, just really like the song, that's all." She blushes. And I tuck the information into my heart—not just because she likes one of the songs I helped to co-write, but also because it is one of those rare overt admissions as precious as a diamond. "But you missed something during the bridge."

From anyone else, it would make me feel like I was under a microscope that they were trying to connect music to my worth. But for her, the truth, sharing this information, is an act of care, not contempt.

Then she instantly tries to correct herself, "Shit. I'm sorry, I shouldn't have said anything. I went on and on about there not being pressure, and I just did the opposite."

"No, tell me. What else?" I urge her on.

I smile as she releases the torrent she's been holding back, "You slowed down too quickly in the second chorus. I get that it's supposed to be dramatic and all, but really, who will sing it that slow? It's the bass drum, right? The one that sounds like a big thump, I think? There shouldn't be as much of that either," she says all this while looking up at the ceiling as if it helps her concentrate better.

There's my girl, never holding back.

"Is that all?" I ask, making sure that my tone doesn't contain even an ounce of venom in it. She looks at me with those gray eyes, waiting for me to shut her down, reminding me of a deer caught in headlights when she realizes she's letting her true self out.

"I think so. But you're pretty good. I guess. Don't go and get an ego, though."

"Do you listen to a lot of music? Like if I played a different song, would you be able to tell me what to do better?"

She stretches, arms thrust over her head. I hate when she does that because it means she exposes an extra hint of skin. "Not really. I don't really listen to music besides the jazz I play in the morning and some oldies."

"And Avery Sloane."

She flips onto her stomach, stars dancing in her eyes, "Yeah. Did you know she has an all-female and non-binary production team?"

Yes, I do know that actually. I know some Avery stories that would probably make Lacey's jaw hit the floor. I would call her up right now if I knew it wouldn't blow my cover.

My cover? As if this is some spy operation and not just a mutual anonymity agreement. Yet, the mere thought of her discovering my identity sends a shiver down my spine.

"Why 'Just for Kicks' then? She has other songs that are definitely much better."

Her head is hanging off the edge of the couch now, cotton shorts bunching at the tops of her thighs, and now it's my turn to stare at the ceiling.

She's about to say something important, so no, this is not the time to become hypnotized by the expanse of her skin.

"Have you ever felt like everyone around you has some ulterior motive? There's that one line that gets me during the bridge, '*Am I a tool to be discarded or a trophy to be won? Does it really even matter when I'll be left collecting dust.*' I think that's what hooked me."

At its heart, 'Just for Kicks' was written out of rage. Avery and I were pissed, mainly at Wesley, when we got to the studio and recorded it. It was generally regarded as one of her least popular songs because the anger didn't mesh well with the lament played out in the lyrics.

"For me, it's '*Are you staying just for kicks or for the story you'll walk away with.*'" It's vain to quote one of the few lines that I contributed to the final cut of the song, but I want to know if it resonates with her on some level, that we've been connected through these scraps of poetry before even meeting.

Music does that, for better or worse.

In the past, fans assumed they knew me simply from listening to Fool's Gambit on repeat. Strangers would approach me with an uncomfortable familiarity. They'd know my face and the trivia spewed in tabloids, but I wouldn't even know their names.

But right now, I need her to know me in that same odd, parasocial way.

Her face goes sullen, and she turns so she's in an upright seated position. "I guess that's a good second-place contender. I've just never felt I give anyone a good story. Plenty of people in my life only find me interesting by association, so I guess that makes me more of a secondary character."

I move to sit next to her, and she arranges her body on the couch so we're almost nose to nose.

"I could never picture you that way."

"In what way?"

"As secondary to anyone." I think of her first, often even before I think of myself.

Her lips part as if drinking in my words. "You never make me feel like that. Here, with you, in some ways, I feel more real. Like you and I are the only real things that exist, and the outside world is some fantasy."

This is the fantasy; that's what she means, but neither of us will admit it.

"I feel real with you, too."

More real than I have for years. It makes me question if I've merely been a figment of everyone else's collective imagination for the past decade.

There's a gap between us, where our breaths intertwine, holding so much possibility. I wish the space didn't exist, but my hands hesitate. It's infuriating that we have to maintain this distance, all because of the flawed notion that living together and being with her is a terrible idea.

But there's always been a loophole because it just says no sex. "There's no rule that says I can't touch you. That I can't kiss you." And God. I might die if I don't soon.

"I thought it was heavily implied." She glances at my lips for half an instant.

"Do you want to follow the spirit or the letter of the law right now? Because I have a feeling we're on the same page. You'll still be a good little rule follower if you let me make you feel good. I want to make you feel good. I want to make sure that every part of you is real."

"I will never stand in the way of giving you what you want." It's a promise that I'm not sure she'll be able to keep. My wants and her needs seem to be at odds.

You. You're everything I want.

But those words would be too much.

"Then can I touch you?" I cup her face and watch the colors in her eyes dance with desire. "I need your words."

"Please," she says, and the one syllable word lifts the invisible wall between us.

She crawls on my lap, straddling me. My hands find their place in her hair, and her lips meet mine with an unmistakable need.

I feel as though I had been crafted for the singular purpose of savoring her touch, her presence. I want to consume her whole, to feel her completely, and I have a feeling that she wants the same as her teeth tug against my bottom lip.

"Mark me, *sconosciuta*," I whisper.

Make my body remember you.

In response, she grinds against me and grips my neck to pull herself impossibly closer.

With a quick motion, I trail kisses down her neck, intending to do exactly as I claim—to confirm that the memories we shared, our first night, and everything in between were more than mere fiction.

My knuckles tease the exposed skin of her stomach, rewarding me with a soft whimper. I don't want anything else from her tonight but the sounds of her pleasure.

My hand makes its way up under the fabric of her shirt. She shudders as I slowly trail my fingers over the soft skin of her stomach. Higher, I cup her breast, my fingers tugging lightly at her nipple. She rocks into me again, ripping a groan from me.

She's going to fucking end me.

Still, I remind myself that this isn't about commanding her body. It's about memorizing it. My biggest regret of that night was not being wholly sober and completely sure that night wasn't, in some part, a dream.

Lacey grabs my hand, attempting to guide it lower.

"You're still so impatient."

"It's only because I remember how good you can make me feel," she purrs, and I give in to her desire.

Gripping her waist, I move her so she's laying on the couch. My hand moves closer to where she wants me, toying with the waistband of the damn shorts she insists on always taunting me with.

"Do you think about that night when you touch yourself? Do you think about how good it felt to be claimed by my cock?" I ask because I have to know if her need matches my own.

"Yes." At the admission, my hand inches lower. The sound that escapes her is barely a word as my fingers brush over the lace that barely covers her pussy.

I continue to make lazy circles, feeling wetness seep through the delicate fabric. God. I love knowing that her arousal is for me, for how I get to make her feel. If this is the second and last time she lets me do this, I'm going to take my time.

"I think about it too. I think about how pretty you looked, taking me so well back when you were determined to hate me. You might not hate me anymore, but I will do my best to make you hate those rules."

"Well, you have your work cut out for you." Her voice turns breathy as I run a finger just under the waistband.

"I'm going to play you like a damn symphony."

"You're not that good of a musician." She's right. Today, I was sloppy, but who wouldn't be if they were as out of practice as I am? But her body is an instrument that I have been visualizing with such regularity that I know exactly how I plan for this to play out.

I hook my thumbs on the sides of her shorts and the strings of her pale lace thong, pulling them down her legs in one fluid movement and tossing them to the side.

With both hands, I hold her thighs open, taking her in. And she's a goddamn sight to behold, wet for me alone.

I brush against her clit, and her hips lift to meet my touch.

"You still have such a greedy pussy," I murmur, my voice low as I sink one finger into her. "Don't worry; I'll give you what you want. What you deserve."

When my thumb presses against her clit she gasps, "Drew."

“That’s my good girl remembering to say my name.”

I work to urge her on, stretching her a little more with another finger, curling them both to hit her exactly where she needs it most. She rides my hand with an unexpected urgency, our combined efforts drawing moans from her parted lips.

This room was made for the sole purpose of making music, and I’m about to create my new favorite song out of her cries of pleasure.

Her thighs begin to shake, and I know that she’s on the edge of release.

It’s so tempting to stop. To leave her on the precipice and beg. To make her say how much she needs me. But this moment is about giving her everything she wants.

Her muscles clench around my fingers as she comes. I pull her back to me as her limbs go limp, and hold her close, cherishing the conclusion of a moment I've craved for countless years. She's everything I've been waiting for.

"You could stay, you know," I murmur softly against her neck, the words slipping through the carefully constructed filter. The ones meant to hide how desperately I need her.

For a while, I thought it was just what she represented—the routine and structure, the knowledge that she saw me as a person and didn't turn away. However, I'm now sure she's irreplaceable, and the thought of letting her go is unsettling.

Her previously boneless body tenses beneath me.

Fuck.

Five simple words uttered without a second thought are all it takes to have her walls slam down like iron.

"Please don't make this into more than it can be." She shrugs out of my arms and walks out without grabbing her shorts.

Without looking back.

25

Lacey

You could stay . . .

Those three words open the door to a future that's never felt like an option.

It was never supposed to be an option; this thing between Drew and me was created with the understanding that it would be discarded once it outlived its usefulness. And no matter how much I've dreaded leaving, I will. At some point, I had convinced myself it wouldn't hurt to walk away from this—that these past months would live on as a happy memory, something I would reminisce about in ten years and wonder how he's doing. Hoping he's found happiness.

But with each step back to my room, I realize how fiercely I've been lying to myself.

What if I stayed? Staying means letting the real world in. Staying means this could end at a moment's notice and not on a set timeline. Staying doesn't mean forever; it means uncertainty.

As I close my eyes, one more thought creeps in, barely a whisper.

What if, instead, I wake up in ten years, wander to the kitchen, and turn around to find him watching me, with nothing but love in his eyes as I prepare our coffee—where I no longer need to wonder what he's doing or if he found happiness because he's happy with me.

It's the only thought I allow to linger as I fade away.

A week and a half passes, and the days feel like they're slipping away from us. And like the fully functioning adults we are, we don't talk about that night. About how he made me feel electric and seen and how I think I did the same for him. Like all of our other problems, we've let the magic of the apartment and our arrangement help us pretend it never happened.

But it did happen, and I still mean every word. Or at least I think I do.

There's a distance between us that there hasn't been before. I try to convince myself that it's a safety net, but it feels more like a cage. No more casual touching or resting my legs on his lap while we watch movies. The space between us says far more than the words we exchange.

Despite the distance, I continue to watch him play, quietly entering the music room upon my return home just to hear him practice. Even as I listen to the familiar infectious beats, I can't help but notice subtle shifts—the music somehow lacking the same magic as before.

Still, I listen, wearing the ear protection Drew insisted I use if I'm going to be there, soaking in every sound and cherishing the simple joy of being in that room with him. And even muted, I still physically feel the sound hum through me. While he loses himself in his music, I sit on the couch and read my paperback horror books.

I'm not quite sure when my obsession with the genre started. Cara once asked me why not choose something happy to escape into?

For me, it's less about escaping and more about knowing that reality is better when I turn off the TV or close the book.

There's something else too. I tend to have inappropriate emotional responses to horror. I laugh in the middle and cry at the end. I cry for the survivors because they got through the nightmares, but they have to live with all they witnessed. For the survivors, the end of the movie or book is just the start of a new life. I cry for their twisted, no-so-happy endings.

I'm about to turn the page to reveal the fate of the final girl when someone taps on my shoulder. I bolt up out of my seat with a squeak.

When I shift to find my tormentor, my field of vision is overtaken by the face of a familiar, currently scowling, blonde.

What is she doing here?

All I know is that Cara looks pissed, her platinum shoulder-length hair frizzing up from the humidity.

"He's playing." I hear Craig's familiar voice somewhere in the background.

I begin to glance back at Drew, but I'm interrupted as Cara looms over me. "I thought you were kidnapped!" she starts, my mind racing as to how she ended up here when, last time I checked, she was supposed to be on the opposite end of the East Coast.

Despite her petite frame, she commands the room, her words bursting out of her with the same force she uses to hold court in a lecture hall. "Why the hell is it that I found out from Craig that your apartment flooded and you've been living in a fucking penthouse? And when you didn't bother to answer your phone, I went to that shitty bar you're always talking about, hoping just maybe I'd find you there. Craig has been a great help during the few moments he spares from staring at my ass. This is what I get for trying to surprise my best friend during the fall study break." It's impressive that she's not out of breath after recounting her journey, but I guess she had plenty of practice.

“Great to see you too. I still think you killed the whole surprise thing.” I stand and go in for a hug, but she immediately pulls away, impressively nimble in her heels.

“Oh fuck no. I'm mad at you. Give me five more minutes to be mad, then you get a hug.” She takes another step back as her glossed lips form into a pout.

I roll my eyes and hug her anyway because Cara isn't capable of being genuinely mad at anyone.

We stay there, embracing for a while as I soak up the moment. It's been months since I last saw her, and now that she's here, I pull her closer to me. I've missed her so much, as well as the spark of feminine energy she always injects into my life. We usually only see each other on our annual summer adventures, packing as many high-octane memories as we can into two weeks.

As she releases me, she turns and takes in Drew. "Holy fucking shit, you're—" She gets halfway through the sentence before Craig scoops her up over his shoulder in a fireman's carry and hauls her across the hall and into Drew's room.

All I hear before the door closes is, "So, I need to catch you up on the rules of this situation."

I turn to Drew, who has his customary cocky grin, and ask, "What the hell was that?"

"I think Craig has a crush and got a little jealous. He's never able to compete with me," he says, standing and making his way to the kitchen. I pick up my book and follow him, closing the door behind me.

"Sure." I furrow my brow, trying to think of what I'm missing. I have a feeling I only have half the story, but that's nothing new, so I try not to overthink whatever the hell dynamic Craig and Drew have going on. "So I guess we're cooking for four tonight."

"Since when did *we* cook?"

“Excuse you. It’s a hard job looking this good and supervising.”

“You make it look easy.” It’s nice to be comfortably joking. The addition of more people in the space seems to have cut through the uneasy tension between us.

I slide onto my place on the counter as we wait for our friends. But ten minutes pass, and there is still no sign of them.

"Should we send out a search party or . . .?" I joke, trying to break the silence.

"You looking for us?" Craig comes out from the bedroom, followed by Cara close behind. "So, what are we eating? Breaking in somewhere always leaves me ravenous."

Drew rummages through the fridge and only finds a handful of vegetables. It quickly becomes clear that we don't have enough ingredients to cook for everyone, so Cara and I are tasked with grocery shopping. The casualness of Drew and I working out the grocery list earns me a raised eyebrow from Cara.

We don’t even make it a second into the car ride before Cara starts firing off questions. It’s a relief to let the truth pour out of me. I tell her about my apartment flooding and my current situation with the email I received two days ago letting me know, I'm all-clear about moving back in. I tense up just thinking about it. By the time I’m done with my debrief, we’ve reached the store, but that doesn’t stop her from digging into the slightly juicer parts of my story.

"How are you not having dirty thoughts all the time? Just standing in the same room as him might have gotten me pregnant," Cara says as she pushes our cart further down the aisle.

Her words have me giving an apologetic look to the young family walking past us at that exact moment.

"Cara, stop objectifying my roommate." I chew on my lip, thinking about how much more about recent events I should divulge.

"God. You do. You are always having dirty thoughts about him. That makes sense because you know exactly how good it is," she groans. "I think I hate you for wasting this opportunity. Like you have been given sex god on a silver platter and have not touched him since that first night, this is criminal behavior, and I'm ashamed to call you my best friend." She continues, her gaze fixed on me, "So, why aren't you sleeping with him?"

"Because he's my *roommate*," I emphasize the last word, not entirely sure if it's to convince her or myself. "And you know that I don't have sex with people I genuinely like. It ruins things." We didn't have sex, so it's not completely a lie, but even the not-sex has put things in a tricky place. Remembering the night has heat creeping up my neck and cheeks.

Cara notices my blush immediately. "Something happened, though! You're holding out on me."

"It's complicated."

"I might be a physicist, but I know chemistry when I see it. It's simple. You like him. He looks at you like you walk on water. Oh, and your apartment is completely fine now, but you're staying longer anyway. What else is there?"

I'm saved from answering as Cara reaches for a package of mushrooms. "No. There's a strict no-mushroom rule in the kitchen."

"Is he allergic?

"No, he just doesn't like them. And by not getting them, I'm saving you from a complicated and drawn-out explanation about umami and how they can eat him when he's dead." I grab the package and put it back in the produce section where it belongs.

"You are so down bad for him. And don't disagree. Don't think that you're getting out of this conversation." Her tone softens slightly as she adds, "I know you've had hold-ups before, with Henry and after your mom, but it seems different with him."

She's right. It does feel different with him; there's no denying that. But just because it's different doesn't automatically mean it won't end the same way.

"How do you do it? Get your heart broken, and just go back out there." Cara always seems so in control of her relationships, moving in and out of them so fearlessly. I've only had one serious relationship, and it's made me feel scared for more. Scared that I'll try again, and the love simply won't be there.

She starts laughing so hard that tears form in the corners of her eyes. "Meeting someone new. Falling for all those little things, those moments make me happy. Why would I deprive myself of being happy again over a little pain?" When she puts it so simply, it doesn't sound all that bad.

"So, the pain just . . . passes?"

"Not always, but the good parts always have a way of making the pain feel small in comparison." I take a closer look at my friend. I've always seen her dust herself off with a smile and never considered how much strength that takes. "The pain is proof you loved before; just because it ends doesn't mean you need to regret it."

"Ok, but even with the good parts, what if this is like one of those reality TV scenarios where the couples only like each other because they're forced to live with each other? And those couples fail almost every time. Maybe it's just because of the situation we're in, seeing each other every day."

"Does it make all the feelings less real, though? Or is this you trying to rationalize your way out of it?"

I don't know is what I want to say, but I stay silent. Apparently, that answer is enough for Cara.

"What if I give you substantial evidence that he is the one?" As she asks, I can practically see the cartoon light bulb appear above her head. It's the look she gives when she has a breakthrough; great for her research but bad for my personal life.

"Cara," I warn as she pulls out her phone, tapping away for a few moments.

"Done. His name is Ben. And don't think I'm pulling any punches. If he doesn't make your stomach flutter on sight, then there's no one else for you besides the man who's been right under your nose."

"You shouldn't be running social experiments on me," I grumble.

She continues, ignoring my complaint, "He's agreed to Thursday dinner, and you should be getting a text from him soon."

"You're terrifyingly efficient, and how do you know I'm free on Thursday?"

"Same way that I knew you were off work today. You still have me on your Google Calendar. And my ability to stay on track is exactly why my students love me."

"I bet you have assignments back within twenty-four hours and have them quaking in their boots because of how brutal you are."

"I like to think of it as constructive criticism."

My phone chimes, and I look down to see Ben's phone number flashing back up at me.

Ben

Looking forward to Thursday. Are blind dates even a thing anymore?

"I'm not going to give you a play-by-play." Then, the thought hits me. "Please tell me this isn't one of your exes."

"We only went on three dates like," she pauses, holding up her fingers and counting one by one, "five years ago and are LinkedIn connections." She waves me off casually as if to emphasize that it's no big deal.

"Then I'm definitely not giving you any details."

Just like that, my fate for Thursday night is sealed.

We're at the checkout line by the time I finally come to terms with Cara's meddling. At some point in the series of distracting events, she snuck a package of mushrooms into the basket, which I'm tempted to throw at her for her various crimes against my sanity. When I hand them to her to put back, she simply cackles like the mad scientist she is.

Still, it's nice to have her here. To let out my feelings and have some plan set in place for what's next.

26

Drew

"You have to come clean," Craig says as he sets down the video game controller and looks over to where I'm prepping vegetables for the stir fry.

"What do you mean by that?" I choose to ignore the obvious. He has a knack for picking conversations I don't want to have.

"Her friend almost ruined whatever delusional shit the two of you are trying to pull. And those domestic grocery runs that have you both so dreamy-eyed? Well, it's only a matter of time before someone takes a picture or comes up to you and says something, and I won't be there to do damage control. You've been lucky, but luck runs out."

"You didn't seem to mind doing damage control just now." I give him a quick look, trying to divert his attention because we both know he wasn't just helping Cara out of the goodness of his heart but because he has a thing for women who could trample him.

"Respectfully, Cara is a beautiful woman, and it's criminal not to appreciate her as if she's a work of art. But seriously, is that how you want Lacey to find out, from a stranger or literally anyone but you?" I hear it in his voice that he cares about Lacey, too.

She hasn't just rooted her way into my life. She's important to him, too. *Fuck.*

"Who says she has to find out?" I ask because that's been my plan.

In my head, it works flawlessly. Somehow, I convince her to stay; the reunion happens without a hitch, and I never have to say anything about my past because she's what's becoming my future. Delusional, but damn, it's a pretty picture. Dancing around the inconvenient parts and only keeping the good.

"Just because you have some cute little list on the fridge that says you won't share any personal information with each other? The entire rest of the world isn't playing along with that. I hate to admit it, but you're a public figure, and it's going to bite you in the ass." He sighs, pinching his temples and forming ripples of skin on his forehead. "She's really fucking good for you. Like you're playing again. Can we take a minute to acknowledge how monumental that is?"

I haven't really stopped and thought about it. I never considered it as something more than practicing. It just happened, and it felt natural. Knowing that when I sit down, it'll be there, safe. I still don't know what it will look like out on a stage, but this is progress.

"Yeah, I guess. It's not really a huge deal," I say, trying to play it off because making a big deal of this too soon might ruin it.

Even acknowledging it makes my stomach roil slightly, like if I say the wrong thing, it'll disappear all over again, but this time, it won't come back. I can't even consider that right now.

Craig wanders off to the bathroom, muttering to himself, "He guesses that some girl coming into his life and helping solve a decade-long problem isn't a huge deal."

As if summoned by Craig, the girls return a few minutes later, proudly clutching the small bag of groceries. “No mushrooms. Though it was a tough battle at the end to save your delicate palate,” Lacey says, unpacking the stir-fry ingredients.

“Not all of us can stomach anything as long as it’s edible and not completely charcoal,” I say.

Cara wears a smirk, a dangerous twin of what Craig looks like when he's scheming. "If you're going to bicker like an old married couple, then I hope you kiss like one, too."

Startled, I drop the knife I've been using to julienne carrots, and Lacey shoots her friend a panicked, wide-eyed glance as she rushes over to me.

"Are you ok?" she asks, grabbing my hand and inspecting it for cuts. It's the first time she's touched me since everything went wrong. Since . . .

She keeps her gaze fixed on me, the only indication that I haven't said anything.

"I'm fine," I finally say, attempting to reassure her.

“God. At this rate, we’re never going to eat,” Craig groans, stretching his arms over his head as he enters the kitchen before turning to Cara. "I could take you out instead so we don't have to swim through the sea of tension between these too."

"In your dreams," Cara retorts before muttering something under her breath and pulling a barstool from under the island.

"Oh. I'll definitely have some good dreams about it." My friend called me starry-eyed earlier, but he should look in the damn mirror.

As the night continues, conversation flows as easily as the wine. It's too easy to picture that this really is our apartment, where it's normal to host our friends together, that this isn't some happy accident that we're all here together.

As a thank you, I offer Cara the guest bedroom. Her immediate recognition of me was unmistakable. Yet, after whatever Craig told her, she remained silent, and I'm happy to show my gratitude in her efforts to play along. After she accepts, Craig jumps at the opportunity to provide a tour of the place.

"That was fun," Lacey says, looking over to me from where she's doing the dishes. Ever since that first meal, she insisted that it's her role. Even on the long days away, she comes back claiming it's therapeutic, though I think she just likes the act of filling every waking moment with something productive.

"What's your money on? Are they fucking or fighting?"

"Both. I just hope he survives."

"Why does it have to be my friend that comes out the loser?" I defend Craig, but honestly, based on the fact that he shaved his head for a girl who couldn't care less about him, Lacey is probably right.

"I think I have a claim over Craig now. I'm going to steal him out from under your nose."

"Have you seen him try to streak down Broadway in Nashville?" I take a sip of the wine left over from our meal. "Once you've wrestled him nude, then you have equal claim. Actually, if you ever wrestle him nude, I'll have to do unspeakable things to my best friend."

She laughs with her entire body, sending a flurry of small, soapy bubbles into the air. My eyes fixate on the ones clinging to her tied-up hair.

I'm always tempted to let it down. To walk over, steal the elastic from her hair, and run my fingers through it. The ponytails and messy buns that threaten to come loose seem to represent the last wall she has shielding her. Though she's almost completely free around me in our apartment, she still has a part of herself tucked away.

But who am I to judge? I'm hiding something that everyone else seems to know about me except for her. I do need to come clean.

But not yet, not when her not knowing me means she can lean against the countertop with little dish soap bubbles in her hair. Not with how it seems like we're starting to recover from the other night. Not with a little less than two weeks left.

27

Lacey

"And for you?" the waitress asks with the universal expression of someone who has already asked a question and would like to move on with their night.

Ace's Sports Bar and Grill is packed with crowds huddling around the TVs broadcasting Thursday Night Football. The occasional clatter of the kitchen cuts through the cheers and commentary.

It's not necessarily a place that screams cute, first date. But the background noise is a great buffer for any awkward silences. And there have been plenty.

"A margarita and truffle fries," I tell her, panicking for the briefest moment before settling on something safe.

I hate restaurants. There's so much unnecessary pressure in the process of picking one thing and hoping it was the right decision—it's just another thing I've spared myself from by avoiding dating for a while. Honestly, even though it was a shitty show of character, I didn't mind it when Henry ordered for me when we were together. It was one less thing to worry about.

"Your orders will be right out." The poor girl slumps slightly with the relief of no longer being caught in customer service limbo.

"I guess we'll have a table full of fries and tequila then." The beautiful man across from me attempts to joke in his Australian accent. I attempt to recall the last few minutes, but I can't remember his order if my life depended on it.

Ever since I started getting ready, it's just felt like I've been going through the motions of what a date is supposed to feel like.

It probably didn't help that when Drew asked where I was going, I told him on a date. It's not like there's a sane way of saying, *I'm going on this date to make sure I want to be with you, and this isn't some weird version of Stockholm Syndrome because I can't trust my own feelings.*

Maybe I shouldn't have said that this meeting with Ben was a date. Maybe I was hoping he would care, even after I walked away from him.

I'm stupid. This is stupid.

Ben is dashing in that classic old movie way, with sun-tanned skin, dimples that poke out each time he talks, and light brown windswept hair. Cara promised not to pull punches, but I wasn't expecting her to serve up a goddamn fantasy. And despite his looks and wry humor, there's no flutter in my stomach, no magnetic urge to touch or be touched. I'm not looking for love at first sight, just a sign of life from my libido.

"Just a sign we have similar taste." The words sound forced as they leave my mouth.

"You look how I feel," Ben says. If I didn't already feel like I was wasting both of our time, I would now.

"And how is that exactly? Distracted? Or like you're making the worst first impression of your life?"

He smiles, not looking at all like I've just made his list of top ten most boring dates. "Like our mutual friend Cara is terribly meddlesome and deserves some sort of prize for her not-so-covert operations."

"I still think I'm still a few steps behind here." Because, yes, Cara is meddlesome, but there's something I'm definitely missing.

"Here's what happened to me, and please stop me if this sounds familiar. I was telling the genius girl I know from an internship I was part of a few years ago about my recent break-up because she gives objectively some of the best advice I've ever received, and she told me the best way to get over someone is to meet someone new. And if she sets me up with her stunning best friend and we don't click instantly, maybe I was already with the person I was supposed to spend the rest of my life with."

I huff a laugh. It sounds exactly like her to be so efficient with her schemes. Why convince one friend they're a foolish idiot when you can convince two friends they're foolish idiots?

"So, how are we going to enact our revenge?"

"I think a thank you letter would do the job."

"I think you might need to reevaluate your definition of revenge," I tell him, suddenly relaxing as the pressure of the night eases. "Tell me about her, the girl that makes you feel like a hopeless daydreamer and makes you want nothing to do with me."

"Only if you do the same," he replies, his eyes meeting mine with a smile. As we wait for our food, he describes her, his gaze going distant as if he's not even here. He's with her, where his heart really is. And honestly, I can't blame him because I feel the same. I don't think I ever truly left the apartment, especially after seeing Drew's expression, and what I'm hoping is pretend indifference.

Ben recounts their first date, which was less of a date and more of a flight that was delayed for multiple hours, only to realize they were both returning to Atlanta from LA. It's serendipity at its finest, people with so much in common that they don't realize it until it smacks them in the face.

"So, did you listen to a word I just said, or were you thinking about your person instead?" Ben's face tilts with a knowing grin.

"Maybe a bit of both," I admit. It's hard to listen to someone talk about their love life and not think of your own and compare. Because maybe Drew and my situation isn't as movie perfect as an airport, but it's something special, and it's ours.

"No, she sounds lovely. I'm glad that this day could at least end in something good."

"You don't think you and your person will be ok?"

"I think there are a few more things that we need to work out before I know that. I wouldn't say the situation is all that simple," I say, my thoughts swirling with uncertainty until my eyes widen, and my heart races as a flicker of recognition sparks within me. Before Ben can even ask about my sudden shift, I catch sight of someone who shouldn't be here, especially considering his earlier behavior.

I immediately think he's followed me, and I can't figure out if it's romantic or not. As I look longer, I see he's handing a paper bag to someone by the bar, and my heart dips a little.

He starts to turn to leave until he turns his head and catches my eye. He pauses there for a bit, as if contemplating, and finally making up his mind, he rushes towards us with absolutely startling speed.

Nope. Nope. Nope.

No matter what happens next, no matter how much Ben and I both don't really want to be on this date, it is destined to be terrible.

I'm not sure what I even try to accomplish, trying to hide, turning my head to shield my face, only to look up and find Drew. Ben, noticing him too, appears as frozen in shock as I am, and I don't blame him. Drew isn't exactly warm and cuddly at first glance. And to have him all but charging towards you is a little frightening.

"Lace, they said you'd be here. I couldn't get a hold of you through your phone, but Aunt May is in the hospital, and we need to head there now," Drew gasps like he's catching his breath from the brisk walk over.

Before I can process the entire scene, he pulls me up, and we're at the host station before I can utter, "What the hell?"

He doesn't say a word until we're outside, my hand still engulfed in his.

28

Drew

"Stop and tell me what's going on," Lacey demands as she moves in front of me on the sidewalk, blocking my path.

I'm not sure where I was planning on going, but my primary thought was getting her away from *him.*

Her date.

"I just wanted to make sure we had ground rules for bringing people back to the apartment. You know, so we're on the same page," I tell her, making it sound like I'm fine with her bringing someone back with her, which couldn't be further from the truth.

"So what? You made up a family emergency featuring the Aunt from *Spiderman.* Really believable, by the way, to tell me that you were worried about not having ground rules about bringing people back to the apartment." She looks more amused than pissed, as if the entire ordeal sounds too idiotic to even be mad about. "This has nothing to do with the other night?"

"This has everything to do with the other night," I tell her point blank. I'm done biting my tongue and biding my time. "And we need to stop pretending that shit didn't happen and didn't matter."

She just looks at me silently, her lips slightly parted as if to tell me to stop. But I continue because she's moving out soon, and I'm done with this stupid dance. "Because it mattered to me. Look at me right now and tell me this all means nothing, and I'll drop it. If I'm wrong and I messed this up, I have somewhere else I can stay until your place is ready."

I wait for her reaction. She would be completely justified to yell at me for ruining her date. Usually, her emotions are plastered across her face, but right now, it's impossible to read what's beneath the surface.

She glances down, hesitating, before she says, "It mattered to me too. It mattered so much that I went on this whole date because I wanted to be sure it wasn't just that I was horny and you were there."

"And?"

"And I realized I wanted nothing to do with the guy from the moment I walked out of our apartment. So, what are you going to do about it?" she goads me, her eyes sparkling with a mix of challenge and anticipation. I can tell simply from the quirk of her full lips that she's trying to taunt me into kissing her. And it almost works.

"I'm taking you on a date."

"Excuse me?"

"I'm taking you on a date the next time you're in town for more than twenty-four hours."

"Drew." My name's on her lips again, but this time it's different, softer, as if she's contemplating all the reasons to say no.

"We do the baby steps. Because this feels right between us. We deserve to give it a chance. And if I'm being honest, I'm so over our damn rules, but I'm open to negotiation." The words feel so good to get out. There's still a trickle of terror because the last time I said anything this real, she pushed me away.

"Yes."

"Yes?" It's the answer I wanted, the answer I needed, but somehow it's still shocking.

"Yes," she echos."I'll be gone for two days starting tomorrow afternoon, and then I'm all yours."

All mine. I like the sound of that.

"Will you kiss me now?" she asks, eyes dancing as they catch the glow of the streetlights. I almost give in, but she tortured me, walking out of the apartment and leaving me with the knowledge of her date. It's only fair to return the favor.

I move towards her so her back is flush against the wall of a building before telling her, "Not tonight. Not until I can do it again properly."

"You're killing me, you know that?" she asks, her voice coming out as a thin thread.

"You've been killing me for two months now. Killing me from the very first night that you said I wouldn't get another taste of you. Killing me after walking out saying this couldn't be anything." I lean in, closing the remaining distance between us. "Those tiny shorts that you used to dance in around put medieval torture tactics to shame. You know how many cold showers I've had to take because of your ass alone? How many times I've had to stroke my cock thinking about how much better it would feel to have your perfect fucking lips wrapped around it instead of my hand?"

Her breath hitches. "I haven't seen those shorts for weeks."

"I'll give them back. Just know that the next time you wear them, I'll be the one taking them off. Just like the last time." The image alone has me growing hard. If it weren't so fun to tease her, to draw out the anticipation, I would throw her over my shoulder right now and fix both of our frustrations.

"Is that a threat?"

"It's a promise. We've done so much of this wrong that I need to do the next part right."

"You better not hold back. I expect the best. I have this roommate who could be a professional chef, and it will take a lot to impress me."

"Sounds like I have some competition. My roommate only knows how to make coffee and toast. Do you want to swap?"

"No, but he's getting on my nerves right now, so I might have to return the favor."

"Do your worst." I flick my tongue out lightly, caressing the juncture of her sharp jaw and the soft curve of her neck. I take some sadistic pleasure in the shiver that runs through her, and I smirk as I pull away.

She flushes, two rosy patches blooming on her cheeks. Her blush might just be my favorite color.

"I plan to," she warns with a glance down to where my cock is straining against my jeans. Thank God I left the sweats at home.

Most of the night, I couldn't shake off the fact that she said yes, that she's willing to give whatever we have a chance. So, I didn't pay much attention to her threat, but she wasn't kidding when she said she'd return the favor.

Fuck.

In the morning, as I head to the kitchen, I'm met with a sight that threatens to unravel my resolve.

There, laid out before me, is Lacey, wearing a new pair of silky shorts as she reaches for something. Her shirt and shorts ride up as she moves, revealing the curve of her ass. We make eye contact the moment she turns in my direction; the slight smile pulling at her lips is an obvious declaration of war on my self-control.

Instead of taking my normal post and watching her go through the motions of her morning, I turn on my heel and close the door behind me.

She's actively ruining me, and she's so damn aware of it.

Hurrying to my bed, I lie on my back, staring at the ceiling until a knock on the door catches my attention. "You okay?" she asks, her question slightly muffled by the door.

"Yeah, I'm feeling a bit off this morning. Might be coming down with something."

"Sure." A slight pause makes me think she's walked away and decided to give me peace, but then she taunts me again, "Give your right hand my regards unless you want to come out and play."

Fuuuck.

I close my eyes, desperately trying to block out the images flooding my mind, teasing me with fantasies of how I could have her, how I could slowly undress her and claim her completely.

All mine.

"Focus," I murmur to myself, struggling to gather my thoughts, especially when the unmistakable clinking of pans lets me know she's settled on the counter—my counter—looking like a fucking meal waiting to be devoured.

Fuck it.

29

Lacey

If he's going to push my buttons, I'll push right back.

I never thought there was anything worse than wanting something off-limits with him. Seeing him and knowing he'd never be mine. It turns out that knowing Drew wants me back and is making me wait is absolutely excruciating.

Why do we have to wait? It's good; we're here, literally across the hall from each other, and for some reason, he wants to wait.

So, what if the tiny shorts were intentional? It's just a way of showing off what he's missing. I hope the image is tattooed right into his brain for the next few days, making him regret hiding in his room.

The victory has a smirk playing across my face as I sit on the counter, sipping my coffee. If I can't have what I want, at least we're suffering together.

I nearly drop my mug as his door flies open, and he stalks towards me. My breath hitches at the sight. How the hell can he look like some vengeful god while only wearing gray sweatpants?

He takes deliberate strides to where I'm sitting. Even though I'm on a raised surface, he still towers over me. His thumb and forefinger delicately grip my chin, tilting my face to meet his agitated gaze.

I hold my breath, sensing the tension hanging in the air. I might have miscalculated my efforts just slightly, but at least now he's right where I want him.

"You're a fucking brat. You know that?" Drew's chest heaves, hungry eyes surveying me as my tongue flicks out to wet my lips.

"Come to your senses about that goodbye kiss?" I hope so. I hope he brands my mouth in a way I could never forget.

"Get on the couch," he commands.

I don't move, still slightly in shock at the shift in mood.

He lowers his lips so they brush against my ear. "If I have to ask again, you're getting nothing from me."

I set down my mug so rapidly that coffee splashes over the counter. I practically slide across the floor to get to the couch. Whatever he intends to do with me, I want it, and I want it now.

He follows, slowly kneeling in front of me, wicked green eyes flashing as they meet mine.

"What are you doing?" I ask.

He raises his hand, tapping his fingers on the top of my waistband. Anticipation swirls low and hot in my belly as I realize what he has planned.

"I'm going to give you a kiss that leaves you dreaming about me tonight. Just . . . not on your mouth. Do you like the sound of that?"

"Yes." Actually, I'm not sure if I've ever heard of a better idea.

When he pulls at my shorts, I lift my hips, resting my hands on his bare shoulders as he guides the silky fabric down my thighs and over my feet.

"*Sconosciuta.* No underwear? How thoughtful. I bet you were hoping that I would come out here to bend you over the couch and fuck your needy pussy until you felt me the entire time you're gone. That I would punish you with what you've been begging for, but I have plans for you so that will have to wait. Lucky for you, I'm feeling generous and hungry," he says as he guides my legs apart.

He kisses his way up my thigh, each touch igniting a tiny fire beneath my skin. His teeth sink into the tender flesh, and I gasp in surprise at the sharp but welcome pain. He plants a soft kiss on the newly red spot he marked. "Another thing to remember me by."

There's nothing tender or restrained about how his tongue plunges into me and the way his expert fingers give my clit the friction I crave. I lean back fully onto the couch, losing myself in the intoxicating intensity.

He's well on his way to coaxing me into oblivion when my phone buzzes on the table. It goes silent for an instant, then comes back to life.

I want to throw it across the room for disrupting my state of bliss.

Drew stops and looks up at me. "Go ahead and answer it." My nerves feel like a million dancing fireworks as he trails a knuckle against my inner thigh.

"But you—" My internal bravado sputters out as my heart races.

"But I what? It won't get in my way, and *it's rude to keep someone waiting*. Be a good girl and answer it, but you better be able to contain yourself." His silky tone entices me to bow to his every whim.

Fuck he's serious. How can he be serious?

I lift the device, staring at the screen. Am I really doing this? My finger trembles slightly as I accept Price's call.

My friend's voice bursts through the moment I hold the phone to my ear. "I'm grabbing coffee from that place you like. Do you want anything for the road?" I bite my lip as Drew lazily trails a finger over my clit and teases my entrance. "They have scones, muffins, bagels, hmm, what else . . ."

"Price," I say, choking on the syllable as it's the exact moment when Drew decides to bury his face between my thighs.

"Oh, and they have these little quiches and croissants."

Why the hell is he listing the entire menu? Fuck. A hand eases up my shirt to pinch my nipple, and I nearly bite off my own tongue to keep quiet.

"Price. I don't need anything. I'll see you soon, ok?" I try to finish the interaction before it's too late. The pressure on my clit recedes, and one of Drew's damned fingers sinks into me. I clap a hand over my mouth to muffle the sound I make. I look down and catch Drew's twisted smirk.

He's having far too much fun with this. A wink is all the warning I get before he adds a second finger. My hand isn't nearly enough to hide the moan ripped from me.

Price's voice forces me back to the issue at hand. "You ok? Are you on a run or something? You sound out of breath." That's one way to put it.

"Yeah. It was pretty intense. I-I should go shower." I can't get the words out fast enough.

"So it's a no to breakfast?"

Before I can form a response, Drew's fingers move in and out at a pace that sends shivers down my spine, drawing me away from reality. Drew inches closer, and I brace myself for whatever he has in store. Just as I'm about to disconnect the call to spare Price from hearing the words Drew is undoubtedly about to say into my ear, until—

"Hey, Price, get her one of everything on the menu. She's really worked up a sweat," Drew says, and my blood sprints faster through my veins.

"Who was—" Price starts before I abruptly end the call, but I don't have a second to relax as I feel Drew curl his fingers, beckoning me closer to the edge. My now-free hands clutch at the couch.

"Fuck. I think I hate you a little right now," I gasp out, barely catching my breath.

He maintains the relentless movement, his voice smooth as silk as he counters, "You don't taste like someone who hates me. And can you really hate me when we're having so much fun together?"

"Yes. Yes, I can." No, I can't. I don't think I could ever hate him, even if I wanted to. Despite all my attempts to not care, he's becoming everything to me.

“I'm only doing my best to make this a memorable goodbye kiss,” he smirks before his mouth returns to working me into a fit of pleasure and torment.

He successfully winds me tighter and tighter until I'm nothing but a ball of whimpering need.

The orgasm races through me so violently that my body threatens to fall forward off the couch. But he holds me in place as the wave crashes through me, only rising when my body softens in the afterglow.

I was so sure that I came out the winner this morning. In some ways, I did get what I wanted, but he's inexplicably triumphant as he says, “I'm starting to think breakfast is my favorite meal of the day.” I stare transfixed as he sucks his fingers into his mouth. “I hope this is the only reminder you'll need of what's waiting for you when you get home.”

The next two days are about to feel so insufferably long.

30

Lacey

It's just a date. I've gone on dates before. Hell, I was just on a date a few days ago.

And it's not like I don't see him or text him every day. Yet, my heart flutters uncomfortably as I adjust my corseted velvet top in the mirror. Everything feels too tight against my skin, making me want to rip it all off and crawl into bed. Why do we need to go on a date in the first place? It's not like it will really change anything.

A soft knock at my door pulls me from the spiral of anxiety.

"Hey, I'm going to pull around front. Come down whenever you're ready." His low rumble flows through the wood dividing us and settles my nerves.

"I can still drive, you know." I was almost depending on it. It would give me a clue of where we were going and take away some of the mystery. I've never seen him drive, I was starting to think he didn't have a car.

"I know you can, but I'm doing this right. I'm picking you up for our first date. You can trust me." There's a slight pause, making me think he's walked away. "I can't wait to see you."

I can't wait to see you, too. It's what I wanted to say, but I hear his footsteps fade away as my heart still wages war inside my body. Doubts and nerves whirl all around me.

It's just a date. Just a date. I repeat over and over again.

I do a final check in the mirror, running my fingers through the soft curls cascading across my shoulders, then nervously tugging at my outfit one last time. The scarlet top and wide-leg trousers that have lived unworn in my closet up until tonight—until I snuck up to my apartment once I landed to drop off a few things and pick up an outfit.

Being able to slip into the same thing every day has been a comfort, but tonight is different. Tonight, I care about the man waiting for me outside. I want to be who I've become around him, and I'm starting to think that outweighs the fear.

Finally, taking a deep breath, I turn to the door.

"Do you know the difference in the likelihood of death by motorcycle crash versus shark attack?" The words slip from me the moment I step out of the lobby. So, maybe Drew doesn't own a car after all.

He's standing beside a sleek, black motorcycle with that cocky grin that makes me want to drag him back up the stairs and convince him that dinner can wait."You scared, *sconosciuta*?"

"No, but I thought you'd be."

I watch as his gaze devours me. We've seen each other in so many different moments, naked, raw, bare, but this is different. We're becoming something new, and I feel it as he takes in every inch of me.

"God, you look devastating. I could stay here all night just looking at you." He holds his hand out to me, and I take it, allowing him to pull me towards him as I let out a girlish giggle that I don't completely hate.

I stop inches away from him, breathing in the spicy scent of his cologne. I don't even try to conceal the smile splitting my face when I ask, "Are you finally going to kiss me properly, or are you going to make me wait until after dessert?"

"It would be criminal to make you wait any longer," he says as his nose brushes against mine, teasing me in the way only he can.

I press up and close the distance between us, his lips finding their place against mine. His hand splays across the small of my back, pulling me into him. Kissing him softly, unhurriedly is a balm to my soul.

I'm not proud of the whimper that escapes as he pulls away. It was too short, just a taste of something perfect.

"Do we have to go? We could go upstairs and order in. I know we'd have plenty of fun," I say because it's honestly a waste that we haven't been doing that this entire time.

He tucks a strand of hair behind my ear and says, "We have time. We don't need to rush this. And don't worry, before the end of tonight, I plan on kissing every inch of you, but we need to get to dinner to make sure we have the energy for it." My skin prickles in anticipation.

"Promise?"

"Promise."

He hands me an extra helmet and leather jacket. I pull them on before sliding on the bike and wrapping my arms around his waist.

As the world rushes past and stray strands of hair whip around me, I feel free. I feel like this isn't something I have to sink my claws in and pray it doesn't slip away, and it's glorious.

We park and walk to the restaurant with his fingers laced through mine. Before we enter, he leans down and tells me, "I think that's my favorite smile of yours."

"Why's that?"

"Because you look so alive, and I love that I have something to do with it." He raises our hands to his lips and kisses the back of mine before letting go and holding the door open for me.

We walk in, and he leaves our jackets and helmets with an attendant before we follow a host up a flight of stairs to a dimly lit room with walls composed entirely of windows. A single table with a cluster of flickering candles at its center stands by the largest wall of glass.

"What is this?" I whisper, even though we're the only ones here.

"I didn't want to share you with anyone else tonight," he explains before kissing the top of my head.

I think I got so used to the penthouse and how he never seemed to need to be anywhere that I forgot that those aren't normal. That he's still a mystery. Well, I guess not for much longer.

He pulls out the chair for me before taking his place on the other side. I look for a menu, but there's nothing there.

I must look confused because he answers my silent question, "I asked for a tasting menu. This place is one of my favorites and one of the few places my parents let me take them because it has some of the only food my mother admits is better than anything she can make. I hope you don't mind."

"Honestly, I hate choosing something at restaurants," I admit, and a weight lifts from my shoulders. "Your mom, she's the one that taught you to cook, right?" And just like that, we're plunging into the personal things that we've been pushing to the side. These things never seemed to matter before, but I'm realizing there are so many things I still don't know.

"Yeah, she tried to teach my sister too, but I swear whatever Evelyn touches is poison. I don't know how she does it, but I guess cooking isn't genetic."

"So she's just as talented as I am?"

"Oh, she'd make you look like a Michelin Star chef." We chuckle. It's just us sharing a laugh together, and it feels good. "But she has plenty of other talents. What about your family?" he asks, shifting the focus back to me. His question is simple yet sincere.

I swallow, feeling the question settling heavily in the air. This conversation was inevitable. I just didn't expect it to happen within the first ten minutes. The waiter arrives, pouring our wine before I can push past the lump in my throat.

Drew's hand reaches across the table, finding mine, and his touch sends comforting warmth through me. "You don't have to tell me if you don't want to. Just because I'm comfortable sharing about my family doesn't mean I expect anything from you," Drew says, his voice gentle yet firm, echoing his genuine concern and understanding. Reassuring me that I'm not alone in this, that I don't have to face my past alone.

"I want to. It's just . . . I've never talked about it with someone new. It's weird to find the words when I do my best to never use them." And it's true.

Usually, the grief that I've become so accustomed to hangs over me like a thin coat. But it has been less present in the last few months, and I'm not sure how to feel about that. It's been nearly two and half years now, but not thinking about my mother every day feels almost like a betrayal. Still, I want to tell him about her. I want to tell him about the good parts, and maybe even though she won't be able to meet him, I can find a way of letting him know her through my memories.

"I don't really know my dad," I start and reality presses down as I glance at his hand, still holding mine, "And my mother died a little over two years ago. It was a car accident." It was one of those freak accidents that occur on rainy, dark nights, with a broken lamppost lurking in the shadows. There was no one to blame, no one to be angry at. At times, I'm not sure if that makes it better or worse. The randomness always has me asking, *why her? It could have been anyone, so why did it have to be her when she was the best person I knew?*

He squeezes my hand and waits a beat, his eyes filled with empathy. "Tell me about her?"

"She had so much love in her. Like she would always be the first person to offer to help someone or make life easier if she could, even when it would be inconvenient. She was as good a cook as I am, so we'd always have take-out nights and watch *Jeopardy!*, even though neither of us were good at trivia. Not because she wasn't smart, though. She just thought there were better things to learn about the world than a bunch of facts. I think she'd like you," I say, and it's not a lie or delusional hope. My mom loved those who care deeply about things.

And I don't know for sure, but I think it's what drew her to Martin. His desire to create.

I think she would have seen the little things in Drew—cooking and waiting up for me on late nights, buying a damn couch because I complained about the one he already had. I think she would have liked to know that someone has been taking care of me as intently as he has.

As the small plates move on and off the table, I learn more snippets about Drew, filling in gaps I didn't even know were there. He tells me about growing up in Tennessee and how he didn't do much except play music in high school, making a point that it was in the nerdy way that ensured he had very few social skills until his twenties.

It's hard to imagine that version of him, but I savor every detail, like the decadent bites in front of us. We go back and forth, trading stories, such as recounting my days playing soccer and how, at twelve, I was confidently convinced I would become a professional athlete.

When my hair keeps falling in my face, he pulls out a hair tie and hands it to me.

"Where did this come from?" I ask as I pull the strands into a ponytail. I had forgotten how inconvenient my hair can get.

He shrugs. "I always have them on me in case yours breaks." I raise an eyebrow, and he continues, "My sister's used to snap all the time. I've literally been shot in the eye by one when I was standing too close. I know how you like your hair. I will say it looks good down too."

"Maybe I'll leave it down more often then."

"I'd like that, but please don't change just for my sake."

I look up at Drew as we stroll down the sidewalk to where we parked. The warm light of the street lamps catches the gold flecks in his eyes, giving the impression of fireflies dancing through a forest. I drink in his serene expression and lace my fingers through his, swinging our arms between us.

Tonight is exactly what it needs to be.

That's until I hear a voice a few feet behind us. And when I hear it again, I know he's headed our way.

Henry.

Of course, out of all the men, it had to be him. Price would never have said it, but I know my work suffered when I was with Henry. That he scattered me because I was so desperate to be the person he wanted. But I couldn't trim myself down no matter how hard I tried.

Only with Drew have I ever successfully given up a slice on the vice grip I've had over my life. From that first night, it's been different.

Hearing Henry now, I have an old familiar desire to shrink away, crawling beneath my skin.

I panic, and I push Drew against a nearby wall and kiss him, hoping that it will hide my face and I can avoid the encounter. It's nothing I haven't been wanting to do anyway.

I sink into Drew, letting my knee scrape up against the rough bricks of the wall as I curl my leg around his. His arm bands around my waist, gluing me to him.

Getting lost in the taste of him is so completely intoxicating. I feel nothing and everything at once. The light movements of his thumb on my hip bone. The way the soft waves of his hair feel between my fingers.

I'm so distracted by Drew that I forget the actual reason for the kiss until I hear someone clear their throat behind us. Maybe it was optimistic to hope that even if Henry saw me, he would be swayed by the tree of a man I've wrapped myself around.

"Lace?" My name breaks the spell, floating to me in a familiar drawl. I inhale and brace myself as I turn to where Henry awaits my attention.

"Henry," I say, resisting the urge to touch my lips, where I still feel the ghost of the kiss.

I smile slightly, taking pleasure in how, next to Drew, Henry is so small. It's not like he's not a fit guy. In fact, he has such a dazzling presence that it usually takes up whatever room he's in. But somehow, Drew sucks away all of that energy, leaving Henry powerless in a way that sends a low hum through me.

If Drew can casually call up people to make meals like we just had, I doubt he's intimidated by Henry the glorified Show Pony. As Henry's jaw ticks in irritation, I can tell that he sees it, too, and absolutely despises it.

Good.

I shift into Drew a little more, finally noticing the girl.

It's as though Henry took every adjective he told me I wasn't and went off and found them all in one person. She looks soft, sweet, and relaxed against his side, a delicate vision in her pastel dress.

The only part that doesn't quite fit is the confused stare that contorts her face when she takes in Drew. It's like she can't quite place him, and it's itching the back of her brain.

31

Drew

Feeling her crash against me with such urgency and need is unexpected, but I love it. Her hands pull me down to her, demanding all of me. How she grabs my shirt feels like I'm the only thing anchoring her to reality. I've written songs about how a kiss can make you feel starlight, but that was before her. Kissing Lacey makes the stars feel dim in comparison.

Tonight has been perfect.

And once we get through this first perfect day, I plan on telling her everything. There's a lingering fear of what my past might change, but if there's one person in this world who won't look at me any differently, it's her.

"Lace?" A male voice rips me from my bliss.

"Henry." Lacey smiles as she says his name, the grin stretching her face. This is a cartoon, plastic version of the joy that is the constant hum I associate with Lacey. I turn from her and take in the man.

He's well-groomed and crisp in an oily way. I turn slightly to Lacey, but her attention is fixated on the arm he has draped around the gorgeous woman pinned to his side. The woman looks like he found her on a laundry detergent ad set where the woman is frolicking in the field.

All I can concentrate on is the scrutinizing gaze the woman fixes on me, causing a ripple of unease.

"You look good," Henry says. His attention isn't on Lacey, though; it's found its way up to me. Lost in his own facade, he doesn't seem to recognize me. He's probably the insecure type who made fun of his high school girlfriend for listening to our music because he was jealous he wasn't the only object of her affection. So, as I tower over him, I relish the moment.

"This is Drew," she says, placing a hand on my chest. The thought crashes into my head.

This is who the kiss was for.

She didn't plan on sweeping me off my feet in the middle of the sidewalk just because. It was all for *his* benefit.

The idea has every muscle in my body going taut. I know it's not the same as what happened with Wes. But the feeling of being used for some other man's benefit twists something deep in me.

"It's good to meet you, *Drew*. I hope you're taking good care of her." He gives me a conspiratorial wink. What an ass, talking about her like he has any claim.

"Who couldn't take care of a girl like her." I brush my thumb across her jaw. I can be possessive, too. I hate the subtext of being used like this, but I'll play out the scene. "Living with her for two months now."

"Lacey can be exhausting to live with, am I right?" His words echo, calling back the memory of the night when this all started. Not the one where we fucked and wanted to be forgotten. The one where we realized we both needed shelter.

I hate that he might have experienced similar moments with her—her mornings, those tender, intimate times, the moments when she lets her guard down and shows her softer side—the ones I prefer to believe are exclusively mine.

"It's completely the opposite. She gives me a reason to wake up each morning." I keep my tone pleasant and even as I continue, "I'd suggest never speaking her name again since you've proven you don't know her well enough to use it properly. Since, anyone who knows her could tell you that she's energizing as hell."

"Well, it sounds like she's finally gotten that stick out of her ass then," he says like it's supposed to be a compliment. Like it's the best thing in the world for her to change.

I feel Lacey start to shake next to me. I look down and don't see even the faintest glimmer of fear.

No, rage radiates off her in waves, her silver eyes glinting like daggers aimed directly at the man determined to make her feel small.

"And it sounds like you still haven't learned how to keep your shitty opinions to yourself." With her words, Lacey moves in front of me, head held high as she stares down her ex. "I'm not above being the one to shut you up. I wonder how those cheap veneers will look after a good punch?"

I can't help the slight smirk on my face. While I'm more than happy to defend her whenever she needs it, watching her tear into him is much more enjoyable.

"You seemed to like those shitty opinions quite a lot. As well as everything else," Henry says, showing me that he's an idiot who just doesn't know when to stop digging his own grave.

"I was pretty good at pretending to like a lot of things." Lacey shifts to direct her attention to the woman plastered to Henry's side. "By the way, his dick is a lot like his personality, disappointing and only gets worse the more you think about it."

I let out a low laugh. "You should probably get going, Henry."

Henry grinds his teeth, irritation evident on his features. But luckily he cuts his losses before Lacey can take another shot at him. "Whatever. We were leaving anyway."

They start to walk away slowly, and relief courses through me. Finally, it seems like we're in the clear to continue with our night, making it my mission to pull Lacey back from the place that encounter with that jerk put her in.

But then, the woman pauses.

And it happens, just as I was warned it would.

Still close, the poor girl adhered to Henry's arm says, "Hey, wasn't that the drummer from that band that was super popular a while ago?" She snaps her fingers, sealing my fate. "Oh, Luca Mariano. Would it be terrible to go and ask for his picture?"

"I don't fucking know. We're going to be late for dinner." They disappear around the corner, leaving us to deal with the fallout of the brief encounter.

Not like this. It isn't supposed to happen like this.

Everything begins to unfold in slow motion as if my brain knows this is the end, even when seconds before, it was only the beginning. So, I try to engrave every feature of her into my memory: the defined dip of her cupid's bow, the graceful curve of her neck, and the strong set of her shoulders.

And I just wait for the dominoes to fall. For everything to shatter. I wait and then . . .

Nothing.

"Well, that was fucking weird," Lacey mutters under her breath. And the world snaps back to normal speed, cars zipping past and pedestrians chattering about everything and nothing.

"Yeah, weird," I agree. The energy around us remains tense as we return to my bike.

The night hasn't been ruined entirely, but it's obvious we're both rattled by the encounter with Henry. Still, even if nothing more happens between us tonight, she's coming home with me—to our home, even if it's only that for a short while longer.

I can feel the stiffness in her posture as she settles behind me for our journey back. The echoes of our carefree laughter seem distant now, fading into the background. But that doesn't matter. I'll be with her through it all, ready to weather whatever storms may come our way.

Once inside the apartment, we both head to our own rooms to change. And even as I shed my clothes, there's still an inexplicable weight on my shoulders.

Now, I have to tell her now.

Tonight was too close for comfort. A glimpse of her walking away is enough to summon the courage to break the remaining barriers and cross that final line.

I step out of my bedroom, ready to find her and confess everything. Yet, there she is, already in the kitchen, her figure illuminated by the eerie glow of her phone. Leaning against the counter, she seems lost in thought.

I steel myself and force a smile. "I want—" I begin, but I'm cut off before I can figure out what to say next.

"I thought I was losing my mind for a moment there. I tried to convince myself it was just a coincidence, something I could solve with a quick Google search." She lets out a small laugh, but I can sense she's retreating behind familiar walls. I try not to look into her eyes, scared of what I'll see. "It had to be a coincidence, right? Because I trust you too much for it to be anything else. But I'm not crazy. You're just a damn liar," she says, thrusting the phone towards me.

My teenage self stares back at me from the screen, and the ground seems to fall away beneath me.

"I was coming to tell you, I swear," I say desperately.

"Were you really? Or were you planning on letting this play out as long as you could," she spits out, venom dripping from her voice.

"I'm sorry. I swear I was going to tell you everything." When I finally dare to meet her eyes, there's no gleam of hunger, no new expectation.

No, it's worse.

Her eyes are a muddle of hurt and confusion. They look like a storm is brewing. A storm *I* caused.

"Lacey, listen to me. It's true. Please, if you think I care for you at all, know that it's true. You know me—the real me," I plead, pointing to her phone. "That's just a name. It doesn't matter," I say because I know it's true. I just hope she can see it too through her anger.

"Of course, it matters. You hid this from me!"

"You agreed to this as much as I did. I have my shit, and you have yours. If you really want to do this, to be with me, this doesn't change anything. It doesn't have to." I point to the list. The list that she drafted herself.

"It changes everything!"

"Why! I don't understand. Is it because of Henry? Are you scared and just trying to push me away? Is this just an excuse? Because I'm not him." My voice rises with desperation and frustration with every word.

"Because I'm Martin Hall's daughter!" she yells as if broadcasting it to the entire world.

"What?" I manage to utter, but suddenly, I'm not in the room anymore, not even in the apartment. I'm standing in the grocery store checkout line with my mother, scanning glossy tabloid covers for anything to break my boredom.

My mind struggles to reconcile the faceless child with the grown woman standing in front of me.

A child who never really knew Martin because he was always with us when we needed him. Lacey is so much younger than me when I think about it. When I was eighteen, trying my hardest not to drop a drumstick on stage during a last-minute, dumb trick, she was probably at her first soccer game. I had all the milestones with the man that was supposed to be there for her.

Now all I can think is, at least I had the chance to kiss her one last time. Because this woman must fucking hate me for what I inadvertently put her through, what I put her mother through.

I look at her, the faint moonlight filtering into the apartment, allowing me to see the silent tears streaming from her eyes.

"If I had told you. If you found out from me and not like this, would you feel any different?" I ask.

"Guess we'll never know," she says, her words cutting the way she intended. "Maybe this is how it was always going to end. Maybe we just don't know each other well enough for this to work." With a sigh, she strides towards her room, and I follow.

This can't be how we leave things. This can't be how we leave us.

"Like hell, we don't know each other. Lacey, you don't just live with someone for two months and not get to know them." My voice cracks, words catching in the back of my throat.

"What's really stopping us from just going back to the way things were at the beginning of the night?"

"I don't know. Common sense. All known laws of reality." She flips her suitcase onto the bed and moves towards the dresser.

"Lacey, what's between us is so good. We don't have to lose it over this. Let's just talk it out," I beg, and I don't give a fuck if she can hear how weak I am for her.

"There's nothing between us to lose. We've been out in the real world for what? A few hours. This isn't going to happen. It's not supposed to be us." Her voice splinters and I'll be damned if I believe her, even as she efficiently moves from the drawers to her suitcase. Each stack of neatly folded clothes feels like a punch to my gut.

"Give me a chance."

"You had your chances. Every. Damn. Day. But times up, and you've lost your right to explain." She's right. I was warned, and I made my choice. She finally turns to face me and halts her painful progression. It's only then, as she stands still, that I notice she's trembling, her chest heaving as she works to breathe.

"It wasn't like that." I grind my teeth, trying to keep calm and not let my frustration take over. This is a mess we made together, and I try not to fixate on that, because it's obvious this is hitting us differently. For me, Lacey learning my identity is the equivalent of splashing around in the mud--for her, it's a wrecking ball demolishing a glass house.

"Then what was it like? You had fun thinking I was some idiot who couldn't see the obvious. I bet you and Craig had a good laugh every time I proved how gullible I was." Her hand goes to her chest as if to steady her heart, and she wobbles. I rush to catch her as her legs give out. We sit in a heap on her floor, with her on my lap.

No matter how much she might want to, she doesn't push me away. I hold her close and softly whisper, "Breathe with me." I reach out to caress her cheek. "Just breathe with me."

But she stops my hand with a gentle touch as she says, "I need to go home."

"You are home," I remind her, pleading.

"No. *My* home."

"What do you mean?"

"My apartment. It's been ready for over a week." Her voice trembles. "I'm not staying," she says, still shaking in my arms.

I force my next words out, even though they feel like I'm driving a knife through my own chest. "You stay here, and I'll pack your stuff. Then I'll drive your car to your place because there's no way in hell I'm letting you behind the wheel right now." I don't want to say what will happen after that, but I have to. If I don't speak the words, I doubt I'll hold myself to it. "Then I'll let you go, but only once I know you're safe. I'll let you go if that's what you want."

I do just as promised. Slowly, her breathing returns to a regular pattern as I gather the bottles from her bathroom and the laptop from her desk, each item erasing another trace of her. If watching her pack hurts, doing it for her is excruciating.

Leaving her for a moment to clean and dry her coffee pot, I try to distract myself, but the silence of the apartment is deafening. All I can focus on is how the counter immediately looks wrong without it, knowing she won't be there sipping her foul coffee, and the couch where we used to watch those horror movies together just to see her smile.

Finally, the sound of the last zipper closing seals my fate.

No words pass between us as I carry her bags to her car, with her trailing behind me. Just before she hands over her car keys, she unhooks the electronic fob and key to my apartment. She hesitates, her fingers lingering as she hands them to me.

"You can keep them, just in case," I offer softly because if she holds onto them, there's a chance she might return—a chance to find her sitting on the kitchen counter or curled up on the couch. But if I take them that's the end.

"I promise I won't need them." She presses them into my palm and then hands over her car keys.

We slide into our seats, the silence between us heavy as neither of us bothers to turn on the radio. The jumble of traffic and blaring horns fill the space, serving as the backing track to our last moments together.

No matter how much I wish she would stay, even if I took the longest route possible, it wouldn't change the inevitable.

Slowing down, I park in the garage and then walk her to the entrance, stopping a few paces away.

"Was the kiss for him or for me?" The question slips out, and maybe knowing will only hurt more, but I have to know. What's one more twist of the knife?

Her brows pinch together as if she's considering sparing me from the truth, but she gives in and says, "It was because of him. But the moment you touched me, you were the only person that mattered."

With the specter of her words hanging in the air, she turns and walks away, leaving me standing there. I just watch and silently plead.

Look back. Look back.

I could run after her, I could beg, but she's already established that the handful of months between us is nothing compared to the years of hurt she has built up inside her.

She hesitates as her hand brushes the door handle, and for a moment, my heart skips a beat.

Look back.

But she doesn't. Really, what else should I have expected? It's so like her to keep moving forward.

It's tempting to go to Half a Memory and drown my sorrows, but that would feel like backtracking, betraying the person she's helped me find within myself. Instead, I go back to the apartment. My apartment, just mine.

Moving through the space, I see our list on the fridge and find the two first names that committed us to this mess—well, her name and my lie.

I leave it there because, if nothing else, it's a reminder she was here, proof that she wasn't just a figment of my imagination. Instead of heading to my room for some semblance of peace through sleep, I find myself standing in front of her door, unsure what to do next.

Walking inside, I find that one of the drawers in her dresser is still pulled open. As I move to close it, my eye catches on a piece of paper—no, not a piece of paper—an envelope with Lacey's name written in unfamiliar handwriting.

Without a second thought, I'm out the door, rushing back to her—to her apartment.

Standing outside her door, poised to knock, I hear her speak from the other side. "I think I might hate him."

All the fight drains from my body as I lower my hand and gently place the envelope on her welcome mat.

32

Lacey

There was always something odd about not being able to talk about which band member I was deeply in love with and was convinced would notice me if I just could be in the front row at their concert.

It was an age-appropriate fantasy. Something I was supposed to hold onto with the determination of a child clinging to the Tooth Fairy or Santa Clause, that yes, a fourteen-year-old on the verge of needing braces was about to catch the eye of one of America's most loved and desired heartthrobs, all of which were at least twenty, but of course, the dreams seemed to always ignore the wildly inappropriate age gap.

It's hard to think of imaginary and improbable popstar boyfriends when your always-smiling mother starts to tear up listening to even their most upbeat songs. The ones that should have been as cheerful as images of puppies and sunshine. Or when she slumps on the couch, not even making it to her bed because her feet hurt from a twelve-hour shift that was supposed to be a ten-hour shift in the ER. Or when you burn yourself trying and failing to make spaghetti from a jarred sauce, then hiding said burn so your mom doesn't have to take care of yet another injury that day.

It's hard to stay young and delusional when everyone else's sparkling escape is what's dragging down the only family you have.

So, it feels like a betrayal to the story I wear close to my heart, to everything I am, to feel anything but disgust towards the man I just left outside my apartment.

The man that's made me feel so acutely aware that I was alive with a single kiss.

I pick up the phone, and Cara immediately answers. I had told her about the date, and she's been on standby for updates, a little cocky about her matchmaking meddling.

"God. I feel so stupid. I think I hate him."

"That's one way to start a conversation. So, I take it you didn't make sweet love to your hot roommate."

"Shit. Drew, I mean Luca. Fuck, I don't know. I just don't know," I mutter, my voice thick with tears and frustration as I sink down the wall until I'm seated on the floor right inside the entryway. I used to like the empty, impersonal feeling of my apartment—the one place I could be completely alone, a blank canvas without any expectations. But now, it feels hollow.

I had gotten used to being welcomed home, to the warmth that came with returning to someone. There was a comfort in sharing space with someone, especially *him*. The apartment we shared only had a few more decorations and personal touches than mine, but it wasn't the decor that made the difference. It was us.

"So you finally figured it out?" I hear whatever show she's watching on the other end of the line turn off, giving me her full attention.

"You knew. Since when?" Her confession adds another layer to the confusion swirling in my mind. I struggle to process it all, unsure if I can even summon the energy to be angry.

"Since I found one of the biggest popstars of our generation in your apartment behind the set of drums he's literally known for playing."

"So, I'm stupid." Yes, every context clue was there, and I didn't pick up on it. Maybe his lie started this, but I was the one too blind to see through it.

"No, you're not. You literally had the band blocked on your search engine. Out of pretty much any person on the planet, you are the one person that I would expect *not* to be able to pick him out of a lineup. Also, he looks different than he did. Better, honestly."

"Why didn't you say anything?" I snap, the frustration bubbling up inside me. I'm torn between needing her and wanting to make this her fault. She had the power to stop it, to prevent me from being a fool, but she chose silence.

She kept his secret, and now there's a painful ache in my chest that won't stop. I just want it to stop.

"Because you looked happy. Like genuinely fucking happy. I haven't seen you look that way in two years. You never put on a face or did that thing where you try and tuck yourself into the corner." She sighs, collecting her words. "I went back and forth cause you know the shit with your dad, but I just couldn't. And would you have wanted to learn that way?" I can hear a slight tremor in her voice, as if this has genuinely been eating her up.

"No. But I would have rather found out from you than all by myself." If she did, maybe my heart wouldn't be hurting so much right now. "Is that happiness worth anything if I can't trust any of you?"

"Lace, if we left you to find your own happiness, you'd never let anyone in. You'd just be stuck in that same cycle of working yourself into oblivion." Her volume raises to match mine.

"Maybe I would, but at least it would be my choice!"

"And you made the choice not to tell each other your names. Maybe you should hear him out."

"Why aren't you on my side? I need you to be on my side!" My voice cracks as I realize that's the real reason that I called. Not to tell her what happened or for any type of pity.

I just need someone to unconditionally be in my corner. If it was three years ago, I know who I would have called, but she's not an option anymore, and that knowledge pierces through me. I've gone through breakups before, but they rolled off my back. I never had the urge to crawl into someone's arms and cry over a boy.

But here I am, an absolute mess, sitting on the floor and just wanting my mom. I want her to stroke my hair and tell me it will be ok, that she's got me no matter what. I want to fall apart and not worry about picking up the pieces because she would take care of it. And I know I'm asking Cara to do the impossible, but I can't help it. I just—

"I am on your side," she stresses. "But it seems like you're the one holding yourself back from what you deserve. Why can't you just let yourself have something good for once?"

"No, you don't get to decide this for me," I spit out. "I'm not asking you to solve this for me. I just need you to be here for me. To tell me I'm right to feel like this. That it sucks, and he messed up, and that I should burn his damn hoodie." The hoodie that I'm still wearing. The hoodie that I don't want to burn at all. "I just want to hate him right now, and I need you to hate him too."

"Lace, I'm just having a hard time. It's a weird situation."

"*Oh, you're having a hard time?* I'm so sorry. Did the man you've been living with for the last few months reveal he's been lying to you the entire time? Then the cherry on top, you learn that he used to work with your piece of shit dad. Oh, and how could I forget? Then your best friend meets the guy once, and that's enough for her to think he deserves a second chance." I'm fuming now. I wouldn't be surprised if my neighbors could hear every word. I don't even care at this point.

"I shouldn't have said it that way. I'm sorry," Cara pleads, her tone softening as if trying to calm a wild animal on the verge of a rampage.

"Well, maybe I should go before you say something else you shouldn't."

"Please—"

I hang up before she can finish. I didn't think it was possible, but I feel worse than I did at the start of the conversation.

I remain on the floor and start flicking through my phone, which is a mistake because I never closed the browser tab with my 'Luca Mariano' search. My finger hovers over a link to an all-about Fool's Gambit page. I give in and am swept to a site with more information than I'll probably ever need. Ignorance has brought me nothing but pain. It's better to be armed with knowledge now that I'm in the thick of this mess.

I see facts I learned earlier tonight, like that he grew up just outside Nashville, but also that he went to high school with all of the band members, and was severely blessed by late puberty that transformed him entirely.

Then I click the first video link, and honestly, I get it. I understand now why the girls would nearly swoon in the halls when they talked about Fool's Gambit. Each of them is magnetic, even on the tiny screen.

As I click the next one, I'm hit with the feeling that the man I know and the one who I see on the stage really are two different people. It's not just that he's older. There's a quality present in the younger version of him that isn't quite there anymore. I see glimpses of it while he practices, but he's different now, heavier, and not just because he's definitely hit the gym since his performing days.

Drew feels far more real than the person in the videos—more real than Luca Mariano, the part of him he hid from me.

In the videos, Luca is never really the focus. He's off to the side, usually with Wesley or Garrett at the center, but my eyes always lock onto him.

When I picked up on the snippets about people's favorite band members, it was rare to hear them talk about Luca as if he wasn't worth being their celebrity crush. Well, they were dead wrong.

The others look completely in control, charismatic, and connected to the audience. But not him. He's lost in the music as if it's about to lift him up and carry him away. What I would pay to go back and take a picture of him as he appears so enthralled by the act of performing, being consumed by his own ability to create something so wonderful.

At the end of one song, his head tips back, sweat dripping from his brow, plastering his grown-out dark waves to his forehead. His eyes closed, with a feral, unrestrained smile on his mouth. I would guess that at that moment, the crowd full of cheering fans, the knowledge of a sold-out show, and the state-of-the-art equipment didn't matter. He would have done it all the same if the stage was just a raised platform in a dive bar with no audience at all.

It feels criminal that he ever stopped.

It makes me wonder why. Someone who loves something as much as he appears to love music doesn't just stop. Even the thought of having to stop working with the team and giving up that rush, makes me sick.

I click on one last video, "Fool's Fall—Luca's Last Performance," and it feels like I've found the missing piece to a puzzle I didn't even know I was trying to solve.

He is on stage, just like in the other clips, but something is off. Despite the vibrant lights and fans cheering, he's pale instead of luminescent. As he starts to rise to join the rest of the band members at the front of the stage, he stumbles, his movements unsteady, before collapsing to the ground. His head hits the stage floor as the fans gasp in shock, their cheers turning to worried murmurs. It takes excruciatingly long moments for the others on the stage to register what's happening before, finally, two burly men whisk him away just as the next song starts without him.

I remember the first time I found him with his drums, frozen in shock, still and unsure. That image doesn't match what I've been watching with so much intensity. I want to find who or what took away that glow of passion. I want to punish whoever dimmed his light.

But most of all, I want to hold him like I did in the shower all those weeks ago and tell him I think I finally do know. I would be shattered, too, if I lost some touch with my purpose on this earth.

With a sigh, I open my messages to finally read the text he sent during my call with Cara. Even when I push him away, he still manages to take care of me before his own feelings.

He's made it clear that the decision to go back is mine, yet I wish someone could help me figure it out.

Standing up, I feel torn between two realities: the one I grew up believing and the one I desperately hope to be true. How do I love someone my father helped build without betraying my mother? Without betraying the little girl who still lives so deeply in my soul and never wanted to admit that she felt like something had been stolen from her.

I look down, re-reading the text as I open the front door.

Luca

I found your letter. It's just outside your door.

I didn't even realize I had forgotten it. It seems to be happening a lot lately. I go to pick it up, my head turning left and right, a small part of me hoping he is there. But he isn't.

I'll let you go if that's what you want.

His words run through my mind, reminding me that there will be no chase.

I'm alone and it's my fault.

33

Lacey

November 20th

Luca

I know we're not talking, but can you still text me when you're safe? I swear, each time I see a plane, I hope it's you coming home and that you're ok.

November 22nd

Luca

Please.

It's been a conscious effort not to automatically check in. Each time the plane lands, I pull out my phone, ready to type, and then shove it back into my pocket before I read too many of our old texts that I can't seem to delete.

"You're fucking kidding me." Tessa's shrill voice pulls me from staring at the texts. Tessa is standing relatively far from everyone, but her words stop all action on and off the ice. The pregame warm-up comes to a complete halt as everyone's eyes lock onto the drama brewing.

She stalks towards me with an agitated gleam in her eye. I stand my ground because it's just Tessa, even if she almost broke the sound barrier.

"You said you couldn't get me tickets. Was that just a lie, or do you actually hate me?" She stands directly in front of me, and I can't quite interpret the anger coming off her in waves.

I feel all eyes on us as I say, "Tessa, I can't." I didn't ask, but it's not like I have the ability to just ask for tickets.

"Bullshit." She thrusts her phone into my face, forcing me to stare at the image.

It's a familiar scene—one that I flash back to with so much regularity that it leaks into my dreams. Drew, or should I say Luca, is positioned in front of me, yelling at Henry. A bold headline streaks across the top of the page: "Drummer Luca Mariano Spotted Sparring with Sports Commentator." It's strange to see how some events in my life can be boiled down into a headline when viewed from an outsider's perspective.

"I—"

"It's you, right? Why did you say you couldn't when you're literally dating a member of the band?"

"I'm not dating him," I say, each syllable forcing me to taste the bitter truth.

A knock on the glass directs our attention away from each other. "Tess." Price saves me with his smiling, non-confrontational face. "Can you come catch a video of a trick shot for us? Aaron won't shut up until you do. It would be a big help."

The question successfully draws her focus because she snatches the phone from me and scrambles on the ice. Price mouths *later* to me as he makes his way back to his place in the goal.

Thank God for Price.

I slump onto one of the bleachers, processing the event that just unfolded. Did that same person see the rest of what happened that night? I don't think I can conceptualize it if they did. I've always hated people taking pictures of me and controlling what they get to see about me, and this only pushes that button. There's no manual for this, no *How to Deal With Finding Out Your Roommate is Famous* I can comb through for the answers.

I guess a benefit of it all is that I get a glimpse of what my mother went through and how her privacy was thrown aside for a good story. But she's not here to ask how to handle this. If she was, I might understand what to do and how to process feeling violated this way.

It's good that I'm finding out about the picture here. Being here gives me a reason not to let loose every rogue emotion fighting for acknowledgment. I remind myself of this and get up, refocusing on why I'm here.

I lift my camera from where it's hanging around my neck and make my way to the perimeter of the rink, not venturing onto the ice because I don't trust my legs to remain stable on the slick surface, despite knowing that means missing out on superior shots.

Granted, my pictures haven't been the same these last couple of weeks. Each time I flip through what's stored on my SD card at the end of the day, I end up frustrated. Technically, they're all usable and fine, but fine is a failure compared to what I'm used to. And because there's no one there to take away my laptop or tell me not to work, I've fallen asleep with my open laptop next to me more than once.

The situation with Drew isn't the only reason I'm on edge today, though. We're in Phoenix for today's game. I haven't been here since last summer when I cleared out and sold my mother's house. Since I found the damn letters. Price has invited me back a few times to stay with his family, but it wouldn't be the same. I nearly asked someone else to travel for this game, but the thought of someone taking my spot with Price in our city made me sick.

"You ready?" Price asks, his tone somber as he starts the rental car.

"Probably not, but I need to do this."

He nods and merges onto the familiar streets of Phoenix.

As we slow down in the suburbs of Mesa, my heart rate accelerates. We pass the turnoff to the cemetery, and a few minutes later, we turn onto a cul-de-sac lined with worn stucco homes. The yards are covered in red-hued rock and speckled with cacti and yucca.

I haven't visited my mother's grave since the funeral. It feels wrong now to go somewhere that I only knew her in death. Even though the house isn't ours anymore. Looking towards it now, I can still picture her walking to the end of the driveway, waving goodbye every morning before I went to school. She would stand there, hair pulled into a messy bun, scrubs on from the night before.

For so long, I've been fine with living on my own. There wasn't any major shift after she was gone. My routine was the same in Atlanta before and after the accident.

I would wake up, go to work, go home, and repeat it the next day and then the next. I fell into the cycle like a lifeline, feeding off adrenaline because it forced me into the moment. And it didn't matter; I was perfectly fine following the routine. Until I forgot how good it felt to wake up and share coffee with someone. And now that it's gone, I realize that old routine was never enough. I wasn't living. I was just surviving.

"Thanks for bringing me here," I tell Price, breaking the silence.

"Always. I'll always be here."

"I know," I say as guilt trickles in. "And I'm sorry."

"For what?"

"That sometimes I forget that you're here."

I've been giving more time to those who are gone in one way or another than those who have stuck by me. They've been there every step of the way, even when I turned down invitation after invitation. Even when I pushed and ran, they showed up like stubborn, loving weeds.

I've been looking at the love in my life as something that would always become past tense when it's been around me the entire time, unwavering and unconditional.

"Lacey, it's easier to remember the people who are gone than those who are here," he says, his tone soft but firm. "And no matter what, I'm here. So is Cara." I flinch slightly at her name. She's called every night for the last three days. It's not like I don't want to pick it up. It's just that I don't know what I'd say. "But sometimes, I really hope that you find someone else."

"Getting tired of taking care of me?" I huff a laugh.

"No, I—that's not what I mean. You deserve to find something more than just us. I know I can always count on you, but with Mari, I'm more myself than I ever thought possible. If everything else slipped away, I know I'd be ok if I had her."

"I don't think I deserve that."

"You don't mean that."

"I do. I really do. I was so close. So close, and then it broke. I shattered it into a million pieces." I stare at my hands. I destroyed something precious between Drew and me; the act felt like smashing a vase out of misplaced anger. Even if I try to fix it, there would still be cracks and fissures, reminding me we can't be the same again.

"If he's the right person, he'll have no problem picking up the pieces with you."

I snort. "God, you should really try to write poetry with all your platitudes. Maybe write a Hallmark movie or two."

"I'm serious. What's stopping you from going back?"

I lean back against the headrest, closing my eyes, realizing that my next words hold a truth I've avoided for years. "Because I left. Because I was so scared that history was about to repeat itself, so I left. I didn't want to go through the same pain she did. But instead, I became just like Martin and walked away."

"You can't be serious right now," Price says, incredulous. "He left and never looked back. No matter how much you believe it, you're not your parents. You watched them implode, and you survived it." He turns his gaze to me. "Do you want to have that same ending?"

I remain silent, shaking my head slightly.

"Then, go back. Maybe not tomorrow or next week, but if you want to be that happy again, you can claim it for yourself."

"How long have you been waiting to say all that?"

"I've been saving it up for months. Mari caught me practicing it in the mirror a few times." He smiles at his own joke.

"Thank you. I needed to hear it," I say, though I'm not sure how I'm going to untangle the Gordian Knot pulling tighter in my gut.

We sit in the car, trading memories until the sun starts to paint the horizon. Just before we leave, I go outside and snatch a rock from the house that's no longer mine and tuck it into my pocket so I can carry something with me even if I never come back. I give a silent goodbye, my heart full of I love you's

I never had the chance to say. As Price starts the car and we drive down the street, I look in the rearview mirror and can almost see her there with the smile that lets me know it will be ok.

We arrive at the car rental agency right on time to meet the team for our flight home. No doubt both of us will be catching up on sleep for the entire trip.

"Have you figured out what you're doing about the reunion?" he asks as we start making our way to our flight. I already told him I was going months ago. So, why would that change?

"What do you mean?"

"Are you still going? I mean, it's like going to a party for your ex-almost-more-than-a-roommate."

My brain is still struggling to reconcile Drew with Luca. No matter how hard I try, I can never see them as the same person—one used to be mine, and one is a stranger.

I sigh. "Shit. I don't know. Maybe I'll walk in, drop off the letter, and leave?"

"Lace, if that's all you wanted to do, you should just mail the damn thing."

"I haven't really thought about it. Haven't really wanted to. It should be a big party. I'll probably have no problem avoiding him—them. I don't know." Trust me, the irony isn't lost on me that the person I was hiding away with is becoming another person I plan on hiding from.

"I'm still not above going as your plus one. Though I think Tessa would murder us both if I did."

"Like going to one of the biggest parties of the year would be a complete chore," I joke, holding open the exit door. "I appreciate it, but this is still something I have to do on my own."

"As long as you're sure."

"I am, but I also—I mean, I don't just want to invite myself. But I miss you and Mari," I say, stumbling over my words.

"God, don't kill yourself over something you don't have to ask for." He rolls his eyes, but I don't miss how his eyes crinkle around the edges. "But now that you've asked, just know that it's baby prep all the time."

"Too bad your kid is going to miss out on the best godmother ever."

Price grins. "Who knows. We might be reconsidering the applicants."

34

Drew

My world is muted, and not just because of my earplugs.

Each of my movements are robotic as I go through the motions of practicing. I've run through the setlist three times since I've sat down. It's not the first time in the last week that I've spent hours playing until my arms protest due to overuse.

Still, it's better to play than to stare at my phone, willing Lacey to respond or, worse, drafting essay-long texts explaining myself.

If she wanted to talk, she would.

After the first week, I bought the same damn off-brand coffee maker Lacey uses, thinking if she ever needs it, it will be there. Like she'll just walk through the door one day.

It's more for me. Going mornings without the smell of her burnt coffee and instrumental jazz would just be wrong. She has fundamentally rewritten the way I know how to live, making getting over her a complete impossibility.

So, now I make a cup of that same coffee each morning and choke it down. If I wanted to escape the memories, I could have moved back into the loft above the bar, but I kept giving myself reasons to stay.

One day, I went as far as calling a realtor to look into selling the place so that I'd never have to look at it again. But I couldn't follow through.

I allowed the excuses to flow in, covering up the truth, fearing that if I returned to my loft, I'd be the same person I was before—before her.

I strike the high tom and the drumstick cracks, splitting the wood unevenly. The top fragment flies across the room from the force of my hit. Craig ducks as he enters the room, narrowly avoiding the projectile. The sharp end of the wood embeds itself in the wall inches from his head.

He begins speaking, but I can't hear a word he's saying. He must realize this because he raises his hands, mimicking the action of pulling something out of his ears.

I remove the earplugs. "What were you saying?"

"That if I knew you were going to try and assassinate me, I would have just stayed downstairs." He winces and rubs the side of his head that would have taken the impact.

"Ok, so why are you up here?"

"The magazine people are here and want to know where to set up," Craig says, and I finally register the clattering downstairs.

Oh yeah. That.

In addition to the meetings and upcoming rehearsals, each of us has been set up for individual interviews to get extra media buzz. Wes and Garrett have been on a handful of talk shows and podcasts recently. Jared did a wholesome home tour that had everyone swooning over his home theater. And showing their lack of confidence in my ability to act interesting on camera, the PR team opted for an interview about the bar. A print interview.

I don't bother changing out the basic black T-shirt and jeans. They're going to have to work with what I give them.

I pose behind the bar as the photographer captures pictures of me mixing and pouring the pink-hued liquid of a Naked and Famous into a decorative coupe.

I make the drink three times before the media team agrees they have the right shot. Granted, I dropped the shaker on the second attempt, probably making a dent in my professional credibility.

The photographers remain poised as I settle into a booth with Naomi Laurent, a popular celebrity culture journalist beloved for her ability to make interviews feel more intimate than seems possible.

She presses the start button on her recording device and turns to me with a casual smile.

"I have to ask. You know this tastes like a French model chewed up a cigarette and spat it in my drink, right?" Naomi points to the cocktail in front of her.

"Yeah, I think you've nailed the taste profile," I agree.

"Thank God, I thought it was just me. Would you mind never serving me one of these ever again?"

"I think I can manage that," I say and start to relax. I guess this is how she's gotten such a following, not caring about the dance of pleasantries so many other journalists subscribe to.

A tide of easy conversation flows around us, covering topics like my journey in developing and launching the bar, my past experiences, and the challenges I've faced along the way.

As the number of questions grows, Naomi pauses thoughtfully, preparing to ask me her first real question. "Even though you've been keeping the dream alive with your bar, I know we're all curious about how you feel after so many years out of the limelight?"

"I guess I don't feel all that different. Ten years feels a lot shorter than it sounds." I lean in conspiratorially. "Be honest with me. Was I ever really the one in the limelight?" I joke, and she lets out a husky laugh.

"Maybe you have a point there. You seem to always be content with letting your bandmates stand in the spotlight. Speaking of whom, do you miss working with them? Or I guess they're here at work with you every day," she says, gesturing to the posters.

"I've always thought of those years with them as the best I'll ever get. I guess I've been doing my best to not forget that."

"What do you think that version of you would think of where you are now?"

I wrestle with the question. "Has anyone ever told you that you're annoyingly good at your job?"

"Maybe once or twice," she shrugs. "You don't have to answer if you don't want to."

"It's fine." I take a minute, tasting the truth on the tip of my tongue. "I think that version of me would be really happy with where I am." Because I'm exactly where I wanted. Playing, about to go back on stage, getting wrapped up in music again. Things that have been out of reach for so long. "But I have to admit I'm not that person anymore. So, even though he would be happy with where I am, I think my priorities have shifted."

"What caused this shift?"

"Sometimes you meet someone who reminds you that there's more to you than your past," I tell her, feeling a wave of nostalgia.

There's no denying that Lacey changed my life for the better. One thing I can't ignore is that, for her, I was someone else.

I liked being Drew with her.

Shit.

I *needed* to be that person with her. And maybe that's the reason it all worked. With her, I didn't have to worry about disappointing or letting anyone down—I could just be.

With her, it was just us. With her, music felt like music again. For the longest time, my life revolved around music, but, at some point, it started to revolve around her instead.

"Anything to do with that recent picture with a certain mystery woman?" I can see that Naomi has noticed me drifting into a daydream as her eyes flicker with excitement.

My heart twists. The day the picture was released was brutal, forcing me to relive the night from an outsider's perspective. It was a moment laid bare for the world to see. A moment when she was still mine.

"I think that it's best to leave that a mystery." Even if she's not mine anymore, I don't think I'll ever want to share Lacey with anyone.

Naomi nods and continues on to safer waters. The interview flies by with the comfortable feeling of spending an afternoon with an old friend.

At the end, she turns off her recording device and holds out her hand. "You know, I wouldn't mind having a drink here again soon."

I start to shake my head to clear up any confusion. "I'm sorry if I gave you the wrong impression, but I'm not really interested. I mean, you're great, but—"

She cuts me off from my rambling nonsense. "Oh no, I just mean you're good company. And I'd love to bring my fiancée. She's a fan of places like this."

"Borderline tacky bars?"

"I wasn't going to say that, but . . ."

I'm not entirely sure what else she says, because my mind is spinning with thoughts about Lacey and everything that's happened lately.

I became someone else with her.

But why can't I just be that person, not just in theory but in real life?

All I know is if I want to make it happen, I'll have to deal with a lot of paperwork.

35

Lacey

"But it's so cute! It could go above the crib." Price begs, holding up a little astronaut.

"No!" Mari and I tell him in unison, and not for the first time since the start of the shopping trip.

"We agreed on the fairytale theme. There are no astronauts in fairytales," Mari says, a hand poised on her hip as she looks at her husband. Marisol is one of those women who glows when pregnant; her medium golden skin is absolutely radiant. In her sage dress, she looks like some sort of goddess. If Price didn't already look at her like she's the sun, I'd knock some sense into him.

"There could be. They could be modern fairytales." It's a similar protest to the ones he's used after we told him no to the dinosaurs and giraffes. He wants to give this kid the world, but it's really messing with Mari's carefully laid-out aesthetic.

So far, Price's only win on our excursion is a huge frog stuffed animal, claiming it could be part of the Princess and the Frog story.

Despite these minor disagreements, Price came prepared with safety ratings for cribs and other baby-related equipment.

The outing has been the perfect distraction, steering my thoughts away from work and the dread of frozen meals that remind me of what I used to enjoy every night.

It has also spared me from immediately returning home and fixating on how empty my apartment feels, well, empty beyond my mother's letter that I haven't been able to stop staring at since I unpacked it. Almost every night, I run my fingers along the seam of the envelope, not quite ready to unseal it. At this rate, I'll probably never be ready. But at least this way, there's one part of my mother that's still out there for me to know, one more story keeping her here with me.

We leave the first store with our arms full of bags, a teenage attendant following behind, carting a crib to the van. I'm fairly certain I saw Price buy the little astronaut when Mari turned her back; he just gave me a wink as I smiled, silently letting him know I wouldn't tell.

I sit back and relax in the second store, watching Mari and Price negotiate the merits of having knights versus princes as part of the decor and what each would subliminally teach their child. Price has another rare victory with the knight, claiming something about chivalry and morals.

Their interactions leave me contemplating how good it would feel to skip the messy beginnings of a relationship and just belong with someone.

However, when Mari leaves to hunt down a bathroom, Price's worried expression catches my attention. Our eyes meet, his brows furrowed in worry. "What if I'm not doing this right? What if I mess up this kid? Mari isn't stressed at all, and I feel like I'm about to run up a wall."

"If there was anyone that was meant to be a dad, it's you. As someone with professional-grade daddy issues, I have full faith that this kid is not going to be messed up. And as for Mari, I bet she's not freaking out because you're the one in this with her." It feels good to say the words, to finally get my shit together and be excited about the tiny life they're bringing into the world. To tell him what I should have said already. "Leave the kid ruining to me. I'm very excited to be the single aunt who drinks too much wine and tells inappropriate stories."

"Oh, no. I have a full vision of our kids falling in love and shit. You're not getting out of that by being a cat lady." He bumps me with his shoulder.

I picture that same image of a house full of light with kids and a chuckling husband. It feels more real than it used to, but my heart sinks when I think about my hypothetical partner, because now he looks a lot like Drew. I thought I was almost there, only to have fate snatch it away. Or maybe I threw it away too quickly. Regardless, it's just life playing its cruel game, and all I can do is pick up the pieces and move on.

"I'll add 'playing matchmaker for our kids' somewhere on my to-do list, but don't expect it anytime soon."

As we leave the store, they head to the cashier to purchase even more toys and decorations. It's as if they're single-handedly stocking up on everything their child could possibly need, and I'm not sure what people will be left to get for them as gifts.

"Are you sure?" Price asks, extending an invitation to come and assemble the crib with them.

"I feel like, despite everything we've gone through, building furniture would tear us apart."

Traffic forces me to take an alternative route on my way home. It's technically the way I used to go, but I've spent the last two weeks going the longer way just to avoid the street with the familiar pink neon sign.

Like a conditioned response, I pull into the all-too-familiar parking lot, repeating the motions I've performed countless times before. It's almost as if my body is betraying me, leading me back to a place I've been desperately trying to avoid.

My grip on the door handle tightens. *I'm here.* I could just get this over with. I could go in and talk. I could finally see him.

But am I ready, or would it just end in a shouting match?

I could just leave, drive away, and pretend like nothing happened. But it did, and now—

Suddenly, a tap on my window startles me, and I jerk the door open in shock.

"Fuck, what's with everyone trying to maim me these days?" Craig hisses, recoiling as coffee spills from the lid of his cup.

"What are you doing?"

"Just checking to see if you needed any help with your stakeout. Can I hop in, or would you rather step out?" He must see the worry and stress etched into my face because he says, "He's not here."

"I didn't come back for him," I echo the same words spoken so long ago, and from the look in his eyes, I sense that Craig remembers.

"Yeah, yeah. So, are you planning on coming in?" he asks, slowly backing away from my car and walking towards the bar.

With that, I push the door open and follow Craig to the bar. Neither of us speaks as he unlocks the door and flicks on the lights.

I sit at the end of the bar on the stool that I can't help but think of as mine at this point. "So, how is he?"

Craig leans against the back counter behind the bar and sighs. "Better than he used to be, but worse than he was with you."

"Care to explain instead of speaking in riddles?"

"Nope. You'll either talk or you won't. Not my story to tell. And even if I tried to tell it I'd probably get it wrong since he's never really cared to share the full thing."

"But he's fine?" I'm not sure if I want to know the answer. Not really.

Craig sets his coffee cup on the counter and crosses his arms over his chest. “Yeah, he’s fine enough.”

“You knew this entire time about everything, didn’t you?” Just like he knew my name that day, he knew Luca’s and the string that connected us.

“Yeah, and sometimes I think I should have stopped this all from happening. But I trust my gut with these things. And I still do despite everything.” His expression twists for a second before reverting to his perma-smirk. “Since you’re here, I’m going to put you to work. You have to pay for all the emotional damage you’ve cost me.”

"Emotional damage?" I shoot him a skeptical glance.

"It's hard playing matchmaker." His grin widens, his eyes holding a mix of mischief and understanding. "Before you unleash your wrath upon me, take it out on the tables instead." With a casual flick, he tosses me a rag, striding away before I can respond.

I stay for the rest of the pre-opening tasks, lugging around buckets of ice and helping restock the front bar. I don't have to, but it does help keep me busy. By the time it's time to leave, exhaustion has dulled the sharp edges of my emotions.

“Maybe I’ll see you around,” I say as I head to the door.

“Maybe, but if I don’t, let me say one last thing. I’ve had so many people sit at this bar and tell me how broken they feel, how they keep running back to old mistakes. Promise me that you won’t let the people who’ve hurt you dictate the way you live the rest of your life.”

I swallow the lump in my throat. "I think I can try and manage that."

I head to my car, feeling better and worse than before. On one hand, taking that incredibly small step towards something brings a tiny sense of relief, yet there's also a selfish desire for him not to be ok.

And I can't help but wonder if, for him, nothing changed. What if my lack of response led him to move on effortlessly, much like I would have months ago? What if my absence meant nothing? *What if?*

With a heavy sigh, I reach my car and pause for a moment, my hand hovering over my phone. And despite the uncertainty clawing at me, I pull out my phone and take one more small step.

December 5th

Lacey

Safe

December 6th

Lacey

Safe

December 9th

Lacey

Safe

December 12th

Lacey

Safe

36

Drew

My cocktail shaker collides with the coupe glass, sending sparkling shards into my well as it shatters.

Fuck. This is the second time tonight that I've had to empty the ice. I haven't broken this many glasses since the first week of our opening.

"Out. Kill your ice well, then get out," Craig shouts to me while working double time to pick up my slack.

"Who put you in charge?" I grumble, knowing damn well that I did.

"You did in one of your few moments of clarity." Without missing a beat, he strains the amber drinks into their glasses. "This bar is our love child, and I won't let you ruin it with your ceaseless yearning."

I shovel the ice into buckets, taking care not to cut myself on any of the glass shards. It's good to have something to do, to force myself to focus. Otherwise, I've been checking my phone incessantly for her single-word confirmations that she's alive and well. Once my well behind the bar is cleared, I set to work wiping down tables and avoiding breaking anything else.

It's Christmas Eve, but that hasn't stopped the locals from trickling in. I told my parents there was an emergency, so I had to stay in the city for the holidays.

I can't stomach being around my parents' unapologetic displays of affection right now. I do feel a little regret leaving Evelyn to fend for herself, but she's always been good at handling our parents.

Craig plans on jetting off on a red-eye tonight to Orlando. He makes it a point to spend as little time with his family as possible, but Christmas and Korean New Year force him back under their roof. It's for the best, though, as our circumstances allow the rest of the staff time off for the holiday.

The front door flings open as an unmistakable feminine voice calls out, "Merry Christmas, bitches!"

Her volume is nearly loud enough to shatter more glasses and contribute to my growing pile.

I immediately pause restocking the cocktail straws as every head in the room swivels toward the woman, her hands flung up in the air, and her head adorned with light-up reindeer antlers that rest atop her long, dark hair.

Shit. Shit. Shit.

"Please tell me that we're all having a shared hallucination," I plead with Craig, who is also struck with a look of shock.

"If only luck was on your side." Craig pats my shoulder before making himself scarce.

Evelyn Elena Mariano is the last person I expected to walk into my bar tonight, but I have to give my sister some credit: she knows how to make an entrance.

"Ev. To what do we owe the pleasure?" I ask as the patrons return to their drinks, and Evelyn slides onto the nearest barstool.

"I thought it was a shame you couldn't join us for Christmas because of your *emergency*, so I convinced Mom and Dad to come here instead. I didn't want you to miss out. Don't worry, it's not worth telling them it's complete bullshit," she says with a twinkle of mayhem in her eyes.

"Did you really not want to be left alone with them that much? You're around them all the time. It's not like this would be any different."

"Normally, they're fine. But I can't fabricate work excuses on Christmas like I usually do when I need to escape." She shrugs. Our parents have never outright said it, but they want Evelyn to be normal. It comes off as overprotective, from encouraging her to live close to home to steering her to a typical career.

"Sorry. I should have at least offered to let you hide with me," I concede. "Where are they?"

"At the apartment. I like the new couch, by the way. Oh, and you better watch out for Mom. She's threatening to throw away that shitty coffee machine on the counter." Fuck. Our mother no doubt has a lecture planned for me about bad coffee. "Mom's nearly done with cooking. I say you have an hour max." Great, that means they've been here for hours already if she's most of the way through the feast she whips up every year.

"While I help Craig shut down, will you make sure that none of my stuff ends up in the trash?"

"I'll take it under consideration. Well, as long as you help with something."

"Depends on what." It doesn't really. I'd do pretty much anything for Ev, but I can't let her know that.

She starts biting her nail. "I'm moving."

"Ok, so do you need help packing?" I ask, wondering what the big deal is.

"No, I'm moving to New York." And there it is.

Dad is a fan of listing crime statistics like they're Sunday night football scores and New York is right up there with the places he abhors. So, I doubt they're going to take Evelyn's news well.

"That's the real reason you needed me for Christmas, wasn't it?" I rest my head in my hands and groan.

"A little. But also because it's been forever since I've seen you."

It's not like I can say no. "Fine. I'll even ask Garrett to help get you situated."

"What?" Craig and Evelyn ask in unison. I understand their confusion.

Garrett is an ass, but he's reliable and cares for Evelyn in a way that I know would ensure her safety. Her look of surprise is somewhat comforting. I guess she and Garrett haven't been getting as cozy as he let on the last time we talked.

"It's worth asking." I shrug.

"It's funny how you called Shawn a slimeball but now want me to hang out with the media-appointed playboy of your band."

"One, I'd take Garrett over Shawn any day. And he's a reformed playboy now." Or at least I think so. "He has that fancy lawyer job and everything."

"Sure. Because powerful men are known for keeping it in their pants." Ev rolls her eyes.

"Well, even if he's still the same, it's not like you're planning on sleeping with him. Right?"

"Exactly," she confirms.

"Good. Now, can you go run damage control while we clean up here?"

The customers aren't too happy with us doing an early last call, but I'd rather face them than keep my parents waiting. I can already imagine the deadly combo of my father's disapproving face and my mother saying she's disappointed that I don't know how to prioritize them.

Craig keeps looking down at his phone as we rush through the cleaning process. Each time he lets out a dramatic sigh, I can only assume he's facing his own family bullshit.

When I return from putting the mop away, he slams down his phone. "Aren't you supposed to ask me what's wrong?"

"Am I?"

"I'm visibly upset," he says with a forced pout.

"Craig, your emotional state changes faster than the weather," I say as he gives me a pointed look until I give in. "What's wrong?"

"Cara just told me that Lacey usually spends Christmas alone and wanted me, well, you, to check on her." I had no idea that the two had been keeping in touch, but it makes sense with how obsessed he was acting during her visit.

"Lacey doesn't want anything to do with me." I've been ravenous for the crumbs of her in her one-word texts, but aside from that, it's painfully clear she doesn't feel the same.

"Well . . ."

"Craig, I swear if you know something." My voice lowers in warning.

"She might have come by a few weeks ago."

"And?"

"And this is your shit. You made this mess. I'm done fucking meddling. You can either go to her or you can stay. I'm not playing God just so you guys can pretend nothing's wrong. Before you start complaining, I told her the same thing. Fix it or don't. That's up to you." I've never imagined wanting to throttle my best friend, but right now, I'm pretty damn close. The only thing stopping me is the intensity radiating off him.

I guess he has a right to be fed up since he called this from the start.

"Fine," I say quietly.

Craig stares at me for a moment, his voice a mix of curiosity and challenge. "So, are you going to get the girl or what?"

My heart pounds in my chest, my mind racing with the weight of Craig's question settling heavily on my shoulders.

Without wasting another moment, I run past Craig, grab my jacket, and bolt out the door. I abandon my bike and sprint the distance to her apartment, praying not to drop my phone as my fingers fumble, hastily typing out a message to Evelyn.

Luca

Forgot something. Be there a little late.

Ev

Better be important.

She absolutely is.

As her apartment building looms over me, doubt begins to trickle in. But I fight through it as I dash up the steps to her floor, each stride pushing me closer to her.

Arriving at her hall, an alarm starts to blare, and the smell of smoke permeates the area. With each step, it becomes clearer that her unit is the source.

I quicken my pace and finally reach her door, frantically knocking on it.

But she doesn't answer.

I struggle to catch my breath and avoid inhaling too much smoke as I continue pounding on the door, the urgency growing with each passing moment, desperate to make sure she's ok.

37

Lacey

I unapologetically love Christmas.

I love seeing stores put out decorations in the middle of November. I love Christmas music playing nonstop wherever I go. Starting December 1st, I swap horror movies for mass-produced cheesy romcoms. I let myself get swept up in the, albeit delusional, optimistic magic of the season, which helps combat the otherwise gloomy short days and long nights.

By the end of practice today, I had to dodge multiple chunks of ice because, apparently, the team wasn't a fan of my out-of-tune humming of "All I Want for Christmas is You."

Despite my general suspension of disbelief that comes with the holiday, a melancholy fills me as I gather my Christmas Eve supplies.

I'm used to being alone for this part. I've spent Christmas Eve alone since I was ten.

Despite how it sounds, it wasn't a sad tradition. Mom would go to work in the ER, taking late shifts so other nurses could spend time with their families.

So, instead of Santa, I waited for my mom to come at midnight. We'd unwrap presents the minute she returned, sipping hot chocolate and putting on a fireplace recording on the television. We'd sleep through Christmas day, eventually eating frozen waffles and icing-premade sugar cookies.

It wasn't perfect or picturesque, but it was ours.

For the last few years, it's felt wrong to spend it with anyone else. I use that as reason enough to ignore the string of texts I've been getting from Cara all day.

As my phone pings again, I glimpse down.

Cara

Just know you brought this on yourself.

I'll forgive her eventually, but right now, staying mad at her helps me justify not running straight back to Drew.

Still, Drew's the reason I found myself deviating from the Christmas agenda. I couldn't help it; when I went to the store a few hours ago, I also grabbed all the ingredients for his red sauce. I've been craving it for weeks now and have the recipe memorized from watching him repeatedly work his magic in the kitchen.

But things immediately go wrong as I put the garlic in the hot oil. Instead of a delicious aroma, smoke billows from the pan. I turn off the stove and start all over again at a lower temperature. This time, the smoke happens after I add the onions. I try a third time and get as far as simmering the sauce and putting the pasta in the boiling water before a stray piece of pasta catches fire.

The fire alarm finally starts to blare, and I blame the smoke and onion for the tears rolling down my face. I guess this is what I get for not including the secret ingredient.

A knock starts at my door, and I attempt to wipe my eyes. *Great.* Not only have I nearly burnt down the apartment three times tonight, but now I have to deal with an angry neighbor, too.

Merry Christmas to me.

Taking a deep breath and hoping it doesn't look like I was crying, I start walking to the door, only for loud pounding to start again. It's confirmed; my neighbors hate me. What else could go wrong?

I swing open the door prepared to hear the complaints, but find myself blinking in disbelief. Instead of an angry neighbor, a ghost stands before me as if summoned out of pure desperation. That has to be it because there is no other reason for a panting Drew to be right outside my door.

"Hey," I breathe.

"Hey," he says, and I want to melt into that single word. Fall into his voice and never let go.

We stand transfixed, hovering on either side of the door frame, neither of us moving an inch. The last time he was inside was before, and I'm so tempted to believe that if he just crosses the threshold, it will turn back time.

Mr. Nash, from two doors down, pokes his head out the door and yells, "Can you turn that damn thing off!"

"Ss-sorry," I stammer, snapping back into the chaos of the current moment. I shift, wordlessly inviting Drew into the apartment because there's nothing else I can do.

I watch as Drew maneuvers around my apartment, turning off the alarm and waving away the smoke. His actions only delay the inevitable conversations we need to have.

The last time I saw him, I was so hurt, and with him in front of me now, I realize that the pain hasn't faded at all. Yet, despite the pain, there's something in my soul trying to fight it—a force that pulls me towards him and him towards me. Maybe that's what called out to him tonight, bringing him here despite everything.

Once the room is cleared, he walks towards me. "What were you doing? Oh . . ." His voice trails off when he reaches me and has a chance to see the crime scene in my kitchen.

It's quite literally dripping red from an earlier fight with the tomatoes. I can see the realization of what I was making register on his face.

Yeah, I missed him, so I risked the safety of everyone in the building by cooking a legitimate meal for the first time in my adult life.

I speak before he can ask something that will sting. "How did you know I'd be here?"

"I didn't," he says, and I can't help but blink up at him. What does he mean that he didn't know I'd be here.

"So what? You were just in the neighborhood solo caroling?" The question comes out more accusatory than I intend. The bite in my voice is no doubt the side effect of endless imaginary conversations I played out in the shower.

"I just know you have a tendency to do things by yourself even when you shouldn't have to. And Cara seemed to know that too." He glances around the room again. "I guess I just didn't expect so much Christmas."

"You expected me to be the Grinch or something?"

"The absolute Grinchiest, for sure," Drew smirks, and I have to bite my lip to stop my own smile. "So, do you have anything left to eat?"

"No. This was kind of the plan."

"Let me fix that," he says, his gaze never leaving me.

"You don't have to do that," I say almost immediately, unsure why.

"Lacey, please. My family is making more food than we can possibly eat," he insists, as if afraid I'll ask him to leave. "It's Christmas, and I couldn't live with myself if I left you here to eat your abominations of frozen food. Besides," his eyes drift back to the kitchen, "you are a danger to yourself." He smiles, his humor wrapping around me, something I didn't realize how much I missed.

"Drew," I say instead of no because I shouldn't accept his offer. But I want to.

His eyes soften as he asks, "Come home?"

Home. My heart trips, stumbles, and unceremoniously faceplants over hearing the word. Because it feels so right, but

I'm scared it doesn't belong to me anymore. Yet, there's a warmth in his invitation that tugs at me, tempting me to accept.

I guess I'm not done crying for the night because a new wave of tears threatens to break free.

I don't see him move over to me, but his hand on my face grounds me.

A thumb brushes away a tear as he asks, "What's wrong?"

I hesitate for a moment, but there's no hiding the tears spilling down my cheeks. "I missed you. I don't think I realized how much. Now that I do, I feel so stupid."

He tilts my face so I'm looking into those perfect green eyes. "You're not stupid. This is a little stupid, sure, but not you. Never you. And I missed you too."

"You did?" I don't doubt it, but hearing it does something to me that I needed.

"Every day. But if you let me, I can fix that for tonight. We don't have to talk about what happened. We can just let Christmas be Christmas. When it's done, we can go back to not talking or whatever you want. Just come with me tonight."

"Are you sure?"

"The thought of you being alone kills me. Please."

I'm scared his words might be more out of pity than desire, but I give in because I'm a little desperate to prolong this.

"I guess, if you need me to be there." I mean for the words to sound playful, but really, if he needs me, there's little else that matters.

As we clean the kitchen, Drew does his best to pull a laugh from me. He describes all of Craig's antics I've missed out on over the last month and a half. As no surprise to anyone, he's threatened to quit at least twenty times. By the time we're done, I'm sure my pans will never recover from the disaster, but at least my eyes are no longer puffy.

Drew catches my shoulder just before we reach my door. "You umm," he says, pointing to his eyes.

I wipe under my lower lashes and let out a little laugh, realizing how I must have looked when I answered the door. "Like Jackson Pollock did my makeup?"

"Maybe just a bit. I just wanted to check if it was intentional."

"You said you forgot *something*. This is an entire person." An elegant woman with a heart-shaped face and pale eyes greets us with a playful expression and an oven-mitted hand on her hip.

"Ev, you're making me look bad, and I've been here for less than a minute," Drew groans.

"No. You're making yourself look bad. I'm only holding you accountable." She moves to me, reaching for a hug. "I'm Evelyn. The better, more considerate Mariano sibling."

"Lacey," I say as she releases me. I'm left slightly unsteady from the sudden enthusiastic embrace.

"So, you give *her* your name on the first try, but I had to wait until you moved in with me? That hardly feels fair," Drew complains.

A woman with streaks of gray in her thick, dark hair calls from the kitchen, "Luca, did I hear you right? That this woman is living with you. How do I not know this?"

"*Was*. Mama, it's complicated, ok?" Drew explains.

"Is. Was. You don't tell us anything. We had to learn about your show from the internet." She looks exasperated, and I guess I'm not the only one that Drew left in the dark.

I can't contain the uncomfortable giggle that burst from me at the scene. It's like a crash course about his world.

"See, she thinks we're funny." Evelyn gives me a conspiratorial look and then walks into the kitchen.

Drew calls to his sister, "Lacey laughs during horror movies, so don't give yourself too much credit."

"While my son was taking his time getting here, we started prepping everything. Dinner should be ready in an hour," Drew's mother informs us before turning her attention back to the stovetop.

Evelyn comes back, holding up two thin, brownish crisps. "I made cookies!"

Drew leans in. "Whatever you do, don't eat one. My sister is very talented at giving people food poisoning."

"I am not!" Evelyn whines.

"You sent Jared to the hospital last time." His tone is flat, like this is a common argument.

"I swear it wasn't the carbonara. He was just sick or something."

"Ev, you're fatal in the kitchen."

I take one from her and take a bite. The wafer-thin confection melts in my mouth. "She might be onto something here."

"I think you should keep her." Evelyn's approval washes over me, and a smile breaks free. Tonight will be alright. Tonight will be good.

"I'll try," Drew promises.

As the night unfolds, there's hardly a moment to collect my thoughts with the speed of everything flowing around me. Before I know it, I'm sitting between the siblings saying grace at the table. The scene is so utterly opposite to how I had planned to spend my night, but not in a bad way.

The seafood feast laid out on the table is my new favorite thing. I thought Drew was a great cook, but his mother's food puts him to shame. When I say this, the woman's eyes sparkle with pride.

For a brief moment, I let myself take it all in, listening to the exchange of jokes and conversations around me.

As soon as dinner ends, the cleaning begins, and before I can even step into the kitchen to offer my assistance, I'm promptly shooed away.

So, I turn to where Evelyn stands with a hot toddy in one hand, cursing at the windows. "I hate this door. Fucking penthouse. Which one is it." She moves, trying another spot.

"Here." I press on the trim one window over from where Evelyn is prodding her finger in search of the invisible balcony entrance.

"Thanks."

"No problem, I've exchanged my own words with this door too."

"I hate this place. It's so impersonal. I like the new couch. That red monstrosity he had before belongs in the trash. I don't care what his fancy interior designer said about it being an investment or livable art. It's a good thing that nobody actually lives here."

"What do you mean no one lives here?"

"Well, he just camps out above the bar, and we stay here when we visit. But it seems like that might have changed," she says. It's one of the things I was initially so torn up about when I was putting the pieces together, but now it feels more like an inside joke.

Outside, we curl into opposite chairs. Evelyn wraps the blanket tighter around her shoulders.

I motion to the top of my head and say, "I like your umm . . . antlers."

"I have extra if you want a pair!" She offers immediately, exuding enough energy to light every Christmas tree in the apartment building.

"I'm good, but thanks."

"So, what are your intentions with my brother?" Her smile doesn't falter as a new hardness enters her voice.

"Like, are we together? No." *Almost.*

"No, I mean this is all convenient timing with everything going on with his career."

"If I'm going to be completely honest. He gave me a fake name the first time we met, and I still haven't officially forgiven him."

"What name did he give you?"

"Drew." It feels odd rolling off my tongue like I'm letting her in on a secret.

"Damn, my brother wasn't creative enough to give you something better than his middle name." She shakes her head, a perfectly manicured nail skimming along the top of her glass. "I guess that could all be true, but why should I believe you're not using him? This isn't the first time someone has pulled some bullshit on him." It warms something in me to see others in his corner.

"Because Martin Hall is my dad." Immediately, her narrow, furrowed expression turns into wide-eyed shock.

"Oof. I'm sorry."

I can't help but laugh as I say, "Not even going to pretend he's a good guy for me?"

Evelyn considers for a moment, but then shrugs. "No. I probably should. The guys idolized him, but whenever I visited, I got weird vibes. They treated him like a god, but he's just some dude who slept with women way too young for him and used to be good at playing guitar. Maybe he isn't a bad guy, but that's all he really is. Just a guy."

"Honestly, thanks. It's nice to hear the truth." It really is.

Everything I've ever heard or seen about my father was so heavily filtered for my benefit. Despite what happened between them, my mom's words were always coated with a layer of affection. And while Price and Cara were always on my side, they were also ready with whatever they thought I needed to hear. Thinking of her now, I really do need to thank Cara for her hand in making tonight happen.

"It's what I'm good at. Letting the truth out really is underrated. I just wish my brother felt the same. He's always been an expert at bottling everything up. He doesn't think we see it, but there's been something off with him for a while now. And I'm not sure if he doesn't want to tell us or doesn't see it himself. But tonight, he was his old self again, and I have a feeling you have something to do with it." She finishes by taking a long sip of her steaming drink.

"Me? I don't even really know him." Though I'm not sure if it's completely accurate.

"I think that might be part of why he's doing so much better. He always hated having so many eyes on him. There are so many people who say they're just in it for the music. Most of them are just fucking pandering liars, but not Luca. He'd play to an empty room if it meant he got to play." I think back to the videos I watched and how different he looked from the others on the stage.

A drop of moisture brushes my cheek, and I look up to see the start of a light snowfall. "Shit. It's snowing." It will probably only continue for a little longer, but snow in the South is a recipe for disaster.

"I guess you'll just have to stay the night." Evelyn's expression turns villainous.

Before I can respond, the balcony door swings open, and Drew joins us in the cold. He's holding a bundle of gray fabric, which he offers me as he says, "Here. I thought you'd need this."

"She does this a lot?" Evelyn asks, watching the exchange.

"You mean make attempts to catch hypothermia? Yeah. It's arguably her worst habit."

"You mean my only bad habit." I grab the thick cotton hoodie from him and pull it over my head.

God. It smells like him. It makes me want to hold the fabric close to my nose and just inhale. But I don't, especially because it would make me look absolutely insane in front of his sister. But it doesn't stop me from wanting to.

He raises one of those full eyebrows. Is it weird that I missed his eyebrows and this expression that's so completely him? "Sure. It's Christmas Eve, so I'll let you believe that."

"Go." Evelyn waves her brother back to the door. "We're still having girl time." Once the glass door is firmly back in place with a slightly grumpy Drew on the other side, Evelyn returns. "Thank you."

"For what?"

"For being important to him and being in his life. It's been a long time since I've seen him with this much life in him. I really missed my big brother."

As she gazes at her family through the glass, she looks less like a grown woman and more like a little girl who's been waiting for someone to come home.

"I haven't been doing a good job of being in his life recently," I admit. But I don't want to get her hopes up because no matter how good tonight has been, I'm not sure what's coming next. I want to be that person for him again, but that's not something we can jump back into.

"I don't completely blame you, but I think he's worth it. Not saying what he did was right, and it might be selfish for me to ask you to try again. I've met plenty of his girlfriends," her nose crinkles in disgust at the word, "and you're the only one that's any good for him. He's different; no, that's not quite it. He's him again. And there's this little part of me that's mad that I couldn't help my own brother work through whatever he's not telling any of us. But I'm just happy he's let someone in." Her eyes meet mine, her voice softening as she says, "So, I guess what I'm saying is make him grovel and work for it a little, but give him a chance."

Under the glow of kitchen lights, Drew and his father clean the dishes, and the barest hum of my jazz playlist reaches us. When Drew turns, he meets my stare, tilts his head, and mouths *come here.*

"You need to talk to him, too, you know. The guilt is probably killing him. He has this tendency to think everything is his fault," Evelyn says, following my gaze.

"I will." He took a risk by bringing me here and letting me meet people I know are so deeply important to him. I'm not throwing this chance away, not this time.

"Luca, you take the couch and give Lacey your room," his mother directs, coordinating the sleep situation now that the roads are unsafe.

The roads themselves aren't the issue; it's the drivers. The drivers, like me, who panic once a single snowflake enters the equation and ruin the roads for everyone else.

"Not even going to try and argue?" he teases me.

"No. We both know you're not a gentleman, so you'd take the bed if I offered," I tell him. But there's a part of me that secretly wants him to sleep with me instead, but that might be too much. Accepting his olive branch to come to dinner was one thing, but we still haven't discussed anything yet.

"You spent one night with Ev, and now she has you on her team! Has anyone considered that this is my home?" He throws his arms up in mock offense.

"She probably couldn't help it. I'm quite lovable," Evelyn smiles from where she's draped on the couch.

He loses the argument by a landslide. At one point, he glances at his father, who simply shrugs. The man hasn't spoken much tonight, letting his wife take the lead with so much love in his eyes.

It should come as no surprise that I don't have anything to sleep in, given how unexpectedly my plans shifted throughout the night. I could probably ask Evelyn for a change of clothes, but I don't.

Instead, I keep his hoodie close to me, not quite ready to let go of it yet.

Despite curling myself into a cocoon of his sheets, I keep tossing and turning, unable to get comfortable. Most kids can't sleep because they're anticipating the presents waiting to be unwrapped. I can't sleep because I can't stop thinking about the man in the living room.

So, I do something incredibly selfish. But it's Christmas Eve, and I haven't gotten myself a present yet.

I slip out of bed and walk into the open living space. Drew's feet poke out from the blanket he retrieved from a linen closet.

"You can come sleep in the bed," I say. It's framed as an offer, but it's truly more of a desperate request.

At first, there's no response, and I'm scared I've come out here for nothing.

Then his form shifts, and he props himself up to look at me.

"You mean my bed, but only if you're sure." His brows are raised in question. It's one of my favorite things about him, the reminder that he'll always give me an out if I change my mind. I've never been more certain of wanting something so innocent as simply sleeping next to another person.

"I am. I promise."

He rises, and I try not to look at his body because all he's wearing is a pair of low-slung sweatpants. The tattoos on his hips that dip below his waistband invite my eyes to look exactly where they shouldn't. I catch myself and force my eyes to look at the stockings hung over the TV, but I have no doubt that my cheeks are the same bright shade of red as the festive decorations.

I wait until he's had time to get under the covers to venture into the room. Maybe if I don't see him, then I won't think about it.

It's worked before. Well, not really.

After he settles under the covers on the right side, I break the spell. "Umm. Can you move to the other side? I can't sleep unless I'm on the right side of the bed."

It's one of the small things that I need on a level that's so fucking embarrassing. I'm a grown woman who has to sleep on her favorite side of the bed, or she physically can't sleep. It's one of the things Henry used to do, get to bed early and sleep on my side, leaving me restless.

But Drew doesn't laugh or complain. He just shifts over and says, "Of course."

As I sink into the mattress next to him, I register the increased warmth of the space. I would normally hate sleeping with this much heat radiating around me, but tonight, I don't mind it. It feels safe.

We each shift a few times in the silence, and I'm acutely aware of how close his limbs are to mine. Close but never touching.

Just before the last tendrils of sleep claim me, the mattress shifts again. I open my eyes and see the outline of him facing me.

"Does this mean we're ok?" he asks, the strain in his voice indicating how hard he's been trying not to ask all night.

"No," I say softly as I reach out, letting my fingertips graze his cheek. "This means we start with today and then start again tomorrow. We'll try to figure this out. And you know what?"

"What?"

"It's past midnight, so it's Christmas, and I've already gotten everything on my list."

"You being here is the best gift I could have asked for," he whispers in a rough voice that does dangerous things to my insides before brushing the lightest kiss on my forehead. It's barely even a whisper of his lips, but it burns straight to my heart.

And I can't resist grasping his face, gently guiding his mouth to mine, and feeling the subtle scratch of his stubble against my palms.

Some kisses are fleeting, meant to be forgotten. They taste like cheap shots with a side of regret. Our first kiss was like that.

But this kiss is different.

This kiss feels like revisiting my favorite memory, the kind you hold tightly during the darkest nights.

He pulls away and nuzzles into the side of my neck. "I would love to do everything I've ever imagined to you right now, but I doubt that would go over well with our current guests."

"I think I can live with just a taste." *For now.*

I can feel a smile forming on his lips as he plants a kiss on my cheek. He holds me close, his body molding perfectly against mine, one of his legs threading through my thighs.

No more distance, just like it should be.

And as I settle into his arms, sleep comes more effortlessly, as if everything is better now.

Maybe it's a Christmas miracle, or maybe, just maybe, it's because I'm a little bit in love.

38

Drew

She's not here when I wake up, and I start to panic as I reach and only find a dark, empty space next to me. My lungs burn as my breath grows erratic. Was it just a cruel dream?

Then, a familiar laugh floats to me from the kitchen, and my heart settles.

She's here.

She's just awake early, laughing with my family.

I take a moment to drink in the sound; my limbs splayed across the bed, and I thank the universe for bringing her back to me. I don't think I've stopped smiling since we walked through the door. Another burst of laughter from the other room urges me up because no matter how good yesterday was, Lacey is still here, and I don't intend to let a single moment go to waste.

I pull on a shirt and shuffle to join the noisy cluster in the kitchen. My chest bursts with warmth at the sight of the most important people in my life, all in one space.

"You did good with this girl, even though she drinks bad coffee," my mom says.

True to form, my family are all sipping on the various artisan-level drinks they've made with my espresso machine, and then there's Lacey.

Lacey, who's still wearing my hoodie and drinking her burnt coffee. Buying that cheap coffee pot was worth it all for this moment alone.

I move further into the room to grab a mug and pour the rest of the pot that Lacey's made into it. "I don't know. It kinda tastes like home." The comment earns me furious chastisement in rapid Italian from both of my parents, but I don't fully register the words. All I see is the smile on Lacey's lips.

Once there's a pause, I ask, "How long are you guys staying?"

"We fly out in the morning. Evelyn and your father have work, you know." I love my mother's not-so-subtle way of saying, *You should be working too.*

I give Evelyn a look, letting her know it's time. If they're busy being annoyed with me, that means they'll be less annoyed with her. She rolls her eyes as if to say, *don't tell me what to do.* But then, she sets down her mug and takes a deep breath.

"So . . . I'm thinking of taking a detour to New York before heading all the way home."

Our father's eyebrows immediately shoot up. "Why would you want to do that? Are you meeting someone? That's not somewhere you should be visiting alone."

Evelyn glances at me before continuing, "I'm looking for apartments. I accepted a job offer there." She hesitates briefly before adding, "And I'll be starting in March."

I jump in before our parents can pounce. "Garrett's there. He'll be helping her out." I haven't exactly talked to Garrett since the last meeting when he essentially told me I'm a pathetic, selfish piece of shit, but they don't need to know any of that.

"Oh, how is he?" my mother asks, her attention diverted. Garrett might be a prick, but they like him on the principle that he was smart enough to get an undergraduate degree and ace the LSAT while we were touring.

"He's good. He'll be there to help, so don't worry."

"Fine, but we're going with you to the apartment," my father decides, and Ev gives me another look. All I can do is shrug. She's won half the battle with my help. The rest is up to her, and I'm done subjecting Lacey to the strategic tactics it takes to placate our parents.

I grab Lacey's free hand and bend to whisper in her ear, "Let's go outside."

I snag the blanket from the couch as we escape.

"Sorry about that," I apologize once the door is firmly shut behind us.

"It's fine, really. It's nice. I've never had a Christmas like this."

"One with so much family drama?"

"One with so much family." Oh. Yeah. The shit that we need to talk about. The shit with her dad and how I know the guy better than she does.

She pulls something from her hoodie and says, "I have a gift for you." She holds out a thick envelope and hands it to me with anxious eyes.

I break the seal and pull out a stack of handwritten pages.

"What is this?" I ask.

"It's everything you should know about me. I know so much about you now. After everything that night, I might have gone down a rabbit hole of old concert footage. I only thought that it was fair. I want us to be on the same page. I got up early and wrote it out."

"Oh, you Googled me. Miss me that much?" From the look she's giving me, the joke doesn't hit the way I hoped.

I set the papers on the slightly damp side table, not caring if they get ruined because I have no intention of ever reading them.

My tone softens as I continue, "Lacey, the way you learned everything, it's an occupational hazard. I've known that for years now. I signed away my privacy the moment I chose this life. Just because all of my stuff is out there, it doesn't mean you have to share everything with me unless you're ready. And I'd much rather learn all of what's in that letter from simply being around you, being with you." Taking her hands in mine, I gently rub my thumb against her knuckles.

"Is that what you still want? To be with me, like really with me? I understand that you might have just brought me here because you saw me cry yesterday, and if that's the case, please tell me," she says, then bites her lip anxiously, waiting for my answer.

The idea that she thinks there's some possibility that the last twelve or so hours were some act of pity burns.

I drop her hands and move from my seat to kneel in front of her, making sure we're at eye level. "There were days when I was so close to selling this entire place because it looked so terribly wrong without you in it. I would stare at my phone, waiting for that single-word text letting me know you were ok. My one regret is not chasing after you that night, not fighting a little harder to explain everything."

She takes my face tenderly. "If you chased, I would have only run faster. But that's never stopped you from being there exactly when I need you. I don't believe in much, but I believe that whatever keeps bringing us together is stronger than anything that could tear us apart. Last night is proof of that. I wasn't ready then to hear you, to really listen, but I am now."

I gently raise my hand to cover hers. "Then, let's talk. But if we're going to do this, we need to be somewhere without an active audience." I glance over to see that my sister is no longer negotiating for her life. Instead, my family is enjoying the show. The noisy fools don't even pretend to act casual when I turn their way.

Ten minutes later, Lacey and I are dressed and out the door, ready to walk and be out of range from the eavesdroppers. She looks like a marshmallow in my coat, the sleeves swallowing her arms.

With the roads clear of any trace of last night's snow, Lacey slides behind the wheel of her car.

"Where are we heading?" she asks.

"Let's go to the bar. I have something I want to show you. And I also left my bike there since I ran to your apartment yesterday."

She shakes her head as an amused smile makes its way onto her face. "You're really such an idiot sometimes."

"So, you just had Grammy's hanging out up here the entire time?" Lacey questions as she points to an award that's coated in a layer of dust.

"Would have ruined the mystery if I showed you this place sooner."

"You mean the average penthouse-owning, bar regular isn't an award-winning musician? Damn. Would never have guessed."

I watch as she continues to inspect the space, examining the artifacts of my past life. I could just tell her, but bringing her here made more sense.

"I don't know what to call you," she finally says as her fingers brush against a framed newspaper clipping of the band. "It feels wrong to call you anything else except Drew, but that isn't who you really are."

"I hope this gives you an answer," I say as I pull my wallet out of my pocket, sliding my driver's license out of its sleeve and handing it to her. I wasn't sure she'd ever see it.

She takes it and sits on the edge of my bed, staring and flipping it over to make sure it's authentic. It better be after the endless paperwork and the fees I had to pay. Her brows furrow slightly as she turns it back and reads it one more time.

Drew Mariano.

Even if I never saw her again, I wanted there to be one less lie between us.

"What did you do?" she asks in disbelief. I sit on the bed beside her, the mattress dipping beneath our weight.

"The only person I want to be is the person you've helped me become. Maybe at first, that name was a lie, but slowly, it became the name of a person who knew you. A person who finally remembered how to be happy in more than just fleeting moments. Even though you were gone, I've never had any intention of letting you go." Maybe it's too much, but I need her to know how far I'll go, even if it means clinging to scraps.

"You didn't have to do that. You're more than just a name to me. But I get it. Sometimes, it felt like I left a part of me in the apartment with you." Relief washes over me, and my mind reaches for where to start. All of my carefully rehearsed speeches are gone now that she's next to me.

As I struggle to reel them back in, Lacey fills in some of the gaps for me, saying, "I know about your last performance. I don't know if that helps or not, but I thought you should know what I know."

"It helps." Now, I don't have to recall the details, just the aftermath. "I guess that night was really the start of everything.

Maybe it was the fact that everyone else got to finish the performance, and I was just left floating without any resolution, or something else entirely, I'm not sure. At first, it was small, like the music was slipping away from me. Then, two years after it happened, things got worse, and I couldn't play for more than a few minutes before I got so in my head and couldn't seem to get out. So, for about eight years, I haven't been able to play or really even talk about it. Three years ago, I stopped trying entirely." The words fall out of me as a rushing, rambling current.

"But you played for me," she says.

I pick up her hand from where it rests on the mattress. "I'll always play for you. That's the thing. You came into my life, and that was so freeing that I didn't want to let it go. Being nobody with you meant everything to me. I guess that's why I put off the truth for so long, even from the start with my name. It was really hard to want to wake up from such a good dream."

"Thank you for telling me."

"I understand if you hate me a little for the past. What you went through because of Martin and us wasn't fair." The knowledge of what I was tangentially a part of still causes an ache in me.

"I want to make one thing clear," she says, tightening her grip on my hand, a part of me worrying that I may have messed it all up by reminding her of my role in her past. "You don't get to shoulder all the blame here. I went into that agreement with just as many things to hide from as you. If you think you stole my dad, I have news for you. He did whatever he wanted long before you came around." Her voice lowers as she continues, "I'm coming to realize that it was less that I was running from you and more that I was running from myself. And I'm still scared of myself. Scared that I'll say the wrong thing or push you away. I'm scared because that's all I've ever done, and I want this to be different. I want to be the person I am with you, but I don't know if that's sustainable."

The joy that I feel hearing she doesn't harbor any hatred for me is offset by how small and unsure she sounds. I think about the first night cooking together in the kitchen when she said she wasn't marriage material and tried to laugh it off as a joke. How her parent's relationship didn't set the same standard as mine. How so many people must have forced such a terrible belief down her throat until she had no choice but to believe it.

"I've already told you I'm addicted to your honesty," I say. "Go ahead, dissect me with your sharp tongue. Cut me open with your words and see that my heart only beats for you. Say the most terrible things you can imagine if that's what it takes to convince you I'm not leaving. And I promise that if you run again, I'll chase after you. I want you, Lacey."

Instead of saying anything in response, she leans in and kisses me.

I swear I'll never get sick of her kisses. Her kisses make me so annoyed that I have to breathe, that I have to obey some basic bodily need instead of completely being consumed by her. With one hand threading through my hair and the other clinging to me, she pulls me closer. The way her lips move against mine feels like they're trying to solve a question, and I'm the answer.

I'm lost in the absolute headiness of the kiss, knowing she's not about to slip away again so easily.

"Say it again," she whispers reverently.

"I want you." I don't just want her; I love her.

I knew it when I saw her in the kitchen with my family, effortlessly fitting in as if she had always belonged. I knew it when we went to the grocery store for the first time, slowly letting go of the rules she used to protect herself. I knew it when she fell asleep on top of me on the couch, her vulnerability and trust peeking through.

And I knew it the moment she walked away, leaving me empty all over again, a void that only she could fill.

I pull her back to me, my lips resuming their exploration of her skin, but the touches remain innocent as we sink back into the rhythm of us.

When I'm at least partially satiated, I ask, "Spend New Year's with me?"

"I have to work." My heart drops before she adds, "But I'd like you to come with me. See what I do and how much I love it."

"Do I finally get to know where you've been mysteriously running off to?"

She responds with a warm smile, her eyes softening as she begins to explain her work with the Cobras and her hesitation to reveal that side of herself to someone she doesn't know well. Just like that, we make plans for New Year's in Boston.

I'm happy that I didn't look her up or read her letter; the excitement in her invitation is something that couldn't have been replicated through ink on paper.

And to my relief, after Boston, she'll come to the first band rehearsal. Knowing she'll be there calms my fears about it. I've been able to play until now, but playing for her does something special for me that I can't replicate alone.

We only start making our way back once I hear her stomach growl, a reminder that we forgot to eat breakfast. As she rattles off a list of places to grab a bite that should be open, I don't stop her. I also want to make this moment with us last a little longer before we head back to my family. I joke about it being a date, earning a chuckle from her—a beautiful sound I hope to always hear.

There's still more to figure out and histories to understand.

But for now, we have a plan and a clearer idea of what we'll be, and that's more than I had yesterday.

39

Lacey

It's so tempting to move back in with him during the handful of days following Christmas. To settle into the routine of who we used to be, but what we were before wasn't built for reality. Despite this, I spend my empty hours with Drew in his apartment or at Half a Memory.

We haven't had sex again. It's infuriating but comforting how serious he wants to take the progression of our relationship.

There's this wriggling feeling in the back of my mind, knowing that, on some level, I share Drew with the world. So many people love him with so much unquestioned conviction when I'm just learning how to care for him out loud.

I barely slept the night before New Year's Eve. Restless from the nerves of bringing someone into my life so completely.

It feels like being with him in Boston will be the point of no return. It's not that I haven't shared my job and passion with people before, but those people never required an invitation. Price has always just been there. Henry's job was so aligned with mine that he understood most things without me having to explain them to him. My mom used to show up to every game I photographed, cheering for Price the entire time and sitting down with me afterward to parse through the best moments.

A body shifts next to me, and I wake with the movement.

"Hey," he says in that rasping morning voice I've recently discovered. "What are you still doing here?"

I look at the clock on the nightstand next to me and shit.

7:50

Why didn't it go off? Why didn't my phone go off? I have less than an hour to go back to my place to get my bags, get ready, and get to the airport. With the anxiety that's now pumping through me, I don't need coffee.

I yank free of the covers, leaving Drew in the bed behind me.

I'm still in the shirt I went to sleep in, but my pants. Where the hell are my pants?

I find a pair of sweats and tug at the drawstring. They aren't mine, but they'll have to do.

"I'm taking these," I tell Drew's half-asleep form.

He waves a hand at me and murmurs, "Sure, they look better on you anyway. I'll see you in a few hours."

I battle traffic on the way to my apartment, not having my usual luck. If I didn't know better, I'd say these inconveniences feel like signs from the universe.

No. Today is going to be a good day.

It has to be.

I manage to grab my gear and pop a slice of toast in my mouth before making my way to the airport. I'm panting a little as I make it onto the plane and settle into the section with the rest of the non-coaching personnel. I'm not the only one buzzing.

Everyone but the rookies are in the zone. We lost the last time we went up against Boston in a shutout. Now they have something to prove.

It's going to work out.

It's not going to work out.

I stare into the partitioned sections of my bag and a hole where my 70-200mm f/2.8 lens should be—the lens I use for most of my shots. Sure, I have my wide-angle and fixed lenses, but those aren't the same.

I mentally trace back to the last time I saw the lens. I took everything out to clean and inspect them, and then . . . Then I saw a text from Drew and left.

Normally, I wouldn't have forgotten something so major, but my stupid, lovestruck brain had been in such a state of bliss and contentment that I wasn't worrying. I wasn't double-checking.

All this time, I have been so wrapped up in prioritizing my job over people, fearing that in doing so, I wouldn't be able to give enough of myself to someone. Or worse, that it would cloud my judgment regarding their intentions. I wasn't on my game when I was with Henry, and I wasn't even in love with the guy.

But now, I have let myself be so comfortable that I'm putting my job in jeopardy. Today, it's just a piece of equipment. What if next, it's something worse? What if I can't focus, and every picture I take goes to shit? I've been distracted before, but those distractions have always been temporary.

Drew is a distraction I want to last.

The hummingbird trapped in my chest is out of control, its fluttering wings building pressure so intense that I can't feel anything else. My arms, legs, and whole being feel numb, while at the same time, I feel like a bundle of nerves that has been set on fire.

A knock on my hotel room door reminds me where I am, and the second knock reminds me that I should answer the door. When I open it, Price is on the other side, and his easy smile drops when he sees what I look like.

"Hey, it's been fifteen minutes since you said you'd meet me. I just wanted to check in. Are you ok?" It's been fifteen minutes since the time we agreed on. That means I've been here an hour, wasting all this time when I should have been finding a solution.

"I don't have my lens," I say, still feeling like I'm in a trance.

"What do you mean? I saw you carrying in that monster camera bag. You even made me hold it for a minute, and it weighs a ton."

"I have some of my stuff, but not all of it."

"Then, we'll just get you a new one." He pulls out his phone and taps away at it before turning the screen to me, showing the nearest camera shop. "It's open and around the corner."

It's a good solution, but I doubt they'll have exactly what I need.

"Can I meet you outside in a minute? I need to make a phone call really quick?"

He gives me one last concerned look before nodding.

"Of course. I'll be waiting." He smiles, a reminder that he'll always be there.

Alone again, I sit on the bed, holding my phone limply before pressing Drew's contact. I hate that I care for him so much that it's messing with my head—how unintentionally he is part of the reason why this happened, why I forgot. But that same care is why he's the only person I want to call, the only voice I need to hear.

"Hey. How's Boston? I saw the pictures you sent of the city."

"I—" I choke before the tears finally come. They roll down my face, hot and furious.

"What's going on? Is everything ok?"

"No. I messed up."

40

Drew

When I picked up the call, I was not expecting the sobs that came through the speaker.

"I just feel like the most major fuck up. They're going to be out there doing their best, and I can't even remember a damn lens. I'm getting a replacement, but it's not the same. The settings will be different, and I just can't be my best like this." Her voice is thin, filled with distress as she explains the solution she's already found. But fixing it doesn't seem like it's enough; it's like she needs to punish herself for missing the mark.

If only she was here for a home game and could run home to get the lens. But she isn't.

And then it hits me. She might not be here, but I am. I can do this for her.

"What if I bring it?" I offer.

"What?"

"I'm flying out anyway, so I'll just bring the lens with me. You're not alone in this. I've got you. You and me in the eye of all our storms. That hasn't changed," I explain the simple logic of my idea so there'll be less of a chance for her to say no.

"But you don't have a key to my place."

"It's a good thing we know someone who doesn't need a key to get in somewhere."

Her voice cracks, a tentative laugh escaping. "Should I be worried that you are about to break into my apartment?"

"I think it's better that you don't worry about that, but I'm also going to make sure you have a better security system."

"You're right. I really don't need to know the details about my lack of home security."

"Don't worry. I've got this," I promise, hoping my words are as soothing as I intend.

"I'm still going to worry, but probably a more rational amount now."

"That's all I can ask for. Now that we have a plan for later, what do you need right now?" I ask, still hearing the tension in her voice.

"Can you just talk to me about your day? I just want to hear your voice for a few minutes."

And I do. I tell her about the fit Craig threw over all the glitter that's still everywhere from a girl's twenty-first birthday last night and explain that I've been researching hiring a new bartender to help make signature drinks.

All the while, I'm rebooking my ticket to get there sooner and reviewing the timeline she's texted me of when game events are and where I can hand off the equipment when I get there.

"Thank you," she whispers.

I want to stay on the phone and comfort her, but the sooner I get this done, the sooner I can be there with her.

Beyond feeding Craig's ego and his desire to dress in all black like a burglar, the plan goes off without a hitch, and I'm in Boston in just under four hours.

I see her the instant I get into the stands.

Before this moment, I could imagine her in action, her attention to detail, and her eyes that appreciate things no matter if they are beautiful or broken.

Seeing it is a whole new reality. She looks like a tiger stalking its prey, powerful as she tracks the players' movements. I know that look well. It comes with the feeling of creative flow. It feels criminal to break her concentration, so I just watch.

Eventually, I give up on looking at the players at all and just watch her.

She's so still.

Usually, despite her perfect posture and controlled sensibilities, she's always moving, whether it's her foot tapping or her finger tracing the seams of her jeans. It's a small thing that is easier to notice while it's absent.

I think I could be happy like this forever, seeing her do exactly what she was put on this planet to do. That's until she relaxes and turns towards me, and then I realize nothing can beat the way she looks at me.

I wonder how she sees me with her artist's eyes. I know she notices my flaws—the cracks and the chip on my shoulder that I can't seem to get rid of—but still, she's stayed.

Not only has she stayed, but she's needed me, finally letting me fully past her walls.

It's a privilege to be on the other side of them, one I won't take for granted.

41

Lacey

There's something nostalgic about having this old camera setup while I shoot the guys warming up. The lens Price and I ended up finding was the same one I used my senior year of college and my first year with the team.

Bit by bit, I've improved alongside them, and now I'm back at the beginning while they are achieving their dreams. It's a full-circle moment that I wouldn't have chosen for myself, but I can appreciate it despite the restlessness I feel in my bones. I trust that Drew will be here in time, but I can't shake the feeling of how I got here in the first place.

I'm determined not to let my initial mistake cause a chain reaction, but I feel like I'm about to detonate from all the worries that have sprung up.

Intrusive thoughts of worse-case scenarios clutter my mind, ranging from dropping my camera to watching Price get a career-ending injury. I reassure myself that neither of those things has happened before in my time with a camera or his years on the ice. But I also have never made a stupid mistake like forgetting half of the contents of my camera bag before.

I can't dwell in my head. If I do, that means I'm not being present enough to do my job. I take one moment to push the fear aside and collect myself.

Photographing these guys isn't a passive task. They are moving over twenty miles an hour on the ice. Sure, I can just click the button a million times and hope for a lucky shot, but that's not why they hired me. If they wanted that, they could have just handed fancy equipment to a kid and called it a day. No, they wanted me because I get in the zone with the guys.

So I release one last breath, feel the ground beneath me, and do what they pay me for. It's only when the guys break away for a few minutes that I can finally relax again. Minutes tick by, and I feel the heat of someone watching me prickle the back of my neck.

Leaning against the railing is Drew. His eyes locked on me, tracking my movements. I'm not sure how long he's been there with a pale blue camera bag slung over his shoulder.

With a wave, I signal for him to come closer, and he swiftly covers the distance between us with his long strides.

"You could have come down once you got here."

"No, hello, or thank you for flying a thousand miles to bring you your stuff. I see how it is," he deadpans, but his eyes glimmer with humor.

"I guess I should give you a reward for all your hard work," I say before pulling him down for a kiss.

He tries to pull me in, but I keep a hand on his chest so he doesn't crush the camera resting between us. Still, we draw out the moment, even through a series of whoops and hollers from the ice. At the sound of the team, I feel his lips curl into a smile as they claim mine.

As I pull away, Drew asks, "Is that all I get?"

"What I want to give you would hardly be appropriate while I'm on the clock," I reassure him.

"I'll be patient then." He punctuates his words with one more kiss before I grab the bag from him and check its contents. It worked out. It wasn't pretty, but it worked out.

"So, does this make me your new assistant then?"

"Having a pretty assistant would be too distracting. Go enjoy the game. I'll find you if I have time between periods." It's an effort to break away, but it's comforting to know his seats aren't that far from my position near the ice.

Even before the puck drop, a layer of palpable tension envelops the stadium. The intensity doesn't let up for an instant; if anything, the collective agitation grows as the teams are tied at the end of the second period with two goals each.

I hone in on the fight in the guys' features, displaying their drive for all those in the audience to see. This is what they've been working for. Right here on the ice, they are proving to everyone who watches that the Cobras are a team to be feared and remembered. They clawed their way to gain respect after years of hard work.

During the intermission between the second and third periods, I'm buzzing with adrenaline as I send the shots for the social media team.

In the last couple of minutes left, before I need to focus back on the ice, I turn my head to glance toward where Drew is seated in the stands.

A small cluster of women about my age are holding up their phones for pictures or asking for autographs. I can tell he's trying his best to humor the fans, but he'd probably rather just sink into the shadows, away from the spotlight.

Momentarily, I entertain a whimsical thought—I wouldn't mind escaping with him for a while. To escape the demands of work and the prying eyes of fans and simply vanish into the distance with Drew.

A flicker of movement draws me back to the ice, and it's time to work again. I'll have plenty of time to daydream about Drew and all the things we can get up to later. Both teams have given it their all up until this point, and it's easy to see that though their energy is depleted, they are being driven forward by pure force of will.

As the clock counts down, my rapid pulse rings louder in my ears. With three minutes left, we scored, putting us in the lead by a single point. All they have to do is maintain it.

The last minute of play moves so slowly, time feeling thick and viscous as it moves around us. For a moment, the entire game flashes before my eyes as Price doesn't block what might be a buzzer-beater from Boston's center. But this isn't the end;

the difference between hockey and basketball is that the puck has to be in the goal by the time the clock hits zero. I don't think I breathe as they review the footage.

I know Price is like me when it comes to moments like this. If they go into overtime and we lose, the weight of the loss will crush him. So I don't just hope for the sake of the win; I hope for my friend.

They make the call, and I rush onto the ice, capturing how the confirmed victory crashes over the team like a wave. Even though this isn't a game that ends with a conference trophy, this represents something monumental, a hurdle that they didn't let discourage them. The guys are cheering, arms in the air, processing their win. I can't wait to look back while I edit and see their faces, studying the expressions from achieving this moment.

We did it.

As the high drains and fans start to leave, I want to sit and never get up, even if it means I freeze in this arena. When I begin to slump, warm, sure hands hold me, and I lean back, not having to think about who's there to catch me. I knew before the smell of spice and sandalwood engulfed me.

"Let's get everything put away, and I'll take you back," he says as I lean my head against his chest.

"I still have the press conference," I groan, feeling the weight of exhaustion settle on my shoulders. I'm usually not this drained after a game, but then again, I don't usually forget things, either.

Despite my weariness, I make it through the clamoring conference, but only barely.

"We're going out to celebrate. You guys joining?" Price's voice breaks through the post-game chaos as he approaches us.

Right here, I find myself standing between the two men who I love most in my life. While I would have liked to introduce them formally, I have no doubt they know who the other is. Being famous like they are has its perks.

Before I can form the words, Drew says exactly what I'm thinking, "We're going to head to the hotel and rest for a bit. Maybe we'll catch up before midnight." I nod to give my own confirmation.

Before we turn away, I tell my friend, "No matter how it would have ended, I'm always proud of you."

"I know," he says, and from the look of relief that flashes across his face, I can tell he needed someone to acknowledge the possibility. To remind him it wouldn't have been his fault if we lost. "Let's do dinner when we're back in the city, ok?" Price asks the both of us, then heads off towards the team when Drew nods.

Instead of joining the team on the bus, I walk with Drew through the halls and towards the parking lot where he parked his rental.

"Hey," a voice calls, but I ignore it. "Hey, Lacey." Damn, I guess it is for me then. I'm running low on energy for anyone else besides the man walking beside me. Still, I give in and turn to see Tessa rushing down the corridor, attempting to wave us down.

When she stops in front of us, she looks right past me. Unsurprisingly, her attention is fixed on Drew. My skin prickles with irritation.

I want us to be normal, not constantly dealing with people trying to pull him away from me. I swallow the feeling. Drew looks down at me with a raised eyebrow, and something passes between us. I can tell he understands. But understanding doesn't guarantee that this will end well.

"You're Luca Mariano, right? I was wondering—"

He holds up a hand to cut her off. "I think you've got the wrong person."

"But you . . ." she starts, her words trailing off in confusion. She looks at me for a moment as if I'll help, but I just shrug.

"I get that a lot, don't worry." He holds out his hand for her to shake. "I'm Drew." A smirk pulls at his features. It's funny to think that he isn't really lying, well, not entirely.

I can tell that Tessa doesn't fully believe him, but it's obvious that if she keeps trying, she'll just look pushy. She stammers something like, "Oh, I'm sorry," then walks away.

Once she's out of earshot, I say, "You didn't have to do that."

"But I did, for both of us. We get to choose who to include in our lives. Anyone who thinks they're entitled to our time just because they know who we are can fuck off for all I care." My heart skips a beat at his words. I'd be lying if I didn't admit it made me feel like the center of the damn universe.

I lean on him all the way back to the hotel and up the elevator to my room. I've never felt like this with anyone else, secure in my own vulnerability. At the apartment, what now seems like years ago instead of two months ago, it was easy to fall into him because I convinced myself he was someone I would end up walking away from. It's easy to tell strangers your secrets because there's no risk to it.

As we get to the room, I'm still unstable and fairly nonverbal from exhaustion. I try to bend down to untie my combat boots, which shine with the sticky residue of spilled soft drinks tipped over by fans, but I start to tip over, losing my balance.

Drew catches me, guiding my back to lean against the wall. "Hey, let me get these." His hands make quick work of the laces, sliding the shoes off, not even scrunching his nose at how rank my feet probably smell. "What next?"

"Shower." I feel a little helpless, my voice coming out airy. I'm not this bad after a game, but the intensity of the last day feels like it's all finally processing.

"You know, I always wondered what had you looking so exhausted and alive every time you came home. God, watching you out there was better than the game. No offense to the guys, but they have nothing on you. What's going on in your head when you're out there?" Drew asks from where he's reclining on the hotel bed next to me.

"I guess I . . ." I have to think about how to put it all into words.

I can't remember the last time I really talked about my job—the last time someone outright asked and genuinely wanted to know about the passion that my life revolves around. Each time I've brought it up in the past, people have cared more about the players and the games.

"When I'm behind the camera, I'm in a different world, outside of my body, almost picking up on the little details, finding the exact right things that would matter to someone if they wanted to look back on the moment. I'm completely focused out of my own head because if I let doubt or any of my thoughts, it always seems to show, not in any way that stands out, but I can tell. I feel like I've been a background character in my own life with my dad and with the team, so it feels right to be just outside of the important things instead of directly part of them." I finish and bite nervously at my bottom lip before looking at Drew.

"That's remarkable. When I saw you, you were so commanding even when those players were fighting for the puck right in front of your face."

"I'm the best."

He skates his fingers along my arm. "I'm happy you know that because if you didn't, I would have put in the work to convince you of it. I've been wanting to reach out to the photographer who did that piece in my apartment. See if they'd do something for the bar, but would you do something instead?"

I can't help but laugh as I remember something I should have told him a while ago. We have so many gaps we still need to fill, and I can't wait to take my time learning everything. "I guess it's a good thing we're one and the same."

"Excuse me?"

"That's mine. Well, it's technically yours because you bought it for way too much money, but that was my piece for the auction. Somehow, without knowing me and without ever being in the same room, you gave me the validation to chase my dreams. If you didn't buy it, I would have probably been doing something boring with my life, something I'd hate."

"Huh."

"You're not shocked?" I ask, absentmindedly rubbing the cotton collar of his t-shirt between my fingers as I search his expression.

"At this point, you shock me pretty much every day, and I might be getting used to it, but I'll never be tired of it. And mostly, I'm just happy I could give you that. That in some way, I could help you achieve this dream. I want to keep giving you everything I can."

I swallow. "I can think of one thing you can give me right now."

"You want to. You're not too tired?" I feel him stiffen beneath me, his voice husky with want.

I turn so I'm no longer resting against his chest. I straddle his hips as I look into his eyes.

I lean in, brushing my lips against his for just a moment before admitting, "I've never done this before."

He tucks a strand of hair behind my ear.

"What do you mean? We've done this before, and as I recall, we're very good at it." I understand his confusion. We have been together before, but it was different. That first time was supposed to help us forget, but this—*this*—I want to remember.

"I've never been with someone I cared about. I've never had sex in a way that mattered."

"Then, if that's the case, I think this is my first time, too." His eyes crinkle with affection.

"Be gentle with me. It's been a few months."

"You mean that all the time we were living together, you were never with anyone else?" he asks, a line between his brows betraying a hint of fear at my potential answer.

"Not once."

During my overnight trips, there were times when I went out with the intention of being with someone, with anyone. But there was something off about each of the encounters. I guess I already had my heart set on Drew, even if I didn't realize it then.

"There was no one else for me either," he says as my chest settles. Because I've never let myself consider that there were plenty of nights when we were in different cities when he could have found someone else.

"You're kinda falling for me, huh?"

"Not falling, fallen. And I've been waiting for you to catch up," he says with fervent intensity.

I expect my heart to skip a beat at his words, but it continues in a steady rhythm, as calm wraps around me.

I used to experience love secondhand through other's vague metaphors and stumbling explanations. Some said it's like being on fire, while others felt like it's like your heart might burst. I guess that's why I didn't realize I was falling at all.

Falling for Drew was a wound knitting back together, a progression so slow and nurturing it was hard to notice while it was happening but seeing it now, I'm certain of my feelings for him.

I'm not ready to say what those words mean out loud. Soon, but not yet. Not while we're still healing.

Pulling his body to mine, I show him instead, intent on carving the words into his soul with my touch alone. The fabric of his shirt twists in my fists, and I trace my lips against the hints of rough stubble on his jaw and then down the stretch of his throat as his head tilts back to give me access.

He helps me pull his shirt over his head, discarding it once he's free. I continue my progression with my hands trailing across his stomach, feeling the muscles ripple under my exploratory touch.

He catches my chin as my fingers start to undo his belt buckle.

"Lace. If you do that, I'm not going to last. Seeing you take me in your mouth will have me coming in seconds, and I need to be inside of you," he groans.

"Just a taste. I want to feel you in every possible way."

I want to feel all of it. Every reaction. Every sensation. And I want it all with him, only him.

"Ok." I watch as his throat bobs and his jaw pulls with tension.

I take my time freeing him from his pants, letting my nails tease the inside of his thigh.

When he's naked before me, I'm reminded of how truly impressive he is. I stroke his length in one hand, lowering my head to swirl my tongue around the tip, flicking it over the salty taste of him.

"God. *Sconosciuta.* You're going to be my undoing." he pants, his hips jerk with the words.

The sound of him only urges me on. I wrap my lips around his cock and take him fully into my mouth. The need to make him feel good overtakes me, forgetting my earlier promise of restraint. I bob up and down as I run my tongue along his cock. He jerks his hips again with a choked moan and wraps his hand around my ponytail. Each noise he makes is a personal victory.

"I need you to stop so we can finish this together." He moves me back so I'm kneeling on the bed again. "But first, we have to do something about these clothes."

He undresses me with the same slow attentiveness as I did with him. Each brush of his hands sends sparks through me.

When I'm in an equal state of undress, he simply looks at me with admiration and a desperate need dancing in his emerald eyes.

He lowers me down on the bed next to him so we're laying side by side. His face takes up my entire field of vision. It's a perfect view.

I hold my breath in anticipation as his calloused fingers ghost across my stomach, moving down to press onto my clit.

"I've pictured this so many times . . . but my imagination could never do you justice." He presses a delicate kiss to the corner of my mouth before lowering himself to swipe his wet, hot mouth against my nipple, teeth lightly grazing the sensitive flesh.

"Let me grab a condom," he says.

"You don't need to. I have an IUD. I want to feel you. All of you." I don't want anything separating us, never again. As I press lightly against his chest, he rolls over flat on his back.

I straddle him, position myself, then sink down each inch of him slowly, finally returning to the sensation of fullness that I have longed for since our first night together. I close my eyes and simply feel him.

"Eyes on me. Look and see what you do to me. You make a mess of me, and I don't want it any other way," he murmurs, his voice a reverent whisper.

Lifting and then lowering my hips, I watch as he becomes as lost as I am.

Hands grip my waist, fingers splaying across my sides, guiding me as we work our bodies in tandem. Slowly, I lean forward to rest my forehead on his chest as he moves in and out of me. A kiss lands on my temple before he shifts us so he's on top, and his hands move over me in an act of silent devotion.

His fingers trace the curves of my lips, the bridge of my nose, the contour of my neck.

If I make a mess of him, he turns me to ruin.

He rocks into me, and with each fluid movement, he takes me further and further. One of his hands finds my clit with the deftness that only he seems capable of.

His other hand lightly brackets my throat, applying just enough pressure to feel his touch against my pulse, reminding me that I'm alive and this is real.

Maybe everyone I've been with before him was doing this wrong. Or maybe they weren't musicians who were the pure embodiment of rhythm and precision. Now that I've found one, I doubt I'll ever go back.

We never make it out to celebrate with the team.

The new year probably starts somewhere between the second and third time we tangle together. Maybe the clock strikes midnight when he's kissing the back of my neck or biting my lip, only to discover the little smiley face hidden there.

What really matters is we made it from one year to the next.

"*Sconosciuta*," he breathes against my lips as we lay in a mess of limbs and sheets.

"Are you ever going to tell me what that means?" I look into the endless layers of the forest trapped in his eyes, seeking an answer.

"Stranger," he says simply.

"But we're not strangers anymore." A reality I might have once mourned, but now, it's become a truth I'm learning to treasure.

"Maybe not, but I intend to learn as much as I can about you for as long as you let me."

I smile as he pulls me in for a kiss, his arms wrapped around me. As my eyes linger on him, I know one thing for certain.

This is going to work out.

42

Drew

Lacey exhales loudly through her nose, one of those almost laughs when something is just funny enough to make a noise but couldn't be called hilarious knowing her books of choice.

"What's so funny, someone getting murdered in a creative way? Was it a bear trap?" I ask, drawing her attention from where she's draped on the couch. The mid-day sun dances across her features and loose mess of waves. She rests her forearms on the back of the couch, watching as I finish assembling the roasted vegetables into the winter salad I've been preparing.

"I was just thinking that it would have been nice to meet you sooner. To have more time. But then I realized if I had met you on any other night, I probably would have hated you." I've thought the same thing. What if Martin and she had a good relationship and we could have known each other for years? Or if we crossed paths in any number of different ways.

"You didn't seem to like me all that much that night."

"I didn't like the world all that much that night. And you were exactly what I needed at the moment."

"Well, I'm glad you don't hate me, but I am a little concerned that you're thinking about me while reading about gore and dismemberment."

"This one is a bit more psychological if that helps," she offers.

"I think it does, but only because I don't know what psychological horror is." She opens her mouth to explain it, but I stop her before she says something that would haunt my dreams. "And I'll be happy to continue not knowing."

A slight chuckle escapes her lips as I bring the plates to the living room and set them on the coffee table. Taking my place on the couch beside her, she snuggles closer, tucking her body into mine.

"So you really think that?" I ask, catching her attention, confusion flickering in her eyes until I add, my tone softening. "You believe that if we had met any other night, any other place, we wouldn't be here?" It's hard to think that's even possible, but so many things had to align for this moment—this late lazy lunch at home on Tuesday afternoon.

"I think that if there are different timelines, different ways that this could have all worked out, then we're the lucky ones."

"I pity the versions of me that never had a chance to fall for you," I whisper, pressing a tender kiss to her forehead, just thankful she exists.

We finish our meal as I mentally prepare myself for what's ahead.

I've already survived a few meetings with the guys, and despite having to navigate minor disagreements and egos, it's good to be back with them in some ways.

As members of Fool's Gambit, we once grew together like those trees that grow beside each other, roots twining together until they're indistinguishable. But now, we don't fit together how we used to. We still have our history, but there are parts we no longer share.

This will be the last rehearsal before the reunion show. I want Lacey there, but I've also told her I understand if she doesn't want to go.

Her bringing me to the Cobra's game was letting me step into something new. I want to do the same for her, but I also know that bringing her into this part of my life pulls her into a complicated part of her past. Yet, each time I gave her the option to back out, she reassured me that she wants to be there. It also makes me feel better knowing Evelyn will be in the city a few days early for the week of rehearsals and for the reunion this weekend.

I ask Lacey one last time as we make our way to leave, "You really don't have to come if you don't want to. You'll get to see us perform on Saturday."

"It's starting to sound like you don't want me there."

"I do. I really do. I just don't want you to feel any pressure to go."

"I want to be there. And who else gets to say that their first concert is a private session with Fool's Gambit?"

"Then let's do this," I beam as we walk out the door together.

She drives us to the rehearsal space we've rented out for the day. Her Subaru pulls in between a cherry-red vintage Mustang and a black Porsche. Good to know that Garrett and Wes got here safe.

I check my phone to check Ev's ETA, but I'm greeted with the information that she caught a ride with Garrett. When I suggested that he help her with her imminent move, I didn't actually think they'd spend time together.

Yells drift our way as we approach the door to our rented rehearsal space. Great. We're already gearing up for an excellent first impression. I look down, and Lacey just winks at me.

"Sinatra?" Garrett bellows down at Wes. "Fucking Sinatra?" Their six-inch height difference adds to the drama of the moment.

"What do you have against Sinatra?" Wes shoots back.

"Nothing. I just asked you who your favorite jazz artist was, and Sinatra doesn't fit the criteria."

"Forgive me if I don't have the taste of a dusty grandpa. Having old cars and playing chess doesn't make you cool and mysterious, you know."

My sister cuts in from the couch in the corner. She's a pop of pink in the otherwise muted space. "And being world-class dicks doesn't make either of you interesting. If you two lovers will stop bickering, we have someone important to introduce you to." She rises and moves to wrap an arm around Lacey's shoulders. "Oh, and Wes, if you so much as think about touching her, I will cut off your favorite body part. Ok?" she issues the threat with a full smile, sending a chill through me.

"Understood." Wes salutes with a sloppy grin on his face.

"Martin's daughter, right?" Garrett reaches out his hand, and Lacey takes it, looking skeptically at my bandmates.

"Yes, but I prefer it when people use my name. Lacey Decker." Her last name is news to me, but I guess it makes sense that she'd take her mother's name.

Garrett appraises her, not as a man drinking in a woman, but as if Lacey is someone worthy of his acknowledgment. Good. I was ready to fight for her to be comfortable here, but it's clear she can handle herself.

The door opens behind us as Jared finally joins. "Sorry guys, the call ran late. Apparently, someone has a crush on the babysitter because she beats him at video games. Let's get this going so I can go home to my kids."

"You don't like us all that much anymore," Wes whines.

"I've known you idiots for almost two decades. I only have a few more years with them before they want nothing to do with me, and I'm not wasting a single minute of that shit." Jared makes his way to his spot on stage, grabbing his guitar from the stand.

Thank God we can get this going.

Evelyn grabs Lacey, directing her where to sit.

The rest of us follow Jared onto the stage and settle into our respective places, Jared and I towards either end with Garrett and Wes splitting the middle.

Once they all give me the nod to indicate they're ready, I tap my drumsticks together four times, setting the tempo for "Ronnie." Wes starts the vocals, and the rest of us build out the instrumentals. Garrett joins as his fingers work a bass line, his rasping voice clashing perfectly with Wes's velvety tone. That is how the song is supposed to be, though, or at least what it turned into.

Fans fell in love with it because it sounded like two men fighting over the same woman— a fantasy supported by the dramatic crescendos and heavy use of tension-filled minor chords.

Did you ruin him like you ruined me?

Your touch my favorite liability.

I'm yours to haunt, Ronnie.

The moment the last chord is struck, Wes whirls on me. "You were behind," he snaps.

He's right, I was behind. No matter how much I've been practicing, I can't fabricate the feeling of playing side by side with others even if I use our old recordings.

"Sorry," is all I can say.

"Sorry isn't gonna cut it. We have to be just as good, if not better. We have to give everyone what they're paying for when we walk out there," Wes fumes. He's a different person when he's performing, his usual laid back demeanor sloughing off to reveal someone who needs absolute control.

Jared takes a step toward us. "It's not a big deal. That's why we're practicing. We'll be perfect. Just let us get back into the groove of things first." I want to believe he's right, but there's something in me winding tight—something more than normal nerves, or should I say more than what I ever experienced when we used to practice together.

Wes huffs. "Fine. Let's start again."

We take "Ronnie" from the top. It starts the same, with me taking the lead and setting the tempo. The movements flow out of me, each hit reverberating up my arms with precise intensity. Then we hit the chorus, and I can feel the anxiety rushing through me. The flood of nerves disrupts my equilibrium.

No. I'm supposed to get through this.

Fuck. I'm supposed to be better.

My eyes flick toward Evelyn. She hasn't seemed to notice. Is this when she figures it out? When they all do? We may have started all this together, but in the end, will I be thrown away so they can keep going? Just like last time?

The thoughts rattle through my brain, and I see Wes starting to turn to me.

Just as he opens his mouth, another voice cuts through the music.

43

Lacey

"Fuck that hurts," I say, then suck my finger into my mouth, my lips covering the imaginary gash. I was lost watching Drew play. Then he started to unfurl.

No one else seemed to see it: his forearms tensing, the drums sounding duller than they did moments before, or his brow forming into the slightest of creases. In the blink of an eye, he went from being the confident, brilliant musician I knew to someone unsure and wavering.

Once the words leave my mouth, everyone pauses. Evelyn is the first to react. "Are you ok?"

I am, but I'm not above lying to get him out of this. I'm not above much when it comes to him.

"Yeah, I think there's just a loose staple or nail in the couch. I should probably find a first aid kit," I say, turning from Evelyn to the guys. "Drew, can you help?"

"Of course," he says, the fear in his eyes is now replaced with worry. I hold my breath as he rises, tracking his movements.

My eyes flick to the others in the room. How don't they seem to see it? The way his hands flex and his jaw tenses?

I meet him by the door and head into the hall.

Drew turns to me the moment we're alone. "How bad is it?"

"I'm fine," I say, dropping my hand and giving up my facade. "But you're not."

"I'm fine," he grits out, glancing away from me.

"Don't insult me by lying. I know you," I remind him, my tone firm but not harsh. "I don't know who was up on that stage, but it wasn't you."

"I'm sorry."

"You can save that for them, but you don't have to say that to me. So tell me, talk to me about what's happening," I urge him, continuing to do my best to walk the line between concern and comfort.

"Lacey, we're in a hallway."

"Hallway, bathroom, I don't give a fuck if we were in a subterranean bunker. It's us right now, you and me. So tell me, what do you need?"

"A second. I just need a second."

"Let's take one together then," I say, pulling his face to mine and lean my forehead against his. With his skin against mine, I can feel how clammy he's become.

Once his breaths become more regular, I ask, "What was different just now?"

"What do you mean?"

"I mean, I've seen you play before. I know you're good. No, you're better than good," I say, still close enough to feel his tension rising. "But in there, on that stage, it wasn't the same. So what's different, what caused this?" I repeat.

"I don't think I can do it anymore," his voice barely a whisper. "The moment I start slipping, it feels like I'm living out that night again. That it's all ending. That it will never be perfect again. Like I'm supposed to fail."

I hesitate and then ask, "What happened? Not the media version, not what you think I want to hear. What happened to you?"

His Adam's apple bobs, and I brace myself to hold his entire world on my shoulders. "One week before our last performance, they told me they were done. No one ever asked me what I wanted, what it would do to my life, but I could see they all talked to each other." He pauses. "I was so sure I was ok with it. That I could just move on. But music was everything to me. *Everything.* I think that day, I was so sure that if I just got everything right, we'd be fine, stay in each other's lives, be friends, stay brothers. But then I saw Wes with Emily, and I knew . . . I knew I was nothing more than a means to an end. I walked on that stage and then . . ." he trails off, but I know.

He fell on that stage, and no one bothered to catch him.

He sold his soul to people he trusted and never questioned the price. He found the knife they buried in his back, and they expected him to brush it off as if no scar was left behind.

"Have you ever told anyone about this?" It's all I can ask, but I already know the answer.

"No."

"Why not?"

"Because I didn't need to. Because it was over. I guess that was the wrong move, huh?"

"Probably," I say, our gazes locking for a moment. "I want to be everything to you, but I'm not sure how much help I can be with this. I know there are people out there who specialize in helping people work through these things. I want you to get all the help you need, even if I'm not the one giving it to you."

"Are you finally admitting you're not perfect at everything?" he teases, and the trace of humor in his tone calms me slightly.

"Just this once." I smile faintly. "Now, do what you promised me you'd always do. Get back out there and play for me because no matter what happens today or at the reunion, I'm not leaving. I don't care about the music; I care about you."

In response, he weaves his fingers into my hair.

"I'll find someone, but on one condition."

"What's that?" Whatever it is that he needs, I'll give it to him in an instant.

"You find someone, too. You deserve to have someone in your corner to help however you need." His hand meets mine. "I will always be here, always, but in those moments when I may not be able to be exactly what you need, I want you to have someone who can. We might not be able to do this by ourselves, but we can do it together."

I nearly cry, and the tell-tale prickle stings the backs of my eyes. I shouldn't have expected anything less.

"Are we making a therapy pact right now?" I ask.

"I think so."

I nod my agreement, taking the first step into a reality where I'm whole, happy, and his. Now that it's in reach, I think it's all I'll ever want to be.

We stand for a long time, much too long for our mission of just finding a bandaid. The band can wait. The damn world can wait for us if it has to.

Eventually, Drew pulls away slightly and murmurs, "I'm ready."

We head back down the corridor and back to the practice room. The guys take a moment to bicker about where to start, but Evelyn pulls me away from the chaos. "No luck with the bandaid?"

I hold up my conspicuously non-bleeding finger for a minute. "Yeah, funny how it stopped all of a sudden."

"Yeah, funny how that happens." She gives me a conspiratorial look as the band starts to play again.

As Drew strikes the first beat, I know it's different. As the song continues, I get a true glimpse of America's Heartthrobs.

They are more magnetic than before; their foundation is more solid. Just like those videos I watched of their early performances, my eyes don't catch on Wes or Garrett; they trail to the flurry of motion and passion, which is all Drew. For the first time in my life, I don't blame my mother for falling so irrevocably for someone whose talents alone were all-consuming.

I don't even attempt to stop the thought that follows.

This is how you're supposed to listen to music. You're supposed to be in love with the drummer.

I've listened to him practice, seen old clips from concerts, and heard the rumble of his voice in my ear as he made me come. Yet, none of those things have prepared me for the silky sound of his voice mixing with the other members of the band. He looks so incredibly alive like he was designed for this exact moment.

His eyes catch mine, and my heart flutters. It's easy to imagine I'm in a crowd of screaming fans, and I was the one lucky enough to have him look at me. Is this how my parents felt when they fell for each other? Did my mother feel this magnetic pull and get completely swept away?

"They're kind of perfect up there, aren't they? Just as good as they used to be," Evelyn whispers in my ear, and I follow her gaze to where it's locked on Garrett and his bass.

Next to Garrett, Wes is looking at us. Well, it would be more accurate to say he's looking through us, trying to find someone who isn't here.

As if reading my thoughts, Evelyn says, "Avery. I invited her, but I guess they still haven't worked through their shit."

Avery. There's only one Avery I can think of, and it's odd to hear Avery Sloane's name thrown around so casually. But that's this world, I guess.

His world.

I look up at him, noticing how completely he's in his element, and I can't help the tight feeling settling within me, replacing the awe I've been consumed by.

What if this pushes him to get back into music? Could we make that work? Even if I can't, there's no way I'll be able to hold him back from a life he loves this much.

I'd give anything for a manual on how to handle our situation.

They run through the whole set and take a break for pizza before they go back and work through some of the transitions. They bicker, but in a way that feels more brotherly than spiteful. Evelyn and Jared take turns yelling at Garrett and Wesley to stay focused. Drew sets the tone for any instrumental adjustments. The way they communicate appears just as rehearsed as their playing, albeit a little more chaotic.

When I check my phone, I'm startled to see how many hours have passed as everyone is packing up.

Evelyn grabs my hand, stopping me for a moment before we get up from the couch. "Let's get ready for this thing together. They just have to throw on suits and walk out the door. We can have fun with it. You have a dress, right?"

"I'd love that. I actually have no idea what to wear to something like this. But it's just a concert, right?"

"It's more of a gala because these people will make an excuse to be absolutely full of themselves, but I've got you covered. I brought an extra dress that will look stunning on you. See you in a few days!" She rises and races after Garrett. That girl is a goner. I should know. I'm in the same boat when I look at Drew coming towards me, hands stuffed in his pockets, sleeves rolled up to reveal his tattoos.

"So, how was it?" He's sheepish now as if he didn't just give me the most stunning experience.

There's that ache in my heart again. Because how do I tell him how perfect it was and still ask him not to go back to that life? If we're going to give this our all, I owe it to him and myself to not bury this concern and risk it causing a rift between us.

"It was amazing," I say, my smile feeling a bit forced. Before I lose my nerve, I ask, "If you had the chance to go back on tour, record new songs, and live it all over again, would you?"

"No. That's not what I want anymore."

"Why not? I've seen you in the videos and just now on stage. You're some type of god up there. It's like if I had touched you, I would have been set on fire by how fiercely the music was running through you. And I know you make people so happy. If you're saying that for my benefit, please don't. Don't make a sacrifice that will only lead you to hate me. I might be able to live a life without you, knowing that you're doing what you love, but I don't think I can live in a world where I hold you back. I just—"

He cuts off my rant, "Those things have nothing to do with why I'm here." With a tender touch, he lifts my chin, guiding my gaze to meet his. "I needed the reunion to say goodbye to my past and move on. I spent so many years trying to change something that was already set in stone, and it was ruining me. Music will always be a part of me, but you're my future, Lacey. You are so damn easy to love, and I'd be a fool to walk away."

"You love me?" I thought if I ever heard those words from him, I'd feel like running. Instead, they fall over me with a sense of security.

"Yes."

"I love you too. I'm sorry I haven't made it easy." Despite the aggressive swarm of butterflies that have taken up residence in my gut, I can't help but push. I need to make sure that his words won't fall apart under pressure.

Drew's face softens with awe as he says, "Loving you is the easiest thing I've ever done. Waiting for you, chasing you, hoping that I'm worthy of being in the same room as you. That shit is hard. I deserve a gold medal for that. But loving you has taught me what it's like to breathe again. So, if you do leave one day, you'll be leaving me a better person."

As if I'd ever dream of leaving. Not again. I had a taste of that once, and I don't really want to repeat it.

"You're so dramatic," I laugh. "Besides, I can't leave now that we have a therapy pact. That shit is binding."

"You make me dramatic," he murmurs, leaning in for a kiss, his lips fitting perfectly against mine. "Are you ready to go home?"

"Yes, please. I have some terribly wicked things I'd like to do to the man I love," I say with a mischievous grin, and I'm rewarded with a groan.

As we make our way to the exit, I feel like I'm five tons lighter. However, as soon as we step outside, we're greeted by blinding flashes that slash through the night.

I squint as my eyes adjust and take in the cameras.

"Damn, could you give us some space?" Drew's voice cuts through the chaos, his hand shielding his face while holding mine with the other. But even as I watch him lace his fingers with mine, I can't feel it. I can't feel my legs rushing to follow. The only thing I can focus on are the relentless flashes trailing behind us.

Finally reaching my car, I tremble uncontrollably as I press the keys into his hand. "I can't drive."

His wide-eyed gaze meets mine briefly before he nods, accepting the keys. I settle into the passenger seat, leaning back in an attempt to relax.

We drive in silence, tension thick in the air, until he parks the car in the garage and turns to me. "Are you ok?" he asks softly.

"I'm fine."

"Lace, you never let me drive."

Damn. Being predictable has its perks, but people being able to read me so easily in moments like this isn't one of them.

"I can't do cameras. Be behind them, sure. Being the one in the picture makes me feel like my body has been stripped away." I look down at my hands, curling and uncurling them, trying to regain feeling.

Drew's hand strangles the steering wheel. "I'm sorry. Someone must have leaked the location, but I should have known that it would have made you uncomfortable."

"How would you?"

"I used to see you and your mom on those stupid check-out aisle tabloids. I never thought about privacy and stuff like that until later, when paparazzi would show up and ruin a perfectly normal day. But for me, that was part of my job. For you and your mom, that wasn't your fault, and you still had to go through it."

"It's ok," I say, not sure if I'm trying to comfort him or myself.

"I'm really sorry," he says, placing his hand on mine, calming me a little. "It'll be over soon. I promise."

I feel at peace when we get home; walking through the door still has the effect of shrugging off the shit from the outside world.

We curl up with one of Drew's documentaries, this one is something about the Roman Empire. I won't admit that I like it when we watch them, not because I get any joy from the droning narrators or endless facts, but because the slow pace draws out the moments, letting me simply exist with him.

As the narrator prattles about war tactics, I trace his tattoos like constellations. "This one. What's it for?" I ask, my finger landing on a black spade.

"It's part of a set. Each of us has a card suit."

"You and the guys? Do you regret getting something permanent with them?" I've been able to piece together bits of their history. For all the good that music and being in the band brought to his life, there were bad parts, too—parts that tore him apart for years.

"No. The past is important. The people we meet, even if they fade away, it's an honor to have memories with them."

I think of the final memory I've been putting off, the little fragments of time I hold close to my heart because I'm scared they will feel too much like goodbye. In a few days, I'll be giving Martin the same opportunity, and I'm not sure what I expect him to do once I hand him his letter.

And then there's my own letter, waiting for me, haunting me. I know I'll have to read it eventually, but I don't know if I can.

I don't know if I will ever be ready to say goodbye to that last part of *her*.

44

Lacey

"You're sure? We can still pull around." Drew asks, his eyes locked on mine in a way that makes me feel like we're the only ones in the world.

"If this is the one time we get to do this. To let the world see that you're mine, then I think I can manage." I smile, trying to suppress my nerves.

After the incident at the rehearsal, Drew warned me that there would be a red carpet of sorts before the reunion, showcasing the big names in attendance. He then asked if I wanted him to arrange an alternative entrance so I didn't have to face the circus of media attention.

Instead of taking his offer, I thought about how to use this opportunity to my advantage. I've never had the chance to control these situations, to be prepared, or to take back some power that was stolen from me. And the smile he gave me when I told him I wanted to be by his side for all to see made it worth it.

Our car pulls up in the queue. We slide out, followed by Evelyn, who chatted with the driver the entire ride over.

As the clamor of the crowd floods my senses, Drew's hand finds mine, and he whispers into my ear, "Say the word, and we'll run the rest of the way."

"I'm done running," I tell him, infusing all the confidence I can muster into my voice.

Tonight marks another step forward, a special night for both of us: the end of running from everything that drove us into hiding.

And there's no one I'd rather face it with.

My legs betray me only twice, once from nerves and the other from how unaccustomed I am to wearing heels. The sequined midnight-colored gown, borrowed from Evelyn, shimmers under the light of each camera flash. Beside me, Drew is in a deep crimson suit; instead of a tie, he's undone the top buttons of his shirt so the edges of his tattoos are visible. And with each flicker, there's an odd sense of pleasure that tugs at my heart each time I catch someone's gaze flick between Drew and me.

Mine.

Not in a possessive way, but in the way that has settled on me like a second layer of skin.

Hand in hand, we make our way through the bustling crowd, surrounded by voices calling out with a million questions. And when I turn to him, his unwavering focus on me is everything I need.

We catch up with Evelyn inside, entering one of the upper boxes that hang above the general admission seats in the venue.

"I need to go check with the tech team one last time before the performance. See you later. I love you." His lips find mine in a casual yet firm kiss. He's been peppering 'I love yous' since the moment we first spoke the words to each other. I thought the frequency of his affirmations would tarnish the feeling that accompanies them. Instead, I believe him more each time.

He turns back. "I know this night is supposed to be about reconnecting with your dad, but I need you to know that there's no way I would be able to do this without you."

"I wish I had my glittery 'Please make sweet love to me Luca Mariano' sign with me, but I think I left it in the car."

"I can still fulfill that request later." He punctuates his words with another kiss.

"God. You two are like rabbits in heat," Evelyn groans next to us. She's slowly becoming one of my favorite people. Still, a barb-like sting hits my chest whenever I remember all the years lost between them.

"Oh no. Is this a text about crime statistics in New York that I'm about to send in the family group chat?" Drew's finger hovers over his phone, threatening the imaginary text.

"I will leak every embarrassing photo I have of you to every tabloid I can think of and celebrate your downfall." Her cool tone gives the impression this is a practiced threat.

Though they make getting under each other's skin a competitive sport, it's definitely comforting to see her in his corner.

Hurrying toward us is a petite Black woman wearing wire-rimmed glasses and a sleek black pantsuit. Her narrowed eyes are fixed on Drew as if she could freeze him in place.

"Hartly, look! I'm here," Drew announces with a dramatic spin. "No hired guns needed."

"Yes, you're *here,* but you're supposed to be *there.*" Hartly points towards the stage. "Your job isn't done until you make a room full of twenty and thirty-somethings feel like teenagers again."

"Fine, I'm coming." With a *what are you gonna do shrug*, Drew lets Hartly drag him away

Evelyn turns to me with the customary gleam in her eye. "I guess that's my cue, too. I'll go save Avery from whatever reporter is holding her captive."

Yeah, her 'good friend' Avery Sloane. Even with my boyfriend being an internationally known popstar, I don't think I'll ever get past it.

Alone in the box, I contemplate what I should do next, trying to figure out where Martin could be so I can track him down. But before I can even come up with a plan, Martin finds me first.

I watch him approach, dressed in a sleek suit with blond hair that has hints of gray around the temples. It's odd seeing him in the flesh, knowing who we are to each other, yet sharing so few memories. Our gazes lock, and it's like I'm staring into my own eyes.

"Lacey. I'm so glad you could make it. I know that it was a pretty big ask for you to be here. I wish we could have had a little more time before this, but I guess you would have ended up here anyway with your relationship." There's nothing but joy in his features. How can someone's smile look so foreign yet familiar?

I glance towards my bag resting on my seat a few feet away. Is this when I tell him? Do I just hand off the letter and hope for the best? I hadn't really thought this far, focusing more on getting myself here.

I resolve to do this later, after the high of the performance has passed. After I get to celebrate Drew.

"It's funny how these things turn out, isn't it?" Granted, if it wasn't for Martin, I would have never been within a hundred feet of that bar in the first place.

I make an effort to push the conversation forward, asking, "So, what have you been up to these days?"

"I've been helping these twins record while on tour; really talented kids. But not as talented as these guys. I don't think anything I do will ever be as great as them."

What about me? I could have been great.

The voice of that little girl echoes in my mind, her words haunting me as I make an effort to keep a smile on my face, trying to swallow the lingering sourness.

He continues, "I'm rejoining them after tonight in Milan. You're always welcome to come to a show. I've been to these cities dozens of times. It would be great to show you around."

"That would be nice."

"Enough about me, though. Tell me how you are. Tell me what I've missed." Yeah, because that's an easy task, but I make an attempt. I tell him about my work with the Cobras and the season so far. He nods politely at all the right parts.

"The award was for this picture that I took during—" My story is cut off by a phone ringing, and a part of me hopes he'll let it go and choose me for once. But he pulls out the device immediately and walks away to answer it without a word.

His actions force me to reset my expectations, reminding me he's still the same person—charming until something more important comes up.

The background pre-show music lowers as Evelyn walks back into the space carrying glasses of champagne. She's followed by a woman who is unmistakably Avery Sloane. Fire red hair flowing over one bare shoulder in old Hollywood waves, the slit in her draping, black silk gown reveals a patchwork of intricate ink.

The image of elegance and mystery shatters as she slumps into a chair one over from me and moans, "Shouldn't heels hurt less if you pay more for them?"

Evelyn looks at me with a knowing smirk. "Celebrities, they're really just like us. You know what they say about never meeting your heroes."

Avery scoffs, "Oh, babes. I shouldn't be anyone's hero unless they want an example of how to suffer alone."

"Makes good inspiration for music." Evelyn balances Avery's dejected state with her optimism.

"Then tell me why I haven't won a Grammy in the last ten years." Avery sighs and raises a hand to massage her temples.

"Don't worry about that tonight. Just drink your champagne." Evelyn turns to me, handing over one of her glasses of sparkling liquid. "Here, I got you this."

Martin walks back into the room, settling into his seat on the other side of me. Evelyn nods, giving my father a saccharine smile. "Martin."

"Evelyn," he says in return.

The lights finally dim, cutting through the awkward pause, and the room falls silent in anticipation.

A spotlight slashes through the darkness to illuminate Wesley's form at the front of the stage, and the first notes to "Ronnie" float into the crowd. Voices erupt with cheers at his appearance. The remainder of the stage floods with light as Garrett's voice joins, and just like in the rehearsal, the opening song bursts with tension.

The crowd's excitement doesn't dwindle for a second, eating up every note, every lyric. It doesn't matter if this is the thousandth time they've heard these songs. This is their moment to relive something magical right alongside the men on stage.

I see that magic in Drew, and my heart catches in my throat. Even as I watch how the act of performing takes over his whole body, somehow, he still looks up to find me. Even in this mass of energy, he only has eyes for me, as if I'm the only one in the room.

Just before the last song, Wesley moves to the front of the stage, and the crowd hushes for the first time since the show began. The energy in his voice is as infectious as it is inviting as he speaks. "Thank you all for being here. Thank you for giving us this world. Without you all, we would have just been some guys playing music in Luca's parent's garage. You gave us the whole world, and we're so happy to relive the highlights with you. We could have never imagined that our music would have such an impact after a decade. You haven't let us become Half a Memory." He pauses to accommodate the applause. "And don't forget you can see me and an old friend of the band, Avery Sloane, on our tour that's kicking off early next year." The reminder garners another round of cheers before Wes steps back into place.

I look to my side as Avery mutters something under her breath as she rolls her eyes. The reaction throws Evelyn into a coughing laugh as the first dissonant sounds play.

You and I were only half a memory.

I think about it all the time.

We were only half a memory, but it's my favorite place to hide.

The mournful lyrics build, ending with each of the guys making their way to the front of the stage. The men look ablaze in the lights; each made immortal by touching the hearts of everyone witnessing the moment.

With one final heart-wrenching crescendo, the room turns black, and another round of applause floods the space.

"Your mother would have loved this," Martin calls over the slowly receding cheers.

"She would have."

"How is she?"

He doesn't know?

"I hope she's doing well," he continues, with a slight smile on his lips.

My heart stops as the realization dawns on me.

He really doesn't know.

Suddenly, everything falls into place: his lack of urgency, his unsettling silence after she passed, and the peculiar locations he'd suggested to meet.

There's no escaping this moment any longer.

I slowly stand up, trying my best to school my features as I ask, "Martin, is there somewhere we can talk?"

Under ordinary circumstances, the private room would have looked magnificent with its crystal chandelier and lush velvet couches. Instead, it feels like my personal purgatory, a place I have to pass through but want to leave desperately.

"How long has it been?" Martin's voice comes out rough as sandpaper.

"Three years this May," I say, the heaviness of her absence intensifying as I reflect on how long it's been. *Three years.* "I don't know how this happened. I could have sworn that someone would have told you."

But really, who was there to tell him? My mother had no family who would have done it, no connections who would have gone out of their way to contact Martin. There was just me.

A part of me envies him. How, for the last few years, he got to live in a world where he thought she was alive and well. A world of ignorance where grief didn't claw at his heart.

"I'm glad you were the one to tell me. Not some phone call." I watch his shaking hands, unsure how to comfort him. I should have the answers. I already went through this. But it's been years, and I still don't understand it. I'm not sure I ever will.

I pull out the letter, the slightly crumpled envelope flimsy in my hand.

"This is yours. This is why I reached out. You don't have to open it—" Before I can finish, he quickly takes it from my grasp and frees the contents without a second thought.

I should let him have this moment to himself. But as I shift to rise, I catch a glimpse of the first page.

Lacey lost her first tooth today. She didn't cry, just walked into my room with a bloody tooth and asked, "Is this supposed to happen?"

I can't stop my eyes from trailing further down the page.

Lacey started soccer today. She was so mad that she wasn't the best. I see your fire in her.

The list keeps going, my mom's delicate words starting to smudge from the tears trickling off Martin's cheeks and onto the paper—my firsts, my victories, and my losses, all in chronological order. Some in blue ink, others in red or black.

As Martin continues to flip through the last three pages filled with what he missed out on, I catch the first line of the first page.

My love, we have lost so many good years.

Still processing my mixed feelings, I finally pull away and shut the door behind me as I leave. This moment isn't for me; it's between him and her.

But as I wander the historic halls, I can't shake the feeling of jealousy creeping in—how easily he took the letter, how ravenous he was for one last scrap of her.

I find an unlocked door leading to a balcony. When I look up, only a few stars wink at me, their light dimmed by the pollution of the city.

My fingers toy anxiously with the corner of my own letter, one that I had no reason to bring. I pull it out and stare at the precise letters on the front.

Lacey, for if I ever leave you.

Grief isn't simple or kind, but it's there whether or not I open this letter, whether or not I give myself this last piece of her. Grief will always be there. But it's my choice to know this last piece of my mom, to read the words she wanted me to have.

To stop running.

To stop hiding.

I run my finger under the sealed flap and draw out the two pages.

The greeting is far less formal than what I saw at the start of Martin's.

Lacey,

I just got a picture of you from Price. You look beautiful! By the way, green has always been one of my favorite colors on you. HAPPY NEW YEAR!

I'm sitting down to write this letter to you like I always do on New Year's Eve. Morbid, I know. But it's the one resolution I always keep. To write everything down so nothing is left unsaid. I see it every day in the hospital. The regrets of a love lost too soon. I guess it's always too soon, though.

If you're reading this, it's too soon.

So many things to say, and maybe I've had too much wine to say them all properly. First and always, you are the love of my life.

You are mine, but I hope I'm not yours.

I hope you find someone to slow you down. I hope they don't try to stop you, though, but I doubt anyone could because you are a force of nature.

I am scared of that sometimes, how hard you push and push. I'm scared about how much of it is for me and how much it is for you. I see you and all the work you have put into your dreams. I'm proud of you. But do me a favor and do things that make you so happy that they make you forget silly things like time and heartbreak.

I know I don't talk about your father enough. For all the pain, I loved him. I loved him, and because of that, I got to love you. Maybe you can forgive him, or maybe not.

That's for you to decide.

But understand that despite all my hurt, I still hold good memories of him, while you only have stories. I just don't want you to be scared of who you are. You're the best parts of us. And that's all a mother could ever ask for.

I feel like this is the part where I should leave you with some sort of wisdom, but I don't think there's much left for me to teach you.

I just hope that one day you figure out for yourself that when you face a brutal storm, the type where it feels like the rain will bruise you, it's a little easier if someone is there getting drenched with you.

Because there's no world where I tell you this enough, I love you. I love you. I love you.

-Mom

I let the tears roll down my cheeks, my heart heavy with regret as I read that last part once more. To feel the cadence of her words. To picture her drinking a cheap red blend at her vintage desk, writing out her goodbye before she was even gone.

Drew's words echo in my mind.

The people we meet, even if they fade away, it's an honor to have memories with them.

Placing my hands over my heart, I remember the countless moments we shared, every genuine smile etched in my memory, every sacrifice she made, and every time she lifted me up when I fell.

"I miss you so much," I whisper.

And I know this ache will never truly stop because that's grief. It isn't the end of love; it's the continuation of it. It's carrying someone with you because the love you shared was so strong that you refuse to let them disappear.

"I love you, Mom. I love you. I love you. Always."

And as I gaze up at the stars that silently watch over me, I can only hope she hears my words.

45

Drew

There's nothing fake about the smile on my lips as we leave the stage. It's a relief to be done. For the first time, I feel like I've tied a bow on this chapter of my life and can finally walk away without regrets.

"I missed that," Wes says, stretching one arm over his head as we walk backstage.

"Sure, cause it's been what? Four months since your last tour," Garrett scoffs at his friend as he pushes his way into the green room. Signatures and posters gild the walls, a defiant contrast to the elegance of the rest of the venue.

"No. I mean, I meant I missed this. Us." Wes collapses onto the couch with a sigh. "It's not the same."

Jared flops down next to Wes, his sweat-soaked red hair falling into his eyes as he exhales heavily. "I get what you mean. Sometimes, I wish we stuck it out a little longer. Made that last album. I love my family, but sometimes I miss how big you can feel out there." He stops abruptly and gives us all a pointed look. "I swear if Alyssa hears any variation of that." We exchange smiles, knowing damn well we weren't going to say anything anyway. "Honestly, I've never felt so stressed over anything in my life."

"You're serious?" I ask.

"Yeah, it's not like we're practicing round the clock like we used to, except for Wes. And they," Jared gestures, fanning out his arm to form the picture of an imaginary audience, "expected us to be just as good. Shit, I even started going to therapy twice a week because I couldn't handle the stress."

"Why didn't you say something?" I press, my voice bordering on accusatory.

"I guess I just thought we were all going through it." Jared shrugs, then lets his body slump. His statement is simple, but it flips a switch in my head. He felt like we were all in it together, but I felt like the only person affected by the fallout. And somehow, both of us went through it without the others.

"Speak for yourself," Garrett says.

"Oh fuck off. Not all of us can be savants," Jared shoots back.

"I guess I just never thought . . ." The words form on my tongue before I can stop it.

"Thought what?" Jared pushes.

"That you guys would understand." I swallow the lump in my throat.

"Understand what?" Garret's question hangs in the air as Jared shoots him a look, a silent *shut the fuck up asshole.*

I hesitate, but once I start, the rest flows out in a torrent, finally ready to let out the messy feelings that have been fermenting in my gut for a decade. I tell them about the last ten years—the highs and lows, the surreal experience of seeing them again, and how I felt that dreadful night years ago.

Opening up to Lacey has been a relief, knowing I have her in my corner. But that was just a stepping stone to get to this moment.

"Luca . . ." Jared's voice cuts through the tension once I finish, and I hold my breath, bracing for their rejection, for them to tell me I'm wrong. That—

"No, you're right. It's fucked that we just kept going without you. We should have stopped and given you a chance to recover before ending things for real," Wes finally says, running a hand through his mess of brown hair.

"I'm not trying to blame you guys," I quickly say, knowing I've always been my own worst enemy. Not them.

"Doesn't mean we aren't to blame." Wes's gaze meets mine. "Fuck, I'm to blame for so much shit that I understand if you can't forgive me."

"I do wish you would have told us sooner, Luca," Garrett says, his gaze softening with a tinge of regret as if recalling our last conversation. But strangely, in a way, I needed his harshness. "We were—We are a family. A crappy one lately, but that doesn't change everything we've gone through." And that's as close to an apology as I'll get from him.

"I'll be fine. We'll be fine."

"Does Martin's daughter have anything to do with it? I promise to keep a healthy distance from this one. I'll even do my best to dull my charm." Wes flashes a crooked grin and immediately holds his hands up in surrender when he's met with glares from all sides of the room. "Ok, too soon."

Jared pats Wes's thigh. "Probably will always be too soon for that."

Just thinking of all she's done makes me grin uncontrollably. "Yeah, she did have something to do with it. And if you don't mind, I'm going to go find her. I'll see you guys at Half a Memory."

They wave me off as Wes enthusiastically starts discussing his upcoming tour, with Jared patiently listening and Garrett pulling out his phone in feigned disinterest. As I watch them, I can't shake the feeling that while some things have stayed the same, tonight, something shifted that needed to change for a long time. I want to believe that I have them back for good, but only time will tell.

And now, all I want to do is celebrate with the person who made this all possible. Lacey helped me find something I had lost, and in the midst of it, I discovered that she was the most precious thing in my life.

My eyes scan the sea of people, searching for her, but there's no glimmer of the blue fabric of her dress or the telltale sign of her perfect posture that makes her stand out like a queen in any room.

I grow slightly frantic as the swarm of people pulls me in, each one eager to express their love for the performance or request an autograph or photo together. The crowd's noise blends into a blur as I try to keep up with the growing number of requests and loaded questions, and I find myself answering automatically without conscious thought.

Finally, Evelyn drags me away, saving me from the people I was brought here to appease.

"Where is she?" Tension leaks into my voice, the question coming out strained.

"The balcony. I think it was something Martin said." Evelyn's pale green eyes bore into me, urging me to go. *Now.*

Ev has never liked Martin or any of the non-band members we've worked with over the years. She's always thought they were just using us to make money, which they were if I'm being honest. But music is a business, even if it does thrive off of passion and talent. What she didn't see were the moments in between and the care they treated us with.

I rush away without even uttering a thank you to my sister, my steps quickening until I catch sight of Lacey's elegant form framed by the windows of the ornate doors leading to the balcony.

I wish I could freeze this moment in amber just to admire her. But as I approach, I notice her body quivering in a sob.

A desperation to fix whatever caused it consumes me, and without hesitation, I pull off my jacket and gently drape it over her shoulders. "What did he say? What do you need?"

"It wasn't him or anyone here."

"Then, what is it? What do I need to fix?"

"Just be here." She trembles. "Just stay with me. That's enough." She curls into me, her back fitting against my chest.

We stay outside, my arms wrapped around her, pulling her into me. Eventually, the people below clamber drunkenly into cars, some of whom I know are destined for my bar and a very cranky Craig. I have news for him when we get there, but right now, this is more important. I'm ready to throw the rest of the night away if that's what she wants.

Her voice breaks the silence, slightly scratchy from crying. "There's this letter from my mom, and I guess I'm not sad or happy, really. I'm just feeling," She gestures at her face, attempting to explain away the tears, "a lot of big things right now."

"Big feelings can be good. Do you want me to stay?" I hope she says yes and continues to let me in.

"Yeah. Someone really smart said I shouldn't handle these things alone."

"They sound really smart," I say, and she smiles slightly at that, holding the letter closer to her chest.

She turns to me and wipes away the smudges of makeup under her eyes. "Don't we have a party to get to?"

"Are you up for it?"

"I've already turned down so many parties because I was hurting. It would be a shame to waste another now that things are starting to feel alright. And I want to celebrate with you. I'm so proud of you."

"Ok, but let's just stay here for a bit longer. And maybe you can tell me more about these big feelings." I gently caress her cheek, wiping the tears rolling down. "You will never be alone in these things. I promise."

"She would have loved you, you know?"

"Sounds like she had good taste," I say with a soft smile, earning a small chuckle from her.

"The best. She was the best."

46

Lacey

Being in the bar with the same band members whose faces are pasted on the walls is a surreal experience.

I'm completely mesmerized watching how Drew fits in with this crowd of flashy people. He doesn't demand attention but instead slips by with hellos and curt nods. They know and acknowledge him with an easy, earned sense of respect.

Craig and the small blonde bartender, whom I remember as Heather, run out of vodka within the first hour. I jump at the chance to grab fresh bottles so I can have a moment to catch my breath. I wasn't lying when I told Drew that I was good to come here, but I'm definitely not at 100%.

With the noise from the crowd and the music over the speakers, I don't hear the voices coming from the storage room until it's too late, and I've already nudged the heavy door fully open. If it were anyone else besides Avery and Wesley, maybe I would have been comfortable reaching through the conflict to grab the bottles. But I just stand there as the scene unfolds.

"I only signed on because I didn't think you would. If it was going to fall through, I was never going to let it be my fault," she hisses at him.

"I guess I should have accounted for your *little pop princess act*. Think you're too good to spend a few months with me? I assume I can't convince you to buy yourself out of the contract?" he snarls back.

She bites out her next words, "If you're so upset, then you fix this. I'm done solving your problems for you."

I shift my grip on the door, and the hinges groan, alerting them to my eavesdropping. With their attention now on me, it takes everything in me to point to the space behind them.

Instantly, they throw on smiles to mask the emotions roiling between them. I shift through the uncomfortable tension, grab what I need, and swiftly retreat.

I drop off the vodka at the bar and return to the small circle of band members and friends.

I lean close to Drew's ear and ask, "If Avery and Wesley are left alone, will they both make it out alive?"

"There haven't been any casualties in the last ten years, so I think it's safe to say we don't have to worry about any tonight," he says with a sigh. So, I guess their yelling matches are a common enough occurrence.

With that, I settle into Drew's side as he goes through the motions of fielding congratulations. This is his victory, and I'm just happy to be a part of it. I stop paying attention as the faces of old collaborators, label executives, and admirers blur together. It's not like there's going to be a quiz.

I'm pulled back into the moment when I hear my own name enter the mix. "Lacey, do you have a minute?" Martin asks. His suit is mussed, and his hair is disheveled, but I don't know what else I'd expect after the state I left him in.

I'm honestly surprised he's here at all.

Drew looks down to where I'm nestled under his arm. "Do you want me to stay?"

"I appreciate what you mean to my daughter, but this is private," Martin snaps, and it becomes apparent he's on edge.

I feel Drew's body tense where it touches mine. "And I appreciate our history, Martin, but if she wants me to stay, I'll stay. And with all due respect, you've been back in her life for one day. I'm not sure you've earned the right to call her that."

Martin's jaw ticks. I can see the words forming on his tongue, the fight building. I brace myself to jump in. Drew has already stepped in for me enough. This is my fight.

But instead of snapping, Martin deflates and turns to me. "Lacey?"

It's my choice how this will play out. I don't have to do this alone, but I want to.

I slide out from under Drew and offer a light smile. "It's ok. I've got this." I wrap Drew's suit jacket tighter around me as I follow Martin out front.

"Thank you for giving me a chance," Martin says, and it's evident that he thinks he's won something. But I won't give him the pleasure of thinking that much longer.

"I never said I was giving you a chance. Drew is right. You haven't earned the right to call me your family. What you do have right now is my attention. I'll listen, but I'm not promising you anything." I stand my ground, crossing my arms over my chest.

It doesn't matter that this bar represents part of Martin's musical empire. It isn't his turf; it's mine. I don't belong here because of him. I belong despite him. I carved out my spot, and I intend to stay.

"I want to try. I want you to come with me. You could be the photographer for the tour."

"No." I shut him down. The offer is almost insulting. Years ago, when I was starting out, that could have made my career, but with my portfolio, I don't need his handouts.

He blinks at me in confusion. "Why not? This would be great."

"You don't seem to get it. I don't need you. I don't want you to give me anything because you finally feel guilty. I already have everything because I worked hard, and she supported me every step of the way. Either find a better reason to be in my life or stay out of it." My blood starts to boil.

I shift my weight, ready to turn on my heel, and go back inside. I didn't come outside for this. If he thinks he can just waltz back into my life now that he's feeling up to it, he's delusional.

He wilts, his demeanor softening. "Look, I don't know you. We both know that." He looks down as if searching for the right words on the sidewalk. "I miss her. I loved her. But I didn't love her the right way, and now she's gone. You have part of her story that I'll never know."

My chest burns. I know how he feels. I know what it's like to grasp for fragments of her as if I can reconstruct her from stories alone. "If I take this risk and share those parts of her with you, will you tell me what she was like before?" My voice cracks with emotion as my confidence falters.

"I think I can. I just hope I do her justice." His eyes meet mine briefly before a gentle smile appears. "I hope to see you soon."

"You will," I say, returning his smile.

With that, we say our goodbyes, exchanging a final glance. As I turn to head back, I note the sense of closure settling over me at long last.

Inside, I find everyone where I left them, talking about the time their bus broke down and how, instead of staying at a hotel, they decided to camp at a nearby national park.

"It was a bear!" Wes shouts.

"It was a large dog, you idiot," Garrett says, rolling his eyes.

"It was a bear," Evelyn adds, slinging her arm around my shoulder and whispering, "I wasn't actually there. I just want to be included." Somewhere, she's found someone's suit jacket to wear over her lilac dress. Maybe not just someone, based on how Garrett's jacket is nowhere to be seen.

I nod, and she turns her attention back to the group, dangling a glass between her fingers. "Oh no, I'm out of a drink. If only any of you were a gentleman."

Garrett snatches it from her and moves to the bar, muttering under his breath.

"Love you too," Evelyn calls out to him, then whispers, "He's just mad cause I told him I'm going to make sure he carries all of the heavy boxes when I move."

"I'm pretty sure he'll just help you find a good moving company that doesn't look like it will steal and resell all your stuff." Drew laughs.

Evelyn pulls a comedic pouty face. "That's no fun. I want to see if all the muscles are for show. It would be a miracle to find out he's not actually all that vain."

"Don't poke the bear after he retreats. I think you've already won this round, Ev," Drew mutters, and his words result in a flutter of drunken giggles from the rest of the group.

"Whatever." Evelyn brushes off her brother's warning, "What about you and Avery, Wesley? I've been hearing a lot of buzz about your fun little project."

"If it doesn't go up in flames after the first show, I will call it a success, but if it turns into a dumpster fire after the first night, I'll say it's a self-fulfilling prophecy," Wesley says before taking a generous swig of his drink.

"Perfect! I can't wait for the bloodbath," Evelyn replies.

"Why is it that every time I try to apologize, she starts yelling?" Wesley scrubs his hands over his face.

"Because you suck at apologizing and are excellent at making bad decisions." Ev really is everyone's little sister. It's evident in how she knows exactly how to taunt each of them for maximum effect.

They are all proof that my father did some good in his life. He had a hand in building these lifelong ties between them.

As the party starts to wind down, the only people who have made it to three A.M. are huddled in corners as Drew, Craig, and I clean up the mess. My heels lay abandoned in a corner as I sweep up glitter and confetti.

"We need to start thinking of bar names," Drew says, breaking the silence we've settled into as we work.

"Come again?" Craig squeaks.

"Bar names. Like for a new bar, or at least for an old one that's in desperate need of an upgrade," Drew explains.

"Lacey, did you convince him? Cause I could kiss you right now," he says.

"Craig," Drew warns.

"Ok, no kissing." Craig throws up his hands.

I shrug and turn towards my favorite bartender. "It's news to me, too."

"It's been a long time coming, as everyone in my life keeps telling me." He eyes Craig, who just smirks. "Tonight was a good end to it. And I'm kind of over the pink." Drew tosses the rag he's been using to wipe down tables into a far bucket before turning to me. "Would you take pictures for the redesign? I want to be able to look up and have a reminder of who helped me get to this point."

"Pictures. Tearing down walls. Testing out drinks. Making fun of Craig," I say.

"Hey. I'm not a punching bag," Craig protests.

"I'm here for all of it," I promise.

"You'll have time for all that? I don't want to wear you down with work," Drew checks.

I smile, ready to give a confession of my own. "I'm going to finish out the season and then slow down for a bit." Drew just stares at me while Craig dramatically looks between us as if not believing his ears. "But that also means I might be looking for a new place. My rent might be a little high if I'm not working for a year."

It's true. I need a break. I need to breathe, and if I can help with the bar, then I won't be sitting around doing nothing. As an added bonus, I can be around for Mari and the baby when it comes to helping Price's tiny family. Showing them all the unconditional love they have given me over the years.

"I know a guy with a room," Drew says, a perfect smile crossing his tired face.

"Does he cook? My last roommate cooked and offered some other services I enjoyed. Set the bar really high for the next guy," I tease, running a finger down the fabric of his shirt.

Drew's voice lowers with his response. "I think something can be arranged."

Craig gags. “I’m all for this, but shouldn’t you guys wait to get some sleep before making life-altering decisions?”

Drew shakes his head. “There’s no point in waiting to make the best decisions of my life.” His voice comes out in a delicious rumble as he fixes his attention on me. “When are you thinking of coming back?”

“Tonight. I want to come home tonight.”

And I don’t ever want to leave again.

47

Lacey

Epilogue

Five months later . . .

"So, does the bar still look like it's owned by a self-obsessed ass?" Drew smirks.

"I was pretty brutal back then, wasn't I?" I answer, not regretting a word I said back then because they all helped me get to this moment. "No. I think we did well to tone it down." I take it all in from where I sit on the shining walnut bar top.

The place is unrecognizable. Pink neon has been replaced with warm-hued Edison bulbs. A small stage rests in the far corner for future open mics and to help support small local artists. Drew wanted to pay homage to his past without outright living in it.

We visited Evelyn last month in New York, and I brought my camera with me, capturing whatever I wanted to—not for work or the bar, just for me. But we did end up hanging one of my favorite shots: Ev's fingers flying in a blur across the black-and-white keys of the baby grand that barely fits in her new apartment.

"Yes. But at least I had the chance to prove you wrong," he adds.

"What do you mean by that exactly?"

"What else did you say about the owner besides him being self-obsessed? Hmm, I think there was a comment about a tiny dick that is now *not* in question."

"I wouldn't say that," I goad him.

"I can prove you wrong again right here."

That's when Craig pops his head out from the prep area. "I swear if you guys do any nasty shit on this bar again, I'm cutting off my ears, then gouging out my eyes, and quitting."

Heat explodes across my face as I remember the unfortunate encounter, but as usual, Drew brushes it right off.

"That'd make it hard to find another job," Drew quips.

"Whatever," Craig says before resuming his preparations for the night.

"I still don't forgive him for being in on it from the start. But I still like him more than you," I whisper.

"You may like him, but you *love me*."

"Oh, do I now?"

"Guys, we open in thirty, and those oranges won't peel themselves. I would prefer not to be missing garnishes on the first night back in business," Craig calls out.

I slide from my perch to help with the final prep. Besides assisting with the design, I've also become a somewhat competent bartender. However, we discovered my recipe-creating skills were on par with my cooking skills after I somehow made a drink taste like 'salty tar.'

Drew makes his way to the back to let in the first act that will be hosted on our little stage. They're a female R&B trio called Hera's Heirs. He helps them set up their equipment as they tune their instruments.

Customers immediately flow in the moment the doors open. The space is exactly how it should be: full of people and music. Familiar faces are mixed in with new ones. Price and Mari are out for a date night; Mari is still not quite over the fact I'm with her childhood crush, but we're working through it. Evelyn and Avery are tucked into a booth, baseball hats and sunglasses covering their features.

I'm caught in the constant movements of pouring and mixing drinks, my arms aching slightly from the constant effort of shaking cocktails. The burn of my muscles is a reminder of the blood, sweat, and tears that brought us to this place—not just the new building but also the people we became because I walked in instead of walking away.

Getting lost in the flow and adrenaline of the bar is almost as invigorating as capturing the action on the ice. There will be more seasons, more pictures, and more victories, but there will only be one night like this. Faces blur together, and stories flow as easily as the drinks. Each time I look at the clock, I see that hours have passed.

I'm grabbing a new bottle with my back turned to the bar when I hear the familiar scrape of a stool.

I start my customer service script before I fully turn around. "Welcome to Perfect Stranger. What can I get you?" A smile rips across my face as I see the man across from me. Not just because I know he has deep pockets and is guaranteed to leave the best tip, but because he's all mine.

Drew rests his chin in his hand as he watches me. "A house whiskey."

It's a familiar scene, but I'd play it out a thousand times with him. Maybe to someone else that would be boring. But we've always excelled at making magic out of the mundane.

"Burning away a bad day?"

"I'd never burn away a day that you're a part of," he says, his eyes scanning me in a suggestive glance, and I almost jump over the bar to kiss him.

Instead, I bite my lip, determined not to break character. "How would you like it?"

"On the rocks."

Acknowledgements

I can't believe my mother still speaks to me after how much I've bugged her throughout this process. Mom, thank you for always picking up the phone any time I needed you and listening for (I'm not exaggerating here, folks) literally hundreds of hours while repeating the same plot points until they finally clicked. Thank you for telling me the original third-act breakup sucked (it did). You're my favorite critic. I love you.

Thank you to my early readers, Ellie, Ashley, Caroline, Stori, Vai, Miah, Zoe, and Katy. You all motivated me so much throughout this process when I needed it most. Without you, I'd probably be laying on the floor, consumed by my own imposter syndrome. Zoe, thank you for coming back into my life for this project; I wouldn't trade it for the world (You can thank her for helping me take out some of the most awful lines known to man). Ellie, your help was nothing less than magic. Katy, cheers to our drummer boys.

I'm so lucky to be best friends with my cover designer, Stef. Thank you for being the reason this dream took its first stumbling steps into reality. You provided me with the first,

"This is my author friend experience," and you never fail to validate and guide me in the right direction. I wouldn't have trusted anyone else with the phrase "Whiskey glass musical raincloud" and hoped to get the work of art that gets to house this story.

John and Stella, thank you for not letting me become a complete hermit while I wrote this.

It's no secret that I'm really just one big, anxious baby. Without my dear friends and fellow authors, Miah and Vai, I would simply be living in a little hole in the ground. They took so much care to listen to every voice memo and tell me that this book is enough, that I am enough, too. Both of these incredible women helped push this story to become its best version.

Vai, there is literally no way this book would have been on schedule without our weekly writing sprints. It's never mattered that you were multiple time zones away because you've always felt so close. Thank you for always talking through the plot points that make me want to bang my head against the wall and for stoking my creative fire.

Miah, you were the first person to reach out to me and have been with me from the start. It feels odd to say we are co-workers in the Wild West of the author world, but the journey of our friendship was a constant hum of comfort in my mind as we've grown together. Thank you for yapping with me.

And, of course, my wonderful editor, Sheisa. I cringe thinking about how this story would be missing some of the most important and impactful moments without you. Thank you for matching my excitement and passion for this story. The story blossomed under your care, and I can't wait for what's next for us.

About the author

Marja is an author from Northern New Mexico, and though she doesn't live there now, she'll always claim the mountains as her home. She writes big stories built on a foundation of essential, small moments. If she's not writing or reading she's desperately wishing to nap in the sun.

For inquiries contact Marja at marja@mjgrahamauthor.com or on Instagram @mjgraham.author

Printed in Great Britain
by Amazon

43446584R00260